Bright
Smoke,
Cold
Fire

Also by Rosamund Hodge

Cruel Beauty

Crimson Bound

Bright Smoke, Cold Fire

ROSAMUND HODGE

BALZER + BRAY
An Imprint of HarperCollins*Publishers*

Balzer + Bray is an imprint of HarperCollins Publishers.

Bright Smoke, Cold Fire

 For information address HarperCollins Children's Books, a division of HarperCollins Publishers, 195 Broadway, New York, NY 10007.
www.epicreads.com

ISBN 978-0-06-236941-3

---

16 17 18 19 20 PC/RRDH 10 9 8 7 6 5 4 3 2 1

❖

First Edition

For Sasha,

who loves tragedy

A glooming peace this morning with it brings,
The sun, for sorrow, will not show his head.
Go hence, to have more talk of these sad things;
Some shall be pardon'd, and some punished:
For never was a story of more woe
Than this of Juliet and her Romeo.

—Romeo and Juliet, *act 5, scene 3*

Such Sweet Sorrow

IF HE DOES NOT COME soon, she may not have the heart to kill him.

For an hour now, she has sat at the foot of her bed, gripping her sword in its crimson scabbard. Over and over she whispers, *I am the sword of the Catresou. I was born to avenge the blood of my people.*

But her traitor throat aches and her coward eyes sting. Once upon a time, she believed she was only a sword. Now she fears she is only a girl.

She hopes he will come soon. She hopes he will never come.

The casement swings open.

She stands. Her numb hands draw the sword and let the scabbard drop.

His dark eyes are wide as he climbs through the window, but

there is no surprise in them when she greets him with the point of her blade, held to his throat.

He looks strangely small. Just a boy, with messy black hair and a sweet laugh she will never hear again.

Her only love, and now her only hate.

"I see you," she says, speaking the ancient words for the first time, "and I judge you guilty."

He sighs, and the corner of his mouth tips up just a little. "I know," he says, and he kneels and bares his neck.

She can smell the blood on him. He is clean: he took the trouble to bathe before coming here to die. But he spilled the life-blood of her kin, and she can smell that guilt upon him—she can almost *taste* it. Her body shakes with the desire to kill him for it.

She wants him to fight. She wants him to beg. To flee, to threaten, or persuade.

Ever since she met him, she has most terribly *wanted*.

"Look up at me," she demands, and he does, his gaze as simple and sure as the night she fell in love with him.

"Why did you come?" she whispers. "You knew what I would do. You know what I *must* do."

He swallows; she sees the muscles move in his throat, and she thinks of the blood pulsing just below the skin. He is a fragile, perfect balance of breath and heartbeat, skin and bones and blood. A little world entire, most beautifully made—he was *her* world, and now she is going to destroy him.

"'Journeys end in lovers meeting.'" She says the words flatly, without tune, but they both remember the sun-drenched afternoon when he sang them to her. "'Every wise man's son doth know.' *Why did you come back?*"

"Because I'm sorry," he says hoarsely. "Because I know you loved him. You deserve to avenge him."

Not because it is her duty. Not because vengeance is written on her skin and the spells that wrote it compel her to obey.

Because she loved her cousin. Because he ruffled her hair and comforted her when she was a little child. Because he is dead and cold now, in a vault beneath their house, his arms sliced open as the embalmers do their work.

And yet even he, her most beloved cousin, never wondered if she wanted to avenge or not.

Nobody ever wondered. Nobody until this boy who kneels before her now.

Slowly she kneels so they are eye to eye, and she lays the sword upon the floor.

"I see you." Her fingertips trace his cheek; her voice is tiny and soft. "I judge you guilty. But you belong to me now. So all your sins are mine."

She slides her fingers into his dark hair and kisses him, kisses her dearest sin, again and again. Her heart pounds with the desire to kill him, to wreck and ruin and revenge, but she only clutches him closer, kisses him more fiercely, and his arms wrap around her as he kisses her back.

She will not be the one who kills him.

She will give everything else to her family, to her duty, to the adjuration written on her skin.

But she will not give them this.

1

THE WALLS THAT KEPT OUT death could drive you mad.

That was the story Runajo had heard, whispered among the other novices: sometimes, when a Sister of Thorn climbed the central tower of the Cloister to inspect the wall of magic that guarded the city, she would go mad and throw herself down. The other novices liked to giggle about it as they sat up late at night in the dormitory, but not one of them ever went up the tower by choice.

Runajo had volunteered for the duty sixteen times.

Some of the novices thought she was already mad. A few probably thought she was brave. Runajo knew she was neither. She just wasn't fooling herself, like everyone else in the city: she knew they were all dying, no matter what they did.

The daily inspection started at dawn. It took nearly half an hour to climb the narrow stairs of the tower; despite the early-morning chill, Runajo was sweating when she finally reached the top. She flung open the trapdoor, heaved herself up, and collapsed to the white floor. For a few moments, she did nothing but gasp for breath.

The wind stirred against her face. She heard a soft rustle and looked up.

There was no wall around the rim of the tower's roof; but there were narrow steel posts, and strung between them, cord after cord of scarlet silk, every inch hung with the slender white finger-bones of those who had been sacrificed to give the wall its power. Each skeleton finger was complete, the bones hung with thread so they could flex in the morning breeze.

Memory clutched at her throat: her mother's fingers, thin and pale as she wasted away with sickness. When Mother died, one of her hands had rested on the coverlet, and Runajo had seen the last color drain from the knobby joints.

A proper daughter would have gazed at her mother's dead face and wept. All night as she sat vigil, Runajo had stared at the bony, bone-white fingers and felt nothing at all.

Well, she thought, *if you didn't have a stone in place of a heart, you might not do so well up here.*

She stood.

If Sisters went mad at the top of the tower, it wasn't the wall that did it, but the world: so vast, and yet so very small.

Runajo wasn't scared of heights, but it was still a little dizzying to look down to the red-and-white domes of the Cloister. Down the steep slope to the white buildings and twisting roads of the Upper City that clung to the sides of the vast, rocky spike. Down to the grimy mess of the Lower City that tangled on the ground of the island around the base of the city spire; and the water around their island shimmering silver in the early-morning light.

This was Viyara, the last city left alive in the whole world. It *was* the whole world.

Because very close to the far shore was a barely visible line in the water: the line where the walls of Viyara—the translucent, dearly bought dome—ended.

And outside the walls was death.

The wind must have been blowing all night, for the white fog of the Ruining had drawn back from the far shore. Runajo could see pale beaches and rocky cliffs. She could see the green of moss and the spreading branches of trees—the Ruining was deadly only to humans. She could even see the peaks of the mountains, rising out of the fog that swirled around their slopes.

On the far shore lay the ruins of Zucra, the city that had once been the bustling gateway to Viyara, when people came on pilgrimages from all around the world. But now it was crumbling and abandoned. Its stone quays were empty, the ships having long ago rotted away as they waited for sailors that would never come.

Something moved in its streets.

At that distance, Runajo could barely make it out, but she still saw the sudden scurrying of a tiny, pale figure in the abandoned streets. No. Two figures.

Revenants. The dead that rose and walked again.

Fear slid up her spine like the touch of a cold finger. Her heart pounded, but she refused to let herself look away, so she watched the two tiny figures scramble down the street until they turned a corner and disappeared.

Runajo let out a shaky sigh.

The Ruining was more than the white fog that killed every person it touched. It had changed the nature of death. Even here in Viyara, behind the walls, the dead would rise again within two days, mindless and hungry for the living. And so the bodies had to be cremated first; the furnaces of the Sisters never cooled.

Outside the walls, there was nobody left to burn the dead. In the early years of the Ruining, revenants had crowded the far shore, hungering for the beating hearts inside Viyara. But over the past century they had slowly wandered away. After all, they had a whole world to walk.

That, Runajo believed, was why Sisters sometimes threw themselves down from the tower. Because standing up here, they had to see what everyone pretended wasn't true: that death had already won. That Viyara's walls hardly made a difference. That in the end, nobody survived.

It didn't bother Runajo. She couldn't pretend she was going to live forever, not after the years she spent helplessly watching her parents die. Up here on the tower, staring death in the face, at least she could fight.

At the center of the tower's roof was a round hole, about as wide as Runajo was tall. Out of the hole—rising up from a shaft that plunged deeper than the height of the tower, down into the heart of the Cloister—grew the wall. Here, near the base, it looked like seven columns of tiny, faintly glowing bubbles, pressed together into a ring. Overhead, it became transparent as it spread out in a vast dome that covered the city, the island, and part of the water.

Gently, Runajo leaned forward, taking a breath through her nose. The surface of the wall hummed against her lips, then swirled into her mouth.

It was lighter than water, thicker than air. It hummed and almost sang against her tongue; it had a bright, mineral taste, like the scent of sunlight on clean, hot stone.

There was no hint of bitterness, no discord in the not-quite-song. Which meant there were no cracks forming in this part of the wall. No need for adjustments in the spell-weaving chambers far below. But the wall felt thin and faint in her mouth. When

Runajo had first tasted it eight months ago, it had been as hot as noon sunlight beating down on her black hair. Now it was barely warm at all.

Tomorrow was the Great Offering, and not a moment too soon. The wall desperately needed the fresh strength it would gain from another human life.

Runajo should have released the mouthful of magic—it was dangerous; if she breathed it in, she would die—but she hesitated, rolling it over her tongue. This was why she volunteered to inspect the wall, again and again. Because the wall had been the last great magic of the Sisters, before they had lost so much of their knowledge. When she tasted it, she tasted those vanished secrets.

Visions flickered through her mind: complex diagrams and blueprints, memories of the foundations of the city. The images were so clear, every line as sharp as a needle's point, she felt sure that if she could just remember them, she would know all the secrets of the city.

But she couldn't keep them in her head. They faded too quickly, though she tried and tried to memorize the patterns. Finally, when her tongue started to feel numb, she leaned forward and opened her lips. The tiny mouthful of magic swirled back into the wall whence it had come.

Runajo had to check each of the streams rising out of the base; she took a few moments to rest and regain the feeling in her mouth before she went on to the next. And the next, and the next.

Each time she waited, trying to read the secrets hidden in the foam. Each time, she couldn't. And each time, the knot of frustration in her chest drew tighter. They didn't know how this wall worked. They had the ceremonies to keep weaving it, to check for simple flaws and make small adjustments, but they didn't *understand*.

They only knew that to keep the wall standing, they had to offer it human lives. And they knew that the need was increasing: in the beginning, they had only needed to sacrifice every seven years. Now, it was every six months.

Her fingers dug into her palms. They were all dying, and nobody wanted to admit how soon. It was the same sort of cowardice that had made Runajo's mother spend all of Father's illness prattling about the things they would do as soon as he was well again. Even at the end, when the tumor in his side had turned into an open wound, Mother still whispered to him that next spring they would sit beneath the flowering trees and she would read him poetry.

For all the years of her father's illness, and her mother's illness after, Runajo had been a perfect daughter: silent, obedient, still. She had smiled and agreed with the lies. Her only rebellion had been refusing to hope for either of them.

When Mother finally died, Runajo had joined the Sisters of

Thorn the next day, because they were the only ones who resisted death in any way that mattered.

And then she had found that they, too, were sick and unwilling to admit it.

Runajo was done with silent obedience. She refused to watch the whole city fall in her lifetime, without even trying to keep it alive a little longer. Without even knowing why the wall was failing.

And she had a plan. She would take the first step this afternoon, at the Great Offering. It was risky, and it was probably going to get her killed.

But at least she would die fighting.

2

IT SEEMED LIKE HALF THE city had turned out to watch a single man die.

Runajo, standing in her place with five other novices, thought all the fuss was a bit silly. People died every day. And the Great Offering was no less regular or essential than carting the dead away to be burned, or tending the sewage pipes that pulled waste out of the city. But because it was done only twice a year, surrounded by the songs and dances of the Sisters of Thorn, it was a great festival, and nobody wanted to miss it.

When they had to kill somebody every week to sustain the city walls, maybe then the thrill would fade.

Maybe Runajo would be able to keep it from coming to that.

"You're looking awfully solemn," said Sunjai, and Runajo startled.

Sunjai just dimpled. She was a plump, pretty girl whose dark braids were always sleek and flawless, coiled around her head. Her gray novice's robe was immaculate as always, her clasped hands primly tucked into her wide sleeves.

"Worried that Romeo has forgotten you?" she asked.

"No," said Runajo, glancing to see if Miryo, the novice mistress, was listening.

It was not Runajo's fault that the idiot son of her mother's childhood friend had spent years fancying himself in love with her, and had kept sending her poems even after she'd entered the Sisterhood. But Miryo was always looking for an excuse to punish Runajo; she'd jump on even a hint of scandal.

"Then you'll be glad to hear that everyone says he's still refusing to look at another girl," Sunjai went on cheerfully. "Perhaps he's just spent all this time working on a really *special* poem."

Probably that was true. Sunjai was the only other novice from Runajo's clan, and she seemed to know just as much of the gossip from their kin as she did of the goings-on among the Sisterhood.

"I don't care what you heard," said Runajo. "And I don't care if Romeo lives or dies, let alone loves me. Why don't you go bother Inyaan? I don't think anyone's told her she's glorious in the last five minutes."

Sunjai patted her shoulder in fake fondness and then went to whisper in the ear of Inyaan, the novice who was the younger sister of the Exalted himself. Unlike the rest of the novices, who were thrilled at the great occasion, she was staring at the crowd with the same blank disdain she directed at everyone in the Cloister.

It wasn't true that Runajo didn't care if Romeo lived or died. He'd been the closest thing she ever had to a friend, and he had tried a lot harder to be kind to her than anyone else ever had. But his delusion that she had thrown herself into the Cloister out of grief for her parents and needed to be rescued? Insufferable.

If he wasn't sending her letters anymore, he had probably found another girl to imagine himself in love with, and that was all for the best. He could write more bad poetry, and Runajo could get on with saving Viyara.

It felt like the whole city was gathered now. The Great Offering was held in the grand court at the center of Viyara. It was, perhaps, the most magnificent place in the Upper City. A broad avenue cut straight into the rising stone slope of the city spire. At the end was a round marble dais—wide enough to hold a hundred men—in which the glowing patterns of the city's magic shifted and whirled. Above the dais, the gargantuan obsidian face of the god Ihom looked out from the white stone wall, as if the rest of his body was sealed into the city itself. Of the nine gods, he had been the first to die, and so it was before his image that human lives were offered now.

The summer sun was blazing and the air was a sodden weight. Even so, people from the Upper and Lower City thronged the court, chattering, laughing, singing, selling sweetmeats and trinkets. Only the three high houses were allowed to stand before the dais. At the center, of course, was the Exalted—a bored-looking young man who ruled the city on the strength of his supposedly divine blood. All around him stood the rest of the Old Viyaran nobility. They were a tall people, dark skinned wth white-gold hair, all of them resplendent in translucent white silks and gold chains.

To the right was Runajo's own clan, the Mahyanai. They looked like a reverse of the Old Viyarans: fair skin, black hair, their silk robes a swirl of colors, their wide sashes heavily embroidered. Most of the men wore at their hips curving swords in lacquered black scabbards, while the women's hair was piled atop their heads, wound about gold or silver headdresses.

At their center stood Lord Ineo, his harsh face solemn. Supposedly he ruled the city in all but name, since the Exalted was too lost in his own pleasures to care. For this, the Mahyanai adored him.

Runajo could never decide if she hated Lord Ineo or not. He was Romeo's father—and no matter how insufferable Romeo could be sometimes, when she thought of how Lord Ineo ignored him, she could happily spit on her clan's beloved leader. But when her family petitioned Lord Ineo to drag her out of the Sisterhood, he had declared she had the right to sacrifice herself. He'd set her free.

To the left stood the Catresou in sullen ranks: still, dressed in black, and dead silent. Every one of them was masked, because they did not believe outsiders worthy to see their faces; at the center of the crowd stood Lord Catresou, robed and hooded in black velvet, his face completely covered in a mask of gold and rubies. Beside him—dressed in a simple red gown, her face half covered by an ivory filigree mask—stood the Juliet, the nameless girl who had been ensorcelled into being their mindless attack dog.

The Juliet was the pride of the Catresou. They didn't realize what hypocrites they were, calling the Great Offering a cruel abomination when they were happy to enslave their own children.

Drums had started beating. At the center of the dais, a young Sister prostrated herself before the face of Ihom. The High Priestess knelt behind her with a silver knife; gently, reverently, she kissed each of the girl's feet and then sliced a shallow line down the sole, from heel to toe.

The girl rose and began to dance, her body twirling and undulating in time to the drums, her bloody footprints spreading across the marble dais. Where her feet touched the marble, light blossomed in the stone, and the glowing patterns bent and shifted toward her. The city was eating up her bloody sacrifice.

The world was made from the blood of gods. The blood of men sustains it now. So said the Sisters of Thorn. Runajo did not believe in the gods, but she didn't doubt the power of spilled blood.

Nobody in Viyara did.

A low note sounded from a horn. The girl paused, swaying on her feet. Runajo couldn't help wincing at the trembling line of the girl's mouth: the volunteers for sacrifice were drugged, but on such a solemn occasion, Sisters were expected to bear all their pain themselves.

The horn sounded again, and then all the people—Sisters, nobles, commoners, even the Catresou—prostrated themselves on the ground. Because this moment was in memory of all they had lost.

The horn sounded again, and they rose. Runajo blinked at the sudden dazzle of light—she had squeezed her eyes shut during the prostration—and when she could see properly again, the young man was being led out to the sacrifice. He was an Old Viyaran this time, which meant he was a volunteer, not one of the condemned criminals that the Catresou dragged out when it was their turn to provide the sacrifice. Golden chains dangled across his bare chest; he swayed slightly under all the drugs.

Runajo thought, *If they don't like my plan, then very soon that could be me.*

They'd make me wear more clothes, though.

She wasn't afraid. Not exactly. But her body felt terribly light and fragile. She was aware of her tiny, rapid heartbeat: the little flutter that kept her among the living and not the dead.

First the young man was brought to the Exalted, who laid hands on him and blessed him; then to Lord Ineo, who bowed gracefully to him; and last of all to Lord Catresou, who remained stiff and expressionless as a marionette as he placed a velvet-wrapped hand on the young man's shoulder.

Then the Sister escorting the young man turned him around, toward the bloodstained center of the dais where the High Priestess waited. He wobbled on his feet, but gave her a huge, dreamy smile. Not every sacrifice died by the hand of the High Priestess herself.

Runajo's stomach turned uneasily. This wasn't the first sacrifice she had seen. Before the illness, her parents had taken her every year, starting when she was a little girl who barely understood the pageant unfolding before her.

But six months ago, she'd missed the Great Offering because she was ill and vomiting. This would be the first sacrifice she saw since she'd truly understood what death meant.

The cold emptiness was back in her chest, and her hands clenched into fists, because she couldn't panic now. She couldn't.

But as the young man knelt in front of the High Priestess, the feeling rolled over her in waves: a cold, absolute emptiness that left her drifting and hollow, watching the world from what felt like an immeasurable distance. She saw—in flashes—the High Priestess carve the sacred signs into the man's skin and whisper the sacred words into his ears. But the splendor in front of her didn't matter. Nothing mattered. She was going to die, and this bright bubble of a world would wink out, and there would be nothing left of her.

Trying to imagine it felt like choking. Her heart pounded—desperately, fleetingly alive.

Nothing. Not even silence. Nothing.

The High Priestess cradled the man's head. The whole grand court was silent, still and breathless. Her knife flashed.

The man's lifeblood poured out, the dais flashed with dazzling light, and a great shout went up from the crowd. Horns and flutes and drums and tambourines rang out, proclaiming that they would all live for another six months.

Runajo realized she was trembling. Her nails bit into her palms.

She was alive. Right now—just for now—she was alive. And she had a plan to carry out.

On the dais, several Sisters of Thorn danced around the body in languid movements of stylized grief and reverence. It was their teaching that those who died in sacrifice—or in dueling, or in childbirth—would go to feast with the dead gods, while those who died of sickness or age would serve them, forever less but not cast out into darkness like thieves and murderers and oath-breakers.

Runajo didn't believe it. Not because of the ancient Mahyanai sages, who said that the gods were a delusion, and that the soul of man was like a candle that guttered in the wind and was gone forever. But because she had seen her mother and father lying dead. She had seen the terrible emptiness in their waxlike faces, and she knew that nothing was left of them in any world.

The High Priestess turned to the waiting ranks of the Sisters and beckoned.

It was time.

Seven of them walked forward: the newest of the novices, who had been with the Sisters only a year and never taken part in any solemn sacrifice before.

The ceremony was simple. They would kneel before the High Priestess, take the knife from her hands, and slice a single cut into their forearms. Their blood would mix with the blood of the sacrifice, signifying their willingness to pour out their lives serving the gods and protecting Viyara through magic that could only be bought in blood.

Inyaan went first, her face a haughty mask. But when she fell to her knees before the High Priestess and took the knife, her hands were shaking. Perhaps she was realizing that even the sister of the Exalted would someday die.

Sunjai went second, and kept her dimples all the way through, but that was hardly surprising. If she had any understanding of her own mortality, Runajo had never seen it.

Then it was Runajo's turn.

She walked forward, but it almost felt like floating. Her arms and legs were cold and numb.

This was the moment. This was the choice. If she carried out the ceremony correctly, it would be her first initiation. There would be seven more years before she became a full Sister.

She couldn't bear waiting that long. To be silently obedient one day longer.

Her fingers wrapped around the handle of the knife. She looked at the blood, at the dead man's gaping wound, at the crowd and the city, the far-off mountains already ruled by death and the blue sky above them.

She raised her left hand. She didn't make the simple slice she was supposed to; she carved the circle of binding as she spoke the oath she was not meant to swear for another seven years: "By Ihom's breath and Amat's silence, I bind myself to the fate of thorns."

It was a sacred and irrevocable vow. It was blasphemy to speak it before the High Priestess had declared her worthy. And Runajo had just done so in front of all of Viyara.

In the silence that followed, she thought, *I hope they at least wait for my trial before they sacrifice me.*

3

AT LAST HIS FATHER WAS going to come watch him duel.

Paris was in the practice yard before dawn, his arms burning as he ran through the parry he always stumbled on.

He knew he should still be sleeping. Weeks ago, he'd made a plan for this day, and it had included a sensible amount of sleep the night before, and only a brief warm-up in the morning, so that he would be in optimal condition to display his skills.

But no matter how carefully still he'd lain in bed, he couldn't manage to sleep for more than a few minutes at a time. He kept thinking of what exactly he would say to his father after he lost. He had worked out his speech weeks ago—had written it down, even, and then promptly burned the paper—but he couldn't stop repeating it to himself, and wondering if there was a better way to say it.

It was a relief to give up on sleeping, get out of bed, and run down to the practice yard. He knew how Master Trelouno would attack: he would use all the techniques that Paris was worst at countering. That was how they trained every day, and the fact that Paris's father was coming to inspect his progress would not make Master Trelouno go easy on him.

His rapier was shaking. With a gasp, Paris lowered the sword and staggered over to one of the benches at the edge of the practice yard.

The sun had just started to rise; light streaked the sky, though it hadn't yet broken over the walls of the Academy. From outside, he could hear the clattering steps of a City Guard patrol—and there was the low note of a gong: they were bringing up bodies from the Lower City.

Paris grimaced and made the sign against defilement. The Guard was coming straight through the center of the Catresou compound, because they wanted to remind them what happened to people who defied the Viyaran laws about the proper disposal of dead bodies. Because they thought—like everyone else in the city—that the Catresou were only one step away from criminals who stole corpses and boiled them down to sell the bones on the black market.

As the sweat dried on his skin, he started to shiver in the early-morning chill. With a sigh, he stood and walked stiffly down the marble corridors to the mess room, where a few other students were already eating corn cakes and tea. Like Paris, they wore the uniform of the Academy: dark trousers, white shirt, and a red doublet, with a half face mask of plain cloth.

He sat by himself, as always. For once the solitude didn't hurt: he needed to be alone, so he could go over the speech he would make after he lost the duel.

Everybody knew Paris was going to lose, because Master Trelouno always made the final exam as difficult as he could, and Paris was—as Master Trelouno liked to say—"perfectly adequate."

No less, but no more.

So Paris was going to lose this duel, just like he would lose his official duel against Tybalt in two weeks. He would never be the Juliet's Guardian.

That was all right. The Juliet was much, much more important to the Catresou than Paris would ever be. The spells laid upon her since birth let her sense anyone who had shed their clan's blood and compelled her to avenge it. And the Accords drawn up between the Old Viyarans and the other two high houses gave her the right to exact that vengeance.

But she was more than their protector, or their guarantor of respect in a hostile city. She was their justice. While she lived, and carried a sword, they were free. She deserved to have the very best to guard and guide and treasure her.

But Paris didn't want to be forced into the City Guard the way the other Academy failures were. He'd seen it happen to other boys. Some came home with broken ribs, flinching at every sudden noise. Some renounced the Catresou entirely, and bought an easy life by losing all chance to walk the Paths of Light after death.

Paris couldn't bear either of those fates. But the only person who could save him was his father.

His speech had to be perfect.

Father, he thought. But no, that might sound impertinent. *My lord Father. We both know I will never be Guardian.*

Did that sound too defeatist? He knew his lack of ambition was a disappointment, but he would have just lost a duel. Father would not be in the mood for false bravado.

But it would dishonor our family if your only son was sent to the City Guard. You see that I have some skill with the sword. And Master Idraldi can tell you that I have read all the lore and history recorded about all the Juliets who ever lived. Surely it would be most honorable to our family—and most useful to our clan—if I were made Tybalt's assistant. I could help him care for the Juliet. I could be useful.

I could be useful.

Possibly he should mention that there was precedent? The Juliet had once had an entire entourage: only one Guardian, but up to seven other men to fight beside her as she dealt out justice to all who shed Catresou blood.

But that was generations ago, before the Ruining and the flight to Viyara. Father had never cared much for tradition.

The city bells started tolling. It was time.

Paris didn't run back to the practice yard. There were rules against running in the halls, and he wanted another moment to go over the plan in his head.

It was going to work. However disappointed his father was in Paris, he cared about the honor of their family, and it was shameful to send a son to the City Guard. Making him assistant to the Juliet's Guardian was the perfect solution.

Paris realized he was nearly running, and he forced himself to slow down before he walked into the practice yard.

Master Trelouno was already there, wearing his customary black and the steel mask that stopped right at his nose so that his drooping red mustache and goatee would be visible.

Next to him stood Paris's father.

Lutreo Mavarinn Catresou was one of the five lords of the Catresou; he wore the sleeveless red cloak of state at all times, along with his elaborate mask of black velvet and silver filigree. Paris had seen his bare face perhaps five times; going barefaced was a gesture of equality or affection, and his father held very few people in either.

Paris's heart thudded as if he were already fighting, but he drew his rapier and saluted smoothly. "My lord Father."

His father and Master Trelouno exchanged a look.

Something was wrong. Paris could feel it, and he tried desperately to think what he could possibly have done. He wasn't late;

the duel was supposed to be at the quarter bell, and it hadn't rung yet. He knew he had saluted correctly, and he knew that here in the practice yard it was correct to salute.

What had he done?

They were looking at him now. They seemed to be waiting.

He took a step forward. "I am very honored—my lord Father—to show you what I have learned—"

He snapped his mouth shut. The words were so inane, he wanted to cringe. He was supposed to be saying something else. He was supposed to be doing something else, and he would happily do anything if they would just *tell him*—

His father heaved a deep sigh. "That won't be necessary."

"Oh," said Paris.

For one dazed moment, he didn't feel anything. It was like the time he had bungled a lunge particularly badly and smacked his forehead against the hilt of Master Trelouno's rapier. Everything felt numb and ringing.

The next moment, he realized that he was less than a pace away from his father, saying, "You cannot mean to withdraw me from the competition. It would be the worst possible disgrace for our family, and yes, I am perfectly aware it is a foregone conclusion that I will not defeat Tybalt, but if you would just let me explain—"

"Tybalt is dead," said his father.

Paris blinked. "What?" he said.

"Don't leave your mouth hanging open, boy," his father said impatiently. "Tybalt was killed last night in a duel with some Mahyanai boy. You're going to be the Juliet's Guardian." He looked Paris up and down. "In two days, may the gods help you."

Paris had spent three months preparing for a duel that didn't happen. He got two days to prepare for meeting the Juliet.

Supposedly, he'd been preparing since he was twelve years old, but since nobody had ever expected—

"Stand up straight, boy," said Father under his breath. "Had you boldness enough to dream of the position, you might now be prepared to take it."

Paris's back stiffened, though he knew he'd already been standing straight; Father just hadn't noticed because he wasn't looking at him as they strode down the corridor together.

"I am ready," he said quietly, "my lord Father."

"Hm," said his lord Father, sounding entirely unconvinced.

But Paris was ready. He *was*. This early-morning meeting would be a simple affair—a formal introduction between himself and the Juliet, before they all went to Tybalt's funeral. It was also a chance for Father and Lord Catresou to negotiate the details of his Guardianship. Certain rewards and prerogatives were due to the family that gave up their son to be the Juliet's Guardian, and of course Father would want to obtain the maximum possible.

Paris wouldn't have to negotiate. He would just have to kneel to Lord Catresou, express how honored he was—and offer condolences for Tybalt; he was Lord Catresou's nephew and that couldn't be ignored—and then he would have to turn to the Juliet and say—

What?

In all his lessons, no one had ever told him how to make conversation with the Juliet.

He knew that right now she was to be addressed as *Lady Juliet*, but once the final sigils were placed upon her and she became fully the Juliet, she would be simply *Lady*, because there was only one woman whom the Catresou held in such reverence. But at that point he would be bonded as her Guardian, and he alone—except for Lord Catresou—would have the right to address her simply as *Juliet*.

But he didn't know how to actually talk to her.

Unbidden, a memory rushed back: the one time he'd seen the Juliet and Tybalt together. It had been two years ago, and entirely an accident. As always, Paris and his family had been invited to attend Lord Catresou's special feast for the Night of Ghosts. It was the first time Paris had come by himself, straight from the Academy, and he had gotten lost in the twisting corridors of Lord Catresou's house.

Then he'd turned a corner, and through a window, he'd seen the Juliet and Tybalt in a little courtyard garden.

They were both unmasked: they clearly didn't imagine that

anyone else would come upon them. The Juliet sat on a bench, her face turned up; Tybalt stood over her, leaning against a tree and saying something. Paris couldn't catch the words, but the Juliet's shoulders hunched and her hand covered her mouth as she started laughing.

Paris wasn't just supposed to replace a master swordsman. He was supposed to replace the Juliet's *family*.

Maybe he wasn't ready after all.

But it was too late now: they were at the door to Lord Catresou's study, and the footman was gesturing them forward.

And then they were inside.

Paris got only the briefest glimpse of red velvet wall hangings and Lord Catresou's imposing height before he was down on one knee, head bowed, as was proper before the leader of their clan. His heart was thudding, but he had practiced this reverence. He knew it was correct, just as it was correct for him to wear no mask before someone who so outranked him.

From the corner of his eye, he could see that Father had remained on his feet, only bowing: such was his right, as one of the five lords, second in rank only to Lord Catresou.

"My lord Lutreo, and young Paris," said Lord Catresou. His voice was deep but soft, like velvet. "Rise. I wish I could rejoice on this day."

Paris rose and, for the first time in his life, stood within a pace of Lord Catresou. He was a tall, austere man, with a long beard that had gone white when he was barely more than a youth. He had never competed in duels with the other highborn boys, but devoted himself to studying the lore of the magi: the sacred words that allowed them to wield magic without shedding blood as the Sisters of Thorn did. Rumor said it was the mystic secrets that had whitened his hair.

One thing was certainly true: after seventeen years in which ten other magi had tried and failed, Lord Catresou had marked a baby girl with the first sigils of becoming the Juliet—and she had survived. The girl had been his only daughter, the child of his old age. By his skill and willingness to sacrifice, he had won the undying loyalty and reverence of all the Catresou. At last they would have a Juliet to protect them again.

And now he was personally receiving Paris into his study, wearing only a half mask of velvet and gold. That familiarity was terrifying enough, but—like Paris—the Juliet wore no mask at all.

She was as lovely as rumor said: skin like moonlight, hair like midnight, eyes as blue as the twilight sky. She was also very young and very clearly human: a seventeen-year-old girl, staring at him with no expression whatsoever.

Paris was supposed to say something now, but for a heart-stopping moment he couldn't remember what. Then he swallowed dryly and said, "My lord, I—"

"Though he has passed into darkness, young Tybalt walks the Paths of Light," Father interrupted. The words were a standard piety, his voice dismissive. "It's the living we must care for now."

"Though we are deeply grieved," Paris added. The words sounded weak and awkward, but he had to say something. It wasn't right to stand here a few hours before Tybalt's funeral and talk as if his death didn't matter.

No one seemed to have heard him; Father and Lord Catresou hadn't looked away from each other for even a moment.

"There are matters to discuss, my lord," said Paris's father.

"Perhaps young Paris and my Juliet would care to step into the garden, and become further acquainted," said Lord Catresou, gesturing at a little side door.

It was clearly a dismissal. Paris bowed, then held out an arm for the Juliet, because he knew that was proper.

She looked at him for a moment, still expressionless. Then she laid her fingertips on his arm, and they went out into Lord Catresou's private garden together. It was a little round, walled space—no windows—with moss on the ground and a fountain at the center.

The Juliet dropped her fingers from his arm immediately and took a step away. She didn't look back at him. Her shoulders were tense; she was clearly furious, as well as bereaved, and why not?

He wanted to slink into the opposite corner of the garden, but he knew what his father would say. *Don't be a coward, boy.*

"Lady Juliet." He could only get the words out by stiffly, carefully pronouncing each syllable. "I am sorry I'm not your cousin."

She looked back then. Her face was still impassive, but he noticed now that her eyes were slightly swollen. She had probably been awake weeping all night, and now Paris felt even worse. It was so wrong that their fathers had shoved them in this garden and pretended Tybalt never existed.

He went on, "I never knew him—he left the Academy the year I entered—but he came back for dueling demonstrations sometimes. We could see he was amazing. And we heard about him too, all the time. Everyone said he was the best of our generation."

Then he realized that he was sounding like the worst kind of flatterer. Or like he'd spent hours each day wishing he could be Tybalt, which wasn't true. Well, not *entirely* true.

"But he was also your cousin," he finished awkwardly, "and I'm sorry you lost him. And I want you to know—I'm not Tybalt, but I've studied very hard and I swear I will fulfill my duty to you. I will help you protect our people."

She flinched at his words, and then she whispered, "Thank you."

Paris couldn't speak.

The Juliet drew herself up.

"What must be, must be," she said. Her voice was quick and rough, like an iron gate clanging shut. "I do not mourn Tybalt. I do not regret his loss. I liked him not; I like you neither. It is all one to me."

4

THE NEXT HALF HOUR WAS excruciatingly uncomfortable. The Juliet said nothing else. Paris kept trying to think of something to say but found nothing; it was a relief when their fathers summoned them back and told them it was time to leave for the sepulcher.

The funeral, with all its elaborate ceremony, was a relief in comparison. Paris knew his place: walking beside the Juliet in the procession. She carried the jar that held Tybalt's preserved heart. Her face—barely concealed by her filigree mask—was stiff and pale; her chin was raised, her back was straight, her every step was precise as a blade to the heart.

She had clearly loved him as a brother two years ago. What had happened?

Before them—carrying the jars with Tybalt's brain and

stomach—walked Lord Catresou and Tybalt's father, Lord Marreus. And before them went the bier, on which Tybalt's embalmed body rested, hands clasped over his chest, face as still and perfect as the Juliet's.

On either side marched the City Guard. This was the price that the Catresou paid for laying their dead to rest properly, instead of burning them like so much trash as the other Viyarans did. Their magi were watched as they performed the sacred rites of embalming—which must be done in only two days instead of the traditional sixty—and they were guarded as they carried their dead to rest.

Their sepulcher was filled with chains.

Paris had been to the sepulcher only once before: when his mother was buried. He had been six, so he remembered little of the day aside from Amando clinging to him, Father refusing to look at him, and the horrible glimpse of his mother's dead, wax-like face. But he remembered the chains: heavy, wrought-iron chains that rattled and groaned as they were drawn around his mother's coffin and locked.

There was no chance of the Catresou rising again. Despite the abbreviated embalming, their magi drained every drop of blood from the body, removed the heart and stomach and brain. Such a hollowed-out, twice-killed body could not be animated by the Ruining's power. And for further safety, the magi placed on every coffin a dead seal: a powerful sigil that would destroy anyone who tried to break it, as well as anything that stirred within it.

But the Sisters of Thorn did not trust the Catresou, which meant nobody in the city trusted them, and so they must chain their coffins shut as if their beloved dead were rabid animals. As if they were not the only ones who could keep their names and remember themselves as they walked the Paths of Light through the underworld.

From outside, the Catresou sepulcher was only a small, round building carved of the same white stone as the rest of the city. But it stood at the highest point of the compound, near the center of the city spire, and it rested on solid bedrock. And into the bedrock, year after year, the Catresou had dug spiraling tunnels down into the earth. They had paid in their own blood to make the Sisters reinforce those tunnels, and there among the cold rock and obscene spells they made a holy place for their dead. Every inch of the pale walls was carved into filigree; as the procession wound through the tunnel, their lanterns made light and shadow dance across the lacy surface of the walls.

Tybalt's family was renowned enough to have their own room. One-half of it was already stacked floor to ceiling with stone coffins; Tybalt's lay open by the door, lined with silk and scattered with flowers.

The veiled mourners keened as they laid Tybalt's body in the coffin. Lord Catresou and Lord Marreus set one jar by his head, one by his feet. Then a magus came forward, hooded in velvet and masked in gold. He touched a golden seal to Tybalt's eyes, his mouth, his hands, his feet, as he whispered the prayers that would awaken those limbs and organs in the afterlife. He tucked into Tybalt's hands a scroll filled with spells for walking the Paths of Light and a stone rod carved with sigils of power.

Beside Paris, the Juliet took a shuddering breath. Then she stepped forward to lay the jar with Tybalt's heart upon his chest.

The funeral was complete. Tybalt had been laid to rest with prayers to the nine gods. His body was embalmed, so that decay would never touch it; his heart and brains and stomach were safely locked in jars, so that evil spirits would never corrupt them; spells and a rod of power had been laid into his hands, so that he could follow the Paths of Light and defeat whatever opposed him. There was no more to be done for him.

Yet the Juliet paused.

Paris had assumed that if anything went wrong with the funeral, he would cause it by stumbling somehow. So he was utterly unprepared to see the Juliet ignore her father's beckoning and drop to her knees. She drew one breath—Paris winced in embarrassment at how raw, how like a sob it sounded—and she pressed her lips against Tybalt's forehead in a kiss.

Then she laid her head upon his chest.

Paris heard Lord Catresou's soft breath of impatience, saw Lord Marreus's lips tighten. He knew that the crowd of mourners behind them was staring. He felt the awful tension in his chest of knowing *someone is about to get angry*.

Still the Juliet did not move.

Paris didn't realize he was moving until he was kneeling at her side. He reached forward—paused—and let his hand drop gently onto her shoulder. He could feel everyone looking at them. He was sure that any moment, Father would reprimand him. But if he didn't do anything, Father would just get angry at the Juliet instead.

"Lady Juliet," he whispered. "Please."

She lifted her head and looked at him. Her eyes were dry; her face was fixed in a stony, blank expression that could be grief or fear or fury.

A moment later she stood, smoothly and decisively. She said nothing, did not look at him again, and Lord Catresou led them out of the sepulcher as if there had been no interruption.

It was high noon when the funeral feast started; several hours later, it was still going strong when the Juliet turned to Paris and said, "Can you take me back to the sepulcher?"

"What?" he said. It didn't seem quite real that she was talking to him.

"The sepulcher," said the Juliet. "I am not permitted to go out alone. Will you take me?"

Paris wasn't sure that he was permitted to take her, but she was looking him straight in the eyes, and he found himself saying, "Of course, Lady Juliet."

There was no going back down into the depths of the sepulcher: the doors were already bolted shut. But the sanctum on the upper level stood open for mourners. There was an alcove with a sacred fire, and on the wall over it was inlaid in gold the swirling lines of *zoura*, the old Catresou word that meant "correct knowledge"—the wisdom and lore of how to preserve the dead.

The Juliet knelt before the fire and did not move. Paris stood awkwardly beside her: it felt like too much of an intrusion to kneel with her, but it hardly seemed reverent to stand like one of the unconcerned guards outside.

"You," she said suddenly, without looking up. "Do you believe in the Paths of Light?"

"Of course," said Paris. That was the whole point of being Catresou.

"I cannot tell if my father does." Her voice was quiet, meditative.

It was such an absurd accusation, it took him a moment to respond. "I'm sure—"

"No," the Juliet interrupted without anger. "He must believe. He is so sure, when he reminds me that he will walk them, and I cannot. But he does not . . . respect them."

Paris shifted uncomfortably. The Catresou were the only people who could walk the Paths of Light, not just because only they knew the spells for traversing the land of the dead, but because their names had been sealed to them by the Catresou magi. So only they could escape the fate of all other souls: to drift a while on the winds of death as a nameless, gibbering ghost, and then dissolve to nothingness.

Except the Juliet. The magic that gave her the power to protect also stripped her of her name. She would be buried with no scroll of spells, no rod of power, and her heart rotting inside her body, because nothing awaited her but darkness.

It was a noble sacrifice. Until this moment, it had never seemed unfair.

"I can bear that," she said, "if I can protect people first."

Paris swallowed and knelt beside her. "Lady Juliet," he began, but didn't know what he was going to say.

"Tybalt used to bring me here," she said. "To see the fire, and the word." She nodded at the golden calligraphy inlaid on the wall. "*Zoura*. It's all I ever wanted, to be correct."

"You are," said Paris. "You make our people correct. 'Justice is the sword of *zoura*,' right?"

Her mouth tilted up a little at the words of the old saying all Catresou children heard a thousand times.

"My father's *zoura* is not mine," she said. "He thinks 'correct' means no more than 'skillful.' He made me the sword of the Catresou only so he could use me."

Paris knew what this was: the wild imaginings of a hysterical Juliet. He'd been told often enough—he'd read in book after book—that Juliets forever wavered on the brink of madness, and so they were ever accusing their families of imaginary crimes.

And yet he heard her voice, flat and unhappy and ruthlessly accepting, and he couldn't disbelieve her.

Juliet finally turned to look at him.

"You have tried to be kind to me," she said. "Thank you."

Without thinking, Paris took her hand and pressed his lips to her knuckles.

"I will serve you," he said. "I promise."

5

"OF ALL THE POSSIBLE REASONS to punish me," said Runajo, "taking a vow to protect our city seems a strange one."

She had been terrified while she waited for the Great Offering. In the two days since—locked in a small cell, awaiting judgment—the fear had come and gone. But now that she was facing the assembled leaders of the Sisterhood, she felt only a cold, heady exultation. She had done what she must. Let others worry about the consequences.

To receive those consequences, she had been brought to the Hall of Judgment. It was carved of cold white stone, every surface flat and featureless—except for the far wall, where the gigantic obsidian head of Nin, goddess of truth, grew out of the stone panels. It was tilted back to stare at the ceiling; from where Runajo knelt, she could only see the crown of Nin's head and the tips of her ears.

Nin was dead, like all the nine gods, and like all the gods did not exist, so she was not Runajo's problem right now.

The ring of women standing around her in judgment was.

The High Priestess raised a single eyebrow, a stark, pale curve against the darkness of her skin. She was an Old Viyaran aristocrat; her hair was such a pale blond it was almost white.

"Oh? For what should we punish you instead?" she asked, with the glacial amusement of one who could order throats cut if it pleased her.

Runajo knew that most of the people in the room expected her own throat to fare poorly.

"Tardiness," she said. "I should have done it earlier."

"You mean disobedience," snapped Miryo, the novice mistress. Like all the Sisters—except for the High Priestess—she had her white cowl pulled down over her head, so that only her chin, with its briar tattoo, was visible. Unlike most of the Sisters, her skin was pale behind the crimson lines of the tattoo. She was one of the few other Mahyanai Sisters, and she had hated Runajo since she had arrived, perhaps because of the way she had defied the whole clan. Or perhaps Miryo was just inherently poisonous; it didn't really matter.

"And desecration," said another Sister—Runajo didn't recognize her, but her white robe had the red bands of one who offered the solemn sacrifices.

"And bringing shame upon us all before the Exalted," said a third.

Everyone knew the Exalted didn't notice anything unless it involved wine or women in much less clothing than Runajo had been wearing. But since everyone else in the room—except possibly Miryo—believed him a descendant of the gods, it was probably a bad idea to point that out.

"It was the time to make our offerings," Runajo said instead. "I could scarcely offer more than myself."

Vima, the black-robed priestess of mourning, raised her bowed head. From her neck hung the symbol of her office: a bone ring with six splinters branching out of it, like a sunburst. The novices whispered that the bones came from a sacrifice, and that Vima had scraped and boiled them clean herself while chanting the sacred laments.

"Thousands have walked this path before," she said. "Why should you run it?"

Runajo knew better than to reply, *Because I couldn't stand to obey you a moment longer.*

"Because," she said, quietly and clearly, "we need to recover the knowledge that built the city walls. We are lost without it. You know it; I know it; everyone who is not an idiot knows it."

Well, every Sister knew it. People didn't talk of it outside the Cloister: Runajo had never been told, until she joined. But anyone could look at Viyara's history and see how the sacrifices had grown more frequent. Hence: *idiots.*

She looked at Miryo. "Only a full Sister of Thorn can descend to the lower levels without blasphemy, but you told me that the Sisters are too precious to throw their lives away. Clearly, you need one who is disposable. One who can go down into the library and discover how the magic protecting our city works."

"The loss of the library is tragic," said the High Priestess, "but we have lived a hundred years without it. We know enough to honor the gods and protect the city, and there is no guarantee that the library could teach us anything more."

The High Priestess's stern, serene voice was nothing like Mother's breathy whisper, but for one moment, Runajo could smell the sick-room stench again.

Her hands clenched, and there was a flash of pain from her left palm. Because of her disgrace, they had so far refused her the normal healing ointments; the sign she had carved into her hand as she took the oath was still a scabbed mess.

"We protect nothing," she said. "We save *no one.* We only delay the inevitable, and that for not much longer. I have looked at the histories. I have helped weave the walls. I have worked the sacred equations for the sacrifice. Soon we will need to offer lives more than twice a year; do not deny it."

"I do not," said the High Priestess. "We will offer of our blood and bone whatever we must to protect this city, and in the end we will all die as offerings. Did you expect any other fate, when you came to us?"

"No," said Runajo. "But I expected that at least some of my Sisters would *accept* that fate. We are the Sisters of Thorn. We are all going to die, and we are supposed to live as if already dead, for the good of all Viyara. So why do we dally and pretend that we couldn't protect our city better right now by risking our lives?"

She wanted to scream. Didn't they realize what they were accepting? In the end, they would have to offer sacrifices every day; they would be slaughtering the city to save it, and even that would not be enough. The walls would eventually fail, and the white fog of the Ruining would flow into the city, and nobody would survive.

"Going back to the Sunken Library is not a risk," said Miryo, in the lecturing tone she had used every day among the novices. "There must be thousands of revenants locked inside, and likely reapers as well. It is suicide, and a waste of blood that could be better spent feeding the walls."

"It is a *fact,*" said Runajo, "that the people who built that library also built this city, and the walls we can barely maintain. And for three thousand years, their library was the wonder of the world. The secrets of the walls *must* be in there. If there's any chance that we could find those secrets, why is it not worth dying for? Do you think we are going to live forever?"

There was a quick hiss of indrawn breath from all around,

and Runajo knew that she had gone too far. Desire for eternal life was the greatest blasphemy; suggesting, even rhetorically, that the High Priestess might harbor it was not going to improve her case.

Her mouth tugged into a crooked grin. *I am not going to live forever.*

"I believe," said Miryo, "that you are a disobedient, blasphemous child who wants us to consider her a hero."

"Perhaps you could consider me a penance," said Runajo. "And I am not a child; my oath was valid. Or do you dispute that I said the words?"

"I do not," said the High Priestess. "I consider you the youngest of our Sisterhood, and therefore now you must obey me. Be silent."

Runajo pressed her lips together and met the High Priestess's gaze. In the end, Miryo had no say here: she could discipline novices, but sentencing criminals and blasphemers was the sole domain of the High Priestess.

If Miryo could, she would sentence Runajo to death in an instant. But the High Priestess? Runajo had no idea what she would choose.

It had been easy enough to be brave when she was arguing. Now, still and in silence, the cold fear started oozing down her body again. She did not want to die.

The gods have died, and in their blood, we live as those already dead.

Of all the sayings she had learned from the Sisters of Thorn, it was the only one that had any power to comfort her.

"Mahyanai Runajo," said the High Priestess, "I do believe that you desire to serve the gods. Therefore I grant you mercy for your disobedience and I accept you as one of our Sisterhood."

It took all of Runajo's self-control not to slump her shoulders in relief.

"But you have not yet proved yourself as the others have," the High Priestess went on calmly, relentlessly. "So tomorrow night, you will have the chance to sit the vigil of souls alone. Should you survive, you will take your place with us."

For a moment Runajo couldn't breathe. It took years of training before a Sister could sit through the night at the Mouth of Death and be alive and sane come morning. She had been prepared to face death, but she knew about the Sisters who failed at the vigil and *didn't* die. Who were carried out screaming about reapers and dead souls, and who spent the rest of their lives tormented by those visions.

She felt like a bubble, curving around a cold gap of fear.

"If you cannot face that test," said the High Priestess, "then you are no more than a foolish child, and you will be punished no more than such a child deserves. You will confess your fault before the assembled Sisterhood and do penance, and in time you will be forgiven."

She wants me afraid, Runajo realized, and the sudden surge of anger burned away the cold emptiness of fear. *She wants me to admit I'm a child and crawl back to my proper place.*

Beneath the edge of Miryo's cowl, her lower lip was visible. Smiling.

There was only one possible choice. The risk was much too terrible, her failure far too certain. Everyone in the room knew that Runajo would have to call herself a child and beg for mercy.

Everyone in the room didn't know her at all.

Night after night, day after day, year after *year* she had kept vigil beside her parents as they died. She had lived at the Mouth of Death her whole life. If she could survive that, she could survive this.

Her heart was pounding in her chest; she was amazed at how calm her voice sounded.

"Then I gladly accept my duty," she said. "I will sit the vigil of souls."

6

SOMETHING HAD HAPPENED BETWEEN JULIET and Tybalt. Something that would make her swear she hated him, and yet stop the funeral with her grief.

Paris wondered about it all that evening, as they practiced for the ceremony. It kept distracting him so that he stumbled over minor details; then Father would sigh in disappointment, while Juliet looked at him so stoically that he was afraid she had decided to hate him after all, and she was only enduring him for the sake of their clan.

Tomorrow he would know. A girl fully became the Juliet when the magi finished writing the sacred word for justice upon her skin. The power of that word was so terrible, it would drive her insane unless somebody could help her bear it. So the Juliet's Guardian was joined to her mind to mind; he could hear her thoughts whenever he pleased, and when her reason faltered, he could rule her with his own.

Paris had vaguely imagined that it would be glorious to have their hearts united in service, but he had never bothered to think what it would really entail. Now—as they knelt together in Lord Catresou's house, her masklike face so close he could touch it—the thought of prying open her mind and reading those fiercely guarded secrets made him sick.

Perhaps that was why Juliet hated Tybalt: because he had died and left her to share her mind with a stranger. And yet she'd said that she could bear even eternal darkness if she could protect her people. What was more terrible to her than eternal darkness?

The question still nagged at him that night, when he had finally gone back home to have a late dinner. He hardly even cared when Father did him the honor of removing his mask—though probably it was only because Meros was there.

Paris's brother was twenty-three now, a great sprawling young man of handsome arrogance, and Father's right hand in running the glassmaking house that made the Mavarinns one of the richest families of the Catresou. Certainly Father's attention stayed on Meros all throughout the meal, as he quizzed him about the latest reports. Meros sat up reasonably straight, answered fairly quietly, and did not get particularly drunk, which as far as Paris knew was a singular act of respect. Unless he'd changed; in the four years since he started at the Academy, Paris had barely been home.

None of that felt important now. Paris couldn't stop thinking of the way Juliet had smiled at Tybalt. What had changed her?

Then a servant summoned Father away to receive an urgent messenger. With a loud sigh, Meros drained his wineglass and flung himself back in his chair.

"Paths of *Light*, that business is boring," he said.

"At least you get to leave sometimes," said Amando. The middle of the three brothers, he was so pale and scrawny he looked younger than Paris, though he was two years older. "I'm old enough to join in your night games, you know."

"Hush," said Meros, waving a hand, as if everyone didn't know about his hobbies. But he was a genius at the glasshouse, not to mention fluent in five languages and a skilled duelist. Of course Father would forgive him for the drinking and the bullying and for being caught so often with prostitutes from the Lower City.

"But look at you, little brother." Meros sat up again, looking Paris right in the eye. "About to become a great man."

Paris stared back at him. He couldn't help tensing a little, but Meros was still not truly drunk, which meant he was unlikely to start throwing things.

"Too bad it has to be someone else's scraps," Meros went on, plucking an apple out of the fruit bowl. "But let's not be too picky, eh?"

Amando snickered. When they were children, he had played

with Paris. Then he had realized that Meros would reward him better for following orders.

"I am honored to serve our people," Paris said stiffly, because if he didn't have a reaction, sometimes Meros would give up.

Meros raised his eyebrows. "A very generous attitude. Or do you just not know?"

Paris couldn't keep the irritation out of his voice. "I am perfectly aware that Tybalt—"

"You really *don't* know." Meros twisted the apple against his knife, peeling the skin off in a thin red ribbon. "Don't you ever lift your head from your books? It must be all over the Academy by now."

"*What* is?" Paris demanded.

"The reason that Tybalt was breathing fire all last week. And the reason why he picked a duel and now lies dead." Meros finally met his eyes. "The Juliet's no more a maid than I. She's bedded a Mahyanai boy. I hope you don't mind another man's leavings."

Paris didn't realize he had moved until he was on his feet, his chair clattering to the floor. "Take that back."

It was one thing to ignore Meros when he was insulting Paris. That was pretty much inevitable, and in the end it didn't matter much. But the Juliet was *important*.

Meros grinned, wide and lazy. "'Your precious Juliet and some Mahyanai filth have made the beast with two backs."

Paris had heard the phrase before; he wasn't as stupid or naive as Meros thought. He knew what it meant. But the vile words were so completely different from the angry, unhappy girl he had met in the garden—the laughing girl he had glimpsed two years ago—the quiet girl in the sepulcher, resolved to protect her people at any cost—that for a moment, his mind refused to understand.

Then he did, and his face went hot. Just hearing the words made him feel unclean.

"If only she'd told me she was so desperate," said Amando, "I'd have been happy to help her." He snickered, glancing at Meros to make sure he still approved.

Meros was snickering too. In a moment, he would tease Paris about blushing. He was slandering Juliet, and he didn't even hate her; he was just doing it to get at Paris.

And Paris was sick of being silent.

He picked up his goblet and flung the wine in Meros's face.

"You are a liar," he said, "and I will prove it on your body."

Paris had tried the traditional challenge to a duel on Meros once before, when he was thirteen. That time Meros had just laughed it off and refused to fight—but that time, Paris hadn't been brave enough to throw wine in his face and his precious goatee.

This time, Meros's face went pinched and angry.

"You little—" His chair clattered back as he stood. "I accept your challenge, little brother. Bare swords."

Meros was going to kill him. Or slice up his face and leave

him scarred for life, which was how he liked to win duels. But for the first time, Paris wasn't scared of him. His heart was pounding, but he *wanted* to fight. There was no point in getting cut up to stop Meros from teasing him, but for Juliet—

"Boys," their father said mildly from the doorway.

Meros turned, all lazy grace again. "The little one is growing teeth," he said. "And losing his respect for—"

"My lord Father," Paris interrupted, "he has slandered the Juliet. He said—he said—" He couldn't bring himself to actually repeat the words.

Meros rolled his eyes. "I told him what is commonly said and known about her virtue, for which he might be grateful, since it will be his duty to keep her under control."

"It's a lie," Paris snarled.

"It is a rumor," said Father, "that was useful when the Juliet was not going to belong to us."

For a moment, Paris couldn't speak. He knew Father wanted their family to wring every last possible drop of prestige that they could from the Juliet. He knew that, but—he'd never thought—

"*You* slandered her?" he said.

"Do not imagine," said Father, his voice quiet with warning, "that you can rebuke your father."

"I'm sorry," Paris said reflexively. He'd said the words a thousand times before, as he failed his father a thousand times.

But now his father wasn't the only one to whom he had a duty.

His heart pounded, but he made himself meet Father's eyes. "And yet with all due respect," he said, "did you spread those rumors?"

Meros barked out a laugh. "I told you he was growing teeth."

Father stared at Paris for a moment; then he nodded slightly to himself, as if Paris had passed some private inspection.

"I spread no rumors," he said, "but I hardly wept to hear them. The Juliet's honor did us no good when Tybalt was defending it. That must now change, and I expect you to be mindful of that, Meros."

"As my lord Father wishes."

Father stepped closer to Paris. "And as for *you*, boy, I expect you to stop giving yourself airs and obey me. You are finally in a position to be of some use to this family, and I expect you to give me satisfaction. Do you understand?"

The Juliet was the honor and protector of their people, and she had never mattered to Father as anything but a pawn.

"I understand," he said.

If the rest of his family was not prepared to do their duty, then Paris would just have to do it for them.

Paris still didn't know what had happened with Tybalt. And he could never replace him. But as he lay in bed that night, trying to sleep, he thought that maybe he could protect Juliet. At least he could help her hunt down Tybalt's murderer. Maybe that would bring her a little comfort. And then—and then somehow Paris would stop the rumors, and he would force Meros and Father and Lord Catresou to respect the Juliet, and he would protect her and keep her happy, and everything would be all right.

He knew he was thinking wildly, that he probably would never be able to do half of it. But he had a chance. Nobody had ever thought he would be useful, and now he had a chance.

It was very late when he finally dozed off, and it seemed only a moment later that he was woken by one of the servants. They were supposed to fetch the Juliet from her house at dawn, so Paris dressed in the pale glow of the lamp, pulling on his best white shirt and the new doublet stiff with gold embroidery, while listening to Meros's muffled cursing through the wall. It took him hours to wake up in the morning, and he had probably stubbed his toe.

Today, Paris thought as he fastened his mask: the first formal, jeweled mask that he had ever worn. It covered his face from his temples to his chin; when he looked in the mirror, all he saw of himself was his eyes—obviously—and his lips, half revealed through the little hole that allowed him to breathe and speak. The rest was beaten gold inlaid with garnets and lapis lazuli. His pale hair, spilling over the top edge, seemed like one more part of the mask. It covered everything that was

"Paris" and "youngest" and "perfectly adequate."

He was going to be the Juliet's Guardian. He was going to *matter.*

When they got to Lord Catresou's house, nobody was waiting for them. The servant who answered the door looked nervous as he said, "Just a moment," and then fled.

It was no surprise the household was in chaos. But as Paris waited with Father and Meros in the entryway, he listened to the slamming of doors, the shouting of voices, and he started to feel that something was wrong. He couldn't make out the words, but the voices were a little too angry, a little too desperate. Was that someone sobbing in the distance?

And there was Lord Catresou standing in doorway. His face was covered in a full mask, but the eye slits were fixed on Paris.

"You," he said. He held a paper in his hand, but he let it flutter to the floor as he strode forward. Paris's heart gave one awful jolt, and then Lord Catresou shoved him against the wall.

"You knew," he snarled. "Where did you take her last night? *Where is she?*"

"I don't know," Paris said. His head was ringing; he didn't know if he had banged it against the wall, or if he was just dazed by Lord Catresou's sudden fury. "I'm sorry. I don't know. I—"

"Stop babbling and tell me the truth!"

"My lord!" Father protested, and he sounded actually angry. Of course he was. The family was being disgraced.

Meros let out a sudden crow of laughter. "I knew it!"

They all looked at him. He had the paper and he was grinning down at whatever was written on it.

Then he looked at Paris and held it out. "Didn't I tell you, little brother?"

Father's voice snapped like a whip. "My lord, cease this unseemly display and tell us what happened."

Lord Catresou let go of Paris and turned away from him as if he didn't exist anymore. In a cold, distant voice, he said, "The little whore betrayed us."

Paris snatched the letter from Meros.

My lord Father:

Mahyanai Romeo, who killed Tybalt, has married me in secret according to the custom of his people. I will accept no duty that compels me to destroy him. Therefore I am going to make him my Guardian, so that he can order me not to kill him. At his side I will protect not only our clan but all the people of the city.

Do not blame Paris. He knew nothing of this, and has only done his duty.

Juliet Catresou

7

"SHE DIDN'T WRITE IT," SAID Paris. He felt numb and hot and cold all at the same time. Nothing made sense.

"She couldn't have," he insisted, and everyone looked at him as if he were insane.

Meros clapped a hand to his shoulder. "Little brother, you'd be surprised and delighted to learn what women will do for a man who kisses them well enough."

"Her mother was always willful," Lord Catresou growled. "I should have known."

"You must see that Paris had nothing to do with it," said Father. "He doesn't have the wit to take her to a secret meeting, let alone the will."

The words shouldn't have surprised Paris, and he shouldn't have cared about anything except the Juliet right now. But hearing them still felt like a kick in the gut.

Lord Catresou barked a laugh. "True."

"What if he kidnapped her?" Paris said desperately. "Maybe—"

"Paris." Father fixed him with a look. "Enough."

Paris could feel the hot flush creeping up his face. But they had all met Juliet—Lord Catresou was her *father*—surely they had to understand that she would never, ever betray them.

Yet there was the letter.

Maybe Paris had never understood. Maybe he just wanted to keep believing that he could be useful to the clan, when really the girl he wanted to protect had never been worthy.

He remembered her quiet, wistful voice in the sepulcher, as they sat by the sacred fire and spoke about *zoura*.

It's all I ever wanted, she had said.

Whatever she had done—however misguided she might be—she must have a good reason. She was still worth protecting. And that meant he had to get to her before the rest of his family did.

"I'm sorry, my lord Father," he said meekly. "What can I do?"

Father never wanted his help. If Paris could just be dismissed because he was useless one more time, then he could go look for Juliet himself.

"Go fetch the rest of the men from your household," said Lord Catresou.

"What?" said Paris, but of course he should have expected it.

Maybe once he delivered the message, he could slip away in the commotion.

"Did you think you'd find her by yourself, boy?" said Father. "We need search parties. Meros, you go with him too."

"Don't you want him to—" Paris started, but then he saw the disapproval on Father's face. He wasn't supposed to question orders. "I'm sorry," he said quickly. "Never mind."

"Come, I'll comfort you along the way," said Meros, slapping his shoulder.

There was nothing to be done but go back out into the cold, predawn streets. Paris tried to walk as quickly as he could, his throat tight with frustration, because Meros was in a talking mood now and he would like as not try to follow Paris even after they had gotten back to the house.

"There are other girls, you know," said Meros. "Prettier ones. I could introduce you."

And though he knew better, Paris couldn't help snapping, "I didn't become the Juliet's Guardian because she was pretty."

"That's right, you *didn't* become her Guardian," said Meros amiably. "But come, now. You really never thought about what you'd do with a pretty young girl who had to obey you?"

It took Paris a moment to realize what his brother had said. "I did not—I could never—"

"And who *liked* you, of course." Meros raised his hands. "I wouldn't suggest you do anything she didn't want. Doesn't the bond mean she has to love you?"

The bond between a Juliet and her Guardian could not force them to love or even like each other. Paris knew this, because he had bothered to read the histories, and there had been some times where the bond went terribly wrong.

Meros wouldn't care if Paris told him, any more than he would care that the Juliet was a girl who had mourned her cousin and—apparently—fallen in love. Who knew she would never walk the Paths of Light, and who said, *I can bear that if I can protect people first.*

Who was now in danger, while Paris ran errands for his father.

What was he thinking?

Meros had started talking again, but Paris paid no attention. It felt like the world was tilting under his feet. He knew that the Juliet was in danger, but he had still thought that he had to carry out his father's orders first, simply because he had always obeyed.

But his duty to the Juliet was more important. If his loyalty to the Catresou had ever meant anything, she had to come first.

For one awful, stomach-churning moment, he was coward enough to hesitate.

Then Meros reached for his shoulder. Without thinking, Paris slapped his hand away and ran.

He was around the corner and two houses down the side street before Meros gathered his wits enough to shout. When he glanced back a moment later, he saw Meros running after him.

Paris gulped for breath and ran faster.

Meros had longer legs, so if it came to a race, he would probably win. But it wouldn't come to that, because Meros would much rather go back and tell Father about Paris's latest failure than run himself breathless.

Sure enough, within a few minutes—and a few quick, skidding turns—Meros was gone.

Paris stopped to lean against the side of the building and gasp for breath. He had to rip off his mask; the mouth hole was too small for him to get enough air. But after only a few moments, he pulled himself back upright, because there was no time to lose.

Father and Lord Catresou would soon have men combing the city. But they thought that the Juliet had betrayed them. They thought she could have gone anywhere to defile the sacred ceremony with a Mahyanai boy.

But Paris was sure that however much this Mahyanai Romeo might have deluded Juliet, she would never willingly defile the ceremony. That meant she must do it in a hallowed place, and with the sanctum of the Catresou magi so full of people, there was only one other place she could go.

The white dome of the sepulcher was exactly as he remembered. But the guards were gone.

As he ran inside, Paris had never been so grateful that the laws of the city forced the sanctum to have an open archway with no door.

But he was too late. The Juliet—unmasked—sat with Mahyanai Romeo at the center of the room, and they had already started.

The ceremony to create a Juliet's Guardian was, in essence, very simple. The Juliet wrote the sacred word for trust on her palm in ink. Then she clasped hands with her new Guardian, transferring the word to his skin. And the word that was written upon them became true.

There were rituals—prayers and meditations and spells—that surrounded the bonding. But the word was what mattered. Only the Juliet, having borne a sacred word for years, could survive the writing of another; when she passed that word to her new Guardian, her strength allowed him to survive it. The other rituals only helped.

Juliet must have wanted to be careful, because she had written a circle of protective sigils around herself and Romeo on the floor. But the lines were shaky, and Paris thought that some of them might be drawn wrong.

Romeo looked up. Juliet didn't. She was already writing the sacred word on her palm.

Everything changed.

The air was suddenly ice cold; it felt crystal clear and razor sharp, as if Paris had spent all his life living in a thick fog that had only just now cleared. The pale morning light that had shone through the doorway was gone. The walls were gone too. The three of them were surrounded by infinite, empty darkness, the only light coming from the sacred fire.

Juliet dropped the brush—the tiny clatter was terrifyingly loud in the silence around them—and reached for Romeo.

And as their hands met, Paris heard the sound of death.

The Catresou magi and the Mahyanai sages and the Viyaran priestesses all told different tales of what would happen after death. But there was one thing every person alive knew for certain. At the moment of death, people heard a song. *Water, singing with many voices* was how they described it with their last breaths. Paris had never been able to imagine what that meant.

Now he knew.

It was liquid and sibilant and wordless as the song of running water. It had all the urgent meaning of a chant from human tongues. It was cold and rippling and relentless, and it was all around him, tugging at his bones and his blood, and it was going to draw him away. He was going to die.

He had to save the Juliet.

Paris realized he had fallen to his hands and knees. He staggered to his feet, and he saw—

He wasn't sure what he saw.

Ripples of darkness and light rolled through the air, shoved at his chest and made him stagger. For a moment he could see Juliet and Romeo, silhouetted against the flashes of light; then everything frayed apart in dazzling lines of light and darkness, but he knew they were still there because he heard a scream, and he staggered forward. If only he could catch hold of Juliet, maybe he could save her.

Fingertips brushed his and then were gone. He lunged and caught a hand. He knew it was Juliet, because he could feel the sacred word written on her palm; it felt like it was burning through his skin, all the way down to the bone. He screamed, and held on.

Then there was nothing.

Paris woke up crying.

He never cried. He hadn't since he was a little child and his mother died. But now he was kneeling on the stone floor of the sanctum, gasping for breath, with tears running down his face.

He couldn't see anything. For a moment he thought the room was still plunged in darkness; then he realized his eyes were shut. He thought, *I have to find Juliet,* and tried to open them.

The world rocked dizzyingly. Suddenly he wasn't kneeling; he was flat on his back, staring up at the ceiling. His body ached all over; his hand still felt like it had been burned. And he wasn't crying; there were no tears stinging at his eyes or trickling down his face.

But he could hear somebody weeping next to him.

Juliet, he thought, with a surge of fear that enabled him to sit up.

Juliet was gone.

The light coming in the windows was still pale and weak; only minutes had passed. But everything in the sepulcher had changed. The sacred fire had gone out. Soot was smeared across the walls. And the Juliet was gone, only Mahyanai Romeo was left, doubled over and weeping.

Paris staggered to his feet. "What did you do to her?" he demanded. His voice felt raw.

It took Romeo a moment to lift his head and look at him. "She's gone," he said, his voice quiet and dazed. "I killed her."

He sounded so desolate, a sudden wave of sadness choked Paris. For an instant he wanted to sit down next to the boy who had destroyed Juliet and weep with him.

Then he remembered that he was a Catresou and he had a duty.

"She's not dead," said Paris. "She can't be dead, all you did was . . ."

All Romeo had done was defile the sacred ceremony.

Paris remembered how the room had filled with shadows and the rippling, insistent song of death. How the many voices had felt like many hands, pulling him inexorably into darkness.

The magi said that sacred magic would avenge itself on those who misused it. And dragging someone into the land of the dead was surely a fitting vengeance.

But surely the magic should have turned on Romeo

instead—not on Juliet, who was Catresou and loyal, but on the boy who had wanted to defile her—

"I was *saving* her," Romeo snarled. "Your people are the ones who would defile her, by turning her into a slave!"

Paris's breath caught. He hadn't said *defile* out loud.

His hand still ached. He looked at it, and his heart turned to ice.

"Show me your hands," he said, and without hesitation, Romeo held them up.

The sacred word for *trust* was written on his right palm, in ink that looked as black as night, ink that would never wash off because the word was part of him now.

The same word that was written on Paris's hand.

He felt sick. Unclean. The bond between a Juliet and her Guardian was sacred. To have a Juliet joined that way to an outsider was bad enough. But for that bond to be ripped away from her and twisted like this—it was obscene.

And it didn't make sense. Only the power of a Juliet could allow a normal human to survive the bond. How was this possible? How were they not dead?

"She touched me first," Romeo said dully. "She screamed. She must have—"

Somehow she had borne the power of the link for both of them. She had saved them and died, when they should have died saving her.

"No." Romeo flung himself back on the floor. "She lives. We are dead."

"What?" said Paris.

"This is the land of the dead," Romeo whispered. "Life is where Juliet is."

The words were ridiculous, but Paris could feel Romeo's grief like a dark wave drowning them both, and for a moment he choked.

Grimly, Paris took one slow breath and then another. He remembered the meditations he had been taught. He built the wall between their minds. He rubbed at his eyes, to get rid of the tears that *were not his.*

"We have to go back," he said. "We have to tell them what happened."

He'd failed in everything else. At least he could tell Lord Catresou the truth about his daughter's death. At least he could face his punishment like a man.

"This room is the last place that saw Juliet," Romeo said stubbornly. "I will lie here until I die."

"This is the sepulcher," said Paris. "Do you think the magi will clean around you while you wait to die of thirst? Get up."

Instantly and without complaint, Romeo stood. And because Paris could feel what Romeo felt, he knew Romeo hadn't wanted to. That his limbs had moved against his will, as instantly and helplessly as his own heartbeat, and he knew that now Romeo's hands were shaking as he wondered if his body was his own again.

Romeo whispered, "What did you do?"

"I'm sorry," said Paris, who hadn't truly pitied him until that moment. "I didn't mean to."

Even when he'd realized they were linked, he hadn't expected the bond between them would include obedience. Probably he should feel triumphant now—he had captured the Mahyanai who stole their Juliet—but instead he just felt sick.

"You meant to do it to Juliet," said Romeo.

Paris's stomach twisted as he remembered Juliet saying, *I can bear that.*

It didn't change his duty. But he could at least try to persuade Romeo instead of forcing him.

"Listen," said Paris. "You have killed a noble lady. If you ever really loved her, you will come back and make amends to her family."

Romeo's anger burned right through the wall that Paris had tried to put between their minds.

"Amends to the family that wanted to enslave her?" he demanded. "Lie down among your precious bones and *rot.*"

Before he knew what he was doing, Paris had left the sanctum and was most of the way down the stairs toward the inner sepulcher. The next moment, his hands were pounding against the locked door. He had to get inside. He had to lie down among the bones—

With a sick, helpless terror, he realized that Romeo had given him an order. And he was obeying. The bond had been twisted to work both ways.

It was one of the hardest things he'd ever done, but he managed to lower his hands and clench them into fists at his sides. He was a Catresou. He would *not* take orders from a Mahyanai boy.

After a few agonizing moments, the compulsion faded. At least the bond wasn't forcing him into complete obedience.

Romeo had followed him down the steps. Grimly, Paris turned to face him.

"We can order each other back and forth all day," he said. "That doesn't change what's right."

From above—probably from just outside the sepulcher's main door—they heard voices.

And to his shame, Paris panicked. He knew he should call out, or bodily drag Romeo up the stairs. But he couldn't seem to move. What if it was Meros up there? What if it was Father?

Romeo didn't hesitate. The stairwell had an alcove on each side, right before the door, where there were hung tapestries covered with sacred designs; Romeo hauled Paris into one of them, covering his mouth so he couldn't cry out.

Paris struggled, but he knew he wasn't really trying, and after a moment he went still.

Up above in the sanctum, there were footsteps, and then silence.

"She actually did it," said Master Trelouno.

It was the last voice he had expected to hear: his dueling instructor, speaking with exactly the same distant disgust as when Paris had executed a technique particularly badly. For a moment, Paris couldn't quite believe he was hearing it.

"So it would seem," replied the last voice Paris had wanted to hear: Lord Catresou, his former fury turned to icy displeasure.

Lord Catresou was here. He was *here,* which Paris should have expected—of course he would know his own daughter well enough to guess where she would go—and he was going to find Paris cowering with an enemy.

Paris wouldn't just be sent to the Guard, he would be thrown out of the clan entirely. He would *deserve* it.

And though he didn't speak out loud, Paris heard Romeo's furious thought just as clearly as if he had spoken it: *You care about* that, *when Juliet lies dead?*

I care about my duty, said Paris, and it seemed wrong, how easily he spoke the words straight into Romeo's mind.

Above, Master Trelouno said, "Do you think she survived?"

"Can't you feel it?" demanded Lord Catresou. "The land of the dead opened up here, not even an hour ago."

Paris wasn't sure if it was him or Romeo feeling that wave of pure, wordless wretchedness. It didn't matter. They had both gotten her killed.

"There must have been something wrong with the revised

adjurations," said Master Trelouno. "I told you we should have tested—"

"And how would we have kept a second Juliet secret?" Lord Catresou asked sharply.

They had changed the adjurations that made the Juliet.

It took Paris a moment to understand what he'd heard. Another moment to *believe* it. Those spells were sacred, passed down for generations. It was Lord Catresou's duty to preserve them unchanged, undefiled.

But he had changed the adjurations. And Juliet had died.

They killed her, said Romeo. *I will tell them what I think of them.*

Now it was Paris holding Romeo back. *No,* he said frantically. *Wait. They must have had a good reason.*

They are villains and they deserve to hear the truth! said Romeo. *Once I have spoken it, I will gladly die upon their swords.*

Master Trelouno was speaking now. ". . . don't fancy telling our Master Necromancer that he has to wait another seventeen years."

And Paris couldn't breathe.

Master Necromancer.

Everyone had heard the stories of necromancers hiding in the city: of men so vile and powerful that they would harness obscene magic to drag dead souls back into the crawling, revenant bodies they had left behind. These living dead were trapped in a miserable half life. They were no longer revenants; they could think and speak and remember those they had loved. But they could not eat or drink or sleep. They could feel no rest or peace. And though they looked like normal men, if their blood was shed, it turned black as soon as the sunlight touched it.

But those stories were filthy lies, spun to bring suspicion on the Catresou. It wasn't possible to call back dead souls, for the dead were either Catresou, safely walking the Paths of Light, or mindless ghosts who didn't know their own names. And despite what the ignorant and the hateful of Viyara thought, Catresou magi learned spells to protect the living and guide the dead, not to rend apart the walls between them.

"Then lucky for you that we can't speak to him just yet," said Lord Catresou, as if necromancers were a normal problem like the City Guard.

Do you still wish you'd handed the Juliet over to him? Romeo demanded, and Paris didn't say anything. He couldn't.

"He'll be back before we have a new Juliet," said Master Trelouno. "It's a pity this one would be useless if we raised her from the dead."

"You're a very fine necromancer," said Lord Catresou, "but those spells are *not* the answer to everything. I learned much from this Juliet; I can make the process faster next time. Perhaps only five years."

This couldn't be real. Lord Catresou, the leader of the entire clan, could not really be saying such things.

Paris could believe there might be good reasons to tinker with the adjurations that made the Juliet. He could even, if he tried, imagine some reason that Lord Catresou might have to deal with necromancers: if they were threatening the clan, the city. If he had no other choice.

But for him to let one of his own clan be a necromancer—that he would use the word so casually, as if it were no more shocking or forbidden than Master Trelouno's other title of *swordmaster*—

It didn't seem possible.

He killed his own daughter, said Romeo. *What did you expect?*

"He won't like it," said Master Trelouno.

"He'll have to bear it," said Lord Catresou. "Remember, we still have the Little Lady." He sighed. "But I will have that Mavarinn boy's hide. He must have helped her."

Master Trelouno laughed. "He doesn't have the wit. I assure you, Paris Mavarinn has done nothing except be a useless substitute for Tybalt. It's a pity. We could bring Tybalt back, but we can't make him the Juliet's Guardian when everyone knows he's dead."

"His fault, for getting killed in public," said Lord Catresou, and Paris felt a sudden wave of hot, wordless grief and shame from Romeo.

"Yes," said Master Trelouno, "but we won't find another who can help us so well in the Lower City."

"If you wanted an easy life, you should have renounced and

asked to join the Mahyanai," said Lord Catresou. "Come on. We have preparations to make."

Their footsteps echoed as they left the sanctum.

Paris and Romeo were alone again.

Paris couldn't move. He felt dazed and numb all over. He could remember every single word that Lord Catresou and Master Trelouno had said to each other—the memories were so burned into him, he wasn't sure he could ever *stop* hearing those words—but he couldn't put them all together in his head.

Master Necromancer. Revised adjurations. Tybalt in the Lower City. None of it made any sense. None of it was possible.

They killed her, said Romeo. *I have to go after them.*

No, said Paris, but Romeo shoved him away and climbed out of the alcove.

"Stop," Paris ordered out loud, and Romeo staggered but kept moving up the stairs. Paris lunged after him, grabbed his arm, and wrenched. They both went tumbling back down the stairs and landed on the floor.

"You want me to live?" Romeo demanded.

"Not really," said Paris, "but—"

"I must die for her, surely you can see that." Romeo's eyes were very wide; he didn't seem to be quite focusing on Paris. "And I cannot avenge her. I swore I would never harm her family again, so I cannot kill her father, no matter that he killed her. All I can do is speak the truth and die."

"That makes absolutely no sense," said Paris. "They'll just kill you and—and go on—"

He stopped, the sheer horror of the situation choking him for a moment. Master Trelouno was a *necromancer.* He and Lord Catresou were working with another, more powerful necromancer. They had betrayed the Juliet. They had betrayed everything.

And for what? Paris couldn't imagine what goal might be worth such a crime to anyone. Yet there had to be a reason that Lord Catresou had turned to necromancy—something he couldn't accomplish any other way, and Paris dreaded to know what it was. Nothing bought at such a price could have any good in it.

"We have to face this logically," said Paris. "We have to stop what they're doing. For Juliet. And for Viyara."

It's my duty, he thought, but for the first time, the word *duty* was not a comfort. Because he had a duty to the Juliet and to his clan, but also to Lord Catresou.

"You mean go to the City Guard?" said Romeo. He seemed to be calming down a little.

"No!" said Paris. "What are you thinking? Of course we can't do that."

"Why not?" said Romeo. "It's their duty to stop murderers. Lord Catresou killed Juliet. Do you want to protect him?"

The thought of Lord Catresou stripped of his mask and bound in chains, dragged before the Exalted for judgment, made Paris feel queasy. Whatever he'd done, people who applauded the murderous blood magic of the Sisterhood had no right to judge Lord Catresou.

But he had to be stopped.

"No," said Paris. "I won't. But I will protect my clan. Tell the City Guard now, and they will destroy us."

Romeo stared at him. "Why do you think they would do that?"

There were so many reasons, Paris didn't know where to start. The City Guard carrying the bodies of the nameless, unclean dead through Catresou streets, again and again. The chains the Catresou were forced to put in their sepulcher, though their dead had never stirred. The looks and the whispers, and the relentless questioning whenever a death was reported the least bit late. Newly grieving households hauled out and questioned even though they had done everything right.

"They hate us," said Paris. "You have no idea how they hate us. They will never believe it's only a few people. They'll declare us all necromancers and use it as an excuse to drive us out of the city, or enslave us, or—if you ever loved Juliet, you won't tell them."

"Then what do you mean to do?" asked Romeo.

Paris had never in his life been asked to come up with a plan for something. He'd had a plan to avoid being sent to the Guard, and look how that had turned out.

"We have to find out what they're doing," he said. "We have

to get evidence, so that we can prove Lord Catresou and Master Trelouno are conspiring with necromancers, and so we can prove they're the only ones who are guilty. Not the rest of us."

Paris could feel Romeo's skepticism, but Romeo wasn't Catresou. He didn't know how unthinkably wrong necromancy was to their people. It was impossible that more than a very few Catresou were part of this conspiracy.

"When we have proof, then we can tell the City Guard," he said, getting to his feet. "Right now, we have to leave the sepulcher. They'll send in people to clean up soon."

Paris realized his hands were shaking, which said shameful things about his courage, but he couldn't help it. He was supposed to stop Lord Catresou. And there was absolutely nobody in the world to help him. None of the Catresou would, because he had lost the Juliet and ended up bound to a Mahyanai. Nobody else would help him, because he was Catresou.

He was pretty sure that Romeo had heard those thoughts, and knew how pathetic and how lost he was.

"You really do want justice for her, don't you?" Romeo asked quietly, looking up at him.

"Yes," said Paris. "I do."

Romeo watched him a moment longer and then said, "I know someone who will hide us."

8

"BEHOLD THE MOUTH OF DEATH," said the High Priestess. "Here you shall sit until dawn, and if you survive, you shall join us."

Runajo crossed her arms. "I imagined it bigger."

She was pretending, of course; behind her crossed arms, her heart was fluttering and her stomach was unsteady with fear. But she wasn't lying, either. She had known what the Mouth of Death looked like—every child in the city had heard about the perfectly round, perfectly dark lake whose waters flowed up from the land of the dead. After all, it was to guard the Mouth that Viyara had been founded.

But she hadn't expected the pool to be barely wider than her own arm-span. It seemed like such a tiny thing, to have once been the prize of empires, to now be the heart of Viyara, to swallow all the souls of the dead.

To be the thing that might kill her.

Miryo's breath hissed in between her teeth. "Do you truly imagine—"

"Peace," said Vima, who would chant laments for Runajo in the morning if she did not survive. "The girl has met her punishment."

It was not normal for the High Priestess, the priestess of mourning, and the novice mistress to all accompany a Sister to her first vigil—but this was not a normal vigil.

"Listen," said the High Priestess. "You are a child, and a foolish one. Perhaps you are more as well. But not less. And the souls you see tonight—they deserve a faithful witness."

"They deserve better than you," said Miryo.

Runajo smiled at her. "How difficult for you, to wish that I both succeed in my duty and fail in it."

"Live as dead, until thy death," said the High Priestess: the ritual farewell between two Sisters of Thorn.

Runajo bowed and made the traditional response: "My blood is as the blood of gods."

Then they left her alone with the Mouth of Death.

The Mouth lay in a tiny valley with steep, ribbed sides, as if a god had reached down and scooped out a handful from the mountaintop. Nothing grew here: there was only the smooth, pale-gray surface of the rock and the slick darkness of the water.

The Ancients had covered the tiny valley with a dome that looked black on the outside but was transparent from within. They had inlaid glyphs—their meaning now long forgotten—into the walls, and as the sun went down, the symbols glowed with a cold, greenish light.

Runajo walked to the rim of the Mouth and looked down at the dark water. As a Viyaran, she had heard about it all her life; and as a Mahyanai, she had been told it was no more than a pond. There were strange and deadly properties to the water, of course, no doubt caused by the ancient concentration of magical powers. But there was no land of the dead, and therefore no procession of souls every night.

So the Mahyanai said.

Runajo had spoken with enough Sisters to believe they saw something when they sat the vigil. But that did not mean they saw the souls of the dead. Or that there was anything waiting for those souls after they plunged into the black water and were unseen forever after.

There was no sound except her own breathing and a faint whisper from the wind. Her heartbeat was fast in her throat. Runajo knelt on the stone floor, carefully tucking her bare feet under her. It was the way Mother had knelt, day after day by Father's bedside.

Sometimes Runajo had joined her in the endless vigil, but she wasn't allowed to speak or help. She could only watch her mother watch her father. More often, she sat alone in the garden. By the time a year had passed, she knew that she was waiting for her father's death.

It took another three years. When Mother finally sobbed over his emaciated corpse, Runajo had felt nothing but exhausted relief.

Then Mother took ill, and it was Runajo's turn to sit by a bed, reading poetry and spooning gruel. To wash a slowly withering body and hold ever-weakening hands. To pretend she was happy to be there, pretend she was sad to lose her mother, pretend she felt anything at all when her heart was a smooth little stone in her chest.

When Mother died late at night, Runajo did the barest minimum of her duty; she sat vigil by the body until dawn. When the sky began to lighten, she ordered the servants to tell the rest of the family, and to call the City Guard for corpse disposal.

Then she wrapped a shawl around her shoulders and walked up the cold, quiet streets to the Cloister. She banged on the door, and when a sleepy-eyed Sister answered, she flung herself to the ground and begged to be admitted.

Her family was outraged that she had left before the funeral rites, but Runajo knew that if she had waited even another hour, she would never have been allowed to leave. She would have spent her whole life as that same helpless, silent little girl, smothered under the lies that people told to make themselves happy.

For the Sisters of Thorn, there was one true law to the world: blood for blood. Life for life. Price for screaming price. They had a word for it: *inkaad*, which literally meant "appropriate payment," but signified the law that governed all bargain and exchange.

If there was one thing that lay at the heart of the world, said the Sisters, it was *inkaad*. It had governed the chaos from which the gods arose, and it would govern the death of the last human after the city walls failed, and when all the world was dead, it would govern death.

Some of the Mahyanai doubted that wisdom, but Runajo never had. She had watched it every day. Her mother could only care for her husband by ignoring her daughter. Runajo could only care for her mother by strangling herself with silence. And she could only get back the least bit of herself by abandoning everything else—including her parents, deep in her heart, long before they died.

She had paid the price willingly, and she did not regret. Not even now.

But she was afraid.

So terribly, shamefully afraid.

The pool before her was dark and still. That was all. There was nothing terrible about it, and yet the longer she stared at it, the more uneasy she felt. If souls really did sink into the water and not return, then this was the hole in the world. This was the gap through which she would inevitably fall, the final darkness from which there was no escape.

Runajo's hands clenched. She felt the warm, living skin of her fingers and palms; she felt the solid bones. She felt the breath in her throat. But all of that was no comfort, because she could see the waiting darkness, and when she looked straight at the dark water, her vision began to swim. It felt as if she were hurtling toward the Mouth of Death.

Toward nothing.

She scrambled to her feet in quick, jerky movements and turned to look in the other direction, at the gold-rimmed doorway into the tunnel that led away down the mountain.

It didn't help. Runajo closed her eyes.

I can pay any price, she told herself. *I can renounce any love. I can bear any terror. But I will not be helpless and silent again. I will know the nature of the world. And I will prove I was right.*

The familiar words steadied her. She could bear the loss of her mother and father. She could bear this vigil.

She opened her eyes. She turned back to face the Mouth of Death, and knelt, and stared it down.

And then the water sang to her.

It was the cold and inhuman and many-voiced song that the dying all heard. That her mother had heard as Runajo watched her die. That would be the last thing Runajo herself ever heard.

She didn't feel brave or stubborn anymore. She felt like a tiny frightened animal, like a flickering candle that the wind would any moment snuff out.

The stone walls were gone. So were the stars in the sky. So was the pool. She knelt on a little round island in the middle of a vast, flat black ocean. She knew the darkness surrounding her was water only because the glowing marks from the walls still remained, floating in a circle around her, and she could see their reflection gleaming.

The song was louder now.

Runajo slammed her fist against the stone. The pain brought tears to her eyes, but it also steadied her a little.

And then the dead came.

They were pale, translucent, like faded memories. They stepped from the space just behind her, and calmly walked the five steps to the edge of the little island. Then they stepped out onto the water, and sank down with each step, until they were gone from her sight.

A child. An old woman. A young man. They walked past her, eyes low-lidded and peaceful, and sank into darkness. Runajo's body shook, and she wasn't sure if it was from fear or from desire to follow them.

She clenched her fists. She thought, *I must live. I will live.*

Runajo didn't know how much time had passed. She didn't know how many dead souls had walked past her. She could not keep a prayerful vigil for them; she could only dig her fingers into her arms and think, *I will not go. I will not go.* It felt like forever, and also no time at all.

And then she heard a quiet breath behind her.

None of the dead had made the slightest sound.

Runajo looked back. Behind her was a girl wearing a red dress in the Catresou style, with a laced bodice and slashed sleeves, but no mask. She looked as solid and real as Runajo, but she walked forward with the same gentle, inevitable steps as the other dead souls.

She looked down at Runajo. Their eyes met, and the Catresou girl's face was alive with helpless fury. As if she knew, like Runajo, how unjust death was—and as if, like Runajo, she could not stop it.

She is not dead, thought Runajo, in baffled wonder. *She can't be dead.*

The girl let out a little huff of angry breath. She turned away, her whole body shifting, as if drawn by strings. She stepped toward the water, leaving Runajo behind. As everyone always left, while Runajo knelt silent and still.

In that moment, nothing she had learned about how to survive the vigil mattered. That moment was every moment she had ever been helpless, and Runajo only knew that she could not bear to be still for even one more heartbeat.

She lunged forward and seized the girl's wrist.

For one moment, her fingers seemed to be closing on cold air. Then she felt warm skin and solid bone, and she threw herself backward, tugging the girl away from the water.

The warmth of the girl's hand turned to fire. It felt like she was grasping a hot coal, and Runajo nearly let go—but the girl had toppled over against Runajo, and her breath was warm and alive against her neck, and all Runajo knew was that she would not let go. This girl was a mystery she had yet to decipher, and was alive and should not be dead.

Nobody who was alive ought to be dead. And just this once, Runajo would spit at *inkaad* and drag someone back from the teeth of Death, no matter the cost.

I will not let go, thought Runajo, and screamed as the fire burned against her palm.

Then there was darkness.

These Violent Delights

THEY ARE SITTING ON THE edge of a roof, overlooking the marketplace. The grimy crowds of the Lower City swirl beneath them, and nobody pays any attention to a heedless girl and boy who want to risk their necks.

They are reciting poetry—the poetry of his people, because hers have little use for it. But the Mahyanai have preserved one hundred and eight poems from the time before the Ruining, and this collection is one of their greatest treasures. With every line he teaches her, the world grows a little wider. She had never known before how words could sing, how a turn of phrase could unlock a window in her mind.

There are six days left until the ceremony. Once she has a Guardian, she will not be allowed near him again. Whatever poems she has not learned by then, she will never know.

He stares out over the city as he says dreamily:

"The moon is alone, and so am I;
My sleeves are wet with tears."

"I don't know that one," she says.

"It does not yet exist," he says, turning to her, "but I will write it for you. Let me write you a *thousand* and eight poems, one for every morning I wake up beside you. Let me cover the whole world in words, and drown in oceans of ink."

She cannot help laughing, though her heart is breaking. She knows what he is asking. She knows the answer.

"My father will never set my hand in yours," she says.

She has never had to tell him, *I will not desert my people.* It is part of why she loves him.

He smiles. "You won't have to. You only have to marry me in secret, before your father can forbid it."

"That is not a marriage."

"It is for my people," he says. "We have an ancient custom: if we spend three nights together, and declare ourselves to your parents on the third morning, then we are married."

Her face heats. "I will not dishonor myself to force my father to marry me."

"You won't," he says. "You will already be married. The first night is the wedding night. And the second, and the third."

Her whole body feels like it is blushing now, and she cannot look in his eyes. She knows what he is asking. She knows what her family would call it.

She knows what she wants.

If they announced themselves in public, before the whole clan, there would be no way to stop the news from spreading. And her lord father would suffer a very great deal, before he allowed it to be known that his daughter had been dishonored. He might even be willing to acknowledge a marriage to a Mahyanai.

She would still receive a Guardian to govern her. She would still be obedient to her duty and her family, and she would still be no more than a sword in the eyes of all who saw her. But she would be *his.*

He knows what she is thinking. He takes her hands, and oh, his smile has all the spark and gleam that she has loved since she met him. "Lady of loveliness surpassing all the stars," he says, "star of the night that until you requite me will darken my heart, and heart that moves the blood in my breast—will you take pity on a pilgrim, and marry him?"

She laughs, and kisses him in reply.

But that night, as she waits for him in her room, wearing nothing but a loosely belted robe, she is afraid. He is kind and he wants to understand, but he is Mahyanai. His mother was a concubine, and it is no shame for him. She does not think he truly realizes what it means for her, to risk her honor.

The Catresou have little use for poetry, but they do have songs for amusement. She remembers one, about a girl seduced with promises of marriage and then betrayed:

He heard her voice, and up he rose
And opened wide the chamber-door;
Let in the maid, that out a maid
Never departed more.

She has locked her bedroom door. She will not leave this room, she will not unbolt that door while still a virgin. But she will not be fully a wife either, not until the three nights are passed. Not until he has declared their marriage to her father. Not unless he is telling her the truth.

He knocks at the window. She is shaking as she goes to the casement, as she opens it wide.

He climbs inside, but he doesn't take her in his arms. His hand clings to the window frame. He licks his lips, and then he says quietly, "Juliet. Do you want this?"

She wants to make him promise again that this is a real marriage. She wants to beg and demand and threaten, again and again, just so she can be *sure.*

She remembers the end of the song:

"Good sir, before you tumbled me
You promised me to wed."
"So would I have done, by yonder sun,
Had you not come to my bed."

But she looks at his wide eyes, and his white knuckles gripping the casement, and she realizes that he is afraid as well. He may not be risking his honor, but he is surely risking his heart.

She says to him, "I trust you."

He whispers, "I love you."

It's barely a kiss that she presses to his lips, the movement is so soft and shy. It's barely a kiss that he presses back. But then she kisses him again, and again, and she knows this: the shape of his mouth, the push of his breath. She knows the way his hands shift across her back, cup her shoulder blades, and dig in.

She is not afraid anymore.

The next time he releases her lips, she says to him, "Sooner or later you will have to undress me."

He laughs and gently slides the edge of the robe off her shoulder, then presses a kiss to the newly bare skin.

Breathless, she says, "I would advise sooner," and then they are both busy pulling at sashes and laces and buckles. They say nothing, but each movement feels like a ceremony, like a vow: *I trust you. I love you. I trust you.*

Until they are both naked, and there is nothing to protect them from each other, and she is not afraid. She is laughing as he picks her up and carries her to the bed.

9

WHEN RUNAJO WOKE, SHE COULD see the pale sky of dawn through the transparent dome. It took her a few sleepy moments to realize that she had fallen asleep by the Mouth of Death. That she had survived the vigil. Then the dazzling rush of relief swept her awake. She sat up—and noticed the girl sleeping next to her.

More memories rushed back: the dead souls, and the girl who was not entirely dead—

But still dead enough to walk into the Mouth, Runajo thought, looking down at her with mounting horror. *And I stopped her. I brought her back.*

Necromancy was the unforgivable sin, the deed most despised by gods and men. It was worse than the Ruining. For the Ruining had only made the bodies of the dead rise again as mindless, hungry things. But to summon a soul back into its body—to rob

Death, to whom the gods themselves had submitted—that was blasphemy against *inkaad* itself, and a knife to the heart of the world. Whoever summoned back the dead must die.

So said the Sisters of Thorn. Runajo had never much cared, because she didn't believe necromancers existed. There were legends that the Ancients had doomed themselves through necromancy. And there were always rumors of unspeakable crimes in the Lower City. But there had never been any clear historical record of necromancy. Nobody had ever been brought before the Exalted or the High Priestess to be tried for it. Runajo had thought that was because necromancy was impossible; that the dead could not be summoned back because they no longer existed.

But she'd also thought that souls didn't walk into the Mouth of Death.

The girl did not look like an abomination that could unbalance the world. But if she had been truly dead, and was now truly alive, then by definition, necromancy had been performed. She must die, and Runajo must die beside her. They would cut her throat open like the man at the Great Offering—

One clear, icy thought cut through her rising panic: *If I die, I cannot see the Sunken Library.*

Runajo took a deep breath and forced herself to think calmly of the consequences. *If I do not go to the library, nobody will. If nobody goes to the library, we will never learn the secrets of the walls, and Viyara will fall in thirty years. And when Viyara falls, it matters not how much we have or have not offended Death. All of us will die.*

From that perspective, everything was very simple. If Runajo wanted the city to live, she must conceal what she had done.

For one moment, she thought about pushing the girl into the black waters of the Mouth. She wouldn't fight. The water would devour her, hide her. No one would ever know. Not even the nameless girl who had looked at her with such fury.

I can sacrifice anything, thought Runajo, but this would be no sacrifice: it would be murder. She couldn't do it.

So she must find a way to deceive the entire Sisterhood instead.

Runajo stood up and looked at the gold-rimmed doorway. There was no lock and no guard . . . but some of the Sisters would already be awake and walking the halls below. Runajo would never be able to drag the girl all the way down to her cell undetected.

But that wasn't the only place she could hide something.

It was a wild idea that had just come to her, but it was better than nothing. She didn't have time for anything else.

Trying to shake the girl awake produced no effect. So Runajo knelt down, grasped her under the arms, and slung her over her shoulder. Though the girl was short and slender, Runajo still staggered under her weight.

She was not going to enjoy this, but she didn't have a choice.

Slowly, Runajo dragged the girl down the tunnel. Her gasps for breath sounded terribly loud in her ears, but she knew there was no one in the tunnels to hear her. She hoped.

The tunnel was made of dead gray stone, the same as the walls of the little valley around the Mouth. But then she turned a final corner, and a neat seam ran around the walls, ceiling, and floor, where the dull gray rock met the white stone that made up all the Cloister and most of the Upper City.

Runajo staggered the final two steps to the white stone. She lowered the Catresou girl to the ground and sank down beside her, gasping for breath.

In a moment she was up again. There wasn't time for rest. She pressed her palm to the wall.

In theory, all the white stone of the city was "alive," able to receive and be molded by the power of the Sisters' spells. But how well it actually responded varied hugely. Down in the city, it would take long hours of work and engraved glyphs to mold a door into a rock surface.

Here in the Cloister, though, where the Sisters had woven their power over and over for three thousand years? The wall practically hummed beneath her touch.

A little silver knife hung at her waist. Even when she was imprisoned, nobody had taken it from her—because to take the sacrificial knife from a Sister was to cast her out.

Runajo drew the knife. As part of her training, she had calculated many blood prices; she had been the best of all the novices at the sacred mathematics. So she knew that even a little blood from her would be enough to create the door.

She was used to sacrifice now. She only needed a quick moment to brace herself before she sliced a neat little line across her forearm, avoiding all the veins, so that blood welled up but did not gush.

Then she pressed her bloody forearm against the door and whispered, "Open."

It was not the proper ceremony. But blood was blood. Elaborate filigree lines of light grew up the wall into an archway, flared, and turned into the cracks, forming what looked like a door.

Then the door opened.

On the other side was a room. It was no more than a cube, with a glowing lamp hung from the ceiling. Not the most friendly place to wake up, alone and confused about no longer being dead, but it was better than being destroyed as the fruits of necromancy.

Carefully, Runajo lowered the girl to the ground. For a moment she stared—the girl looked terribly small and fragile, crumpled on her side—then she rolled the girl onto her back, straightened out her limbs, and left.

"Close," she whispered, and perhaps because her blood was already in it, the door did not demand a second price. In a moment, there was no trace that the door into the room had ever been there.

She spun around and started running—despite the exhaustion dragging at her legs—because she had to be back beside the Mouth before the High Priestess got there.

She barely made it in time. Runajo had just knelt down when the High Priestess, Miryo, and Vima all arrived together.

Miryo looked furious, Vima looked amused. The High Priestess just looked thoughtful.

"What is the wound on your arm?" she asked.

"A sacrifice," said Runajo, trying to keep her breathing steady.

"And what is the sign on your hand?"

Runajo's heart lurched, and she looked down. On her right palm was a strange little design of twisting black lines.

She remembered how holding on to the Catresou girl had hurt like a brand.

"It must have grown as I sat vigil," she said. "Perhaps the gods sent it."

"Because you have loved them so much," Miryo said sarcastically, which was a bit hypocritical, given that she was Mahyanai herself.

Vima grasped Runajo's hand. "It is a little like the glyphs on the wall, but I have never seen this symbol before."

Runajo smiled in the way that she knew Miryo found insufferable. "Perhaps it means they want me to read the lost words in the Sunken Library."

Three pairs of eyes examined her. Runajo examined them right back. She could tell they all found the mark strange or suspicious to varying degrees—but what could they accuse her of? It was obvious the mark had been made by magic, and what magic could she have found last night except that of the vigil itself?

That didn't stop her heart from beating faster and faster until the High Priestess nodded thoughtfully and said, "Very well. You may rise, youngest of my Sisters, to shed your blood until you die."

For the rest of the day, Runajo was not alone: there were rites that must be observed for a newly made Sister. There was the briar tattoo to put on her chin, blood offerings for her to spill. Her eyes ached from exhaustion; her skin itched and ached from rapidly knitting itself back together under the healing ointment.

She tried not to think of the Catresou girl waking up alone. She thought of little else.

Even before I caught her, she was not like the other souls, Runajo told herself stubbornly. *There has to be a reason. I will find it, I will get proof that I did not perform true necromancy, and then I will tell the others.*

Finally, well after the sun had gone down, she was allowed to rest. No longer would she sleep in the wide dormitory with the other novices, waking in the night to hear their rustling and snoring. Instead, she was sent to a proper cell: a small, white-walled room, furnished with no more than a woven mat to sleep on. When the door closed behind her, Runajo sank to the floor with a sigh of relief.

For the past few hours, the constant attention had been like bugs crawling over her skin. Now she was alone. She was free.

Runajo would sleep in this room every night until she died. Every day, she would have this freedom to look forward to, instead of the jostling and whispering of the other novices, Sunjai's endless prattle and Inyaan's infinite glares.

Even if there had been no Ruining, perhaps Runajo would still have become a Sister, just for this solitude. This peace. Mahyanai girls were expected to take husbands or at least lovers, so they could provide heirs for their families. They had to share bedrooms with their kinswomen and handmaids. Runajo thought that if she had to share her life with anyone, husband or friend or servant, she would eventually despise that person and go mad.

That probably made her quite terrible. But it also made her useful for the mission she had set for herself. She had nothing to hold her back.

Except a not-quite-dead Catresou girl hidden away inside the walls of the Cloister.

Runajo waited nearly an hour, just in case somebody came by to check on her, or Miryo wanted to mount a surprise inspection. Nothing happened.

She rose and traced her fingers over the wall of her cell. She could feel the room she had fashioned, lurking within the structure of the Cloister.

"Come back," she whispered, and pressed her lips to the wall.

For a moment she thought she had lost it. Then the door grew out of the wall and slid open, and Runajo stepped inside.

The girl was gone.

Runajo only had time for one gasp of surprise before she was knocked to the ground, and she found herself lying on her back, looking up at the wild-eyed Catresou girl, who had seized Runajo's knife and was pressing it to her throat.

10

PARIS HAD KNOWN THE LOWER CITY would be dirty and dark.

He hadn't expected it to feel so *dead*.

In the Upper City, the power of the Sisters of Thorn—the power that they fed with unholy sacrifices—lingered in every surface of the rock. It caused the dancing lights in the surface of the great dais when human blood was spilled upon it, and it made little stone flowers glow inside every home in the Upper City. It made the water run and the doors lock. And always, there was an indefinable sense that the city was alive, breathing, humming to itself, though the walls made no sound.

Not so the Lower City.

Here, the buildings were carved of dead gray rock. Some were colorless and grimy; others were painted with garish designs, still coated in a thin layer of grime. The streets were narrow, and stank: some of them because they had gutters full of refuse, others because they didn't *have* gutters.

It was a dead city. And it was riotously alive.

It was like one of the great festivals, a hundred times over. The street swarmed with people, and it seemed that no two spoke the same language or had the same features. Crowds of children ran together through the streets. Sleek, well-groomed men in embroidered robes strode past ragged beggars. Mangy cats yowled for scraps or stalked pigeons across the rooftops.

When the Ruining covered the world in death, whole kingdoms and peoples had perished. A small fraction had found their way to Viyara in time—but they had been thousands, and they had become more in the hundred years since. Only the Mahyanai and Catresou had come in enough numbers, and with their leadership intact, that they could sign the Accords with the Old Viyarans and win a place in the Upper City. The rest had to make their homes at the base of the city spire, and within a generation, a small cluster of buildings had become an enormous, writhing city.

"Where now?" he asked.

Romeo was standing still, staring around the street as if he had never seen it before. He'd been focused enough while helping Paris slip through one of the minor gates into the Lower City, but now he seemed like he might be turning back into the wild-eyed, senseless boy who had wanted to lie down in the sepulcher forever.

And Paris had decided to trust him. He had followed him down into the Lower City, where he had never been before—and where he might get robbed and stabbed any moment.

What had he been thinking? It was one thing to take idiotic risks with his own life, but if Paris died down here, there would be nobody to stop Lord Catresou. Nobody to save the Catresou clan from horrifying punishment when the City Guard found him out.

"I want him stopped too," said Romeo, looking back at him, more alive and resentful than he'd seemed a moment ago. "I will see it done."

"I didn't—" Paris started, but fell silent, because even if he hadn't said it, he'd thought it. And his thoughts were no longer his own. Every time he remembered that, he felt another little nauseous shiver.

"And you're her kin," said Romeo. "So I will get you to safety. I owe her at least that much."

He started walking again, and dubiously, Paris followed him. The breeze was cool against his cheekbones and temples. He had taken off his mask during the desperate race to the sepulcher, dropped it sometime during the disastrous attempt at a bonding ceremony, and he had not remembered to grab it again as they escaped.

It probably would have been a bad idea anyway, to run around the Lower City in such an elaborate, formal mask. But he was acutely, humiliatingly aware that his bare face was on display to everyone in the street, as if he were the lowest of servants, or not a Catresou at all.

Suddenly memory caught him by the throat: Juliet, taking the white filigree mask from her face, and smiling with a kind of tremulous happiness that he had never seen in her.

It wasn't Paris's memory.

"Stop it," he muttered, trying to build up the wall between them, but the clatter and bustle of the street kept distracting him. Romeo didn't seem to have heard him; he turned down one of the narrow side streets and kept striding forward, remembering *Juliet's lips, warm and soft and parting as he kissed her—*

"Stop thinking of her," Paris snarled, grabbing Romeo's shoulder and wrenching him back around.

Romeo flinched, his eyes going very wide, and cold horror clutched at Paris. He had ordered Romeo how to *think*. If it broke his mind—

Then Romeo huffed out a laugh and said, "I can't. I can't stop thinking of her." He smiled. "Your magic isn't strong enough for that."

"You have no right," Paris muttered, relieved and ashamed at once.

He felt Romeo's flicker of anger at the same moment he saw his mouth tighten.

"She was my *wife*," Romeo snapped, and remembered something that Paris had never, ever wanted to see.

The next thing Paris knew, he was three paces away from Romeo, his face burning, palms pressing into his temples. He stared at the cobblestones, trying to imagine them lining his head.

Romeo must have realized what had happened, because he sounded rather strangled when he said, "How—how do we stop it?"

Paris took a slow, deep breath and didn't meet his eyes. "Imagine a wall," he said. "Between us."

There was a short, awkward silence as they both tried. Paris didn't feel any more overflowing thoughts from Romeo, but that might just be because his own wall was so solidly built. He never wanted to feel any of Romeo's thoughts again.

He never wanted to *look* at Romeo again, but he didn't really have a choice about that. So he raised his head.

Romeo was slumped against the wall on the opposite side of the alley, and there was such flat despair on his face that Paris would have pitied him, if he didn't know far too much about what he'd done.

"Still remember where we're going?" he asked.

"Yes," Romeo muttered. Then he looked up and said stubbornly, "Despise me all you like, but don't think such things about her."

"I don't," said Paris. "I despise *you* for—for seducing her with false promises." His face went hot all over again as he said the words, but he managed to keep looking at Romeo.

"Is that what you call a marriage?"

"It's what we call a 'secret' marriage," Paris gritted out. "How many other girls did you promise as much and then abandon?"

Romeo gave him a look of pure disdain. "How many other girls have you enslaved for your family?"

"Only as many as you've killed," Paris said, and regretted it the instant after. He didn't know which one of them was feeling this grief, sharp and breathless as a knife between the ribs. Maybe it was both of them: the image of Juliet, smiling unmasked, danced in his mind, but so did the memory of her voice: *It's all I ever wanted, to be correct.*

She was supposed to have lived. They both rightfully should have died so she could live. And instead they had let her die.

"If you want me dead," said Romeo, "you can do it. You have the right."

Paris shook his head. "Just find this friend of yours," he said. When Romeo didn't move, he added, "You do still remember the way, don't you? To this—"

"Apothecary," said Romeo. "He's an apothecary. He helps the people of the Lower City. He helped us."

Paris probably shouldn't be surprised at any foolish thing Romeo did, but he still said, "You took the Juliet *here*?"

The corner of Romeo's mouth turned up a little. "She liked it." He turned away and started walking again; Paris barely heard the final words: "She loved the cats."

It took them another half hour to reach the apothecary. He lived in a neighborhood where the stone of the buildings had a more golden cast; it did not look rich, but it was a bit less dirty and crowded than some of the spots they had walked through on their way there.

Romeo pounded on the door. A moment later it swung open, and there stood a short, sharp-nosed man with brown hair turning gray. He wore a tailored shirt and trousers, like a Catresou, but no mask; Paris could see the fine little lines about his green eyes.

He could see, also, the way the apothecary's expression moved swiftly from surprise to examination, and then to grim acceptance.

"My dear boy," he said gently. "Come inside."

At first glance, the apothecary's front room was a cheerful place: scrupulously clean, with bright-red designs painted on the pale walls. Chests were stacked in the corners, and there was a shelf filled with herb jars. But then Paris looked again, and he realized that the red symbols were Catresou sigils, the kind meant to keep sickness and rats out of a house.

Dread was a heavy lump in his chest. They were Catresou

sigils, but no true Catresou would be living maskless and alone in the Lower City.

Romeo halted a few steps into the room. "We're being hunted," he said. "I can't—you've already done so much. If you don't want the risk, I won't blame you."

"Her family," the apothecary said heavily. "What happened?"

"Who are you?" Paris demanded, wondering if it was too late to drag Romeo out and flee.

The apothecary looked at him. "My name is Justiran, and yes, I was born a Catresou."

Paris had heard of renouncers, of course—everybody knew that sometimes there were Catresou so evil or so weak that they didn't care about *zoura*. Who abandoned both their clan and the names that would allow them to walk the Paths of Light. But he had never met anyone who had actually done it.

"Why did you renounce?" he asked.

Justiran raised an eyebrow. "Why did you?"

Paris was excruciatingly aware of his shamefully bare face, but he still met Justiran's eyes as he said, "I didn't. I will die a Catresou."

"Then I'm sorry you've been driven here," said Justiran. "I know you've been raised not to believe it, but I will help you if I can. What happened?"

"She died," said Romeo, his voice quiet and desolate. "We went to the sepulcher—"

"Don't tell him that!" Paris snapped. "We can't trust him!"

It didn't matter how smoothly Justiran spoke. He was still an enemy.

"Yes, we can," Romeo protested. "He helped me and Juliet. He told us to get married!"

"Then he clearly has no honor," said Paris. He could feel his heart speeding up. Justiran doubtless wanted to destroy the clan, and the news about Lord Catresou would let him do it.

Paris should never have come here. He should never have trusted Romeo.

Romeo's mouth worked for a moment. Then he looked back at Justiran and said carefully, deliberately, "We went to the sepulcher. We tried to—"

"I *order* you not to tell him," Paris said desperately, and Romeo's mouth snapped shut. "And leave. We're leaving."

Romeo turned toward the door.

"Stop," said Justiran. The next moment he had shoved Paris into the wall, his thumb pressing painfully into his collarbone. "What did you do to him?" he asked, and there was nothing gentle in the way he bit out the quiet, icy words.

"I—" Paris started to say, and then Justiran's free hand was tracing a pattern on his forehead with one finger. It was just the barest hint of pressure, but his head suddenly throbbed with a terrible ache. All the strength went out of his legs; a moment later he was on the floor.

He couldn't move.

Magic. And not the kind practiced by the Catresou magi, with its elaborate sigils and formulae. Nor was it the misbegotten magic worked by the Sisters of Thorn, paid for in copious amounts of blood. It was something else, something Paris had never heard of before.

What if Justiran was the Master Necromancer?

"Wait!" said Romeo, throwing himself between them. "Don't hurt him!"

"A friend of yours?" Justiran's voice was detached and clipped.

"No," said Romeo. "But I've seen his heart. He's a good person."

"Do you know he put a compulsion on you?"

He forced me to, thought Paris, but he couldn't get the words out.

"Yes," said Romeo, "but . . ." His voice grew soft and wondering. "He loved Juliet. I'm sure of it."

Romeo was an idiot. Romeo thought nothing mattered besides who had what kind of pretty feelings about Juliet, and he was going to get them both killed by a necromancer.

Justiran knelt before Paris and looked straight into his eyes. "For Romeo's sake, I'm trusting you," he said. Then he pressed three fingertips briefly to Paris's forehead. Instantly the pain and weakness were gone. Paris sucked in a deep breath and scrambled to his feet.

"I'm a loyal son of the Catresou," he said desperately. "I will live and die for them. If you want me to renounce, if you want me to help you with necromancy, you had better just kill me now."

Maddeningly, Justiran's grim face cracked into a smile. "I'm not a necromancer, and I would never ask you to renounce."

"Then what are you?" Paris demanded. "And what did you just do? Why shouldn't I run and report you to the City Guard?"

"You can't—" Romeo started, but Justiran silenced him with a wave of his hand.

"I told you," he said calmly. "My name is Justiran, who was once a Catresou and is no longer. I have read an ancient book or two in my time, and that is all you need to know. And you won't report me to the City Guard because you are a Catresou still, and trust them no more than I do."

Paris wanted to shout that it wasn't enough, that he couldn't ever trust Justiran. But he had nowhere else to go. And if Justiran had wanted to do terrible things to him, he already could have.

"If you mean no harm," said Justiran, "then you are welcome here. And I will help you."

Please, Romeo said into his mind, breaking the silence between them. *Please trust him. He will help.*

Paris didn't trust Romeo's judgment at all. But he didn't have another choice.

"All right," he said awkwardly.

Justiran nodded. "So tell me what happened with the Juliet. You two boys were rivals?"

Paris's face heated. "Not like that!"

"Tell me, then," said Justiran, who was clearly finding this amusing, "just how you did love her."

"With *honor.* I was to be her Guardian."

"He swore to serve her," said Romeo. "I saw it."

"How could you—" Paris stopped. Of course he knew how: the bond, and Paris's own pathetic inability to control it. "She loved *zoura,*" he said to Justiran. "I wanted to protect her."

If the man had ever truly been a Catresou for one instant, he would understand that.

And maybe he had, because Justiran nodded. "I see," he said. "I'm sorry."

"Thank you," said Paris, but inside he was seething again, because what right did a renouncer have, to sound grieved over the death of the Juliet?

"Lord Catresou is working with necromancers," Romeo blurted out. Hearing the words aloud made Paris's heart jolt in his chest.

Paris looked Justiran in the eye. "And we know for a *fact* that he is acting in secret against the will of the clan. That's why we didn't go to the City Guard. They'd never believe it wasn't all of us without proof."

Justiran nodded. "Sit down," he said. "Tell me the rest."

Paris wasn't sure if he'd ever been more uncomfortable at a table. Justiran brought out tea and corn cakes, but neither of them ate anything. Romeo was obviously too wrapped up in his grief, while Paris was far too aware that he was the only Catresou among enemies.

To make things worse, Justiran kept looking at Paris with an expression that was probably meant to be gentle and comforting, but was only infuriating. He wasn't a child. He was quite aware of what Lord Catresou had done. And he was capable of bearing the knowledge without betraying his clan and *zoura* itself, unlike some people at the table.

But when he tried to say the words—words that any renouncer would enjoy hearing so very much—they stuck in his throat.

So it was Romeo who ended up telling most of the story, and Paris only broke in occasionally to add clarifications. (She was not a slave. She was not truly married. He hadn't wanted to drag her back; he had wanted to persuade her to come willingly, so that her father would show her mercy.)

"Perhaps it is a good thing you failed," said Justiran.

"A good thing she's *dead*?" Paris demanded.

Romeo didn't say anything, but his breath stuttered, and Paris could feel his ragged, oozing misery.

"I can guess what sort of mercy she'd have gotten from her father," said Justiran. "I doubt she'd be alive now anyway."

"What would *you* know of Lord Catresou?" said Paris without thinking. Justiran just looked at him. And Lord Catresou truly was evil, and when Juliet had said as much, Paris hadn't listened.

Someone else should be avenging her. Somebody who wasn't so stupid.

"It doesn't matter," Romeo said dully, staring at the table. "It's my fault. If I hadn't fought Tybalt—"

For one brief moment, Paris caught a flash of memory: sunlight and the glint of steel. The smell of blood and the bitter, helpless taste of grief and rage.

"You're right," Romeo went on, looking at Paris. "I did defile her, the moment I came to her with blood on my hands. I swear to you, I asked her to kill me then, but she was too kind. And now she is destroyed."

There were tears sliding down his face. Right there at the table, in front of both Paris and Justiran, he was crying like a child.

"I shouldn't have light in my eyes, I shouldn't have breath in my mouth. But you're her kin. You can set it right."

Paris wanted to flee, or at least cover his face in embarrassment. He had never seen anything like this outburst, and he would have thought it was a bid for pity except that he could feel raw grief rolling off Romeo in waves, and he knew that Romeo sincerely meant every desperate word.

It was so strong, he could hardly think. With a last, violent effort, Paris managed to slam the wall back between them. Then he looked at Romeo and said the very first thing that came into his head.

"You are completely useless. Who cares about your broken heart? We need a plan to bring Lord Catresou to justice."

Romeo stared at him, as if he couldn't believe that anyone would still have a grasp of what was important.

Paris plunged on, "We need to know what he had planned for the Juliet—what he's doing with necromancers—but we can't break into his house and spy on him. At least, I can't. But he said that Tybalt had been doing something for them in the Lower City—"

"I don't care," said Romeo, quietly but very distinctly. His eyes were wide, his mouth a flat line; he was no longer crying.

"If we investigate Tybalt," said Paris, "we might be able to find out—"

"I already know about Tybalt," said Romeo. "He was a brute who tried to kill me for marrying Juliet, who *did* kill my only friend, and who probably would have gone home and beaten Juliet if I hadn't killed him after. I regret killing him. I would have let Juliet kill me in revenge. But I don't regret him being dead."

"He would never have laid a hand on her," Paris protested, but the words came out weak, because they knew that Tybalt had helped Lord Catresou work with necromancers.

"I brought you here," Romeo went on, terribly calm, "for Juliet's sake. And for her sake, I won't try to harm her family.

But you can go on a quest to save them by yourself. I am done."

"Done?" said Paris. "I thought you wanted to avenge her. I thought you cared for her!"

"Do *you* really want to avenge her?" Romeo demanded. "Or just exonerate your clan? What will you do if you have to choose?"

As if Paris hadn't already betrayed his family. As if he weren't sitting at a table with a Mahyanai and a renouncer.

"I don't think—" Justiran began, finally speaking up—but Paris was not willing to hear any more of his gentle condescension.

"Enough." He shoved back his chair as he got to his feet. His heart was beating very fast. "I should have known better than to trust a Mahyanai and a renouncer. Sit here and cry like a coward if you want. I'm going to go get justice for the Juliet."

And before Justiran could stop him, he had shoved his way out of the house.

11

"WHO ARE YOU," THE CATRESOU girl demanded, "and what have you done to me?"

She had slammed Runajo to the ground. Now she crouched on top of Runajo, pressing the knife to her throat, just a fraction of pressure away from murder. One twitch of the girl's hand would send Runajo's blood flowing across the floor of the room she herself had created.

She had expected to be afraid when she died, and the cold running down her body probably had something to do with fear, but it felt like calm.

"I'm a Sister of Thorn," she said, "and you used to be dead. You do remember being dead, don't you?"

The girl flinched.

"Trying to kill me won't get you any answers. It will just get you dead of starvation, because I'm the only one who can open the door to this room."

Abruptly, the girl scrambled off her. Runajo sat up, and now she could feel her heart beating, her fingers trembling. But she still didn't feel exactly afraid. Apparently she was braver in the face of getting killed than she had expected, which would be useful in the Sunken Library.

"Where are we?" the girl demanded. She was crouched a little over a pace away from Runajo—out of reach, but easily able to lunge forward and gut her with the knife.

"In the Cloister," said Runajo. "Why were you dead? Never mind that, why were you only *almost* dead?"

The girl pressed her lips together. She had those exotic blue eyes that the Catresou were so proud of, and they were narrowed in suspicion.

"At least tell me your name," said Runajo.

The girl recoiled as if the question were a hot iron, but she still answered immediately, all in one monotone breath: "I am the Juliet." Then she grimaced and met Runajo's eyes as she said, "I am the sword of the Catresou. Do what you will, you cannot break me."

Runajo knew she was staring, but all she could see was the memory of the girl standing at the Great Offering. Juliet had been stiff and solemn then, her face hidden behind an ivory filigree mask—and tiny with distance, like a little doll set out on display. Nothing like this furious, terrified girl crouched in front of her, hair in a tangle, who seemed an inch away from hissing like a cat.

"I don't want to break you," said Runajo. "I want to know what happened to you."

Juliet's voice was toneless. "I died. That is all. Let me go."

"That can't possibly be all," said Runajo. "I was sitting vigil on the dead souls, and believe me, you were a good deal more living than they were, if not entirely alive. I pulled you out. That shouldn't be possible. How did you die?"

Juliet's mouth twisted.

"Tell me how you died," said Runajo.

The words snapped out of Juliet in short, sharp bursts. "It was my fault. I tried to make Romeo my Guardian. The magic went wrong. I do not know why. He is dead now, and I do not know why. It was my fault." Then she pressed a fist to her mouth, as if to stop the words.

It took Runajo a moment to understand what Juliet had said. "Romeo?" she demanded. "Do you mean Mahyanai Romeo? Son of Lord Ineo?"

Juliet stared at her for a few moments with a flat, impenetrable expression. Then she said, "He is my husband."

It had to be a lie. Romeo was nine kinds of foolish—he'd more than proved that, in the years he'd spent trying to make Runajo fall in love with him—but he didn't want to die, and he would never give his heart away to a Catresou girl . . . let alone the Catresou's barely human attack dog.

But then she remembered Romeo's stubborn smile as he befriended her when they were both just children. How long he had kept visiting her, even after everyone knew her house was filled with sickness. How much he loved a challenge, how many times he had sworn that he loved her, and how stubbornly—in defiance of all evidence—he had believed she had a soft heart hidden away.

She looked at Juliet's pretty face and grim expression, and she realized that actually, falling in love with Juliet Catresou was exactly the sort of thing Romeo would do.

And then she thought, *Romeo is dead.*

She didn't mourn him. She couldn't. She had renounced him along with all the world, and she had been happy at the thought that she might never see him again, and it *was not possible* to miss what you didn't have.

But she did regret that he was dead. That was all this cold, hollow ache inside her chest could be. Simple regret that he'd thrown his heart at this girl and gotten killed for it.

Juliet said, "What's on your hand?"

Runajo raised her hand, palm out. "Why don't you tell me?"

Juliet stared at her, dark eyes wide. "I am going to kill you," she said, standing. "I am going to kill you all." And this time Runajo could see that she wasn't just angry, she was drawing herself up for action. As if the sign on Runajo's hand was terrible enough to tip her back into violence.

And suddenly everything made horrifying sense. Juliet had been trying to make Romeo her Guardian, and the magic had gone wrong. She had stopped trying to cut Runajo's throat when she told her to. The same mark was on both their hands.

"I order you not to kill me." The words snapped out of her mouth. "Or kill any of the Sisters. Or try to escape my orders. Or kill yourself. Or maim yourself. Or provoke anyone into killing you."

Juliet swayed slightly on her toes. Her face was expressionless.

Then she dropped gracefully into a deep obeisance, knees and hands to the floor.

"Does my mistress have any other orders?" she said, and Runajo couldn't help grinning at the perfectly modulated sarcasm even as her stomach churned with disgust. Because Juliet was her slave now. Runajo hadn't tried to become her Guardian, hadn't had a choice about giving her orders, but it didn't matter. She still had absolute power over her.

If she didn't set this right, she would be as bad as the Catresou.

"Sit up," said Runajo. "I have no interest in owning you."

Juliet sat up. "My clan will not negotiate to save me from death or torment." She recited the words coldly, precisely, as if they were made of metal. "I am the sword of the Catresou. I was meant to be broken before I betrayed them."

Runajo rolled her eyes. "Stop pretending you're in the middle of a war. Nobody cares enough to destroy you, and also, none of us are oath-breakers who would violate the Accords. Not to mention that it's much more useful to keep your clan alive and having babies who can grow up to shed blood."

Juliet stared back at her expressionlessly. Of course it was no use talking sense to her. The Catresou trained all their children to believe the entire city hated them; it made it easier for them to hate the entire city. No doubt their precious Juliet had been more thoroughly indoctrinated than anyone.

"Do you know what happened when you died?" asked Runajo.

"No," said Juliet, her shoulders slumping slightly. "We did everything right. And if we hadn't—we should have died, but not like that. The dark lands appeared around us while we still breathed." Her fists clenched. "That should be *impossible*."

"Then I will find out why." Runajo stood. "Stay here. I'll bring you food."

"As you wish," said Juliet, with a meekness that was clearly meant to cut like a knife. "Mistress."

12

SO FOR THE NEXT FEW days, Runajo had a pet Catresou.

It was uniquely awful.

Stealing food and water and smuggling them to Juliet was bad enough. So too was trying to get answers from her—it didn't seem right, ordering her to respond whenever Runajo wanted her to speak, but if she wasn't ordered, she wouldn't say a thing. She would only glare silently at Runajo as she ran through what looked like fighting forms. Probably she was practicing for how she would slaughter all the Sisters of Thorn, the moment she slipped Runajo's control.

Runajo could be killing everybody in the Cloister just by keeping her alive. If she had been truly dead. If Runajo had, however unwittingly, performed necromancy.

The question nagged at her constantly. But she couldn't ask

anyone for advice, because if the Sisters knew what she had done, they would never allow her into the Sunken Library.

If she had any chance to begin with. As each day passed, Runajo was less sure. The High Priestess didn't let her do anything different now that she was an actual Sister of Thorn. She slept in her own cell, instead of in the dormitory with the other novices. She sat with the other Sisters at meals. But she was given no chance to study previous attempts to enter the library. For two days, they drilled her on her new part in the prayers and chants; on the third day, they sent her straight back to the weaving room where she had worked before.

Three floors below her, in the heart of the Cloister, the raw material of the city walls continuously gushed from the sacred stone and flowed up through the pipeline that formed the Cloister's spine. Here, in the weaving room, the hundred-year-old spells performed the first refinements on the pillar of flowing light, splitting it into twenty-eight glowing strands and weaving them back together into the pillar that—very far above—would spread out into the vast dome that protected the city.

Not without guidance, though. There must always be three Sisters or advanced novices to shape the flow of power. So when Runajo went back to the weaving room, she found Sunjai and Inyaan waiting for her just like always.

"All hail the noble and wise Sister of Thorn," said Sunjai,

flashing her a big smile. "I'm glad you got yourself back in one piece."

Runajo rolled her eyes as she knelt to take her place. "Nobody's around, you don't have to pretend."

"Maybe I actually like you," said Sunjai, which was the most bald-faced lie Runajo had heard since her mother had said *everything will be all right.*

From the corner of the room, Inyaan glared at Runajo and then looked away without bothering to say a word. She had never bothered pretending to like anyone.

It didn't matter. Runajo was not in this room or the Cloister to make friends.

She hooked each of her fingers around a glowing strand and pulled. Light danced around her hands.

Weaving was not the same as tasting the wall up above. No glimpses of the ancient lore flickered through Runajo's head. There was not the same frustrated bliss of feeling infinite knowledge beneath her tongue and beyond her grasp. But the light was alive in her hands; its song hummed through her skin and into her bones. At every moment it tugged against her grip, dancing with her fingers and resisting them at the same time. And at every moment, she shaped it to her will.

In the weaving room, she was never silent. The wall became her words. It was joy and it was freedom, and it could almost make her forget that she hadn't yet gotten into the Sunken Library. That she had become a Sister, and it wasn't enough.

On the other side of the room, Sunjai did the same with her half of the strands, while Inyaan pressed her palms to the glyphs inlaid on the floor and controlled the flow. After Runajo, they were the best of all the novices at weaving. When neither of them was speaking, she was grateful to be working with them.

The problem was that Sunjai almost never shut up.

"Or maybe I'm just glad you didn't succeed in killing yourself," she said now. "And impressed. How did you make that tattoo?"

Light trembled in Runajo's hands, even though there was no way anyone could guess what the sign on her hand meant. The Catresou fiercely guarded the sacred words they used to work magic; nobody in the Cloister could have seen the mark before.

"The novices are all wild about it," Sunjai went on. "Some of them even believe the gods gave it to you." She looked at Runajo from under her eyelashes. "I didn't disillusion them."

"Because you love me so *very* much," said Runajo, yanking the strands of light back into order. Usually Sunjai just chattered about the other novices or teased her about Romeo. She didn't trust this . . . directness.

"Mm," said Sunjai. "And because I want you to remember me kindly, when you're talking to Lord Ineo."

The words were so unexpected, it took Runajo a moment to respond. "Why would I talk to him?"

"Why would he offend your family to get you in here?" said Sunjai. "Do you think the rest of us didn't notice what he did for you?"

And Runajo couldn't think of a thing to say. She'd been relieved when Lord Ineo had allowed her to stay in the Cloister. She had never wondered why. It had just been so obvious that it was the right decision. But there was no reason for him to do it.

Had Romeo begged on her behalf? He'd tried to convince her to leave the Cloister, but he was the only person in Viyara who might dislike it if she was dragged out by the hair.

"And now you're the youngest Sister ever to survive the vigil of souls," said Sunjai. "We all expect great things from you. I'm sure he does too."

"What sort of things?" asked Runajo, trying not to think of Romeo reciting poetry, his stupid face alight with joy. Trying not to think of how he was dead.

"I don't know," said Sunjai. "I'm not clever enough to survive the vigil. But I *am* your closest friend, so I hope you remember me when you reach your inevitable heights of glory."

"I'm not—" Runajo stopped as another, worse thought hit her. Sunjai didn't believe a single thing unless it had been gossiped first. If she thought that Runajo had sat the vigil for the sake of ambition—

"Do they all think that?" she demanded. "All the Sisters, do they think that's why I sat the vigil?"

"Well, there are a few who think you did it out of despair, now that Romeo is condemned to die for killing a Catresou in a duel," said Sunjai.

Romeo had already died, because he was a lovesick idiot who shouldn't cause this heaviness in Runajo's chest.

"But I told them you didn't love him," Sunjai went on. "And reminded them that the man he killed was a Catresou and probably asking for it, because we Mahyanai have to stick together."

They all thought she had done it for fame, and for the power that fame could bring.

Runajo had known that Miryo despised her and would always believe the worst of her. She had vaguely known that a lot of other Sisters and novices disliked her. But somehow—because she was stupid, stupid, *stupid*—she had thought that proving herself in the vigil would matter.

It had only proved to them that she was determined. That was why the High Priestess had not let her make any progress toward the Sunken Library. Why she never would. She thought that Runajo had only sat the vigil for glory.

Never in her life had Runajo cared what people thought of her. But now it mattered.

And she was going to lose her chance at the Sunken Library because of it.

"Did you not know about Romeo?" Sunjai asked, her voice dripping with sudden fake pity. As if she actually cared.

"I knew," Runajo snapped. She felt numb and cold; it was only bone-deep memory that kept her fingers moving in the pattern. "But I didn't care. Just like I don't care about you. If I ever do see Lord Ineo, I'll tell him that you gossip when you're meant to be weaving and your divine little friend still needs your help on the advanced patterns."

There was a short silence. For nearly all the time they'd been weaving, they'd had a truce where Runajo pretended not to notice Sunjai covering for Inyaan's faults—the girl was wildly talented, but only at half the weavings they did—and Sunjai didn't try to destroy Runajo.

"Don't make me hurt you," said Sunjai, all the sweetness suddenly gone from her voice. It was not an idle threat.

"Concentrate on the weaving," Inyaan droned, her voice as colorless as her hair.

Sunjai fell silent, because she always obeyed Inyaan. Because she was a fool and she accepted the divine right of the Exalted's family as no Mahyanai should. And yet she had seen something idiotically obvious, which Runajo hadn't even noticed.

Everything she'd done had been for nothing. She had possibly committed necromancy, and it had been for *nothing*.

That night, Runajo couldn't sleep. She stared at the dim ceiling of her cell and tried to make a plan.

If the High Priestess wouldn't allow her to enter the Sunken

Library, Runajo would have to force her way in. That was obvious. There was no other choice, except giving up and waiting for death.

That meant she would have to get down to the door—easy enough—and break open the spells holding it shut. That would be hard. The magic had been woven to keep revenants in, not keep Sisters out, so it wasn't impossible. Unweaving spells had been part of her training. But Runajo had never tried to undo any magic so powerful before.

And then she would need a way to keep the revenants from tearing her apart before she managed to get the books out of the library. Runajo had always known that was a risk, but she had hoped to get help from the Sisterhood. She had hoped to at least die knowing that others would follow in her steps.

Now there was nobody who would help or follow. So she could not afford to die.

There was another part to that problem: if Runajo died now, then Juliet would be left locked in that hidden room until she starved to death. But she couldn't smuggle Juliet out of the Cloister until she knew for sure if she needed to die for being undead. And she *still* couldn't ask any of the Sisters for advice, because if she was locked up for necromancy, she'd never be able to sneak down.

With a sigh, Runajo finally gave up on sleeping and stood. She couldn't solve the whole problem tonight. But she could at least examine the door into the Sunken Library and start to get an idea if she could open it.

So she slipped out of her room and through the quiet corridors.

The most direct way down went through the heart of the Cloister. It was a huge, round room where glyphs and patterns shimmered as they swirled ceaselessly across the stone walls. At the center, on a great round dais whose surface glowed with a pattern of ever-shifting lights, sat the sacred stone. It was a dark, knobby lump of rock, as wide as Runajo was tall. Legend said it had fallen from the sky; another legend said it had been dragged up from the land of the dead, when the first Sister walked down to bargain with Death.

Whatever its origin, it now had a single purpose: to weave the walls around Viyara. The glowing, translucent foam of the walls drifted up from the surface of the sacred stone, and farther up through the pipelines that channeled the raw material, all the way up to the platform where Runajo had tasted the walls.

There was a faint, soft humming in the air, as if the city were singing. For this was not the heart of just the Cloister, but of all Viyara: this shining, singing column of light that drank up the blood of the sacrifices and made the city alive with magic in return.

The normal solemn sacrifices were held in the grand court, outdoors beneath the sunlight. But once every five years, a Sister herself must be sacrificed, and that was done here, where her blood could pour across the dais and dye the base of the sacred stone red.

Runajo swallowed, feeling a little sick.

You cannot raid the Sunken Library if you can't face death, she told herself. *You will just have to learn to be brave.*

She started walking around the room. First things first. On the other side was a stairway that would take her down to the door of the Sunken Library. All she had to do was examine the door. Find a way in. Find a way to survive.

Find out if she had to kill Juliet or not.

No matter what Juliet thought, the idea of cutting her throat made Runajo feel sick. Of course she had known that as a Sister, that duty might fall to her someday, but she had thought there would be more time to get used to it, time to stop being afraid, time—but there was no time for anything now.

Maybe Juliet had never really been dead. Maybe Runajo would find a way to break the bond between them, so that Juliet could be sent home and Runajo could live out the rest of her days in peace.

Or maybe everything would end in blood. Runajo felt another wave of nausea—she could almost smell it—

She *could* smell it.

Her heart gave an awful lurch. There were alcoves all along the wall, and now she realized that there was a dark puddle seeping out from one of them.

Some of the Sisters came down here to make offerings. Maybe one of them had not bothered to bleed in the right place, had not bothered to clean it up.

She knew she was thinking nonsense, but she couldn't help hoping as she ran forward.

Then she looked into the alcove.

There was blood everywhere—puddled on the floor, splattered across the wall, but also dribbled in a great spiral around the dead body. It took Runajo a moment to recognize her: Atsaya, the Sister who taught the novices how to offer their first penances. She always stuttered, hands gesturing wildly, as she tried to explain how glorious it was to perform sacred penance.

Her throat had been cut from ear to ear.

Runajo didn't remember the next few moments. The next thing she knew, she was in the hall outside, gasping for breath and trying not to vomit.

Atsaya had been alive yesterday. Romeo had been alive a few days ago. Everyone was dead. Bloody and dying and dead.

Her ears were ringing; the world seemed to have gone blurry around her. She knew that she was panicking. It didn't matter, because they were all dead. They were all going to die.

Hands grasped her shoulders and shook her. Somebody was talking. Runajo blinked and saw the person's neck. She remembered the raw, red edges cut into Atsaya's throat, and that was when she gave up and lurched to the side to vomit.

"—tell me what you are doing, you disgusting little—"

It was Miryo. Of course. The one person in the temple who hated her most would find her when she was being unforgivably weak. No Sister of Thorn should ever flinch from blood or death.

Runajo pushed her hands away and managed to straighten up.

"Atsaya," she said. "She's dead." She pointed back toward the great hall.

Miryo huffed out a breath. "Don't be ridiculous—"

Runajo held up her hand. She must have touched the wall of the alcove to steady herself, because her palm was smeared with blood.

"Stay here," said Miryo, and ran for the hall.

Runajo leaned back against the wall. She thought of the dead woman in the hall nearby, and the living girl hidden in the walls, and she tried to breathe.

And she thought of Juliet's voice: *I am going to kill you. I am going to kill you all.*

13

THREE HOURS LATER, PARIS WAS lurking outside Meros's favorite pleasure house and thinking about the flaws in his plan.

As soon as he'd gotten far enough away from Justiran's house to calm down, he'd panicked. Paris didn't know anything about the Lower City. He didn't even know where he was. He certainly didn't know where Tybalt had been, much less how to discover what he'd been doing for Lord Catresou.

Pretty much all Paris knew about the Lower City were the stories that Meros had told of his exploits. The way Meros talked, all the young Catresou lordlings went to the same pleasure house to drink the same liquor, watch the same dancing girls, and purchase the same prostitutes. It didn't seem possible that Tybalt would have done such filthy things, but it didn't seem possible that he would help Lord Catresou work with a necromancer, either.

No part of the situation made any sense. What could Lord Catresou mean to accomplish by tampering with the adjurations upon the Juliet? What could any Catresou even want with a necromancer? They were supposed to be the people who didn't fear death.

They were supposed to be *better* than everyone else. Not worse.

Meros liked to boast that his pleasure house was the most elegant spot in the Lower City, and Paris could believe it. The street was wide, and many of the people thronging it were dressed in clothes just as finely made as Paris's now-rumpled formal outfit. The pleasure house itself was not made from actual white stone, but it was painted white, and the lines of the eaves and windows had the same gentle curves and sudden curlicues as buildings in the Upper City. The doorposts and lintels were painted gold.

Paris realized he had no idea what to do next. He was pretty sure he'd need money to get inside, and he didn't have a single coin. And if he did get in, how would he know whom to question? Tybalt wouldn't have told his secrets to any of the staff, and who knew if he even had any friends, let alone if they came regularly to be entertained at this house.

He felt like an idiot. He'd spent the last few hours trudging through the city, sweating in the humid afternoon heat, asking for directions and getting snickered at. And it was all for nothing, because he had no plan, and really he'd never had any hope of succeeding, just like Father had always—

Paris drew a breath. He had to try. Whatever it cost him, he had to try.

His one comfort was that—whether because of the distance, or because they had both been trying so hard to block the other out—he couldn't feel anything from Romeo at all. No matter what happened, at least he wouldn't have Romeo weeping into his mind.

Paris forced himself to walk toward the door. His pulse was racing, and he knew that his face was flushing more than the afternoon heat could excuse.

There was a stout, heavily muscled man at the door. Paris bowed slightly to him, the way he would to a doorkeeper at a house where he had come as a guest, and then wondered if that was wrong.

"I'm supposed to meet a friend here," he said. "His name is . . ." He remembered that all the Catresou boys—or Meros, anyway—used false names while they were in the Lower City. "Lurien," he finished, after probably much too long a pause. It was Meros's false name, which would probably cause problems if Meros was down in the Lower City right now, but he had to still be helping with the search for Paris above, didn't he?

The man stared at him with an expression like the giant stone toads in the grand marketplace of the Upper City.

"I'm his brother," Paris added hopefully, and then remembered that he had already said he was meeting a "friend."

"Do you have coin?" the man asked flatly.

"No," said Paris, "but if you let me in to wait for him—he'll be along any moment, and I won't make any trouble, I promise—I just need to meet him. I told him I would be here and it's very important."

He knew that he was babbling, and that it was pointless trying to get in because he had no idea how to investigate anyway, and he'd probably have to bribe the girls with money he didn't have to make them say anything. But he couldn't give up. He had to get justice for the Juliet. He had to stop Lord Catresou and the necromancers.

"If you don't have coin," said the man, "you don't get in."

For one wild moment, Paris thought of yelling that there were necromancers about and trying to run inside during the confusion. But nobody would believe him—nobody would believe anything that had happened today—and he didn't think the man in front of him would panic even if the Ruining breached the walls.

Maybe he should just admit that this was a pathetic, useless attempt and go away.

Maybe there was a back door he could sneak in.

He turned away and had taken two steps when an arm landed roughly on his shoulders.

"Terrible thing," a man announced cheerfully in his ear, "locking up pretty girls behind a wall."

"And charging what almost no man can afford," another chimed in from the other side as they dragged him forward.

"I—thank you, but I don't want—" Paris tried to slow down, but they were pulling too hard; he only stumbled over his feet.

"Never you mind, we know a place where the girls are cheap," said the man with his arm over Paris's shoulder. "You'd like that, wouldn't you?"

"No," said Paris. "No, I don't want that."

"Ohhh," said the other man, drawing out the sound, "the boys are cheap too. I know you Catresou like to keep that kind of thing secret. We won't tell."

They were already off the main street and turned down an alleyway. It was both clean and quiet, and it would have been a relief from the busy street except that Paris was now alone with the two men. And he realized that it didn't matter how respectable the narrow alley looked, it was dangerous.

He lunged forward, and for a moment he twisted free. Then one of them caught his arm and wrenched him back so sharply that it felt like the arm was coming out of the socket. Then came a punch in the stomach, and for a few moments Paris couldn't focus on anything except the pain and trying to breathe.

When his lungs started working again, he was on the ground with a knee in his back.

"Don't damage the clothes," one of the men was muttering.

"I have done this before," the other one snapped, and then

there was the prick of a knife at Paris's throat. "We don't want blood on all this nice cloth," the man went on, a little louder, "so just stay quiet and be good and we can all walk away from here, eh?"

The whole world narrowed down to the tiny sharp edge against Paris's throat. His breath, rushing in and out faster and faster. He was going to die here.

"Just look at the embroidery on the collar," said the man holding the knife to his throat. "Ever seen the like?"

"No," said the other one thoughtfully. "This boy comes from money. D'you think the captain will want to see him?"

The man whistled. "He probably will." Then he eased the knife back a little and said, "Xinaad smiled on you today, boy. You're going to live long enough to be ransomed."

Paris had a hysterical impulse to point out that they had just promised to let him live if he was only quiet, and it wasn't logical to keep changing the rules like this, but he managed to keep his mouth shut. Maybe, if he stayed calm, he could get a chance to run.

They hauled him back up, but kept him pinned between them, one arm twisted so painfully behind his back that his eyes watered. Without dislocating his arm, there was nothing he could do except keep walking where they pushed him.

There was going to be a chance. He just had to wait for it. But after they had dragged him down two more streets, Paris realized that there might not be a chance. He might actually have to dislocate his arm if he wanted to live.

He thought, *Now or never,* and before he had time to get any more terrified, he kicked at the man holding his arm.

The man staggered, and for a moment Paris thought it was going to work, but then the other man punched him in the gut, and Paris was on the ground again, trying to breathe.

And there was a knife pressing at his throat. Again.

"Do I need to teach you a lesson?" the man growled.

"That doesn't look friendly," someone called out from above.

The knife left Paris's throat. He twisted his head to look up.

Quite casually, as if it were nothing, a boy Paris's age balanced on one of the ledges of the building above them, one hand hooked on a windowsill. The next moment, he had leaped to the ground below, as light as a cat.

"You'd better let him go," the boy said pleasantly, drawing two sticks painted in a swirling pattern of blue and black. They were a little longer than his forearms, and not half as wide; they didn't look like they would be of much use against the two men, who were both larger than him.

"Or we could skip to the part where I thrash you," the boy added.

The man who wasn't holding Paris gave a growl, and lunged at him.

The boy moved so fast Paris could barely see, but he could

certainly hear the sharp crack as one of the sticks bounced off the man's head, followed by two thuds as they slammed into his middle.

Paris felt the pressure on his back lift as the man holding him wavered; with a sudden burst of energy, he wrenched himself to the side. A moment later the new boy was bearing down on the man. But he didn't try to fight; he grabbed his whimpering friend by the arm and hauled him into one of the nearby buildings.

"Sloppy," said the boy, watching them go. "They could have used you for a hostage against me, if they'd been thinking." He looked at Paris. "You all right?"

"I—" said Paris, and couldn't get any more words out. He realized he was trembling and gasping for breath.

"Lean against the wall," the boy advised. "Your first fight?"

Paris nodded. He knew he looked pathetic, but for once, he wasn't embarrassed; he was still too shaken. And the boy didn't seem interested in sneering at him. He was almost the same height as Paris; he had dark-brown skin and a head full of tiny black braids. He wore a black tunic and coat with a bright-blue kerchief around his neck, and blue beads dangled from his braids.

"Well, don't worry," said the boy. "They're just fetching the rest of their gang. From their headquarters in there." He jerked his head at the dingy building they had disappeared into.

"Gang?" Paris asked faintly. "Shouldn't we run?"

"You can," said the boy cheerfully, "but if you do, I can't

protect you. I've been hunting them all day; I'm not giving up this chance." His voice suddenly swelled to a shout. *"Are you here yet, you filthy cowards?"*

As if in answer, the door swung open. Out came the men who had tried to rob him, followed by at least ten others, all wearing yellow kerchiefs, including one really large and angry-looking man carrying a huge cudgel.

"Who's the boy who thinks he can mess with my men?" he demanded.

"Nobody," said the boy. "Just the King of Cats."

The words made the gang draw up short; obviously the title meant something to them, though Paris had never heard it before.

"It's a very simple situation," the boy went on. "You can join the Rooks and follow my orders without question. Or you can immediately decide that your territory starts east of here. Screaming as you run is optional."

Paris suspected that it would be a good time for *him* to scream and run, but the situation had a sort of awful fascination. The boy was definitely, absolutely mad, and they were both going to be pounded to death, and he couldn't look away.

"*Or* you can fight me over it," said the boy. "Care to wager your gang on a duel?"

The leader hesitated a moment; then he sneered, "So long as you fight fair."

"Nobody gets anything but what he earns from me," the boy

said pleasantly as he strode forward. He bowed like a duelist; the leader of the gang grunted. Then the boy's sticks whirled into motion, tracing out an elaborate flourish of defense around him. It looked exquisite, and skillful, and not terribly useful, and Paris was about to give up and run while he could, when in one swift motion the boy tossed his sticks up in the air and kicked the leader of the gang in the neck.

He collapsed. The boy caught his sticks out of the air and said, "Anyone else?"

There was a moment of strained, incredulous silence.

"I should warn you that the rest of my crew is here now, so you'll need to fight them as well," the boy went on. Paris looked back, and coming up the alley behind them was another group. They were all wearing bright-blue kerchiefs, and most of them were openly carrying short swords, in blatant violation of the law.

Not that anyone in the alleyway except for Paris seemed to care about the law.

The men from the other gang hesitated; then four of them grabbed their leader and fled. The others reluctantly tore off their kerchiefs and dropped to their knees.

One by one, the boy went to each of them, hauling them to their feet and clapping them on the shoulder. "Welcome to the Rooks," he said. When he was finished, he called out to the rest of his gang, "Take them inside and start explaining things to them."

As they streamed past, he turned to Paris and said, "Let me guess. This is your first trip to the Lower City."

"Yes," said Paris. And this boy clearly led one of the gangs that infested it.

"Good." The boy's mouth was tilted up slightly, but his dark eyes were cool. "Run home and don't come back. You aren't going to survive around here."

Paris felt his spine straighten. "I'm not dead yet," he said.

"Because I helped you," said the boy. "But I'm not planning to follow you around the city. And I'd rather not trip over your dead body."

"Who are you?" Paris demanded.

The boy grinned, all white teeth and sudden glee. "Didn't you hear? I'm the King of Cats."

"Stop being so mysterious, Vai," one of his own men called over his shoulder.

"Also known as Vai the Bloody, Vai the Terrible, Vai the Bloody Terrible, and more importantly, Vai dalr-Ahodin, captain of the Rooks."

"And King of Cats," said Paris, who still had no idea what that meant. The Rooks were clearly Vai's gang of blue-kerchiefed men; Paris would think that there was just another gang called

Cats, but everyone seemed to think the title was even more important somehow.

"Yes," said Vai, "and I really did mean what I said. Get home or learn to survive."

"I didn't come here for fun," Paris said, and then a thought struck him. Some of the gangs in the Lower City were really powerful; if Tybalt had been organizing something for Lord Catresou down here, he had probably met with at least a few of them.

"Have you ever met Tybalt Catresou?" he asked.

"Met him, defeated him, and why do you ask?" said Vai. He was still smiling, but there was a sudden edge of menace to his voice.

"I . . ." Paris trailed off, realizing that he hadn't bothered to plan out how he was going to ask people questions about Tybalt without revealing what was going on.

The next moment Vai had shoved him against the nearest wall, and it didn't matter that they were of a height. Paris could feel how strong he was, and he knew which one of them would win in a fight.

"You seem pretty naive, so I'm going to go easy on you," said Vai, his voice pleasant but deadly. "Down here, this is my city. Catresou who want to live had better stay out."

Then he shoved Paris away and strode after the rest of his gang.

Paris knew he should follow him. Vai had fought Tybalt and

hated him, and that meant he probably knew something about him. But Paris's feet didn't care; in a moment he was limping back the way he had come as fast as he could.

Vai was clearly not going to talk to him. If he died in an alley, he would never get justice for Juliet. Paris told himself that, but he knew the simple truth was that he was afraid.

Paris had trudged across the city and nearly died, and all he had to show for it were scrapes and bruises, and a reminder of his own cowardice. Short of Lord Catresou appearing on the street, he wasn't sure how things could get worse.

And then he heard Romeo's voice in his head, calling, *Paris?*

Paris nearly turned and fled in the opposite direction. There were only two problems. One was that he didn't know where Romeo was.

The other was that he felt a horrifying need to walk straight toward him.

Where are you? Romeo asked.

Paris slipped back out of the alley onto the main street. He couldn't remember its name, so he tried to send Romeo an image of the spot.

You went there?

Paris felt his face heating. *I was trying to find someone who had spoken to Tybalt! I didn't know where else to go because* you *wouldn't help! And what is it to you, anyway? I thought you were planning to just lie on the floor and weep while cursing our clan.*

For that matter, why did Paris care what Romeo thought? Of all the people he'd disappointed in his life, surely the Mahyanai who got Juliet killed was the least important.

I know, said Romeo, and there was something strangely quiet in his voice. *I'm sorry. I was angry, but I should not have pretended that you didn't care about Juliet.*

That was . . . the last thing Paris had expected to hear.

I'm nearly there, said Romeo, and now Paris could feel his presence approaching: a faint, directional warmth like the winter sun.

A minute later, he heard steps and turned to see Romeo. For a moment they stared at each other.

Then Romeo squared his shoulders. "I'm prepared to help you," he said. "Please come back."

"Why?" he asked. "I thought you hated the Catresou." He could still hear Vai's voice, telling him to stay out.

"You were right," said Romeo. "She'd have no use for me, if she saw me being such a coward. And she loved her clan. She would want me to help them."

"So just for that, you're going to help me? What happened to weeping forever?" Paris knew he shouldn't be trying to drive Romeo away, but he couldn't seem to help himself.

"For Juliet," said Romeo, "I would do anything. Wouldn't you?"

He sounded naive and sentimental and stupid and . . .

completely in earnest. And he was right: Paris would do anything to make up for failing Juliet.

He would even work with a Mahyanai.

Paris shouldn't be feeling this kind of desperate relief at being helped by an enemy. But he had no one else.

"Let's go back," he said.

14

THEY BURNED ATSAYA'S BODY THE next morning. Like every other Sister who died, she was not sent to the great furnaces where all the other dead of Viyara burned; rather, she went to the sacred furnace reserved for Sisters and the royal family. It was in a huge round room whose white walls and floors were inlaid with a dizzying pattern of black stone stripes. At the center was a great bowl of the same black stone, ribbed with pale metal; here Atsaya—washed and anointed and naked—was laid to rest. At a gesture from the High Priestess, the metal ribs of the bowl grew, writhed, and then folded together like the legs of a dying beetle. When they had tightened themselves into a lid, the fire leaped up to devour the body.

All four hundred fifty-eight of the Sisters were present, and together they sang to Atsaya. Runajo didn't even try to join in.

Her eyes were swollen; her head felt too heavy and too light at the same time. She hadn't slept after finding the body. Miryo had questioned her, and then dragged her away to be questioned again by some of the other senior Sisters, and then she'd had to wait for the High Priestess to speak with her. And then the bells were ringing, calling for the Sisters to wake.

She wasn't sure she could have slept, anyway.

Atsaya was dead. Atsaya had been *murdered.*

And the murderer was in the Cloister.

Juliet couldn't have done it. Runajo had specifically ordered her not to kill any of the Sisters, and even if she had found a way around the order, she was locked in a room that only Runajo could open.

But that meant one of the Sisters must have done it. Nobody else was allowed past the outer visiting rooms; it was why they held the Great Offering outside in the grand court.

A Sister had cut Atsaya's throat and dribbled her blood into a spiral. That wasn't just murder; that was a ceremony. Magic. Somebody in the Cloister wanted a terrible amount of power—enough to feed the city walls for half a year—and she was willing to kill for it.

Runajo had thought she had already faced death. Her father. Her mother. The top of the tower. The Great Offering. But those deaths had been, if not arranged, then known in advance. They had been nothing like this.

She had always thought she had a heart of stone, but maybe it had only been ice, now melted to water. Because when she thought of the murderer lurking in the Cloister, ready to strike again at any moment—when she thought of facing the revenants, of them ripping her throat open with their bare fingers—

She couldn't bear it.

For the first time, Runajo wondered if she was too much of a coward to accomplish her plans. But if she couldn't . . . then there was no point to anything she had done.

The song ended. The High Priestess spoke into the silence, her voice clear and ringing: "For love of the gods and the city, Atsaya offered her own life. Let us remember her, for we live in her death."

Then she began to chant the prayer for someone who has died in sacrifice, buying the city's life with her own blood.

In the hours before dawn the High Priestess had said, *You are distraught. Atsaya died by her own hand.*

The memory burned: not that the High Priestess had lied to her, but that for a moment Runajo had thought she wasn't lying. She had actually tried to convince her.

Did you see the body? she had demanded. *How could she have done that?*

There is much about sacrifice that you don't understand, the High Priestess had said calmly. *If you repeat these wild ideas to anyone else, you will be punished.*

And that was when Runajo knew her for a liar, and knew she should not have protested. Better to have held her tongue and let the High Priestess think she was fooled. Now she was being watched, to make sure she didn't try to tell anyone.

Runajo would obey. She could not afford to be punished now. But she fumed in silence as the High Priestess continued with her lying prayers. Much that she didn't understand? She understood quite well that Atsaya could not have spread her blood in a spiral after cutting her own throat.

The High Priestess's prayer ended. As one, the Sisters all prostrated themselves in silence.

Runajo pressed her forehead to the cold floor. There was no sound except the muffled crackle of the fire. She was surrounded by women who were supposed to be as sisters to her, and she was all alone.

She was running out of time.

That was all Runajo could think, all day long. Somebody in the Cloister was murdering to gain magical power, and the High Priestess was doing absolutely nothing to protect the rest of them. That meant everyone was in danger, especially Runajo, since she had found the body. Somebody would gossip. And then whoever killed Atsaya would have reason to want Runajo gone.

Runajo didn't have a hope of catching the murderer first. So it didn't matter how much of a coward she was, or how unlikely she was to survive the Sunken Library. She had to go now, while she was still breathing. Even if the thought made her hands go numb with terror.

But what was she to do with Juliet? It was no use leaving a note in her room, telling the Sisterhood to get Juliet out of her prison if Runajo didn't come back. Since Runajo's blood had made the room, only Runajo's hands could open it.

She didn't want to be a murderer. But that was what she would be if she left Juliet locked in the room while she herself perished in the Sunken Library.

"What is it?" asked Juliet that evening. "Working yourself up to send me out for my first kill?" She threw out the words flippantly, as if they were nothing to her, but she didn't meet Runajo's eyes.

"No," said Runajo, and remembered a throat torn open. She swallowed convulsively.

"Then what happened?" asked Juliet.

Runajo shrugged, trying to look like she didn't care. "One of the Sisters is dead."

Juliet shrugged. "So?"

"She was murdered. I know, because I found the body." Runajo's fingers twisted together and clenched.

"So?" said Juliet again, loud and irreverent and drowning out the memories. "Aren't you all supposed to live as if already dead? What does it matter to you?"

Runajo looked back at her. "I didn't know your people ever bothered to learn how we live."

"'What you would destroy, first love,'" said Juliet, in a prim voice that made it clear she was quoting something.

"Is that why you married Romeo?" asked Runajo.

She'd meant the words to sting, but for a moment Juliet's expression was nothing but openmouthed pain, as if she were being gutted.

Runajo sighed. "Atsaya was murdered. Her throat was cut from ear to ear. But the High Priestess told everyone this morning that the gods inspired her to sacrifice herself. It's not right. And people are going to die for it, because the murderer is still at large. Is it so very strange to you, that I might care?"

"Yes," said Juliet. "What is one more death to you?"

"Well, you have only your ignorance to blame for that," said Runajo. "And I know you were trained to kill, so you should stop pretending we are somehow more heartless."

"I'm the sword of the Catresou," said Juliet. "I was *born* to kill."

"Anyone Lord Catresou tells you to," said Runajo. "I know."

"No," said Juliet. "Anyone that justice tells me to. That's what makes me different from you."

And then Runajo remembered the enchantments that the Catresou placed on the Juliet.

"You can sense when somebody is guilty of spilling Catresou

blood," she said. "Could you tell if a person was guilty of *anyone's* murder?"

Juliet shrugged. "Probably."

"How close do you have to be?" asked Runajo, sitting up. Her exhaustion was melting away, now that she had the start of a plan.

If Runajo could use Juliet to find the murderer, then the High Priestess might finally listen to her. She might permit Runajo to enter the Sunken Library, might help her find a way to survive it. Even if she didn't—if the murderer were stopped, then Runajo would have time. So she could prepare for the library, so she could decide what to do with Juliet, so she could think about danger without shaking again.

Runajo was afraid. She was desperately afraid of the murderer. But if she could stop her, then maybe she would find her courage again.

"Why should I help you?" asked Juliet.

Because I order you to, Runajo nearly said, and then felt sick. Was it really so easy, to start using this girl as a slave?

Of course it was easy. Juliet's own family had all managed it.

As if she could tell what Runajo was thinking, Juliet said, "You've already enslaved me. You shouldn't flinch at a few more orders."

"Your family enslaved you," said Runajo. "And what choice do I have but to give you orders? You said you wanted to kill me and all my Sisters. You really should have lied to me from the start."

"I never lie," said Juliet.

Runajo raised her eyebrows. "You took a secret husband without ever lying?"

"I did not always tell the whole truth," said Juliet. "That is not the same as lying."

"Well, if you want to slaughter the entire Sisterhood, you'll have to learn at least a little deceit," said Runajo. "Tact, as well."

"You've thought about what it would take to kill them?" asked Juliet.

"I think about everything," said Runajo. "And a good deal more than you seem to. Will you help me or not?"

Silence stretched between them. Juliet stared at her, and though her face was resolutely set as always, there was something tired in her shoulders, her eyes.

"You still haven't told me why I should," she said.

"Because it's unjust," said Runajo, "for anyone to be murdered. Even one of us. Don't you want to see all murderers punished?"

Juliet stared at her for a moment longer. Then her mouth tilted up. "All right," she said.

15

PARIS WAS GLAD TO HAVE Romeo's help, but he felt a sense of dread as they trudged back to Justiran's house. He had declared that he didn't need help from a renouncer when he stormed out. He could guess the sort of raised eyebrows and condescension he was going to face when he came crawling back.

It was for Juliet. He could bear any sort of humiliation to get justice for her and save his clan from being bound to necromancers.

He still kept trying to make the wall around his mind stronger, because if he was going to be humiliated, at least he didn't want Romeo to know how much.

But when Justiran opened the door, he just looked them up

and down and said, "If you want dinner, you'll have to help with the cleanup."

Romeo smiled and said, "I can show him how."

Paris didn't say anything. He followed Romeo into the house for a second time, feeling like he was sneaking in, and then stood awkwardly on the edge of the room, watching Justiran go into the kitchen and Romeo wipe off the table. They had clearly eaten together before; they knew the rhythm to move around each other.

He didn't belong here.

"Paris," said Justiran. "Come give me a hand."

Reluctantly, he walked into the kitchen. "What?"

"Stir this," said Justiran, handing him a spoon. He didn't immediately start another task.

"This is just an excuse to make me talk with you, isn't it?" said Paris.

"Yes," said Justiran, not sounding the least bit ashamed.

Paris drew a breath. "If you're going to tell me I can live without my clan or some such nonsense—"

"No," said Justiran. "I'm going to tell you that those clothes are going to get you robbed, and you'd be better off selling them while they're still in one piece."

"You were thinking that nonsense, weren't you?" said Paris.

Justiran smiled ruefully. "Maybe. I don't claim I'm perfect."

"I don't need you to tell me what I'm strong enough to live

without," said Paris, wishing that Justiran would get angry at him or at least openly contemptuous, so that he wouldn't feel quite so ridiculous lashing out.

"You're right," said Justiran. "You don't."

And it sounded . . . honest, when he said it.

"But you do need to keep stirring," Justiran added, "or you really won't like what we have to eat. I'm guessing you've never sold used clothes before?"

"No," said Paris, stirring the pot. Steam puffed up in his face; the soup was heavily spiced, and he was suddenly aware of just how hungry he was.

"I'll do it for you," said Justiran. "And I have some spare clothes that might not fit you too badly."

Paris's hand tightened on the spoon. He shouldn't be taking help from a renouncer. He shouldn't be relieved that the renouncer was treating him with respect.

But he was.

After dinner was over, and Justiran had gone out to sell Paris's old clothing, Romeo looked at him over their tea and said, "I will tell you everything I know about Tybalt."

"All right," said Paris. He knew he should feel triumphant, but instead he felt uneasy. He was sitting in the house of a renouncer, drinking tea. He was unmasked, wearing not Catresou clothing but an ill-fitting tunic and trousers. He was about to discuss, quite calmly and civilly, his kinsman's death with the murderer.

Romeo might have caught a bit of that last thought, because his fingers tightened on his teacup as he said, "I know it doesn't matter, but I am sorry."

It didn't matter. *Sorry* was such a little word for killing Tybalt and helping get Juliet killed. But when Paris looked at Romeo, slightly hunched over his teacup—while he felt the faint, persistent ache of Romeo's walled-off grief—he couldn't seem to feel exactly angry.

"We have to stop Lord Catresou," he said. "That's all that matters. When did you . . ." He realized that he was about to ask, *When did you last see Tybalt?*, which was idiotic, because they both knew the answer.

"Did you ever see Tybalt in the Lower City before?" he asked instead.

Romeo shook his head. "I never knew he came down here."

Paris didn't want to ask, but he wanted to stop being the sort of coward who had heard the Juliet say she was in danger and done nothing.

"You said he was a brute. Did he really—did you ever see him—"

"Juliet never said a word against him," said Romeo. "I never saw him hurt anyone in the Upper City. He had a reputation for being friendly with everyone. Courteous, anyway. He must have said good morning to me half a dozen times. But when we dueled . . . I never saw anyone so angry. I do believe he might have hurt her afterward."

"If you hadn't killed him," said Paris, and wished he didn't feel just the tiniest bit relieved at that. Because if Tybalt had lived—if Romeo hadn't accidentally thrown Lord Catresou's plans into disarray—then Juliet might be in the hands of a necromancer right now.

"Yes," said Romeo.

He wasn't meeting Paris's eyes. He also wasn't sinking into a wild display of grief, which Paris found a great relief but also unnerving. He wasn't sure what to do with a Romeo who wasn't wailing aloud.

He'd known him less than a day. Last night, he had still thought he was going to be the Juliet's Guardian.

"You fought him in the Lower City?" said Paris. He'd heard that much from his father.

Romeo's voice was barely above a whisper. "The south market."

That was why the City Guard had known to look for Romeo: the duel had happened in one of the largest marketplaces of the Lower City. There must have been a hundred witnesses to name him.

"What happened?" asked Paris.

Romeo pressed his lips together for a moment and then said, "Makari. My tutor."

The memories were overwhelming. Paris caught a glimpse of a

lean, lined face, slouching shoulders, and a wry half smile; he felt a hand on his shoulder, heard a voice warm with pride. An enormous rush of mixed affection, admiration, and desperate desire to please swept over him. And grief. Bitter, aching grief wrapped around the thought, *He was like a brother to me, and I will never see him again.*

Makari was dead. Paris knew it, without having to ask.

"Tybalt knew about me and Juliet somehow. He said . . . utterly vile things. I tried to explain, but he wasn't listening, and Makari got angry. He could always shrug off any insult—he grew up in the Lower City himself, he's only half Mahyanai, and a lot of the clan looks down on him for all he's one of our best swordsmen—but that time he got angry. For my sake. He told Tybalt to shut up, and when he didn't, he said he would teach him a lesson. They fought, and I tried to stop them, because Juliet loves Tybalt—"

Romeo stopped.

"Loved," he corrected himself dully. "She loved him, so I tried to drag Makari away, and Tybalt killed him while I was holding his sword arm."

"Tybalt *cheated*?" said Paris, and he probably shouldn't be surprised at anything anymore, but he was.

"Or he was aiming for me," Romeo said, his voice quiet and hollow. "I'm not sure. And then—I hardly remember. I picked up Makari's sword. You know what happened next."

Somehow Romeo had killed Tybalt, the best fighter of his generation.

"I think I met somebody down here who knew Tybalt," said Paris.

He didn't want to tell anyone, let alone Romeo, about how useless he was on his own. But Romeo had been willing to talk about his own shame, and Paris could hardly do less. So he resolutely explained everything that had happened since he got angry and stomped out of Justiran's house.

"Do you know what the King of Cats is?" he finished.

"He's the champion duelist for the Lower City," said Romeo, as if everyone knew.

"But it's illegal for commoners to duel," said Paris.

Romeo snorted. "Of course it's illegal. They do it anyway. Anyone who brings a weapon can fight, and the one who wins is the King of Cats."

"Do you know where they meet?" asked Paris. If they could track down Vai, maybe they could make him talk.

Romeo shook his head. "They'd never tell someone like me."

And obviously, nobody would want to tell Paris either. They could still try to hunt down Vai, but given the size of the Lower City, it might be almost as hard as hunting the Master Necromancer.

There had to be a way they could learn more about Tybalt.

"When you dueled Tybalt," said Paris, "did he have any friends with him?"

Romeo's eyes went distant. "Maybe," he said. "There was a girl—a Lower City girl, she looked like she might work in a shop. She ran to Tybalt when he fell. She was crying over him, until somebody dragged her away. I suppose she might have just been tender-hearted, but . . ."

"Would you know that girl if you saw her again?" Paris asked, his pulse quickening. Because this could be it. This could be the clue that would lead to them stopping Lord Catresou.

"Yes," said Romeo.

"Then we go back to that market," said Paris. "We find her. And we find out what she knows."

When they set out for the south market the next morning, Paris had two goals: to find the girl who had cried over Tybalt and to *not* storm away from Romeo in a fit of anger.

Five minutes after walking out Justiran's door, he didn't feel confident he'd achieve either one. Romeo had not had any more fits of grief, but he was incapable of taking two steps without thinking about Juliet. He had taken Juliet to sit on that rooftop. He had walked down that street, the day after meeting Juliet. That woman's dress was the same blue as Juliet's eyes. This morning's sunlight would be so beautiful on Juliet's hair.

And he was terrible at keeping his thoughts to himself.

"I can't help loving her," said Romeo. "Maybe you're just terrible at not listening."

Of course Paris was terrible. He had never been meant to be Guardian. He tried to crush that thought before Romeo could hear it.

"Love her?" he said. "How much did you even *know* her?"

He remembered Juliet in the garden when he met her, the anger hiding her sadness, and her resignation in the sepulcher. Her determination to protect her people. *It's all I ever wanted, to be correct.*

How could Romeo have taken that from her?

"Or did you just see she was pretty, and decide you needed her?" he demanded.

"She was lonely," said Romeo. His voice was soft, wistful. "And kind."

And you used her loneliness against her, Paris wanted to say, but he could no longer convince himself that Romeo had manipulated her on purpose. And he was trying not to start a fight. He hoped Romeo hadn't overheard that thought.

If he had, he didn't react. But after a few moments he said, suddenly, "It was just a stupid bet, the first time I saw her." He laughed softly, ruefully. "Not even really a bet. We were joking about what you Catresou had hidden behind those walls, and Makari said I was too scatterbrained to sneak past the guards, and I wanted to prove him wrong. So I got inside. I climbed the walls of a garden. And there she was, as lovely as the stars and just as bright, and all the daylight seemed as night compared to her—"

"You can't have thought that," said Paris. "Not at first."

Romeo hadn't even known her name. Paris knew that he himself had never understood her, but at least he'd exchanged words with her.

And strangely, Romeo seemed to listen to him. He paused, lips pressing together, and Paris felt a flicker of uncertainty before he half laughed and said, "No. At first, I thought she was terrible and strange and pitiable. She was practicing the sword, and she looked not quite human."

And Paris saw it, a secondhand memory so vivid that for a moment he felt like he was there himself: Juliet in her garden, unmasked, her dark hair swirling free and her face set in stubborn, angry concentration as she worked through a set of sword forms. Her blade gleamed in the sunlight; her mouth was set in a not-quite-smile that was just as ferocious and sharp.

He saw it, and he thought *Juliet* and *zoura* and *protector of our people* . . . but he also felt what Romeo had thought in that moment: *alien* and *victim* and *wrong*.

"And then the cat came," Romeo went on.

"What?" said Paris.

Romeo shrugged. "I don't know its name. It was barely more than a kitten—"

And again Paris saw the memory, saw the white fur dappled with orange and black splotches, heard the shrill, plaintive meows.

"—and she picked it up. Cradled it."

The words were short and abrupt. But in the memory Paris saw, it was an entire dance: Juliet slowly laying down her sword so the cat would not startle. The fingers she held out for the cat to sniff, the gentle scratch she gave its cheek. The cat trilling and rubbing its cheek against her hand, then arching its spine under her fingers. Another meow, and she ran her fingers down its spine again, scratched its cheek again—and then, at last, she cupped her hand around the cat's chest and lifted it up. She cradled it in her arms, whispering something that Paris—*Romeo*—could not hear. But the gentle delight on her face was something anyone could read.

"Then the guards came and I had to run," said Romeo. "But I wanted to know how she could be so ferocious and so kind. And I loved her. Because of that moment, I will always love her."

He said the words as simply as if he were describing the sun going up and coming down.

"No matter that I live and she is dead," Romeo went on earnestly. "It is nothing to me. Were she a revenant and ripping the flesh from my bones, I would love her still, and still I would try—"

"Stop it," said Paris, and then quickly added, "if you want.

But I really don't care about your beautiful feelings."

He couldn't help thinking, though: Romeo had loved Juliet for what he knew of her. Who among the Catresou had done the same?

Paris didn't know much about the Lower City, but even he had heard of the south market, because it was the one marketplace in the city where *everybody* went. Because—as in so many shops and markets of the Lower City—half the goods were stolen from workshops and transports in the Upper City. If you wanted something elegant and didn't want to pay full price—or if, like Paris's father, you wanted to know what your competitors were crafting—you went to the south market and searched through the goods. People were always complaining, both about how much stolen material was in the market and about how high the prices were, and everyone always agreed that the City Guard needed to do something about it. Not much ever got done, though, largely because most members of the City Guard liked to shop there too.

The shops lined a large avenue, and at the south end, the avenue turned into a wide stairway that spilled down into one of the main squares of the Lower City. The stairs were almost impassible because of the crowd of vendors who had jammed their stalls, carts, and blankets spread with goods onto the steps. The crowd oozed slowly between them, admiring, chattering, bargaining.

It did not seem like a good place to duel someone.

"We were down in the square," Romeo muttered, looking unhappily toward the huge fountain at the center. There was more space down there; Paris could see how it would be possible to fight a brief, awkward duel.

"It didn't take long," said Romeo.

"Stop listening," said Paris, trying to shore up the walls in his mind. "Do you remember which direction she came from?"

"That way," said Romeo, pointing toward a knot of vendors.

It took them several hours, but finally they determined that the girl was not working at any of the shops or carts nearby in the marketplace. At least, she wasn't working that day. Most people hadn't been talkative, and there was no way to ask questions about absent employees without sounding suspicious.

"We'll just have to wait for her," said Paris. "She came here once. She'll come again." He looked around the square. "We'd better sit apart, so that we can see more at once."

It was a sound plan, but when Paris settled into his corner alone, he was uncomfortably aware of what had happened last time he'd gone off without Romeo; and while the other boy was close, Paris knew quite well how quickly it was possible to be dragged into danger.

He wished that, like Romeo, he had brought his sword to the sepulcher. He didn't like being defenseless.

The morning wore on. And then the afternoon, and so far the only real danger had been from boredom. Romeo must have been feeling the same, because he started reciting poetry to himself—not out loud, but saying it in his head, and Paris couldn't help hearing it.

Pale flowers like snow have covered the ground, said Romeo in Mahyanai, and waited.

It was a very pointed silence. He didn't need a word or a look to let Paris know that he was waiting for a response.

You know what comes next, said Romeo.

No, I don't, said Paris.

Except he did. He could hear the next line in the back of his mind: *The year has turned to spring, but the ground is still cold.* If he just opened his mouth, the words would flow out in perfect, unaccented Mahyanai.

Yes, you do, said Romeo, sounding gleeful. Because even though Paris had trained for years, somehow Romeo was able to slip past his walls and speak in his head.

Is there a point to this? Paris demanded.

To pass the time, said Romeo. *Do you Catresou never play at turning phrases?*

I have no idea what that means, said Paris, craning his neck to examine a new clump of people forcing their way into the marketplace.

It's a game. One of us says a line from a poem, the other says the next. Back and forth.

Sounds like a game for girls, said Paris.

Juliet liked it, Romeo said agreeably.

Juliet liked you, said Paris. *I don't.*

The next moment, someone stumbled into him. "Sorry!" Paris said without thinking, catching at the person's shoulders.

It was a girl his own age. She was quite pretty, with a heart-shaped face, a bronzed complexion, and sleek black hair.

"Thank you," she said breathlessly, sliding out of his hands.

And then he felt Romeo's shock as he said, *That's her. That's the one.*

16

EVERY EVENING, THE SISTERS ALL dined together. Around the top of the great hall ran a gallery full of storage cupboards. It was the perfect place for Juliet to hide and watch them. All Runajo had to do was go to dinner with the rest, then announce that she felt ill once the food was served. As soon as she was into a corridor with an empty wall, she pressed her hands to the smooth white surface and pulled open the door to the room she had crafted for Juliet. Then the two of them slipped up the stairs into the gallery.

"Can you see them all?" Runajo whispered. They were in one of the most shadowed corners of the gallery, so they shouldn't be visible from the floor, but echoes carried.

Juliet was silent.

Runajo touched her shoulder. "Is one of them guilty?"

Still silence. Every moment was another risk.

"Tell me and do not lie."

"Her," Juliet said promptly, pointing at the High Priestess. "And her." She pointed at Sunjai. "And her, and her, and *you*." She turned on Runajo with a terrible, teeth-bared smile. "You live in a charnel house, and you're all guilty and dripping red."

Runajo felt the slow burn of resentment start. "You said you would help," she said.

"I did," said Juliet. "I can't see any difference between them."

"I told you not to lie!"

Juliet huffed out a breath. She said, "Look again."

Without thinking, Runajo looked down into the hall.

Blood.

Everywhere below, blood.

She didn't exactly see it. She could look at every individual Sister, at every plate and cup, and see only the colors that they should be, not red. And yet the whole room seemed to be dripping crimson, and every Sister was drenched. Sunjai threw her head back to laugh, and spattered the floor with red; Inyaan hunched in on herself, crimson lines dribbling between her eyes.

Runajo could smell it. She could practically taste it in the air, and it felt like being drenched in all the blood she had ever seen spilled: Atsaya's sliced throat. The sacrifices at the Great Offering. The tumors on her father's body, split open and bleeding and foul.

She realized that her breath was coming in desperate, sobbing gasps.

I thought the bond had failed, said Juliet, and her voice wasn't in Runajo's ears but echoing in her head, cold and calm and full of disdain. *But you simply don't know how to use it. You were blocking me without even knowing it. But this is what it means to be the Juliet's Guardian. You hear what I think. You feel what I feel. You see every guilt that I see.*

Runajo pressed a hand to her mouth, trying to get control over herself. This wasn't possible. She had heard rumors, yes, that Juliets and their Guardians could speak mind to mind, but there was no such magic known to the Sisters, so she had always assumed—

Not rumors, said Juliet. *Truth.*

She could feel Juliet's emotions: fury and grief and sheer, burning determination. They were all around her, washing over her skin, sliding down her throat and choking her. There was no escape.

You can feel it now, said Juliet. *You know what we have to do.*

She did, and she didn't know how Juliet wasn't already mad. It was like a hot wind, swirling around and around her, whispering in her ears: *Kill the guilty. Kill them. Kill.*

Give me the order, said Juliet, *and I will kill them all in minutes, and then we can surrender ourselves to the Catresou. They will use us for justice.*

It wasn't the vision of blood or the whispering need for vengeance that nearly made Runajo say yes. It was the simple, absolute certainly in Juliet's voice as she said the word *justice*: as if it were holy, and as if it were hers. Runajo felt like she was slipping, sliding, sinking into and drowning in that fathomless conviction.

Get out of my mind, said Runajo. She meant it as a command, but it was more like a plea.

I can't, said Juliet, ruthless and strong as Runajo had always wanted to be. *We can never escape each other.*

Runajo couldn't lose herself like this.

She *refused.*

Grimly, she made herself look Juliet in the eyes and say, *Then go back to the way you were this morning.*

Instantly the pressure was gone, and Runajo staggered with sudden relief. She could still feel Juliet's emotions, but they were something separate from her, nearby but not overpowering.

Go sit by the door to the gallery, she said. *Don't talk to me until I come near you.*

Without another word, Juliet walked around the corner of the gallery to the door. Runajo sat down with a thump and gasped for breath. She felt ragged and hollow and slightly sick.

Not her mother nor father, not Romeo nor the rest of her family, not even the entire Sisterhood of Thorn had ever been able to change her mind about anything. They spoke and she rendered judgment—in her head, if not out loud—and acted accordingly. Her mind was a fortress that no one had ever breached.

Until Juliet walked in without even a battle. For a moment Runajo had been—she had nearly—

She commanded you to feel as she did, and you felt. She enslaved you, as you enslaved her.

The thought was cold, and it was comforting, because she knew this was her own self speaking: this was the ruthless analysis that had brought her to the Sisterhood, that had brought her to the vigil. That did not fear anything, not death or even the truth.

She is a warrior and there is war between you, and she will always take whatever advantage she can.

Maybe she was listening right now.

Let her listen. Runajo was no warrior, but she had never been defeated, and she was not about to hand the keys of her soul to a bloodthirsty Catresou who thought mass murder was justice.

I will be stronger than her, thought Runajo. *I have always been stronger than her.*

And now, as her heartbeat slowed, she could finally grin as she admitted to herself: that had been a ruthlessly determined attempt. She could almost like Juliet for it.

But she didn't intend to die for her, so it was time to get her hidden again before anyone found them. Runajo got to her feet, took a breath, and went to Juliet.

The other girl sat formally by the door, her pale face as much a mask as the gold and silver contraptions that Runajo had seen the Catresou wearing. Her feelings were muted; Runajo could still sense that they were there—she wondered if their earlier communion had destroyed some fundamental separation between them, so that neither could ever fully shut out the other again.

Juliet looked at her, but did not move or speak.

Stand, Runajo told her. *Come with me.*

Juliet stood and followed. There was a terrible . . . *containment* to her motions, as if she were concealing a storm, but Runajo wasn't sure what it could be. Another plan to rend her mind open?

Perhaps it was time to test this new bond.

Once the door to the gallery had been eased shut behind them, Runajo turned to Juliet and pressed two fingertips to her neck. She felt warm skin, and the muscles shifting as Juliet swallowed.

She felt what Juliet felt.

There was grief and anger, but also fear. Enormous, all-encompassing fear that had probably been there all along, but that Runajo had been too dazed to feel.

She remembered the vision Juliet had given her of the blood-spattered hall. For the first time, she wondered what it would really mean to be so convinced of the Catresou beliefs, and yet be trapped among the Sisterhood.

Juliet had died, and then wakened to a world of monsters, and found herself enslaved to one of them.

"Satisfied?" asked Juliet, meeting her eyes.

Runajo couldn't tell if she knew what Runajo had discovered or not.

"There are no secrets between us," said Juliet. "Very well, I am afraid. What is that to you?"

She didn't sound angry now, just . . . weary.

"I'm surprised you thought slaughtering the entire Sisterhood was a good idea," said Runajo. "Satisfying, I'm sure, but aren't you supposed to live for duty?"

"You are all abominations against justice," said Juliet. "It is my duty to kill you."

And how had Runajo missed the desperation in those words before? Juliet had to kill them all because that was the only part of herself that she had left.

"What about your duty to the Catresou?" asked Runajo. "If you, their holy Juliet, were to slaughter the Sisterhood, nobody would ever believe your own family hadn't ordered it. You would all die by the knife before the next sunset, and then all the justice in the world would not matter to them. Not to mention that without the Sisterhood, the walls would fail and the Ruining would overtake the city and not a soul would be left alive."

Juliet leaned her head back against the wall. "We should never have accepted that bargain," she said.

"And died outside the walls of Viyara? That's a harsh fate to wish on your own people."

"I wish we had undefiled honor," said Juliet, and thought—not at Runajo, but too loud to miss—*I wish that I did too.*

"What defiled you?" asked Runajo. "That you wedded Romeo or that you bedded him?"

Juliet flushed, but she still met Runajo's eyes as she said, "That I thought I should be more than the sword of the Catresou. It is a lesson I will not soon forget."

It was not a threat so much as a promise.

"Well, for now you're *my* sword," said Runajo. "I can't change that."

"You don't have to kill them," said Juliet. "Take us out of here, submit to the Catresou—"

"No," said Runajo. "Submit myself to superstitious fools, who wish they were necromancers, who cannot find the courage to accept death or break the law? I'd rather die."

Juliet showed her teeth. "I have died. It was not helpful. And none of us wish to be necromancers."

"And yet you cannot stop devising spells you hope to use after death," said Runajo. "Do you truly think—"

A hand landed on her shoulder. Someone had found them. Runajo's heart thudded as she whirled.

And found herself face-to-face with a nightmare.

It was not a Sister. It was not a revenant. It had never even once been human.

Two arms, two legs, one head: it had the accoutrements of being human. But the skin was chalk white, stretched taut over the bones of a face a little too long and narrow. A web of white threads covered the eye sockets, while a single new eye, yellow and baleful, had burst open in the center of the forehead. Instead of lips, it had a polished gray beak. Small, dark feathers grew along the arms, the neck, the cheekbones. Every finger was tipped with a long, slender claw.

It was a reaper.

Revenants were the dead that had inevitably risen again, dragged into a parody of life by the Ruining. They were terrible, but they were known. They were history and current fact.

Reapers were a legend. They were practically myth: tale after tale said they were the children of Death herself, spawned when she made love to the uttermost shadows. Runajo didn't believe that—not even all the Sisters did—but one thing was certain: reapers had never been human. They did not rise from graves; they formed themselves out of the shadows in places overrun with revenants—outside the walls of Viyara, or down in the Sunken Library. Not here in the very heart of the Sisters' sanctuary.

Clearly the theory needs adjustment, thought Runajo, unable to breathe, unable to move, unable even to fear.

Then Juliet knocked her to the side. Runajo slammed into the wall, and for an instant she was dazed with the pain and sudden movement.

Then she realized she was on the ground, that the feeling like icy spikes was fear, that she might be about to die. She staggered back to her feet to see Juliet fighting the reaper.

Gone was the stillness, the weariness, the expressionless face. Juliet fought like she was dancing, ducking and whirling and slamming kicks home, and she was smiling in pure delight as she danced.

Runajo knew the delight was pure because she could feel it, and it was the same absolute satisfaction that she felt when she helped to weave the city's walls.

The reaper grabbed Juliet by the shoulder and lifted her off the ground. Runajo felt an echo of the pain as claws sliced into skin and muscle, but it didn't seem to affect Juliet. She gripped its wrist to brace herself and kicked the reaper in its one working eye. The creature screamed; Juliet kicked it twice more, then wrenched herself free as it staggered. An instant later she had seized its head; there was a crack as she snapped the neck, and then an awful tearing sound as she kept wrenching, and the head came off. Dark gray blood spurted everywhere.

Runajo turned away suddenly, gasping for breath. She wished she hadn't seen that. Heard that. It was nothing like the dead body she had found last night—it didn't *smell* like blood, it smelled like old water and leaves rotting in the gutter—but the pattern of the droplets was the same, as they splattered dark across Juliet's face.

Hands gripped her shoulders, and she flinched.

"It's all right," said Juliet. "Breathe. It's dead."

Runajo sucked in a breath, then shoved Juliet's hands away. It didn't matter that she was shaking all over; she had a situation to evaluate.

She forced herself to turn and look at the twisted body, the head lying next to it, unattached. Ignore the nausea; focus on the situation.

Juliet had killed a reaper.

Runajo had heard stories, read *histories* of how terrible they were, how they had harried the refugee caravans as they fled toward Viyara. Revenants killed from hunger; they would eat one victim before moving on to the next. Reapers did not eat, only destroy; it was said they had torn apart half the Mahyanai before they made it to safety.

That was why people called them the children of Death: because they had no desire but to make the whole world dead.

And Juliet had killed one with her bare hands.

"Now you know how *my* people survived," said Juliet, "and in somewhat better numbers. We only lost one in four."

"Are you always going to know what I think?" Runajo demanded.

"Only until you learn to put your shield back together," said

Juliet. "You really are a terrible Guardian."

But for once there was no bitterness in the words.

The reaper shivered. Runajo bolted to her feet, heart pounding, but it didn't try to stand; it writhed, like a burning piece of paper, and then it crumbled into ash and then even the ash was gone. They were alone in an immaculate hallway.

Runajo looked at Juliet. The blood splattered on her face was flaking away, turning to dust and disappearing.

As if nothing had ever happened.

"I suppose that means it's no good telling anyone," said Runajo.

"Don't you have other reasons to keep me secret?" said Juliet.

Runajo waved a hand. "If they needed to hear about this, I would tell them and take the consequences. But they'll never believe me without proof, so I might as well save my death for another occasion."

"Did it kill the Sister?" asked Juliet.

Runajo wanted to say yes. It would be neat and nice and comforting if they had just dispatched the killer. But reapers killed their prey as fast as they could and kept on killing. They didn't stop at one victim, and they wouldn't ritually bleed their victims like a sacrifice.

"Yes, that's definitely the work of a Sister," said Juliet.

"I do not like it when you do that," said Runajo.

"I'm not *doing* anything," said Juliet. "You're the one who can't stop shouting your thoughts. I suppose you could order me not to hear them."

"Could you stop?"

Juliet shrugged. "Sometimes."

"I would appreciate it," said Runajo, "if you would try not to."

It wasn't an order, but she didn't want to be giving orders more than she had to; and though Juliet's face didn't even twitch, she could feel the other girl's shock through the bond, and that was more than enough reward for her.

"You'd order me fast enough if you had a need," said Juliet, obviously not heeding her requests quite yet.

"If you had to, by which I mean if you had the chance, you would slit my throat," said Runajo, and Juliet grinned at her.

Juliet had killed a reaper with her bare hands.

The Sunken Library was full of them—and Runajo knew where she could get a sword.

Her whole body was trembling, but it felt more like exultation than fear. She had faced the ancient nightmare of her people. She had survived. And she had an ally.

Maybe she could survive the Sunken Library. Maybe she could be brave enough.

And if Juliet was at her side in the library, they would live or die together. She might get Juliet killed, but it would be a clean death in battle, not walled up alive and starving.

Before she could say anything, she heard voices in the halls.

The Sisters were leaving dinner. She and Juliet were about to get caught.

She pressed her hand against the wall and opened the door for Juliet.

17

"WAIT!" PARIS CALLED, BUT THE girl was already vanishing into the crowd.

I see her, said Romeo. *Come on.*

Together—taking turns edging close enough to keep her in view—they followed the girl as she went into three different shops: she bought bread in one, argued in another, and burst into tears in a third. After she had stopped crying, she paid what looked like quite a large sum of money for a huge butcher's knife, and then slipped into one of the alleys.

Paris slipped in after her, wondering if she was actually a robber and he was about to be knifed. But the girl was apparently just going home: she hurried down the street, hunched over a little, without looking to either side or behind.

She didn't live far away. It was only a few minutes before they saw her go into a huge, ramshackle tenement. It was not particularly dirty, but old; the designs once painted on the walls had nearly faded away, and many of the shutters on the windows were cracked or broken. Paris slipped in after the girl, trying to move as quietly as he could; behind, he could hear and feel Romeo running faster to catch up.

One set of stairs. Two. Three. Then the girl turned down the hallway, fumbled with the lock on a door, and slipped inside.

Paris paused. He could feel Romeo running up the stairs half a floor down.

You should wait, he said. *I'm going to talk to her alone.*

Why? asked Romeo.

She wept for Tybalt, didn't she? And she saw you kill him. She might remember your face.

Of course, said Romeo. He didn't sound upset, just weary and defeated.

Besides, I'm Catresou like Tybalt, Paris went on. *Maybe that will make her trust me.*

It was very logical. But as Paris knocked on the door, he couldn't help being aware that he had never, even once in his entire life, persuaded anyone to do anything.

Well, he had persuaded Romeo to help him. That was something, though really it was Juliet who had done that. Paris had only benefited from it.

With a loud creak, the door opened just a crack and the girl peered out. "Yes?" she said suspiciously.

There was nothing for it but to try.

"Did you know Tybalt Catresou?" Paris asked.

Her eyes widened as she took in his face and accent. "You're his kin?"

"Yes," said Paris, and her face crumpled.

"Thank the gods," she said, tears trickling from her eyes. "I'd lost all hope."

Over her shoulder, Paris could see a small, dingy room with one door leading to a second room. It seemed like a dismal place.

"Tybalt . . . did he make you a promise?" asked Paris, hoping that Tybalt hadn't seduced the poor girl.

In the distance, one of the neighbors started banging on the wall.

"Yes," she said. "You're here to redeem it, aren't you? To take me to the Night Game?"

Paris felt sure that his bafflement showed on his face, but she kept looking at him with hopeful expectation.

The banging was getting louder. It sounded like it was coming from the other side of the door behind the girl, but that didn't make any sense.

"Do you know where it is?" Paris hedged, not willing to make promises he couldn't fulfill.

She shrank back, suspicious again. "You're not—"

And with a crash, the door burst open. On the other side was an old man, his gray hair a tangle, his mouth wide and gasping.

No. It was not an old man, but a thing that had once been an old man.

A revenant.

Paris had heard all his life about what the dead were like when they inevitably rose again, mindless and furious and hungry. This revenant wasn't like the ones in the stories: rotting or half mummified, naked with their skin peeling, their hair fallen out. This one was fresh. From a distance, from the corner of an eye, it might have passed for human. But so close—

Paris had only seen an unembalmed dead body once: his mother, before she was carried to the magi for her funeral preparations. He had been very young. But he still remembered how *empty* she had looked. In her final illness, she had been pale and still as death, and he had frightened himself a dozen times by thinking she had already died. Once dead, she had no longer looked like a woman at all; she had been like a hollow doll made of wax, and Paris had feared her—feared *it*—in a way he had never feared anything before.

The revenant had that same quality—that utter, absolute emptiness.

It hissed at them and lunged forward.

"Father!" the girl shrieked.

Paris grabbed her by the arm and hauled her outside, then slammed the door shut just as the revenant slammed into it. The door shook, and he pressed himself back against it.

"Why's your father—"

"I tied him up," the girl gasped, also throwing her weight against the door. "I swear I tied him up."

"Why do you *have* him?" Paris demanded. It took two or three days for a dead body to turn into a revenant. The City Guard should have taken him away long before this.

Icy dread pounded through his veins. They couldn't hold this door forever. But if they ran, the revenant would be able to follow them. Or hunt down other people.

Then Romeo came hurtling up the stairs.

Paris had never been so glad to see a Mahyanai sword in his life.

"You," the girl said, in a voice of terror and loathing, but Paris was already hauling her aside. The door flew open and the revenant stumbled out.

Romeo drew his sword, but as he swung, the girl threw herself in front of him, crying, "No!"

Just in time, Romeo pulled the strike. Through the bond, Paris felt his mind flash white-hot with something too stark and all-encompassing to be called fear.

Cold fingers gripped his arm. The revenant hissed in his ear.

Without thinking, Paris flung himself back against the wall. He heard a crunch; then he flailed, kicked, and sent the revenant staggering back. It was the perfect moment to kill it—but Romeo was three paces back, still as a statue and eyes wide.

"Use the sword!" he yelled at Romeo, and finally Romeo came back to life, lunging toward the revenant. But it was too late; it dodged back and skittered down the stairs.

Down toward the street and the crowded marketplace full of people.

Revenants loose in Viyara, rending the city apart with their ceaseless hunger for human flesh. It was the nightmare that everybody dreaded, and for one moment, that dread held Paris in place. Then he bolted down the stairs after the revenant, calling silently to Romeo, *Come on!*

Whatever had kept Romeo from attacking properly was done now; he ran just as fast as Paris did down the stairs.

Why didn't you kill it when you had the chance? Paris demanded, still silently because he didn't have the breath to spare.

She nearly died, said Romeo, and there was a shakiness to his voice that Paris had never heard before. *I nearly killed her.*

Two memories welled up between them: the girl flinging herself in front of Romeo, and Romeo flinging himself in front of Makari, along with a horrible, paralyzing sensation of *not again not again.*

He hadn't thought that Romeo truly regretted anything except the loss of Juliet, but maybe he did.

They nearly caught the revenant at the base of the stairs, but it slid away from them and out into the street. They ran after it, past one corner and around another, but Paris was starting to feel a horrible certainty that they wouldn't catch it. His lungs burned and his legs felt heavy. He had trained in dueling, not in sprinting, and he could tell that Romeo was the same.

With a last, desperate burst of energy, he lunged forward, trying to grab the revenant. His fingers grazed its arm and closed on the sleeve. Paris threw himself back, his arm jolting. *Now!* he called silently to Romeo.

Then he heard a rip. He stumbled back, clutching the remains of the sleeve, while the revenant bolted forward again . . . out into the busy marketplace.

As Paris lost his balance and tumbled to the ground, Romeo charged past him. He could feel Romeo's exhaustion through the bond, but also his desperation. He was going to stop the revenant or die trying.

Then Paris saw the gray-and-red uniforms of the City Guard.

Even now, his first thought was to call *Look out!* to Romeo, because seeing the City Guard never meant anything good. When one of them heard the screams and turned, his heart jumped in alarm.

But the City Guard had a purpose besides persecuting the Catresou—and it was not to fight the living that they carried swords at all times.

In one fluid movement, the nearest guard drew her sword and swung. The revenant's head fell to the ground. The body wavered on its feet a moment after, fingers clutching at the air, and then it too toppled to the ground.

As Romeo skidded to a stop in front of the staggering body, Paris climbed back to his feet. He looked away from the shuddering body and took a deep breath. It had already been dead. He didn't know if that made it more or less sickening.

Now that the chase was over, he was shaking. He also very much did not want to face the City Guard, but he couldn't abandon Romeo, so he marched forward, shoving his way through the crowd.

The guard who had killed the revenant was barking out orders for the others to search the surrounding area. She had the mark of a subcaptain embroidered on her shoulder, which meant she had responsibility for this whole section of the city.

"You were chasing it," she said to Romeo. "Where did you find it?"

"Ah . . . ," said Romeo.

He noticed, which meant Paris noticed, that the girl had followed them. She was squeezed between two stalls, staring at her father's corpse with both hands pressed over her mouth.

"We were walking down the street that way," said Romeo, pointing roughly the direction they had come. "It just . . . leaped out of an alley."

"'We'?" said the subcaptain.

Paris stepped up beside Romeo. "I was there too."

"Is that true?" she asked, looking down at him.

She was tall. Her white-gold hair, a bright contrast to the dark skin of her face, was wrapped around her head in a six-strand braid. Her nose and cheekbones were as elegant as her accent. She wasn't just Old Viyaran, she was clearly an Old Viyaran aristocrat. If she wanted to, she could certainly lock them up and throw away the key.

We can't turn that girl in, said Romeo. *I already hurt her too much.*

People who hoarded corpses deserved every punishment they got. Paris had grown up knowing this. But if the girl was dragged away by the City Guard, they would never be able to find out what she knew.

And he couldn't forget the way she had cried, *Father.*

"Yes," he said. "We were just—just that way. Not very far down, I can't remember now." He knew that he must sound shamefully frightened, with the way he was stumbling over his words, but the only thing that mattered was the subcaptain believing him.

Of course, if they started searching in that direction, they would sooner or later look into the girl's tenement and hear about the commotion. But at least she would have a chance to clear out.

"Just walking down the street," said the subcaptain, and Paris remembered with a sick sort of terror that they were both fugitives. Well, Romeo was; his own family probably hadn't wanted to report him.

"Just walking," he said quickly. "I know it looks odd, but we didn't come to the Lower City for trouble."

"We came here for love," Romeo said earnestly.

"Love," the subcaptain echoed, sounding faintly amused.

It was like the time when Paris was a child, and he'd accidentally knocked over a pile of expensive dishes waiting for the servants to clean them. The pile had tottered for several moments, but Paris hadn't been able to grab and steady them, or even flee before the crash gave him away. He'd been too entranced by the oncoming disaster.

It was like that now. Paris knew this was going to end badly, but he couldn't seem to get his mouth working, and meanwhile Romeo was rambling enthusiastically.

"Yes!" he said. "It's my friend here—he fell in love with a girl who worked in his family's kitchen, and she loved him in return, but when his father found out he was furious and had her cast out into the Lower City, and then he lied and forged letters and tried to make him believe she had renounced him. But my friend loved her too dearly and trusted her too deeply, and he discovered the truth, and so we've come to find her!"

Paris found that his panic was turning into a peculiar sort of calm. They were doomed. If he was lucky, he would be executed along with Romeo. If not, he would be handed back to Lord Catresou.

"And you, a Mahyanai, are helping him?" asked the subcaptain.

"Because I love her as well," Romeo said earnestly, "and I will see her happy though it breaks my heart in two. Lovely, kind Maretta with eyes like the summer sky at twilight. Have you seen her?"

"No," said the subcaptain, "but I'm not sure I've ever seen anyone so bad at lying, either."

Romeo looked uncommonly like a bird fluffing itself up for a mating display. "My love is as true as the stars are bright," he said with terrifying intensity. "So is his."

The subcaptain's mouth quirked. "Tiny and flickering and easily clouded over?"

She doesn't believe you, said Paris silently, *so can you stop humiliating us?*

There is no shame in love! It shouldn't have been possible to shout silently, but Romeo managed it.

"I don't much care if you're stupid enough to think you can win duels down here," said the subcaptain, "or if you think the liquor is better, though I can assure you it's not. I need to know where that revenant came from."

"We really don't know," said Paris.

The subcaptain sighed and rubbed her forehead. "Then you're free to go," she said. "Try to stay out of trouble; I don't particularly want to explain your bodies to anyone up top."

And she turned away from them to direct the guards who were clearing out the body.

Paris risked a glance at the girl. She was still in the same spot, but had sunk to the ground and was hugging herself.

Romeo took a step toward her, but Paris grabbed his shoulder.

No, he said. *Wait.* Then he realized he'd given an order again, and said, *Sorry.*

You're right, said Romeo. *They might be watching us.*

So they sat on the rim of the fountain. They watched the City Guard clear away the body and move out to form a search for any more revenants. They watched the marketplace return to its normal ordered chaos. Paris was surprised that everyone seemed to forget about the attack so quickly, but then, he knew that the Lower City was not as well-ordered. Revenants were not unheard of; there was always somebody who died in a corner, or whose family refused to deliver up the body, whether because they couldn't bear to say good-bye, or they were too afraid of the City Guard, or they wanted to boil down the corpse and sell the bones for black-market charms.

"You didn't turn me in," said the girl quietly, from right next to Paris.

He started; then, trying to stay calm, he said, "No. Why did you keep him?"

The girl gave Romeo a poisonous look. "Because Tybalt promised me a chance. Why are *you* running about with your kinsman's murderer?"

"He promised to help me set things right," said Paris. "Please. We know that Tybalt was mixed up in something bad. We have to know what it was. Or a lot more people will get hurt."

"It wasn't wrong," said the girl, still softly, but with a passionate intensity. "He wanted to make things right for all of us. He said—"

Her voice cracked and she pressed her lips together. Paris stared helplessly, wishing he knew what to say.

"Did Tybalt—" Romeo began, but broke off when the girl went rigid.

"I will not speak to you," she said to the cobblestones.

"I'm sorry," said Romeo. "I'll be silent."

For a few moments none of them said anything. Then the girl said to Paris, in a very small voice, "I owe you. I'll answer your questions."

She hesitated for a moment longer. Then she sat down beside Paris.

"I work in a tavern," she said. "He came for drinks a year ago. He liked me. I liked him. And my father had just started dying. Tybalt told me he was King of Cats, and then he told me he was more."

Paris swallowed, terrifyingly aware that one wrong word could make the girl stop talking and flee.

"What kind of *more* was Tybalt?" he asked.

The girl sniffed. "He worked with the Night Game." She gave Paris a fearful look, as if she had just said something terrible.

"What's that?" asked Paris.

She stared. "You don't know?"

"I've never been to the Lower City before," said Paris. "I don't know about anything down here. Please, what is the Night Game?"

The girl shrugged. "Nobody who's seen it has ever said much. But the people who run it can . . . if you've lost someone. You know." Her gaze flickered away for a moment, as if checking for anybody standing too close. "They can get that person back."

The afternoon sunlight felt cold. Paris had already known there were necromancers in the city—but to hear it again, not in the secrecy of the sepulcher but amid the bustle of the crowds, with the City Guard one street away, the revenant's blood still sticky on the cobblestones—

"But you have to pay," said the girl. "And you have to know how to find them. I had no hope. But Tybalt said something great was coming. Very, very soon. And once it was done, the Night Game would be so powerful, even he would have the power to save anyone. He said my father would live again and never die." Her shoulder slumped. "But he died first."

Paris took a deep breath. He had already known that he would have to fight necromancers. He wasn't going to panic now that he had a chance to do it.

"The Night Game," he said. "Where does it meet? Who runs it?"

The girl shook her head. "Tybalt never told me any of that. It was more than his life was worth."

His fingers curled in frustration. Then this day had all been for nothing. They had already known that Tybalt was doing something with necromancers in the Lower City. Of course that meant he was helping raise the dead. Knowing the name "Night Game" was something, but if nobody who had seen it was willing to talk, how would that help them? They didn't even know whom else they might be able to ask—

Wait. Vai had probably defeated Tybalt to become the new King of Cats. Suddenly his anger was more than simple suspicion of the Catresou, or loathing for a rival. And while Vai had definitely not wanted to talk to Paris, at least he didn't seem like he would be afraid of the Night Game.

"Do you know where they hold the duels for the King of Cats?" Paris asked.

"East quarter," said the girl. "By the face of Xinaad. Every day at dawn."

"Thank you," said Paris. "I'm sorry about your father."

The girl didn't respond. She let out a shaky breath, still staring at the ground.

Suddenly Romeo stood, and before Paris could stop him, he knelt before the girl.

"I'm not asking your forgiveness," he said, quietly and calmly. "But you deserve to hear this: because I killed Tybalt, I lost everything, including the girl I loved. And I am probably going to die myself. So I am punished. And I am sorry."

Without waiting for an answer, he rose and strode away into the crowd.

The girl started crying. Paris couldn't move. It seemed wrong to leave her, but he had no right to comfort her. He was about to give up and flee when she grabbed his hand and squeezed it so hard it hurt.

"Thank you," she said.

"I'm sorry," he said helplessly.

She looked at him then, wiping tears out of her eyes. "He doesn't deserve your friendship," she said.

"We're not friends," said Paris. "I just . . . I need his help."

The girl drew a shuddering breath. "He still killed Tybalt. I'll probably do my best to make trouble for him."

There was nothing Paris could say to that.

"But for now," she said, "you can thank him for me."

18

RUNAJO WAS AN IDIOT.

Admittedly, she was still rattled from nearly dying at the hands of a reaper. But that was no excuse. When the Sisters started emerging from the dining hall, the solution was simple: open the door to Juliet's room, leap through with her, close the door behind them. She could then open the door again, this time to her own room. Nobody would know she hadn't really felt ill and gone to lie down.

But she didn't think. She shoved Juliet through the door and closed it from the outside, which effectively saved Juliet from discovery but left Runajo out in the open.

The next moment the hall was full of Sisters, one of whom was Miryo.

The woman's eyebrows went up. "You seem to have recovered swiftly," she said.

And that was how Runajo ended up facing the High Priestess once again.

"It worries me," said the High Priestess, "that you seem to regard all our laws as your personal playthings."

Skipping dinner was not a terrible offense, but lying to her fellow Sisters was. And Runajo had already proved herself far too willful to deserve mercy. She was not surprised when her punishment was a shift of heavy penance.

"Now," said Miryo, "lest she *disappear* again."

"That seems like a wise precaution," said the High Priestess, and looked at Runajo. "Remember this lesson in future, and perhaps you will not have to do it again."

The message was clear enough: *Remember not to tell the truth about Atsaya.*

Runajo made a perfect bow, then looked up at them with a perfect smile as she said, "I am honored to serve my city."

Happy acceptance was always the best way to infuriate Miryo. By the tightening of her lips, it did a pretty good job at irritating the High Priestess too.

So an hour later, she was back in the heart of the Cloister, standing before the sacred stone and trying not to think of the body she had found in this very room. She had stripped off her long-sleeved robe and now stood in a simple, sleeveless shift.

Before her was one of the mouths of the city: a bowl carved into the floor, with a little rim of woven stone cords around it.

This would be her first time offering heavy penance. The novices whispered about the pain, how it was much worse than any cut with a knife. But most of them took months to stop flinching from the simplest little offerings.

Runajo had never flinched from anything. She wasn't going to start now, when it might make Miryo happy. Maybe her heart beat a little faster than usual when she knelt before the bowl, but her hands were perfectly steady as she took up the knife. Beside her, one of the Sisters had begun a quiet chant: a simple invitation to the city, to the gods, to drink of her blood and honor her sacrifice.

Runajo traced three straight lines on the inside of each forearm. When the blood welled up, she held her arms over the bowl.

Drop after red drop splattered against the pale stone. For a few moments, nothing else happened.

Then the slender, pale cords of stone that formed the rim of the bowl moved. They unwove themselves and reached up, swaying, toward her bloody arms.

Runajo had watched other Sisters do heavy penance before. She knew how the city drank the blood that sustained it. But for the first time, it struck her how alive the writhing cords looked as they nuzzled her arms, and yet how unnatural.

The cords went still, and she had just enough time to clench her teeth before they punched through her skin and into her arms.

She didn't cry out, but for a few moments all she could do was breathe slowly through her nose, blinking back tears. When she could see clearly again, the white strands growing out of her arms had begun to blush pink. The city was drinking her blood.

It hurt with a slow, cold burn that went right to her bones. It hurt and it went on hurting, much more than the simple cuts she had learned to make, and her body couldn't seem to get used to the feeling. But that wasn't what made her heart beat faster and faster, what made cold, queasy fear roil in her stomach.

It was just seeing the cords: slender white stone, brought alive by magic, eating its way into her arms. There was something unspeakably *wrong* about the alien strands plunged into her skin, as if she weren't human at all, but just a piece of wall drilled for drainage pipes.

She knew that the spells were safe, that the city would not drink too much of her blood. But she felt like it was draining out every drop, like it was going to leave her a shriveled husk. Like the strands were still pushing deeper into her arms, and she couldn't stop herself from imagining them pushing all the way down to the bone and burrowing up her arms to her spine. It took all her strength not to rip her arms away from the cords; she tried to hold them still, but they trembled sometimes, and the slightest movement made the pain even worse.

The world is bought in blood and pain. That was the teaching of the Sisters. That was *inkaad*, the absolute and obvious truth.

I can pay any price, Runajo told herself. *I can renounce any love. I can bear any terror. I am that strong, and that ruthless.*

Her right arm spasmed, and she had to bite back a cry. *I am that strong,* she told herself again, and then she did something she had often done when Father was sick, when Mother was sick, and the weight of death was too much around her.

She closed her eyes. She thought of her skin as a wall around her—and yes, it was breached, but only where she chose, to let out what *she* chose—and she thought, *What happens outside is not your business.*

Pain happened in the heart. The dead didn't feel pain, because their hearts had stopped beating. And she was not her mother, breaking her heart anew every day over things that couldn't be changed. She was Mahyanai Runajo, and her heart was carved of stone. She imagined it in careful detail: a sharp-edged chunk of obsidian, nestled inside the circle of her ribs. The world could cut itself upon her heart and she wouldn't feel a thing.

Her heartbeat slowed. There was still pain, but she was choosing not to let it matter.

Runajo opened her eyes and stared at the spine of the city. She breathed. She was still afraid. But she was just calm enough now that she could make herself think about something else.

It was unheard of for there to be a murder among the Sisters of Thorn. It was absolutely impossible for a reaper to get past the protective spells and into the Cloister.

The two could not be coincidence. Either Atsaya had been killed to summon the reaper or else she had been killed in an attempt to keep it out. In the latter case she might very well have been an actual sacrifice, killed by the High Priestess's decree, the reason for her death covered up to prevent panic. Though it would have been foolish, shoddy work to leave her body lying out like that.

And if Atsaya had been killed by a necromancer who wanted to summon reapers, then Runajo bringing back the wherewithal to strengthen the walls would make her a target. Which meant she wouldn't have to bother hunting down the murderer; she could wait for her to come find Runajo.

Somebody tapped her shoulder, and she startled, again jostling the strands in her arms.

"It's time," said the Sister who had chanted for her.

Runajo looked down and saw that the strands had turned bright crimson. She took a deep breath (her heart was stone) and thought at the strands, *Release me.*

Quite easily, they did, and slithered back into place. Runajo was free, and all she could do was tremble and gasp for breath while the other Sister wrapped her bloody arms in lengths of white bandages.

"You'll want to go see one of the healers," said the Sister. "Since you're new."

Runajo nodded. Something in the city's bite helped clot blood and speed healing, once it had released its grip. After enough sacrifices the body grew attuned to it and barely needed care after. But Runajo was not yet at that point.

There were footsteps, and she looked back. Miryo stood in the doorway, come down just in time to see if she had fulfilled her penance properly.

She still felt weak and wrung-out, but she clambered to her feet. She wasn't going to give Miryo any satisfaction.

"Thank you for permitting me this honor," she said, and managed to bow.

"We are not here to win glory," said Miryo, looking as friendly as always. "You might try remembering that."

Runajo nodded obediently. "May I go to see the healer?"

"You may come with me," said Vima from the doorway. "I will take care of you."

Miryo frowned, but there was no objection she could make to that. A few minutes later, Runajo and Vima were in one of the little healing rooms, and Runajo was sitting on the bed while Vima searched in the cupboards.

"I didn't know you were trained as a healer," said Runajo.

"I have been a Sister for twenty-eight years; I have learned a thing or two." She turned around, holding the little jar of healing cream. "And this is a simple operation. I don't think you even need bloodwine; you didn't give that much."

"Why did you want to heal me?" asked Runajo.

"You interest me," said Vima.

"Why?" Runajo asked carefully.

Vima raised an eyebrow. "Perhaps because you survived a vigil unprepared?"

"Oh," said Runajo, hoping she didn't sound too relieved.

Vima took one of her hands and turned her arm so that the bloody inner skin was visible. She began to wipe it with a damp cloth; Runajo breathed carefully and tried not to flinch.

"During that vigil," she said, staring at the bone pendant that hung from Vima's neck, "I was wondering."

"Yes?"

The cloth caught at a bit of half-clotted blood, and for a moment Runajo had to just breathe. Then she went on, "The souls that walk through that room, into the water. They're dead. But they're not *in* the land of the dead yet." Probably because there was no land of the dead, but Runajo had already gotten in enough trouble debating that point with her fellow novices, and the question didn't matter right now anyway. "Are they . . . does that mean they could be brought back to life? Unlike the true dead?"

"Child." Vima touched her cheek, and there was a strange compassion in her voice as she went on. "Whatever joins that procession is truly and utterly dead."

But I could touch her, Runajo thought desperately. *That has to mean something.*

Vima took the cream and started to spread it across Runajo's arms; it burned cold, and she couldn't help the little hiss that escaped her.

"You learn strange things, as the priestess of mourning," said Vima. "There's lore that we've lost everywhere except where it's mentioned in ancient laments. There was a time when three Sisters sat vigil together, and two of them tried to walk bodily with the dead souls, to speak with Death herself and then return. But joining the procession made them dead, and they could not be saved."

The burn of the cream on her arms suddenly stopped mattering. Because Juliet was dead. She had already been dead when Runajo pulled her back. That meant she must die again.

"That's a fable," Runajo said numbly. "That Death has a face and can be spoken to."

"Is that what your parents taught you?" Vima asked gently.

"It's truth," said Runajo.

All those stories of ancient heroes traveling to speak with Death, to bargain with her for the return of their loved ones—lies. And none of those stories had ended well, anyway.

"Believe that if you wish," said Vima. "But do you understand what I am telling you?"

"Yes," said Runajo.

Juliet was dead, and Runajo was a necromancer. She hadn't realized, until now, how much she'd started to believe it was otherwise.

"You could not have saved your mother or your father, once the breath left them. Mourn them, but do not blame yourself."

"I," Runajo choked out, *"do not mourn them."*

The dead were dead and didn't matter. Nothing mattered except that she was a necromancer.

Miryo would be so delighted when she found out.

They would kill Juliet. Would they kill Runajo? They would certainly never let her down into the Sunken Library.

Vima was saying something else now, but Runajo couldn't hear her. She was staring at the wall and thinking, *The past is outside you. It can't hurt you unless you allow it, and your heart is made of stone.*

There was no time for grief over what she'd done. Or what she would have to do. She had to get down to the Sunken Library, prove how important it was to get the books—and that she could—and then she would deal with Juliet. Then she would accept her punishment.

You are pure obsidian inside your chest.

When Runajo got back to her bedroom, she didn't want to see Juliet again. She wanted to curl up on the mat that served as her bed, hug her half-healed arms to her chest, and sleep. She did not want to face a girl who hated her, and who would be searching Runajo's mind for anything she could turn against her, and whom Runajo would have to kill.

But Runajo had not joined the Sisters of Thorn so she could do whatever came easiest. She pressed her hand to the wall and opened the door.

For all that she'd expected anger, she staggered under the wave of raw fury that she felt from Juliet. A moment later it was gone, locked away as Juliet obeyed Runajo's earlier order.

"What?" asked Runajo, and then realized there was one answer. "You heard, didn't you?"

"I *felt*," said Juliet. "It was impossible to block." She crossed her arms and looked Runajo up and down. "I know your people are twisted, but I cannot comprehend how they could make you think that *good*."

Runajo's spine straightened. She might deserve hatred, but scorn?

"You were trained to kill revenants yourself," she said. "Isn't that one of the Juliet's duties?"

"So?" said Juliet. She stood with her chin planted, her feet forward. Against the featureless white walls of the room, she was a gash of vivid, living color.

"So you can hardly object when I do the same to you." Runajo's voice slid into the sweet, placid tones that Miryo found most infuriating. "Unless you believe revenant-killing is a virtue to be practiced only by your clan and not others, and that hardly makes sense. The dead are all alike in death, no matter their family, so surely the living are all alike when it is time to dispatch them."

Juliet stared at her, forehead wrinkling. "What has that got to do with anything?"

Runajo realized that her heart was beating very fast, which made no sense, considering that Juliet could neither harm her nor offer logical objections.

"I mean," she said, "that I do not particularly want to kill you. But if you've heard what Vima said, you must know I have no choice. And you can blame me if you like for bringing you back, but it's beyond hypocrisy to despise me for setting it right."

"I heard nothing," Juliet said after a moment. She was looking at Runajo now with a wide-eyed, disdainful bafflement. "You told me to stay out of your mind as much as I could."

"Oh," said Runajo.

Juliet's eyes narrowed. "I only felt what you did with the knife," she said.

Runajo winced. It had never occurred to her that Juliet might be sharing in her punishment. She only hoped that Juliet hadn't felt her fear as well as her pain.

"I'm sorry," she said.

Juliet waved a hand. "As if *that* matters. But what's this about killing me?"

And Runajo felt sick. She'd thought the truth was out already. Knowing that she still had to say it was—

It doesn't matter, she told herself. *You are Mahyanai Runajo. You can sacrifice anything.*

"You're dead," she said. "I talked to one of the Sisters, and she says that if even a living person walked into the procession of souls, that person would instantly be dead. I performed necromancy when I pulled you back, and for that we must both pay. I'm sorry."

Two apologies in one conversation. If Miryo were here, she would not believe it.

Juliet shrugged. "You didn't kill me."

"Then . . . you're not angry about it?"

"No," said Juliet, her voice suddenly low and shaking. "I am furious that you are fool enough to believe cutting your own arm open is right and just."

It took a moment for Runajo to find her own voice. "I thought you hated me."

"I do," said Juliet, calmer now. "But it's still obscene."

"If I cared about you at all," said Runajo, "then *I* would be angry that you don't care about being killed soon."

Juliet shrugged. "I am the Juliet. I have always known that my life would be spent for others. But you—you *chose* this. How could you choose it?"

"How did *you*?" Runajo asked.

"I didn't," said Juliet. "I was born to this life. Or near enough, anyway."

"Near enough?" asked Runajo.

Juliet shrugged again, and when she spoke, her voice had the inevitable, singsong cadence of somebody telling an ancient story.

"Nobody is born the Juliet. The sigils must be applied in infancy, and they often fail. I was the first in seventeen years to survive. That's why my father is counted as one of the greatest magi now alive."

Runajo had thought she knew all the horrible things the Catresou did to their own. But for a moment, this one took her breath away. "Your own father did that to you?"

Juliet rolled her eyes. "As if your father has not handed his own kin over for sacrifice."

"Unlike you," said Runajo, "we have volunteers. Do you think it makes you less evil, somehow, to live by the blood of your criminals?"

"They have earned their deaths," said Juliet. "Your victims haven't."

And then the silence stretched knife-sharp between them, because Juliet was going to be one of her victims.

"If I'm already dead," said Juliet, "I'm not one of your victims."

Runajo flinched. "I told you to stay out of my head."

"I did. It wasn't hard to guess what you were thinking." She paused. "I told you: my life has never been my own. You and your people are an abomination against justice, but I don't resent you for my death in particular."

That was pretty nearly the last thing Runajo would ever have expected from her. From any of the Catresou, because everybody knew how desperately they wanted to live forever. Perhaps their abuse had done Juliet one kindness: she had learned to be brave.

"You must be planning something first, though," said Juliet. "Else you'd have come with all your Sisters."

"Yes," said Runajo. "How would you like to kill some revenants?"

"Where?" asked Juliet.

Runajo grinned. "In the Sunken Library."

After a moment of Juliet utterly failing to be daunted or impressed, Runajo realized that the Catresou probably didn't know that much about what lay within the temple.

"You know that the Ruining didn't touch Viyara, right?" she said.

Juliet smiled faintly. "Are you about to tell me the sole exception?"

"Deep beneath the Cloister," said Runajo, "there's a massive vault. Once, the Sisters used it as a library, and they had three thousand years of books within it. All the knowledge of all the world. But when the Ruining came . . . a second Mouth of Death opened up at the bottom of the library. The one you saw, at the very top of the Cloister, that's the mouth that the dead use to leave. This one, the dead use to come back. Hundreds—maybe thousands—of revenants swarmed through. We barely stopped them. The entire library is now locked away under triple seal. They used to try, now and again, to send somebody down, but nobody ever came back alive."

"Why do you want to go there?" asked Juliet.

"Because three-quarters of the Sisters died in the first week of the Ruining, including all the oldest and wisest. And because the walls of the city are failing." She paused. "Do you know about that?"

"I am not a child. I understand the doom of our city," said Juliet. "Do you think you can do something about it?"

"I think I can try," said Runajo. "We've lost so much knowledge—we barely understand how half the magic in this city works. But the High Priestess thinks it isn't worth the risk of going down into the library. Which is a ridiculous assessment when we are all doomed anyway. And that reaper in the hallway—if somebody was able to summon it, then the protections have grown very weak. If it crawled in here by itself, then the protections are practically gone. Either way, we don't have any time to waste. So I'm going down there. I want you to come with me and help keep me alive long enough to find a way to save the city."

Juliet pressed her lips together thoughtfully. For a few moments there was silence.

"Well?" Runajo said finally.

Juliet looked her in the eyes. "You're not going to order me?" she said.

It would be very easy. And expedient. And probably the right thing to do, but this girl had been angry when Runajo spilled her own blood. It seemed wrong to force her—and in all honesty, she really doubted Juliet would turn down this opportunity.

"No," she said. "I am asking you."

Juliet dropped her gaze, saying nothing, and Runajo's heart lurched. Had she just made a terrible mistake? But she couldn't go back on her word now.

"You never answered my question," said Juliet. "Why did you choose this life?"

There were several answers, and Runajo wasn't sure which of them Juliet would believe. Which one she would even be able to understand in the slightest.

"Do you know the history of Viyara?" she asked.

"Blood, blood, blood, and more blood," said Juliet promptly. "With a little evisceration."

Runajo snorted. "Do you know about the Ancients?"

"They were very much the same, weren't they?" said Juliet. "As far as blood goes."

"They found the Mouth of Death," said Runajo. "And yes, here they learned to work blood magic, and they used it to build an empire across the whole world."

"And then," Juliet said with relish, "the gods judged them as they will judge all murderers."

"They used slaves," said Runajo. "The blood that made their empire did not flow willingly. And then they tried to find a way to undo death itself. When the disaster came upon them and their powers failed, one princess of the imperial house fled to Viyara with her handmaidens. She prayed to all the gods for mercy, and then she flayed the skin off her feet and danced before the Mouth of Death."

When the Sisters told the story, they usually continued, *And then Death herself appeared and bargained with her, and she alone has treated with Death and not been cheated.* Runajo did not believe that, but in a metaphorical way, it was true.

"So the first spells protecting Viyara were laid. That princess became the first High Priestess, and her son became the first Exalted."

According to the Sisters, the first High Priestess had not sinned by breaking her vow of virginity. The god Xinaad had seen her beauty and her bravery, and through a game of dice he had won permission from Death to visit the priestess for one night. So the royal line of Viyara was begotten.

Runajo thought that if the legendary princess had even existed, she must have loved a handsome servant and lied when she was found with child. But in this case, what mattered was the story, and what that story had made Viyara.

"So we have lived under this covenant ever since," she said:

"that only those who shed their own blood shall rule us."

Juliet looked curious. "You said 'us.' I thought the Mahyanai didn't believe in gods."

"We don't," said Runajo. "*I* don't, and I don't believe half the other things the Sisters teach, either. But I do believe them when they say that the fundamental truth of the world is blood for blood and price for price. I am not a fool who thinks any blessing comes free. I want to be the one who pays the prices. I *will* pay all the prices that we need."

She broke off. She wasn't sure she could explain it any better: the anxious, insatiable need to be the one who was not a protected child, who knew what the cost was, and who paid it in full. Who fought against the inevitable defeat, instead of waiting helplessly.

"You," said Juliet, "unlike the rest of your people, I might not entirely hate. Yes. I will help you."

Runajo let out a breath. *Thank you,* she thought, and wasn't sure if she wanted Juliet to hear that or not.

"I will still have to kill you afterward," said Runajo.

Juliet's mouth curved up. "My husband is still dead. I welcome it."

By Any Other Name

THIS TIME SHE GOES TO meet him.

This time she puts on her simplest clothes, her plainest mask, and slips into the streets. Nobody stops her, because nobody expects the Juliet to flee her duty.

She does not expect it, though she has planned it; when she meets him on a quiet street corner, when she takes the mask from her face, she feels as if she is dreaming.

He kisses her bare cheeks before he kisses her mouth. To walk outside unmasked, where the whole world can see, is to become nobody and nothing. Every Catresou child knows this. But with him holding her hands, her face exposed to his—she almost feels as if she finally has a name.

(She will never have a name. She will never get to keep him.

There is only this moment, this sun-drenched afternoon. This kiss, and the next, but not too many after.)

He leads her down to the Lower City. She has been there before, but only as the Juliet, needed and despised. Now she is just another girl, hand in hand with just another boy; the sellers in the market cry out to her, and the scrawny cats sniff her and rub their cheeks against her hand.

It is as if she had been a ghost, and now is alive.

Her eyes sting. He must see it, for he presses a hand to her shoulder and says, "Race me?"

"Where?" she asks, and he grins at her. A moment later he is clambering up the side of the nearest building, and she follows him. Side by side, they race across the rooftops, leaping between the houses, careening off ledges. They do not laugh only because they are running too hard. The air and the wind and the sunlight are their laughter.

At last they stop on a roof overlooking one of the many little squares of the Lower City. This one has a public fountain, and beside it sits a musician, singing and playing his lute for the coins that the passers-by throw at him. She can catch scattered bits of the tune, but she cannot make out the words.

"What is he singing?" she asks.

He listens for a moment longer, head tilted; then he begins to sing along with the musician:

"O mistress mine, where are you roaming?
O, stay and hear, your true-love's coming,
That can sing both high and low:
Trip no further, pretty sweeting;
Journeys end in lovers meeting,
Every wise man's son doth know."

Below, the song ends abruptly as a pair of children start to argue with the musician. She wonders if they are pickpockets working with him; she has heard of that trick, when her family was telling her that the Lower City was a terrible and unclean place where she must never go.

She is not blind now to the dirt and the poverty, the anger and the tricks. She loves this place anyway.

"How do you know that song?" she asks.

"They sing it all over the Lower City," he says. "I've heard it often." Then he starts the song again:

"What is love? 'Tis not hereafter;
Present mirth hath present laughter;
What's to come is still unsure.
In delay there lies no plenty,
Then come kiss me sweet and twenty;
Youth's a stuff will not endure."

"That is a wicked song," she tells him, when his voice has drifted away on the wind.

"Oh?" he says.

"We know what comes after," she says, "and this life is only to prepare us for the Paths of Light."

This is why she loves him: because he does not believe in the ways of her people, and yet she sees pain in his face as he says, "But the Juliet will never walk those paths."

"No," she admits, and the word holds all the loneliness of childhood, and all the loneliness that she knows waits for her hereafter.

He does not tell her she is wrong. He does not tell her she should be resigned. He listens, and waits, and she loves him so very much.

"You could walk those paths," she tells him. "If I gave you the spells, if I taught you the knowledge. If you were willing."

He takes her hand, wraps his fingers around hers. "Not without you," he says, and the words are pure foolishness—foolish and stupid and wretchedly foreign—but nobody has ever been foolish for her sake before.

"I should disown you for that," she tells him. "But I won't."

His thumb traces a circle against her knuckles. "Then will you kiss me sweet and twenty?"

He is folly and sin and everything she should not want, and

yet in his eyes she has a name, as she can never have among her people. With him, she is only a girl, and he is only a boy, and that is enough. In this fragile, fleeting moment, it is enough.

With her free hand, she brushes her fingertips against his cheekbone. She will never get used to the way his face is so open and free, never masked, never hidden.

She will never get used to the way he looks at her as if she is the world, and yet that is how she has the courage to lean forward and press her lips against his.

They kiss.

She has never kissed him like this before: long and slow and sweet. She is still kissing him, and now he has let go of her hand; his fingers are tangled in her hair, and her hands are gripping his shoulders, and there is nothing, nothing, nothing in the world that matters except this easy, heart-stopping joy between them.

19

IT WAS TOO EASY TO get down to the door into the Sunken Library. If Runajo survived the revenants, then before she was executed, she would have a little talk with the High Priestess about making it more difficult. Surely there should be guards. Locks. Spells to sound an alarm when anyone even got close.

Runajo stared at the smooth white stone of the door and wiped her palms against her skirt. Her whole body prickled with hot-cold fear.

Because it was quite possible that the door didn't need anything but the spells on it to keep her out. It was quite possible that trying to break the spells would bring the High Priestess down on their heads.

And it was also pretty likely that if they got inside, they would die.

Live as dead until thy death, she thought. *That won't be a problem, surrounded by revenants.*

Really, it was surprising the whole Sisterhood wasn't down here.

"Well?" said Juliet.

Runajo glanced at her: the other girl looked more relaxed than Runajo had ever seen her, the double short swords that Runajo had found for her gripped easily in her hands. They were crafted in the Old Viyaran style, with wide, straight-edged blades; Runajo had been worried that Juliet wouldn't know how to use them, but Juliet had said that she'd trained with some very similar swords, and liked them.

"Unless staring is how you open it," said Juliet. She was rocking very slightly on her feet, just a fraction forward and then back, as if she couldn't wait to charge.

Unlike the pain of the bloodletting, fear was inside Runajo's mind. But fear still had to be felt in the heart for it to matter, and Runajo knew how to cast things out of her heart. She thought of stone, cold and hard and razor-edged, and she thought, *You are still alive. Therefore you will die. Therefore you have no excuses.*

She sliced open her palm and laid her bloody hand against the door. Beneath the stinging pain and the wet trickle of blood, behind the cool surface of the stone, she felt a soft, living vibration, like a heartbeat.

My blood is as the blood of gods.

There were no gods. That aphorism of the Sisters was a lie.

But it was true in one way: blood was blood was blood. There was no difference between what flowed in Runajo's veins and what had laid the foundations of Viyara. Between what had sealed the door a hundred years ago and what she brought to unlock it now.

At first Runajo thought she wouldn't be able to do it. The spell on the door was dizzying in its complexity, with twists and turns that folded it in on itself over and over. She had no idea where to even start.

But then she realized: the seal on the door was a mirror of the walls that she had helped weave. They were both created to keep death out.

Slowly, carefully, she unwove the seal. Every time another trembling strand of magic loosed itself, she held her breath, wondering if this one would set off an alarm. Every time she started to pull on a new thread, she fumbled at first for a grip, wondering if this one would be immovable.

As Runajo undid the magic in her mind, the door unwove itself as well. Solid, smooth stone peeled up in slender white ropes that spiraled gracefully upward to form an arch, layer after layer, until all that was left was a thin film of white dust clinging to her hand. She shook her fingers, and the dust fell away.

Runajo let out a breath. *I did it,* she thought. Her shoulders were cramped and aching, there was sweat trickling down the back of her neck—she had no idea how long she'd been working—but she had done the impossible. She had opened the door into the Sunken Library.

Perhaps this plan would actually work.

Through the door was a dark, narrow hallway. Runajo could see only a little way inside, because the only light came from outside, where she stood with Juliet; but that was why she had brought along two little lamps—white stone spheres that glowed with a cool, steady light—each on a chain that could hang from the neck, so they could have their hands free.

She had also brought a little jar of healing ointment, which she rubbed against the cut on her palm. Once the hot tingle of rapidly healing flesh began, she tucked the jar back into her robe.

"You're the one with the swords," she said to Juliet. "You first."

Juliet nodded and stepped inside. Runajo was right on her heels. This time she only had to tap the archway, and the door wove itself back together. It liked to be closed.

And they were in the Sunken Library.

"Well," said Juliet after a moment, "it's smaller than I expected."

"This is just the vestibule," said Runajo. "It wasn't even part of the library, back before it was closed off."

And we'd better keep to talking silently, she added. *So the revenants don't hear us.*

Juliet raised her eyebrows.

Yes, I rescind my order to stay out of my head, said Runajo. *You enjoy making me clarify everything, don't you?*

I'm the sword of the Catresou, said Juliet. *Slavish obedience is my specialty.*

There was something inexpressibly warm about her sarcasm. It was like . . . Runajo was actually not sure that anyone had ever talked to her that way, and probably Juliet was hearing her think this right now.

How do we keep our thoughts separate? she asked Juliet.

You make a wall inside yourself, said Juliet. *And then you practice for at least five years.*

But Runajo had already had a lot more than five years' experience locking herself away. Again she imagined the obsidian inside her chest, wrapping around her heart and mind and soul, keeping what was hers safe from prying eyes.

How did you do that? asked Juliet.

You're not the only clever one, said Runajo. *Come on.*

Together they walked down the narrow hall. It turned twice, and then there was a little square room that seemed to have once held a number of potted trees, judging by the pottery shards, the thin layer of dirt scattered around the floor, and the withered, broken branches.

There were two bodies. The tattered remnants of their robes still clung to them, as did the shriveled remains of their skin.

Some of their hair still clung to their skulls; some had fallen to the floor.

Swallowing, Runajo strode quickly across the room, Juliet at her heels.

And there were the main doors into the library: dark bronze, carved with the faces of the gods, and glinting faintly in the light of their lamps. There was no handle on the doors, no visible lock or bolt. When Juliet pushed against them, they didn't move in the slightest.

Runajo laid a hand against the doors. *I am a Sister of Thorn,* she told the metal, and she felt a tiny spark of something answer. *These doors are mine by right, and I need them to open.*

With no sound except the soft sigh of moving air, the doors swung open.

Before them was the great stairway down into the library. Runajo had heard of this: a vast, white spiral staircase that curved ten times through the air before it reached the floor of the main library.

It was not white anymore.

When Runajo had heard about the last, desperate stand on the staircase, about the Sisters who had cut their own throats to seal the spell that stopped the swarming revenants from setting one foot on the stairs, she had imagined it as something terrible but glorious. But she had not imagined it like this: withered bodies sprawled everywhere, their clothes rotting, their bodies shriveled, their long hair shed onto the floor in circles around their wrinkled heads. She had not imagined how the blood that the Sisters poured out would not remain crimson, but instead turn to dark stains.

This was, indeed, hers by right: blood and death and withering. It was the only birthright anyone ever had.

You are not a cheerful companion, said Juliet.

You can't tell me you like this place, said Runajo as she started to pick her way down the staircase. She didn't want to look down at the bodies, but there was no other way to avoid stepping on one. Or on the occasional head or hand that had come loose and rolled down a few steps. Around them, the darkness yawned; she could feel the slight drift of air currents, could hear the echoes of every step they took, but she couldn't see a thing beyond the stairs just in front of her.

I have a battle to look forward to, said Juliet. *And then a grave.*

She did actually look—not exactly eager, but strangely at ease as she descended the stairs beside Runajo. Maybe that wasn't surprising: she had been a prisoner before, and now she was, if not free, at least in her element.

I'm still a prisoner, said Juliet. *I just find holding swords a very great consolation.*

Will you stop that? Runajo demanded, thinking of stone again.

I can't help that you make it so easy, said Juliet. *You're getting better, though. You'll be able to do it without thinking about it soon.*

Really? Runajo asked, and the beauty of silent speech was how much skepticism she could put into one unvoiced word.

Well, Juliet allowed, *in a year or two.*

They walked in silence for a while longer, and then Juliet asked, *Do the Sisters have any idea what caused it? The Ruining?*

No, said Runajo. Her foot landed in a path of dried blood, and she swallowed. *Mostly they think it is simply the end. The sacrifice that the gods poured out to give the world life has run dry, and since the blood of men can never equal the blood of gods, the world must falter and fail.*

Do you think that? asked Juliet.

Runajo had seen souls walk and she had performed necromancy. She didn't know what to think anymore.

I don't think it matters, she said. *Everything dies anyway; I don't see how dying from a cloud is any different.*

Being torn apart by revenants, I'm sure that's different, said Juliet.

Two steps below Runajo, a withered, bony hand lay by itself on the pale stone. Runajo's heart thudded as she stepped over it.

They say that it started in the peninsula where our two peoples once lived, she said, trying not to think how soon they would be down in the library. *Do* you *have any ideas about it?*

Some say it was the Sisters, said Juliet. *That you went too far, seeking dominion over death. Others say a lone necromancer called it down upon us.*

We don't seek dominion over death, said Runajo. *And it can't have been a necromancer. Because—*

Necromancy doesn't exist? The mockery in Juliet's tone was almost affectionate.

There's something I don't understand, said Runajo. The withered eye sockets of a dead Sister stared up at her, and she stared back, refusing to shudder. *If necromancy was possible, then in all of history, more than one person must have figured it out. There's no power anyone has ever wanted more. If it were done, then it would be done again and again, no matter who tried to stop it. Nobody would be dead anymore.*

You are more arrogant than my father, said Juliet. *Do you imagine that death has so little power? That whatever is wanted enough, can be obtained?*

Runajo huffed out a breath. They were surrounded by the corpses of Sisters who had died buying a protection that wouldn't last much longer. Of course she knew how futile trying usually was.

That's my point, said Runajo. *For all of history, nobody has been strong enough to defeat Death. Perhaps necromancy is only possible* now *because the Ruining broke down the walls between life and death.*

Or, said Juliet, *perhaps the first time necromancy was accomplished caused the Ruining.*

It was a strangely plausible thought. If the Sisters were right when they said that necromancy was worse than the Ruining, then perhaps it was the one thing powerful enough to cause it.

Had that first necromancer meant to cause destruction? Or had he thought that he was bringing a blessing, by conquering the foe that even the Ancients could not stop?

Maybe he hadn't cared. Maybe he had been like Runajo's mother, so desperate for just one person to live that he didn't care if the whole world burned to achieve it.

Runajo had never thought highly of her mother, but she supposed that at least she could be thankful that the woman had never even dreamed of necromancy. If she'd had the idea, she would have tried it.

What had that necromancer thought when he saw the white mist appear? Had he even realized it was deadly?

Regardless, he had probably been one of the first to die, for which he should count himself lucky. Living with the burden of destroying the balance of life and death was not a fate that Runajo would wish on anyone.

And now here she was, one hundred years later, cleaning up his mess.

They were over halfway down the stairs now. Runajo stubbed her toe against a corpse—it didn't hurt, of course, but she still sprang back as if burned, and Juliet had to grab her shoulder to steady her.

Had something made a noise in the darkness just now? Or was that only an echo of the corpse shifting when she kicked it?

We need to go faster, said Juliet. *When they attack, we can't get caught on this stairway. They won't be able to hurt us here, but we'd never break through their numbers.*

Runajo's back prickled. *Can you sense them coming?*

Not exactly, said Juliet. *I don't know where they are, I don't know how many. But I know they are somewhere close.*

Her heartbeat picking up, Runajo found her way down the staircase faster and faster. When her feet hit the floor, she let out a little sigh of relief . . . even though now the danger really began.

And then the lights came on.

She had known about them: the one hundred and thirteen stars, floating in the upper air of the Sunken Library. She had assumed that they were destroyed, or that their power had withered and faded. But now the glowing orbs blossomed above her, so bright she could barely look at them.

And she could see the Sunken Library.

It was huge. It didn't even feel like she was indoors. The vaulted ceiling so far above them could just as well be the sky; she could see why the lights in it were called stars. Far away before her, she could see the looming face of Ka, god of memory, growing out of the walls. The bookshelves looked tiny in comparison to the rest, and yet they were easily four times her height, every one of them equipped with two sliding ladders.

All across the floor were scattered bare white bones. Nothing had escaped the revenants' teeth.

Do you know where to go? asked Juliet, and there was a strange sense of calm to her voice.

Yes, said Runajo. She had pored over every record she could find. She was almost sure.

Then start running, said Juliet.

Far off to their right, something rustled.

Runajo didn't need to be told twice. She bolted forward, feet light and swift, straight toward the face of Ka. Bones clattered and crunched beneath her feet, and she wanted to cringe at the sounds, but the revenants were coming and there was no time.

They reached the first rows of bookcases, and with a hiss, a pair of revenants leaped out at them. They looked, horribly, like people: hairless, eyeless, naked people whose skin had in some places turned shiny and crinkly, in others rotted away.

Because they had once been people, before they died. And then returned.

Juliet spun into motion without missing a step. Her blades whirled, sliced, and then two heads fell to the ground. The bodies of the revenants swayed a moment longer before they also collapsed.

Keep going, Juliet snapped, and Runajo started running again.

The problem was, she was getting near the end of her strength, and Runajo cursed her own foolishness. She should have known that this quest would involve running away from monsters. If she'd been thinking, she could have spent the last six months running up and down the stairways of the Cloister. She could have been ready for this. Instead she was going to die and get Juliet killed as well, just because there was one way she hadn't thought to prepare.

Suddenly Juliet grabbed her arm and yanked her back. Runajo stumbled, flailing, and by the time she had gotten her balance again, Juliet had finished off a revenant in front of them.

Runajo had nearly run into it headfirst.

Thank you, she said, and felt a sudden wave of shock and fear from Juliet.

Like Juliet, she looked back.

There were hundreds of revenants. Perhaps thousands. Runajo didn't know and didn't much care; all she knew was that they were swarming through the library like ants driven out of a nest, utterly silent except for the rustle of their feet against the floor as they crept forward, drawn by the sound and smell of human flesh.

Keep running, said Juliet, and there was nothing now in her voice but pure, ruthless determination.

They ran. Runajo didn't feel tired now. She didn't even exactly feel afraid. She felt like her body had turned into pure light and fire, or like it was being whirled forward by a mighty wind, and all she could do was watch. Watch, and think, *We aren't going fast enough. We're going to be dead.*

They were starting to get close to the face of Ka. But the

revenants were running faster.

Are we running for someplace defensible? asked Juliet.

I hope so, said Runajo.

And then they were there. They were skidding to a stop right beneath the huge chin of Ka, and there was a short little hallway burrowing into the wall, and at the end of it was a door.

Defensible. Slightly. The revenants couldn't rush them as badly here, which meant Runajo might be able to get the inner door open in time.

Then they'd find out if there were any revenants on the other side.

Juliet whirled to face the main library as soon as she was inside the hall. *Get to the door,* she said, and there was a razor-sharp grin in her voice. *See if you're good enough to save us.*

20

"WE NEED TO BE SUBTLE," said Paris that evening, as they sat together in Justiran's spare room. Sheaves of extra herbs hung from the ceiling; the smell tickled at Paris's nose. "And we need to agree on a story ahead of time. Not like with the City Guard today."

"What was wrong with that?" asked Romeo, and blew on the tea he held cupped in his hands.

"She didn't believe you," said Paris. "*And* it was completely embarrassing. What possessed you to spin that story?"

Romeo half smiled. "There's nothing shameful about love."

He had been very quiet as they made their way back to Justiran's house, and he had remained quiet all evening as they ate dinner, as Paris told him about his first meeting with Vai, as they made their plans to find him again. But now that Paris was annoyed with him, at last he seemed to be cheering up.

Maybe Paris should have pitied him a little longer.

"There's something shameful in thinking all the world lives your story," said Paris. "Didn't it occur to you that not all of us are busy getting ourselves killed for feelings we fancy are love? Think of all the other people you've known."

"I don't really know anyone," said Romeo, "except Juliet and Makari and Runajo and Justiran. And you too, I suppose. But I can't conceal your identity by telling people about your own life, and I don't think you want me telling people that you drink as much as Makari does, and I never understood Runajo to begin with, and nobody would believe that either of us was an apothecary. So that leaves me and Juliet."

The words were cheerful enough, but they were accompanied by a wave of wistful sadness that Paris felt he had no choice but to completely ignore.

"Don't be ridiculous," he said. "Sorry."

Romeo grinned. "You can't order me on that one. I really can't stop."

"You weren't raised in a cage," Paris went on. "Even if you don't have friends, you have family."

He expected Romeo to say, *No, of course I have friends, they flock to hear my poetry*. But he didn't.

"Of course I have family," said Romeo, and there was an uneasy sort of cheerfulness to his voice. "But it's all on my father's side and *they* could hardly be expected to have that much time to waste on me. That's why I had Makari for a tutor. Anyway, most of them didn't like my mother. They say that's why she killed herself—I don't know, I was only a baby. I mean, my father liked her very much—that's why his other women hated her—but of course he was too busy."

"Your tutor raised you," said Paris.

"Well, not from a baby," said Romeo. "Obviously." And Paris caught a flickering memory of nannies and quiet attendants. Of watching a tall, silk-robed man from across a courtyard and thinking, *Father.*

It was only to be expected. The high-ranking Mahyanai took several concubines along with their wives, and of course it would lead to jealousy and neglected children.

Paris was uncomfortably aware that he had seen his own father hardly more often. But he, at least, had been a legitimate son. There had been a way for him to earn his place in his family, even if . . . he hadn't ever really been good enough.

"We don't have illegitimate children," said Romeo. "Keeps things simpler. Besides, isn't your family supposed to want you whether you earn it or not?"

"What would you know?" Paris demanded, not liking how gentle Romeo's voice had gotten.

"Because that's how Makari was with me," said Romeo, and Paris could see the man's face clear as daylight as he felt Romeo's overwhelming rush of affection. "He didn't always have time—he was only my tutor, he couldn't always be attending to me—but when he did, he was . . . well." Romeo rubbed at the back of his neck. "Also I have read poems, and it's very clear. If your family didn't want you, they aren't worth poetry and therefore aren't worth worrying over. Right?"

But they *were* worth worrying over. Paris didn't know what sort of irresponsible butterfly soul Romeo might have, that he could just forget his family didn't want him, but Paris wasn't—couldn't—*did not* have it in him to ignore and despise the family that birthed him.

"I could write a poem for you," said Romeo. "To make it clear."

"That wouldn't help," Paris said stiffly, wondering how this conversation had gotten out of control.

"A poem of comfort."

"No." Paris desperately wished that he had gotten stuck in this situation with somebody who was . . . anyone but Romeo. "Look, when we meet Vai, just . . . let me do the talking."

There was one god face in the Lower City: Xinaad, the god of luck and lies. His upside-down features protruded out of a giant mound of red-gold rock that rose up in the middle of the Lower City, and around him was a round courtyard with several old fountains. As with most open places in the city, scrawny, ragged cats swarmed the courtyard, sunning themselves and scuffling with each other.

Romeo marched forward to one of the nearby buildings and rapped on the door. A hulking, one-eyed man opened it and gave them an absent-minded glower.

"We're here for the duel," said Romeo.

"Don't know of any duels," said the man.

Romeo drew a breath, probably about to make an attempt at lying their way in. Before he could do anything irreparable, Paris stepped in front of him and said, "Look, I don't know whatever ridiculous code you people may use. We're here to see the King of Cats. It's important."

There was a moment where the man just stared at him and Paris felt horribly certain that they were about to get laughed at and thrown out on the street.

Then the man pulled the door wider and said, "Inside."

They stepped inside the house and promptly discovered the two other men waiting, who quickly and efficiently searched them and confiscated Romeo's sword, then grabbed them quite tightly by the arms and marched them down into the house's cellar.

The cellar had a door.

The door went down into a passage, which opened out into an underground hall that was made of the space between the foundations of several old buildings—each of the five uneven walls was a different style of stonework. On one of the walls, somebody had carved a rough copy of Xinaad's face from outside.

And dueling right beneath Xinaad's nose was Vai. He was fighting again with the short sticks, this time against a man wielding a long staff. And this time he was using no elaborate tricks; their weapons clattered against each other as they struck and parried.

The staff's reach should have given the challenger an advantage. But Vai moved like a cracking whip, fast and flexible and strong. As Romeo and Paris watched, the challenger's staff whirled toward his head. Vai dropped to the ground, and his arm lashed out, slamming one of his sticks into the man's knee. There was a sharp crack of breaking bone; the man howled and fell.

Vai stood up, grinning wildly. "Anyone else?" he called.

This was probably not going to end well, but they had come too far to back out. Also, they were being held by a pair of men with grips like steel, so they really *couldn't* back out.

"We need to talk," said Paris.

Vai's smile disappeared. "I told you to go home."

"We have no home," Romeo declared, sounding like he was delivering the start of a poem.

Paris cut him off before he could say anything else. "We're not working for Lord Catresou," he said. "We're trying to stop him. We know that Tybalt was the previous King of Cats. Do you know anything about what else he was doing down here?"

"Yes, boy with a Catresou accent, I'm clearly going to believe you on that," said Vai. "Run along now."

"No," said Paris. "You have to help us."

"You're either working for your family, in which case you're lucky I'm not breaking your bones, or you're not, in which case you're a naive little boy who's going to get killed," said Vai. "Whichever it is, I have nothing to say to you."

"I'm not Catresou," said Romeo. "And they want to destroy both of us."

Vai gave him a skeptical look.

"We need your help," said Romeo, "so we can avenge a noble lady they have wronged most terribly."

That appeal was not going to work. Paris didn't think Vai was entirely without honor—he had saved Paris, after all, when he didn't have to—but he clearly wasn't going to help them just because Romeo was very, very earnest and almost speaking in verse.

He remembered how Vai had faced down the other gang in the streets and offered them a wager.

Paris stepped between Romeo and Vai. "I'll fight you for answers," he said.

Vai's narrow eyebrows went up a fraction. "Will you, now?"

"Give me a sword," said Paris, "and I'll fight you. If I land a hit, you have to give us answers."

Do you think you can? Romeo asked silently.

Probably, said Paris. Vai was clever and an amazing fighter, but he couldn't possibly have had training with a sword. That was a noble's weapon.

Vai's grin was like a razor. "Andrvad!" he called out. "Two swords!"

It wasn't a good sign that one of Vai's men had two swords on hand. When Vai drew one of them with an easy, fluid grace, Paris felt the familiar, nauseating certainty that he was about to fail humiliatingly.

Are you sure? said Romeo.

You're not helping, said Paris. It didn't matter how good Vai was. Paris had been useless at everything else so far; he was *going* to succeed at this. No matter what it took.

"I promise not to throw things at you," said Vai.

"Do you do that often?" asked Paris.

"It's how I won the title. Threw my stick at his head and knocked him out. Fastest victory on record."

Paris suddenly remembered two months ago, when Tybalt had disappeared for a week and everybody said he had been injured tangling with brigands in the Lower City. He had heard gossip about how *Paris must be hoping he won't get better,* but he'd known that Tybalt would recover. And he did.

And then he died in a duel. As Paris now might.

"I'll call out the start," said Romeo. "Three. Two. One."

Vai struck like the wind. Paris had barely realized that he was moving, and then the point of his sword had scraped his arm.

"I win," said Vai, turning away. "Good-bye."

"Wait!" said Paris. "That—that wasn't the bargain."

"Oh?" Vai looked back.

"It was if I scored a point, you answered our questions," said Paris. "Nobody said anything about when *you* scored a point."

Vai's grin was absolutely delighted. "Keep thinking that way, and you'll almost be worthy of this court." He fell back into dueling stance. "Come at me, then."

In the next flurry, Paris lasted a bit longer. But then he tried to duck away from the sword and ended up landing on his back. A moment later the sword point was just above his nose, with Vai looking down at him.

"Yield," said Vai, sounding positively friendly.

"No," Paris said, and rolled to the side.

He was growing fairly sure that Vai didn't want to kill or maim him, and that meant all Vai could do was injure or humiliate him. Paris had been humiliated by the best, and he didn't mind bleeding. Not if it meant he could avenge Juliet and stop the necromancers.

In the next round, he didn't bother trying to parry; he lunged at Vai without any sort of finesse, hoping that it would at least be unexpected. All he got was a really nasty scrape along his left shoulder.

The next time he tried to attack, Vai cartwheeled away and then kicked the sword out of his hand. Doggedly, Paris picked the sword back up and attacked again. And again. And again.

"Yield," Vai said each time, and each time Paris said, "No."

He was being played with. He was being shown his place. He was being publicly humiliated, but Paris was used to that, and he wasn't going to stop for anything except death or maiming.

Sooner or later, Vai was going to realize that, and then he would have to make a choice.

There was sweat running into his eyes; his breath was coming in ragged gasps. He'd gotten two more cuts.

"Yield," said Vai, and he wasn't smirking now.

"No," said Paris.

"That's enough," said Romeo, and wrenched the sword out of his hand.

"No," Paris gasped, but Romeo ignored him and attacked.

Suddenly the game was a duel. The swords flashed and clattered, as Romeo drove Vai back with an easy, relentless grace. Paris stared at him, realizing he had completely forgotten that *this boy defeated Tybalt Catresou.*

It didn't take him long to defeat Vai. A few moments later he had Vai backed against the wall with the sword at this throat.

"Yield," Romeo said calmly.

Vai smiled over the sword point and said, "You're very impressive. But not as much as your friend."

Then he kicked Romeo in the stomach. Romeo doubled over, and Paris gasped as he felt a faint echo of the breathless pain.

He still managed to call out, "He scored a point. Will you answer *his* question?"

Vai's smile was almost fond. "You really don't know how to quit, do you?"

"No," said Paris. "Do I need to fight you again?"

Before Vai could reply, Paris heard the door behind him slam. There were audible gasps. And then someone called out, "I challenge the King of Cats!"

Paris had heard the voice before, but for a moment he didn't recognize it. He was too dazed by the sudden wave of overpowering dread that flowed over him from Romeo's mind.

And then he looked.

It was Tybalt.

He was several inches taller than Paris, with broad shoulders and dark red hair. He moved with an easy, fluid confidence as he strode down the steps into the main part of the hall; his unmasked face was set and grim.

He was *dead*. Paris had seen his embalmed body, and he felt sick as Tybalt walked toward them, moving as naturally as if his heart and brain and stomach had not been scooped out of his body and put in jars.

And he was alive. He was nothing like the revenant they had seen yesterday. This was not his dead body, writhing back to a semblance of life as all corpses did if they were not burned first. This was Tybalt himself, summoned back into a body that had been dead and cold. This was necromancy.

Everyone in the room had gone silent, staring. But nobody was screaming. Nobody was running from Tybalt or trying to hack him to pieces. As Tybalt strode toward them, his boots echoing against the stone, Paris realized: nobody knew the previous King of Cats had been Tybalt Catresou. They knew that the previous king had lost his place to Vai. But they didn't know he was the Catresou boy who had died a few days ago.

Master Trelouno and Lord Catresou had lamented that they could resurrect Tybalt, but they couldn't use him, because everyone knew he was dead. Evidently, they had found the loophole.

"Lock the doors," Vai called out, and there was no fear in his voice, but he was watching Tybalt with an absolute attention. "It's another dead one."

Of course. Vai had known Tybalt's name. He knew what they were facing.

The men scrambled to obey, but they weren't panicking, and Paris realized that Vai had said *another*. They had faced this kind of threat before.

"You have defied my masters," Tybalt said flatly, looking straight at Vai. "For that offense, you will die. But I came for these two." He turned toward Paris and Romeo. "That girl did not lie."

For one nightmarish moment, Paris thought that Tybalt had been talking to Juliet's ghost in the land of the dead. Then he remembered the girl from the day before, saying, *I'll probably do my best to make trouble for him.* She must have gone to Lord Catresou and told him what she knew about Romeo.

"What happened to her?" he asked.

The girl hadn't minded necromancy, if it would bring back the ones she loved. But Paris couldn't imagine she would like to see Tybalt like *this.*

"When she had told us where you were, she was no more use to us," said Tybalt, his voice dry, disinterested, and Paris shivered. "You will die now."

"Wait!" said Romeo. "Tybalt, you can't do this—you loved Juliet, didn't you? Lord Catresou had her killed."

Tybalt looked at him as if he were an insect and said, "So?"

Paris finally found his voice. "You had a duty to her," he said. "You were the best of us. I don't care if you've died, that's no excuse."

He only realized after he had said the words that he had moved to stand beside Romeo, even though he didn't have a sword. Though it probably didn't matter, because there was no way Paris could ever beat him in a fight.

"My duty is to my master," said Tybalt, and though Paris had hardly known him before, he could tell there was something wrong about his voice.

Tybalt moved. He was *fast*, and Paris would have been slashed open and bleeding to death an instant later except that Romeo shoved him to the side. They both went tumbling to the ground, as Paris heard the clatter of steel on steel that meant Vai had started fighting Tybalt.

"Don't hurt him!" Romeo yelled, sitting up.

"He's already dead!" Vai shouted back. His next stroke sliced across Tybalt's cheek. For just an instant, as the blood welled up from the cut, it was bright red. Then as it dripped, it turned black as ink.

Black blood. The sign of the living dead.

Two other men lunged forward with swords, and Paris knew that Tybalt was a master swordsman, but the magic that brought him back must have changed him. No normal person could dodge and parry *that* fast against three opponents at once.

Tybalt snarled and lunged, and this time he knocked the sword out of Vai's hand.

Paris didn't think. He rolled, flinging out his legs to catch Tybalt's ankles and trip him.

Tybalt went down, and in a heartbeat Vai was on top of him and had gripped his head—

And with a sharp crack, snapped his neck.

Paris flinched. Beside him, Romeo had gone very still.

Vai looked at them. "Thank you," he said.

Paris swallowed. Tybalt had been raised from the dead by a necromancer. Paris had helped kill him again.

"It was nothing," he managed.

"I think we need to talk," said Vai.

21

THE REVENANTS SWARMING FROM EVERY corner of the Sunken Library didn't scream or howl as they closed in, ready to kill. They only hissed: a dry, whispering chorus from every direction.

Runajo's hands shook as she drew the knife.

Then Juliet yelled as she attacked. The next moment, Runajo had slashed her palm back open and pressed it to the door. She burrowed her mind through the locks, layer after layer. The spells were archaic; they felt old and dusty and full of hidden razors, but it didn't matter if she sliced her mind open on them, she had to get the door open. She had to get them out of here.

She heard Juliet's harsh gasps as she attacked the revenants, the pounding of her feet against the floor as she jumped and dodged, the thumps of limbs and heads falling to the ground.

The endless, hungry hissing of the revenants.

There were so *many*.

Then Runajo found the turn of the lock, and she felt the spells on the door unraveling, and it swung open.

Juliet! she called, and a moment later Juliet came charging down the hall. She grabbed Runajo without losing speed and shoved her through the doorway, then whirled to slice and stab at the two revenants that had followed.

Now, said Runajo, and Juliet leaped inside just as the door slammed shut, chopping off one writhing revenant hand.

Gasping for breath, they turned around.

They were in a round, domed room. The walls and ceiling were covered in woven strips of brass, so that every surface glittered. There were no bookshelves, but there were rows of low racks full of softly glowing white cylinders with brass on either end.

She had read the descriptions. This was the heart of the Sunken Library.

And there were no revenants inside. Until they opened the door again, they were safe.

"What is this?" asked Juliet, poking a finger at one of the cylinders.

Runajo grinned. "You've never seen a scroll? Since the Ruining, we've lost the art of making them. But in the old days, the Sisters of Thorn didn't need paper."

Gently, she removed a scroll from the nearest rack. It fit

snugly into her hand, her fingertips curving comfortably around the rim. She said "Open," and glowing words hovered in the air before her. It was in one of the more obscure ancient languages; she knew the alphabet, but not the words.

Juliet prowled around her in a circle, her gaze shifting suspiciously between the glowing scroll and the shadowed walls.

"And you think," she asked, "those Sisters wrote down the knowledge you need?"

Runajo whispered "Close" to the unreadable scroll, and the glowing letters vanished. She put it back on the shelf.

"They built Viyara, and they also wrote the scrolls," she said, running her fingertips along the cool, smooth cylinders. "So perhaps. At any rate, our odds are better taking scrolls than books. They could put five or ten of our books into a single scroll. More chance of bringing away something useful."

"Hm," said Juliet. She laid down her swords—they were smeared with something black and thick—and with a sigh, sat down on the floor and leaned back against the wall.

As if she'd been given permission to feel it, Runajo was suddenly dragged down by exhaustion. Her heart pounded and she could barely breathe.

She had nearly died.

Still, she had to keep working. She knelt by one of the racks, but her hands were shaking.

Juliet cracked one eye open. "You're not going to be much use for a while," she said. "I've seen men come back from duels where they nearly died. Everybody needs a rest."

"How come you're all right, then?" Runajo demanded crossly, but then she noticed the slight tremble to Juliet's hands, and she realized that some—not all, but *some* of the shuddering relief-exhaustion-fear in her veins was Juliet's.

When she nearly dropped a scroll on the floor, she had to admit that Juliet was right. With a sigh, she sat down beside her and crossed her arms, tucking her hands under her elbows so that they would stop shaking.

For a while they sat in silence together. Then Juliet said quietly, "Romeo would love this place."

Runajo thought of Romeo: sweet, enthusiastic, not terribly bright. (Dead.)

"Why?" she asked. "There aren't any pretty things for him to babble over."

Juliet gave her a disgruntled look. "Words," she said. "He loved words."

Runajo thought about that. Yes, Romeo had always been in love with the pretty phrases he could string together. She'd always assumed he just loved the sound of his own voice, but maybe he liked the words themselves as well.

"Anyone's words," Juliet went on. "He wanted to know the poetry of my people, though we have hardly any. He taught me the poetry of his. He would have . . . been so delighted, to read the words of the Sunken Library."

"Is that why you loved him?" asked Runajo. "He wrote you poems?"

"You don't believe I loved him," Juliet said flatly.

Runajo winced. She hadn't meant to let that slip through the bond. Maybe it had just been obvious in her voice.

"He was begging me to run away with him three months ago," she said. "Whatever happened between you two, it wasn't—"

"It was real." Juliet's voice was unyielding. "It was swift and it was foolish, but it was *real*."

"Then what was it?" asked Runajo. "Because if it's just that he treated you as a girl and not a weapon—"

"No," said Juliet. "It wasn't just that."

She was quiet for a few moments, and then she began to speak, very slowly and softly. "The Catresou say . . . nothing is important unless it lasts forever. That's why outsiders don't matter: you will all perish in the darkness outside the Paths of Light. This world only matters because the duties we undertake, the knowledge we obtain, unlocks the world beyond for us."

Again Juliet was silent for a few heartbeats. Then she went on, "I don't think I ever entirely believed that. I couldn't, not when I was the Juliet. But I didn't understand what I thought about it, until—he recited a poem for me. He wanted to tell me that I was beautiful, and he recited a poem about blossoms falling from a tree each year. How the same flowers never fall twice."

"Every six-year-old learns that poem," said Runajo. "It's the first in the lexicon."

Juliet shrugged. "That things can be beautiful, that they can *matter,* even as they vanish—I never had words for that before. He gave me the words. That's why I love him." Then she smiled faintly. "And, yes. He did write me poems."

"I should hope he did, if he spent the night with you," said Runajo. The courtesy of a morning-after poem was what made a tryst honorable and not a mere seduction.

Juliet was blushing bright red now and not meeting her eyes, and Runajo couldn't help a soft snicker. She had forgotten that the Catresou were so peculiar and full of shame about their love affairs.

That thought must have leaked through, because Juliet flinched, the blush fading from her face as some sort of cold, sick fear swirled around her.

"Tell me the truth and I will know if you lie," said Juliet, speaking rapidly and not looking at her. "He told me that if we spent three nights together and declared ourselves to my parents, that would be a marriage. Among your people, at least. Is that . . . was he . . ."

Juliet was terrified, far more than she'd been when facing revenants. Runajo remembered a year when the Catresou's offering had not been their usual condemned criminal, but a "volunteer": a young woman disgraced for losing her virginity to one man when she was betrothed to another.

Suddenly Juliet's shame and fear didn't seem amusing at all.

"Yes," said Runajo. "It's an old custom. I don't know of anyone alive who's done it. Usually, to take a wife, men negotiate beforehand. It's lovers they go to without asking the family. But if he declared himself for your hand on the third morning—yes. You would be his wife."

Juliet didn't respond. She was staring straight ahead, her lips pressed together, her mind locked away as if behind glass. Finally she nodded and whispered, "Thank you."

"*Did* he declare himself?" asked Runajo.

"The third night," said Juliet, her voice raw, "was the night after he killed my cousin Tybalt. They'd have slaughtered him on sight. But we were going to—after I made him my Guardian, we were going to go back to my family together. Only." She shrugged. "I left a letter for my family, declaring what we'd done. I don't know if that counts."

The Catresou wouldn't consider it a marriage, and the Mahyanai wouldn't care. Runajo didn't bother saying it, because they both already knew.

For the first time, Runajo truly wanted to comfort this girl.

"He would have done it if he had the chance," she said. "I can't say I ever much liked Romeo, but he would never betray a girl. He's too stupidly earnest for that." She paused. "And he tried to make *me* love him for near on five years, so it's not as if he gives up easily."

Juliet gave her a withering look. "I already knew about you."

"I hope he told you that I never did kiss him," said Runajo. "I'm really not competition."

And then Juliet was blushing again, and Runajo probably shouldn't still find that amusing, but she did.

"What did you mean," she asked, "when you said you couldn't believe your people because you were the Juliet?"

"Because justice is for things in this world," said Juliet. "Even the things that are lost forever."

"I thought your only duty was to avenge the Catresou," said Runajo.

Juliet gave her a look of infinitely patient disdain. "You don't know anything about the Juliet, do you?"

"I know they put spells on you," said Runajo, "to compel you to avenge them."

Juliet sighed. "You outsiders can't think of anything but our obedience. As if that's all we care about."

"What else is there?" asked Runajo, genuinely curious.

Juliet stared at the shelves and the glimmering scrolls. "You Sisters are renowned for your knowledge of the Ancients," she said. "Do you know they had the power of sacred words?"

"Yes," said Runajo. "That was one of their sins, presuming to know the language of the gods."

Juliet smiled crookedly. "You call it a sin, to blaspheme against the gods you don't believe in?"

Runajo felt her own mouth tugging up. "I call it a very bad idea. As proved by their destruction."

"Well," said Juliet, "that language wasn't all lost. Many of our sigils and sacred words are derived from it. But we have two words of that language preserved unchanged. One of them is on your palm. It's the word for trust. That's how we make the bond between the Juliet and the Guardian. And that's how we make the Juliet. The word for justice is written on my back. All but the final stroke."

Runajo looked up from her palm to stare at her. She didn't know whether to be thrilled or horrified: the sacred, forbidden language. Here. On her skin.

She had to know everything about it.

"And that's what makes you compelled to avenge them?" she asked.

Juliet shook her head. "No. There are other seals and spells for that. They're almost done too. The word for justice is . . . I can *feel* it. Not just as an idea in my head, something I was told or that I made up. It's like the way the sun rises, or stones fall to the ground. It's infinite and eternal and closer than my heartbeat. And when people are hurt—even people who die and are gone and become nothing in the darkness—people my family would say I should care nothing about—I can feel justice scream against it. Nobody in my family understands that. They all think justice is just for use, some kind of—of instructions on how to keep us safe and headed toward the Paths of Light. It's not. It is real and it *wants.* It wants to reach into every corner of the world, and I want to make that happen. That's what I wanted. To bring justice to the whole city, and not just my people." She drew a ragged breath and fell silent.

Oh, thought Runajo. *Her too.*

She hadn't known there was anyone else.

"You think I'm foolish," said Juliet. She was hugging herself now, her gaze shuttered, fixed on the floor.

"No," said Runajo. "No. Do you want to know why I joined the Sisters of Thorn?"

"I thought it was some sort of nonsense about wanting to spill your blood."

Runajo waved a hand. "That's part of it. But." She took a deep breath. She had never told anyone this before, because she had been sure that nobody would ever understand.

"I was a little girl," she said. "I think maybe nine years old. It was one of those spring days where the sky is bright, bright blue but the air still tastes like winter. I was sitting in my family's garden." She closed her eyes and she could see it all again. "The sun was glowing through the grass and the flowers on the trees, and there was a little gust of wind and—it was as if the skin of the world peeled back, and I could see . . . I felt like I could *almost* see the very heart of the world and it was something impossible and perfect. It was so beautiful, and I could almost see it. All I've ever wanted since is to find that thing, that infinite, perfect truth, and understand it." She grimaced. "But I was my family's only child. It was my duty to take a husband or at least a lover, and bear children to inherit. I didn't want to waste my time on that. The Sisters protected me from that fate, and they also—they know something about the nature of the world, even if they don't know everything. I wanted to learn from them."

Juliet looked up, her mouth puckered in a way that might be wry or contemptuous or affectionate. "And you didn't mind murdering to do it."

Runajo's heart didn't skip a beat. When had it become comforting, to hear Juliet call her a murderer?

"Sacrifice," she said pleasantly. "And remember that *your* destiny was killing as well."

"Did they teach you anything?" asked Juliet. "Besides their magic?"

"That's the whole point," said Runajo. "Magic only works insofar as it understands the nature of the world. When they say that everything is bought in blood, that is true. Only, I am not sure it is the only truth." She paused. "The Sisters of Thorn say there is a word that lies at the heart of the world, and that word is *inkaad*. It means . . ." Runajo struggled to sum up the concept.

"Both cost and price. 'Appropriate payment,' maybe."

"That is not quite the same as justice." Juliet clenched and released her hands. "My people would say it is *zoura*. Correct knowledge. Because it is knowledge of the correct spells that allows us to walk the Paths of Light."

"That's a cold-blooded way to view the world," said Runajo.

"And the way of the Sisters isn't?"

"Blood is hot when you spill it," said Runajo, and Juliet laughed suddenly, her head tilting back.

"Would the Mahyanai have an answer?" she asked. "For what word lies at the heart of the world? Or do they not believe in that, any more than they believe in gods?"

"We don't believe in *nothing*," Runajo said mildly. "We have our own sages. I suppose they would say it's *monyai*. It means both 'dust' and 'river.'" She paused, trying to think how to explain it to someone who had not grown up with the words of the sages, or the hundred and eight poems they had saved from the Ruining.

"The Sisters of Thorn will tell you that all things move by the blood of the gods. This is false." Runajo's voice was soft, yet it echoed among the shelves and the scrolls. "The sages of our people tell a different story. They say that everything in all the world is made of particles like motes of dust. They spin and cling and part, and we are formed of their patterns."

Runajo's throat tightened. She remembered her mother telling her this long ago, before any illness had touched their family. Before she had known what it meant for things to vanish forever.

She drew a breath and went on. "Like a river, the particles are ever-moving, ever-changing; we are the ripples in the river, that vanish in a moment and never return. But while we are here, we are like dust motes caught in the afternoon sunlight, dazzling before we fall into the darkness."

The words had been beautiful and comforting, before anyone she knew had died.

"So the sages say," she finished dully.

There was silence between them. Runajo stared at nothing and wondered how much dust floated in the air of the Sunken Library, and how much of that dust was made from bones and dried flesh.

"And you?" Juliet asked finally. "What do *you* think lies at the heart of the world?"

She couldn't believe in the nine gods and the feasts they held for the sacrificed dead. She couldn't believe that the world was nothing but dust. She definitely couldn't believe in the superstitions of the Catresou.

Buried beneath the temple of the Sisters, surrounded by revenants and ancient lore, remembering that she had sat at the very Mouth of Death and watched the souls walk in, Runajo said quietly, "I don't know."

There wasn't time to go through all the scrolls, but Runajo did the best she could. As she picked through them, trying to decide what to leave and what to take, Juliet paced back and forth by the door.

"Don't take too many," she said. "We'll have to run."

"I know," Runajo said regretfully, examining a scroll that seemed to be mostly folktales about people meeting Death herself and trying to bargain. She nearly discarded it, but she supposed there might be some useful hints related to the Ruining.

"If they're waiting for us by the door, we're dead," said Juliet. "If not, we're going to run for the shelves and climb them as fast as we can. I didn't see any of them up high, so maybe they're too stupid to work out ladders. You'll need to strip off your outer tunic."

Juliet—whom Runajo had dressed in the simple gray of a novice before they started this adventure—started to pull off her robe.

Runajo stared at her.

"I've talked to men who had to hunt revenants. It's part of my training." Juliet pulled the tunic over her head, leaving her only in her shift. "They don't see like we do; they mostly rely on sound and smell. If we drop something that smells like us near the start, it might distract them. On second thought, we should drop the shifts and wear the robes."

"Right," said Runajo.

A few minutes later, they were ready. The packs that Runajo had brought were full of scrolls and slung over their backs. Runajo held the shifts; Juliet had her swords drawn.

"See if you can open the door just a crack," Juliet said.

Runajo did. The hallway outside was empty.

Run, Juliet said silently, and they did.

There was one revenant still near the door; Juliet dispatched it instantly, and the next moment they had dropped their shifts and were swarming up ladders to the top of a bookcase.

Then there was nothing for it but to run across the tops. Runajo had never been scared of heights, but up here in the yawning emptiness of the Sunken Library, running across a surface half as wide as she was tall, knowing that if she fell, she would break her bones and then be torn to pieces—

She didn't like it. But she ran faster.

Noises from below. The revenants were on the move. Hunting them. *Hungry.*

Ahead, the bookcase they were on came to an end. There was a short gap, and then another one started up. It looked possible to jump—it would have to be if she wanted to live—and Runajo didn't let herself slow down as she approached the ledge, just flung herself into the leap, because she knew that if she hesitated, she would never be able to make herself do it.

For one moment she was flying; then she landed, hard, and went down to her knees, grabbing at the wooden surface for purchase. Her heart was pounding. She was still alive.

She thought, suddenly, of the poem Romeo had recited to Juliet, the first poem that any Mahyanai child ever learned, about how beautiful things were when they were about to die. She didn't think the poet had imagined *this*.

Juliet landed beside her and slapped her shoulder.

Up, she said, and then they were both running again—and maybe there was something beautiful in their silent, desperate race.

They crossed that bookcase. And the next. And now there were revenants following them below, waiting for them to fall or climb down.

It's not going to work, she told Juliet.

Yes it will, Juliet said, and jumped to the next bookcase. Runajo jumped after her, but this time her feet skidded and she nearly fell. Juliet caught her by the hand as she wobbled and steadied her.

They were on the last bookcase. They were nearly there.

I'll go down first, said Juliet. *You follow after.*

She didn't climb down the ladder; she jumped, and landed with her blades out. There was something terrifying in the way she fought: fast and fluid and utterly relentless.

The Catresou had made her into this.

The Catresou would use her against the Sisterhood, if they ever got the chance.

Stop hating my family and get down here, said Juliet, and Runajo clambered down the ladder. One of the revenants lunged forward, jaws snapping; Runajo ducked, and Juliet sliced its head off.

And then they ran. It felt like there was no strength left in her legs, but Runajo ran. And they were getting close to the stairs. They were nearly there, and they seemed to have outdistanced the revenants, which was strange but she wouldn't complain—

Behind them came a long, low moan.

They both looked back.

Two reapers were running toward them with long, easy strides. Their limbs were harsh white against the shadows of the library; light glinted off their shiny gray beaks and claws.

They were just like the one that Juliet had killed up in the Cloister. And they were utterly different. The one in the Cloister had been nightmarishly out of place. The two reapers running toward them now were in their own kingdom. They moved like kings, and watching them, Runajo couldn't move. She couldn't quite be afraid, either. They were going to kill her because it was their nature. She was going to die, because that was hers.

They were close enough that she could see the tiny feathers sprouting from their necks. And then she realized that they had wings: great feathered wings that were made of shadow, or perhaps only indentations in the air. The wings pumped with a slow, enormous, inevitable motion, and Runajo could only stare in helpless fascination.

That was when Juliet picked her up bodily and threw her at the base of the stairs. With a horrifying dry crunch, she landed on one of the bodies.

It felt like her mind flashed white, unwilling to accept what had happened. A moment later she was on her feet, shaking off dry flakes of—

There wasn't time to think about that.

"Juliet!" she called.

Juliet didn't answer, because she was fighting two reapers. She was fighting them because she hadn't run fast enough, because she was too busy saving Runajo. She wouldn't survive, and Runajo was never going to forgive herself.

But then Juliet sliced off the leg of one and bolted toward the stairs. They were quick—even the one that was now missing a leg and had to run on its hands and foot—but they weren't fast enough. Juliet vaulted onto the lowest step.

The reapers clawed at the air, their mouths stretched wide as they keened their love for death, and all around them the hissing of the hundreds of revenants rose up to the ceiling—

But the spells on the stairway held. The dry, withered corpses around her had not died in vain.

Juliet was bent over, gasping for breath, but after a moment she lifted her face and grinned at Runajo. It was the purest happiness she had ever seen on Juliet's face.

"That was fun," she said.

Runajo turned away. She was shaking. She felt obscurely angry at Juliet, and furious at herself.

"You nearly died," she said as she started climbing the stairs.

"You shouldn't have been so scared," said Juliet.

Runajo rolled her eyes. Her heart was still pounding against her ribs. "I know, I know, you're the fearsome Juliet. Forgive me for thinking even you might struggle against a horde of the dead."

"Actually," said Juliet, "I meant you shouldn't have been scared, because I'm already dead. And going to die again, when you turn me in."

"Of course," Runajo said faintly, and tried not to think about that for the rest of the climb up.

22

"NOW," SAID VAI. "WHAT DO you know about the Night Game?"

He had taken them into a small room off the side of the main hall. There were bright-blue designs painted on the wall, and a wooden desk at the center; Vai had perched on the edge of the desk and leaned back on his hands. The slant of his shoulders was relaxed, but his eyes never wavered from them.

Paris squared his shoulders. "First things first," he said. "What are you doing with Tybalt?"

"Me?" said Vai. "I'm done with him. Two times over."

"I mean his body," said Paris. "He needs to be buried." He was painfully aware of the scrapes he had gotten in the duel, of his humiliatingly bare face. Of the strength concealed in Vai's lazy posture. But he couldn't back down now.

"Doesn't seem like burial agrees with him," said Vai, grinning as if the desecration of the Catresou sepulcher was hilarious. To Vai, it probably was.

"Look," said Paris, "I don't know how much choice Tybalt had, getting mixed up in this. Maybe he did deserve to die twice. But he's Catresou. He's my kin. I have to see him properly buried. You have no idea what it means to us."

Vai tilted his head, examining him. Paris stared right back.

"Please," said Romeo, his voice soft and rough. "It really is important."

"My men are already burning him," said Vai, and now he wasn't smiling. "If the necromancers could steal his body once, they could do it again. And raise him again. Trust me. There is no fate that's worse."

But there was. Tybalt's name had been sealed to him by the Catresou magi, but if his body wasn't properly buried, then he would never be able to find the Paths of Light. He would keep his mind, as the nameless, gibbering shades did not, but he would be forever lost in the darkness. *That* was the worst of all fates.

Vai would never believe him. And it was too late anyway.

"I'm sorry," said Vai, and for once he didn't sound mocking at all. "Truly. I know what it means to owe a duty to your kin."

The worst thing was that Paris couldn't hate him, because he truly seemed to mean it. He just wasn't Catresou. So he couldn't really understand.

Paris looked at Romeo. *Please* was the first word he'd spoken since Tybalt died. His shoulders were slightly hunched, his hands clenched into fists. His mind was completely walled off.

Romeo couldn't have understood either. But he'd still pleaded.

"I would pay you blood money for him," said Vai, "if I thought you were civilized enough to understand it. But I can help you track down the necromancers that made him one of the living dead."

"Blood money?" Paris echoed, startled out of his horror.

"The custom of my people," said Vai, "which no one else in Viyara understands. It's very disappointing. Ever try telling the City Guard that you've paid off the family of the man you killed? They don't care at all."

Paris knew that a hundred peoples had ended up in the Lower City. He had never heard of this custom, but there was no reason to believe it didn't exist. There was also every reason to believe that Vai was mocking him.

"Do you think killing people is a joke?" he asked.

"Not a bit," said Vai, half smiling. "That's why I'm going to hunt down and destroy the necromancers. How did you know Tybalt?"

Paris thought about demanding that Vai start making sense, and gave up on the idea. He did seem genuinely willing to help them, and that was more than Paris had hoped for.

"I didn't know him," said Paris. "He was out of the Academy

before I entered. I only saw him a few times. But he was never . . . like that."

Romeo sighed and straightened. "Even when he was killing Makari, he wasn't like that. Something happened to him. Besides rising from the dead. The necromancers changed him."

"Raising him was enough," said Vai, and now his voice was grim. "No one ever told you? Necromancy can raise the souls of the dead back into their bodies. But it also makes them slaves to the ones who raised them. They cannot even think rebellion. I've seen them murder family without a second thought."

It took Paris a moment to fully realize what Vai had said.

"How often does this happen?" he asked.

Vai's mouth twisted. "Far too often. But not to anyone important enough for the City Guard to care."

He spoke the words bitterly but easily, as if he were talking about the number of beggars in the Lower City.

For a moment, Paris couldn't speak. He wasn't sure how many more of these revelations he could take. How large was this conspiracy? How much had Lord Catresou and Master Trelouno done?

How many living dead walked the streets of Viyara right now?

"Is that the Night Game?" said Romeo.

Vai spread his hands. "All right, tell me if you've heard this before. There are some people in the city who can grant your every wish, if your every wish is to have somebody brought back from the dead, and if you can bring somebody else as a sacrifice. They hold a grand party once a month, and at the end of the night, the guests turn over their sacrifices and draw lots. One lucky person gets a resurrection. The rest just get to know they helped support the Night Game for another month, and next time they may get better luck."

"We've heard . . . part of that before," said Romeo.

"But in any given month," said Paris, "there can't be *that* many people who are that desperate and that ruthless and have the means to obtain a sacrifice *and* know how to get into this party."

"And there aren't that many who want a resurrection each month," Vai went on. "A lot of people attend just for the thrill. Dancing with necromancers is apparently quite exciting."

"What was your offense against them?" asked Romeo.

"Apparently, even the donations aren't enough," said Vai. "Some previous Kings of Cats have helped pull people off the street for them. I said no. They were surprisingly slow to start the assassination attempts after that."

Paris frowned. Now that the first daze of horror was fading, he was starting to have more questions. "I can see why they'd try to kill you. But all those other people that you say they've killed—why?"

"Offhand?" Vai raised his eyebrows. "Because they're evil."

"I mean, strategically, what's the purpose?" said Paris. "However corrupt the Guard is, they don't want necromancers infesting the city. You're not the only one who's met the living dead, right? And every time they're seen, that's a risk."

As he spoke, Paris grew more confident. Because he knew about this: the nagging awareness that at any moment, with the least excuse, the City Guard might decide you were a problem. He had few memories of his mother before she died, but one of them was her telling him what to say if the Guard ever came to their door and accused them of being necromancers.

"You're not all stupid," said Vai. "They've been a lot bolder the past five years. I don't know why, unless they're experimenting. Preparing for some plan that can't be too far from accomplished." He leaned forward, lacing his fingers together. "Which makes me very interested in what you two did to earn their undead fury. If they were willing to send a man publicly known to be dead after you, they must have been furious indeed. Please tell me you did something good."

"No," Romeo said bleakly. "I did something terrible."

Wait, Paris said silently. *You can't tell him about that.*

Don't we have to? said Romeo.

We don't know anything about him! How do we know he won't sell us out to the City Guard?

He leads a gang, said Romeo. *He's probably not on speaking terms with the Guard. And do we have a choice?*

"Does it have anything to do with the marks you have on your hands, which look strangely similar to the marks worn by the Juliet and her Guardian, and the way you stare at each other silently like you're talking mind to mind?" Vai asked innocently.

They both flinched. "How could you—" Paris started, and then realized that speech had been a trap.

"I didn't, but I'm good at guessing games," said Vai, only a little smug. "And I've suspected that the Catresou were involved with the Night Game for a while. Of course I did some research."

Paris decided it was time he faced the facts. They were far past the point where it was possible to avoid risks.

"It's not all of us," he said. "It's Lord Catresou. He's working with somebody called the Master Necromancer. And he was planning to use the Juliet for . . . something."

He went on to tell Vai everything they knew. Vai listened and nodded and watched him, his dark eyes never flickering, and Paris felt uncomfortably like he was revealing more than he meant to. When Paris had finished, Vai was silent for a few moments, still watching with that terrifying directness.

"What worries me is Tybalt telling that girl they were going to be more powerful soon," said Vai. "If the stories are true, the Night Game's been running practically since the Ruining started. And all that time, they've had the power to raise the dead. What was going to change for them?"

"Juliet," said Paris. "The adjurations and the training make it possible for her to survive magic that would kill anyone else. They must have been planning to use her for some sort of spell.

That's why Tybalt told that girl it would be soon. Because Juliet was nearly ready."

"But a spell for *what*?" said Vai.

"Evil," said Romeo.

"Obviously, yes, but there is a whole garden full of evil delights they could have chosen from. We need to know which one they picked." Vai gave them a measuring look. "How do you feel about some burglary?"

23

PARIS HAD HOPED TO RETURN to the Catresou compound. With Juliet dead, there was nothing else for him to want. He hadn't imagined it very clearly, but he had vaguely thought that once he exposed Lord Catresou and vindicated the rest of the clan, perhaps he would be able go home.

He had never imagined that he might creep in disguised as a servant, with the King of Cats at his side to help him burgle Lord Catresou, and Romeo's silent voice in his mind.

"What's your friend see?" Vai asked under his breath.

Anything? Paris called silently to Romeo. He was also lookout because Paris and Vai could pass for servants in the uniforms they'd obtained—Paris because he was Catresou, Vai because sometimes they did hire help from outside the clan. But nobody would ever believe a Mahyanai was a legitimate servant.

All quiet, said Romeo, and for a moment Paris could see through his eyes: the sloping roofs of the compound, the empty paths between the buildings.

"Nothing," said Paris.

"Lovely," said Vai. "Which way?"

Paris had not often been to Lord Catresou's home, but most of the clan's houses were laid out in a similar fashion. He knew that the corridor to the left probably led to the kitchen, and a memory burst upon him: sneaking into the kitchen as a little child, sitting in a corner among the warmth and clatter. The servants were willing to let him stay if he was good, and the cook would sometimes slip him treats. She'd been a kind woman; he still remembered her smile as she coached him in the proper way to make the sign against defilement before eating.

He'd been so proud, learning to make the sign right. He knew it was part of being Catresou, part of being *good.*

He would never quite be a proper Catresou again.

He squared his shoulders. "That way," he said, pointing down the hall.

Above the door to Lord Catresou's study was a carved wooden statue of Azu, the sixth god, who governed hearths and memories, food and children. He was portrayed as a chubby man, smiling happily at those beneath him; without thinking, Paris made the sign of reverence.

Vai cocked his head. "You worship the nine gods?"

Paris bristled. "Of course we do. We just don't believe the lies you people tell about them."

The Catresou alone knew the truth: that the gods were dead, yes, but not in any obscene ritual of sacrifice. At the beginning of time, they had walked the Paths of Light to show humanity the way. And they would never for an instant accept human sacrifice as worship.

"My people don't tell lies about the nine," said Vai. He knelt and slid a piece of wire into the lock on the door to the study. "Or truths, either. We don't worship them at all."

"You can't mean you're like the Mahyanai," said Paris. One clan denying the gods was surely enough.

Vai twisted the wire, his eyebrows drawn together in concentration, the tip of his tongue peeking out of his mouth. Then there was a click, and the door swung open. He stood and smiled at Paris in triumph.

"Oh, no," he said. "My people, we save our reverence for our ancestors. I expect to have a shrine someday, with flowers and dancing girls."

Paris rolled his eyes. "The City Guard would never allow that kind of blasphemy."

"You'd be surprised how many things go on in this city that the City Guard don't know about," said Vai, and slipped into the study.

Paris followed him, and for a moment all he could see was

memories. He'd met Juliet in this room. It had been just days ago, and it felt like forever, and now she was dead.

Tears prickled at his eyes, and then he realized that they were Romeo's.

"I like the decorations," said Vai, looking around at the tapestries and carved wooden paneling. "Maybe I'll steal some for my shrine." He reached toward the plaque on the wall, where *zoura* was written in burnished letters.

Paris grabbed his hand.

"Don't," he said. "That's holy."

Vai looked at him, and there was a sudden lack of mockery in his eyes. "All right," he said quietly. "I won't."

Paris stared at him, waiting for the inevitable joke, wishing he had words to explain how much he could love his people while still trying to stop Lord Catresou.

But Vai didn't say anything.

He did wiggle his fingers, and then Paris realized he was still holding Vai's hand.

"Sorry," he muttered, letting go.

Vai just grinned and turned to look around the room. "Right. If you were an evil Catresou, where would you hide your secrets?"

"I *am* Catresou, and we're not all evil," said Paris, going straight to the desk, which was the only logical place, except that it was also an extremely obvious and stupid place, and there was a reason that he had never managed to get his things back when Meros stole and hid them. "It's just Lord Catresou."

"Evil or not, I'm impressed you're turning against him." Vai went straight to the wall. "You know, down in the Lower City, they say your clan puts spells on all their babies at birth so they'll be obedient?"

That's just the Juliet, said Romeo.

Stop eavesdropping and keep watching for guards, said Paris, rattling vainly at the locked drawer in the desk. He'd have to wait for Vai to pick it.

I can do both at once, said Romeo.

Paris sighed. "If you're stupid enough to believe that, I don't know how much use you'll be as an ally," he said, hoping Romeo heard that as well.

"I don't," said Vai. "But I do believe you're all just about that loyal. I've seen it."

"Because half the city wants us dead, so we have to stick together," said Paris. "Do you think that would make us all turn necromancers?"

"I don't know," said Vai. "If it were me, I might be tempted. I'm my family's heir, you see. It's my duty to protect us."

"By leading a gang," said Paris.

"Your family dabbles in necromancy," Vai pointed out. "Anyway, I'm not leading *a* gang; I'm taking control of all the gangs so that I can run the Lower City. You people up top are doing a terrible job."

First Romeo, now Vai. Was Paris ever going to be around people who were remotely practical?

Though the really terrifying thing about Romeo was how far he had gotten with his dreams. Maybe Paris should be scared of Vai.

There was a soft click, and Vai said, "Here we go."

Paris turned. One of the panels of the wall had swung open, revealing a steep narrow stairway that twisted down into the shadows.

"How did you find that?"

Vai shrugged. "It's what I would do. Come on, grab the lamp off that table."

They went down. The air in the stairway was cold and stale; outside the dim glow of the lamp, there was absolute darkness. Paris knew that they hadn't gone far, but it still felt like they were descending deep into the earth, and he couldn't help wildly imagining that this was a stairway down into the land of the dead, and they would never be seen again.

Then they reached the bottom. Their boots suddenly echoed when they stepped onto the stone floor, and the lights blossomed around them: little stone flowers glowing bright white, like the lights that lined the city streets.

"Your family is stranger than I thought," said Vai.

They were standing in what was clearly the laboratory of a magus. Paris had never been trained in the arts of the Catresou magi, but he knew enough to recognize the signs: the sigils painted on the floor for safety, the brass sigil-wheels for experimentation, the piles of scribbled paper on the tables.

But that wasn't what he and Vai were both staring at.

At the center of the room was a huge glass box. And inside the glass was a girl.

She looked Catresou; she had long golden curls, and her sightless, staring eyes were blue. She wore a dress of ruffled white, and she sat on a little silver chair.

For a moment, Paris thought she was an impossibly perfect statue, a doll with the most exquisite painting and wig ever made.

Then she blinked.

Paris flinched.

Vai strode forward and picked up the nearest stool.

"No!" Paris shouted.

"Do you see any problem besides a girl inside a cage?" Vai asked.

"Yes," said Paris. "Look at the upper rim of the glass."

Tiny sigils were painted in silver around the top—and while Paris had no idea what most of the sigils in the study meant, he knew these. All Catresou children could recognize a dead seal.

"Those are the signs that the magi put on coffins," he said. "It takes at least an hour to put them on. Another to take them off. Break them without ceremony and it'll probably kill you."

Vai let out his breath in a hiss. "She's living dead, isn't she?"

Paris swallowed. "Probably."

It had been bad enough knowing that Lord Catresou was working with necromancers somehow, somewhere. But the thought of a girl forced back into her corpse and held prisoner, right here beneath the floor of the Catresou compound, was absolutely sickening.

"I hate the living dead," said Vai. His voice was low and unsteady. "I really, absolutely hate them, and that's why I kill them dead again. But I can't stand people who torture them."

"Torture?" Paris echoed.

Vai gave him a weary look. "He has her locked up in his magical workshop. Do you think he just takes her out for tea and cookies?"

Paris wanted to say, *He wouldn't,* but he wasn't sure there was anything that Lord Catresou wouldn't do.

When he'd met Juliet, this girl must have been sitting in her glass coffin underneath them. Had she also been here two years ago, when he glimpsed Juliet laughing with Tybalt? When he was a child, begging for treats in the kitchen?

How much of his life had been a lie?

Vai let out his breath in a hiss. Then he looked at the girl. "We are going to come back for you," he said, "and put you to rest. I promise."

Then he turned to the desk of papers. "Come on," he said, his voice quietly vicious. "Let's ransack the place."

24

AS SOON AS THEY GOT back into the regular levels of the Cloister, Runajo opened a door in the wall and shoved Juliet through into her room. She also dropped the bag of scrolls, since there was always a chance that Miryo or somebody would demand to search her room.

She thought that she would at least have an hour to sleep. But when she finally lay down on the mat, she closed her eyes and all she could see was revenants, swarming through the library.

It wasn't like a nightmare. She didn't feel afraid. She just couldn't stop seeing them, and her body couldn't stop tensing and preparing to run. She couldn't stop wearily, hazily wondering where Juliet was and if she would be able to fight off this wave.

An hour later, she was still awake, staring into the darkness of her room and thinking of revenants. So many, swarming beneath the Cloister. She had thought that she understood how doomed they were. She had thought that she was the only one who completely understood. But it was different, now that she had seen it. Now that she knew exactly how it would look when they finally breached the stairs.

The spells won't fail that fast, she told herself, as she imagined for the hundredth time how she would dodge to the left, how she would run. *You don't need to be afraid yet.*

But she was wrong. Because less than an hour later—just as she had started to drift off—Sunjai banged on the door. When Runajo staggered up to open it, Sunjai said cheerfully, "If you killed her, you'd better hide the knife."

"What?" said Runajo. She wasn't fully awake yet; the memory of the surging revenants still flickered behind her eyes.

"Stay away from Inyaan and it's nothing to me," said Sunjai. "But I have never seen Miryo wanting so badly to blame you for something."

"Why are you here?" Runajo demanded.

Sunjai's mouth twisted in a bitter smile. "To summon you to the funeral. Lurra was inspired to offer her life."

Lurra was one of the Sisters who worked at cooking. She was not terribly bright, but Runajo had always admired that she'd managed to get from the Lower City to the Sisterhood.

She remembered how Atsaya's blood had looked, how it had

smelled, and her throat closed up.

Sunjai tilted her head. "Work on looking more distressed," she advised. "People don't mind me being cheerful because it's sweet, but when you go cold like that, they get worried."

Cold was exactly the word for how she felt—a vast, shivering cold ocean of fear. The murderer was still among them. A reaper could appear right next to her this moment, and there was no Juliet to protect her. There was only Sunjai, weak and ignorant and . . . for once, not trying to get her into trouble.

"Why do you care?" Runajo asked suspiciously.

Sunjai rolled her eyes. "We're comrades, aren't we? Get dressed. We'll be in trouble if we're late."

The funeral was the same, and so were the High Priestess's lies. Runajo knelt and prayed as obediently as she had before, and felt like a terrified fool. She'd been so wrapped up in the library, she'd briefly allowed herself to forget that there was a murderer among the Sisters.

It was not the High Priestess, for all that she was lying, because if she had done it, she wouldn't need to lie. She wouldn't need to murder, either: she could simply order any Sister to take her own life, and be obeyed.

It *might* be somebody else trying to renew the protections on the Cloister. She had considered that at first, but the more she thought about it, the more she doubted it. Reapers only appeared of their own accord once death already ruled, as in the Sunken

Library. They wouldn't walk the corridors of the Cloister until revenants did as well.

So the murderer had summoned the reaper. That meant she was somebody who wanted to master death. A necromancer.

And apparently nobody but Runajo was interested in catching her.

But how could Runajo even start? She knew nothing of how to track necromancers, and with four hundred fifty-eight Sisters—no, four hundred fifty-seven now—there was no possible way to find out who had been where at the moment the murder was committed. *If* she could even find out when and where the Sister had been killed. And if the necromancer had even been there at the time; she might have just summoned a reaper and sent it off to kill for her.

The problem was that Runajo did not know enough about necromancy.

Well. She did have a set of ancient lost texts, didn't she? Maybe one of them would have the answer.

It seemed like very long odds, but it was the only hope she had.

After the funeral, Runajo was supposed to have her normal duty weaving the walls with Sunjai and Inyaan. But instead, they were all summoned to speak with the High Priestess. Runajo went warily, wondering if Miryo *had* found a way to blame her for the second death.

"Your duties are changing," the High Priestess told them.

"We have three promising novices who are ready to start weaving. Sunjai will work in the water gardens below. Runajo will assist Vima and begin learning the laments from her. Inyaan will enter ascetic seclusion and engage in the penance that befits her rank."

It was not bad news. It might even be good news, because Vima seemed to know a lot of obscure lore. Perhaps she even knew something about reapers and necromancers. At any rate, she did not actively hate Runajo, which put her ahead of most of the Sisterhood.

It might also be an attempt to put Runajo under closer supervision, because they suspected her of being involved with the murders or being likely to talk about them. But then, Runajo was planning to be in trouble for necromancy pretty soon anyway. Not to mention that the *other* necromancer might very well kill her first.

Inyaan didn't react any more than she usually did; she stared at the wall, not deigning to look at any of them. "As the gods wish," she said, her voice soft and bored.

But Sunjai crossed her arms, lifted her chin, and said, "Why?"

"The water gardens are the life of the city; we can never have too many Sisters who know how to tend them—"

"No," said Sunjai, and this was the first time that Runajo had ever seen her interrupt someone who outranked her. "Why must

Inyaan do more penance? Surely you don't need her blood to keep the walls up."

Runajo thought of the shriveled bodies on the staircase into the library, of the reapers that were summoned into the Cloister anyway. And she imagined one appearing among them right now as they were squabbling.

"Of course they need her blood," she said. Her heart was beating faster than usual; her voice sounded just a half-note off in her ears. "They need every drop from every person in the city. And it still won't be enough."

"Do you desire eternal life?" The High Priestess raised an eyebrow at her. "Only for that is our magic not enough."

Runajo carefully remained still, her chin up. But it felt like she flinched inside her chest, because she suddenly remembered falling onto the corpse on the stairs of the Sunken Library. Paper-dry skin crunching beneath her hand. The crack of fragile bones.

She wanted to live forever. The most wretched and wicked of all sins, and she wanted it.

"No," said Runajo, because that fear might have rotted its way into the center of her heart, but she was still—she *could* still set it aside, could be stone and steel beneath her skin, if she chose. And she chose. "I do not wish it. Therefore I can admit what fate awaits our city."

"The fate of the gods," Inyaan said disdainfully, no doubt

thinking of her glorious ancestry.

"Indeed," said the High Priestess, and looked back at Sunjai. "The gods demand Inyaan's blood. As they demand yours, and mine. Need I remind you of our purpose?"

What the High Priestess ought to remind her of was that undergoing ascetic seclusion was a sure way to glory among the Sisterhood. Those who had done it were reverenced forever after. Sunjai had always been ferociously ambitious on Inyaan's behalf; it was surely all she could want for her.

But Sunjai didn't seem to think so. She said, "Our purpose or yours?"

"Enough." Inyaan's voice was still soft, but it might have been a slap across the face, for how Sunjai flinched and went silent. "The blood of the gods is in my veins," she went on—as she had a hundred times before—and the High Priestess nodded in satisfaction. "I will do as the gods command."

So that was that.

The gods had gone down into darkness, and in darkness they died one by one. So Vima mourned them not in the heart of the Cloister, where light danced around the altar of sacrifice; she mourned them in a room that they called the Navel: an almost perfect sphere of a chamber, with only a little flat circle of floor, only one little door half as high as a grown woman. Runajo and Vima had to crawl through on their hands and knees; then

Runajo curled herself against the curving cup of the round walls—it was the only way to leave enough room—while Vima lit one little candle.

A novice slid the door shut from the outside. There was no light left but the tiny spark of the candle.

Runajo did not believe in the gods. She did not mourn them. But she believed in death, and in this dark place, she felt the weight of it dragging down upon her. She knew she was just as fragile as that candle.

And then Vima began to sing.

Runajo had heard and sung many chants about the gods, but this one was different. Perhaps it was just the beauty of Vima's voice, low and sweet—but the soft, sad repetition of the tune, in the nearly complete darkness and silence, felt at once tiny and vast. For once, Runajo was not thinking about idiotic superstitions; she was listening to the story of the song.

This lament was for Nin, the goddess of truth. She had been the second of all the gods to die; when the earth had been formed by the blood of Ihom, but the sky was dark and fathomless, Nin cut out her own heart and called for Death.

Death came. Death smiled, and kissed her bloody heart, and set it in the sky as the sun. She cut out one of Nin's eyes, and made it into the moon, and scattered Nin's tears across the sky as stars. And then she took Nin by the hand and led her across the water into the land of the dead.

Ihom, her husband, waited for her there. Runajo had seen sculptures of them feasting together, king and queen of the dead gods. But the lament ended with Nin still walking into the underworld, alone except for Death.

She remembered the dead souls she had seen in her vigil, how none of them had seemed able to see each other or her, and she thought that much of the song, at least, was true.

When Vima had finished singing, she did not move to blow out the candle or open the door.

She said, "I think you will do well at mourning."

There was, in fact, nobody who could be worse, but Runajo supposed she didn't need to tell her. Vima would learn her lesson soon enough, the same way as everyone who thought Runajo might be useful.

"Will I have to scrape the flesh off the bones of a sacrifice, so I can have a pendant like yours?" asked Runajo.

Vima laughed softly. "Is that the tale the novices are telling? This is an heirloom, which you may inherit from me one day, along with my post. But that's not your true question, is it? Tell me, my brilliant, disgraceful child. What do you want to know?"

Her voice was strangely thoughtful. It almost sounded as if she cared—as if she expected more questions than *How do I hit the right notes?* As if she wanted more than mute, mindless obedience.

So Runajo obliged.

"I would very much like to know how to summon a reaper," she said.

Her body hummed with tension. She knew this was a risk—Vima could think she was the necromancer, Vima could *be* the necromancer—but Runajo was running out of time. And she was tired of being afraid. Everyone died, even the gods.

Vima laughed. "And when do you plan to do that?"

"I don't," said Runajo. "But the more I know about them, the longer I'll survive in the Sunken Library."

It was not even a lie. Runajo did mean to go back if she could, and knowing more about reapers would certainly help. It was just more important to find the murderer first.

"Oh? That's still your plan?" asked Vima. "I was beginning to wonder, since you hadn't demanded to do it for two whole days."

There was something insufferably affectionate about the way she said the words. As if Runajo was hers to indulge.

"I never go back on my plans," said Runajo. "Unless I find better ones."

"I'd advise you to go back on this one," said Vima. "They are the children of Death herself, and she does not take kindly to seeing them dragged away by force."

"You believe that story?"

"I am not a liar," said Vima, with quiet dignity. "I could not lament the gods, did I not believe in them."

Runajo couldn't help wincing. It was expedient to obey the

Sisters and make little mention of how she regarded the gods, but it was not honest.

"Comfort your skeptical heart with this," said Vima. "It can't be done by the living. Do you not know the purpose of reapers? To restore the balance of death and life, by killing all they find alive. It is the presence of death in life that summons them."

Dread seeped through Runajo's chest. "Like ghosts?" she said numbly. "Or necromancy?"

Her fingers curled as she remembered the procession of souls, the warmth of Juliet's hand in hers. Had *that* been what summoned the reapers and killed two Sisters?

"A Mahyanai girl, believing in ghosts?" said Vima. "Truly, the end of all things is upon us."

"You had me sit a vigil for ghosts," Runajo said tartly.

"It's true there are stories of lingering souls," said Vima. "But I don't know of any power that could allow them to resist being pulled into the Mouth of Death. And I don't know how long a single act of necromancy would take to draw reapers. Truly, your best hope would be a great horde of revenants. It has never been known to fail."

Runajo kept her breathing even, careful not to show how desperately relieved she was. "Then if I summoned revenants, I could summon a reaper."

"Be more direct," Vima advised. "Become a revenant, then summon the reaper yourself."

"If I could do it and keep my mind, I would consider that plan," said Runajo, and was surprised when Vima laughed softly. Usually people didn't take so kindly to the way she talked.

"*Is* it possible?" she asked after a moment passed and Vima still hadn't reprimanded her.

"I doubt it," said Vima. "Even those raised body and soul by necromancers are pitiful, ruined things. Nobody comes back whole from death. There was a time when nobody came back at all, but the world is broken now, and we are running out the cracks."

Runajo remembered dark water all around her, and the spirits of the dead striding silently past, and her fingers tightened on the edges of her sleeves.

The world was made from the blood of gods. The world was bleeding out.

"You say the world is broken," said Runajo. "Do you think, then, that someone *did* this? That the world isn't just running out?"

"It has always been running out," said Vima. "The gods do not possess infinite blood, so their power to sustain the world must someday end. But this living death that nibbles away at our world . . . I wonder if it is something else."

"What?" asked Runajo, leaning forward.

But Vima shook her head. "Whatever it is, we can do nothing but shed our blood and die like the gods."

Runajo's shoulders slumped. "That's not enough."

In the dim light, she could just see Vima's lips curving in a smile. "Do you know why I asked for you as an apprentice?"

"I didn't know you did," Runajo said cautiously, wondering what this meant.

"Oh, I demanded you. Because I looked at you and I thought, Here is a girl who will become either a blood Sister or a necromancer. You have that will, to slice the world until it suits your purposes."

Runajo felt sick. She had already become a necromancer. She would become the nearest thing to a blood Sister—one who cut open the neck of a sacrifice—when she brought Juliet to be killed.

"I thought it was honorable," she said, "to cut throats for the solemn sacrifices."

"I notice you don't deny the necromancy," said Vima, and Runajo's heart thudded painfully, but there was only amusement in her voice.

"That will to sacrifice and to do what you must," Vima went on, "it's not a bad thing. But I have seen girls with that will break themselves upon it. And you, I think, might fight so hard you would break the world."

It shouldn't be a disappointment that Runajo had yet another keeper who wanted her to sit quietly and be uselessly good, but it was.

"So I should kneel in the dark and mutter lamentations instead?" she asked bitterly.

"Since we all are dying," said Vima, "yes."

Vima kept her busy studying the lamentations all day. They never got past the first three lines—which were the same in every lament—because Vima wanted every note and syllable to be perfect before they went further. So over and over, Runajo sang the words:

"Down and deeper, lost into silence,
Beneath the light, beyond the sun—
Alone, O my beloved, where have you gone?"

The song had been beautiful when she first heard it, but by the end of the day, she was completely sick of it.

At last she was free, and that evening she slipped away to Juliet's secret room. Juliet had been quiet all day—Runajo had felt very little through the bond—but when Runajo entered the room, she was on her feet and looking restless.

"Where do we go?" she asked.

"Nowhere," said Runajo, handing her the food she had smuggled out of the dining hall. "I need to read the scrolls. Did you look at them? Before the Ruining, scholars came to the library from all over the world; they're not just meant for

Sisters." She pulled open the pack. "Wait. Can you read?"

"We are neither imbeciles nor barbarians," said Juliet. "I can read. But I have no training in the old tongues."

She was still standing, still holding the little basket of food, looking strangely awkward.

"Well, then sit down," said Runajo, and hastily added, "if you want."

She didn't notice whether Juliet did or not; she was too busy sorting through the scrolls. The first one she pulled out seemed to be damaged: the metal caps on its ends were dark and corroded, while its body shone with a dim, greenish light. When she said, "Open," the letters that appeared were flickering and blurred. She wasn't even entirely sure what language they were in.

That had been a waste of nearly dying. She had grabbed a few extra scrolls at the end without properly examining them; this must be one of them.

But the other scrolls were no better.

She had tried to take everything that mentioned death and revenants. The first scroll was nothing but laments for the dead gods—the names were different, but it used the words of Vima's chants: *Down and deeper, lost into silence.* She skimmed through it very quickly—she didn't need to know how much the Ancients loved the gods.

The next scroll recorded the trial of someone who had

attempted necromancy and raised a revenant.

So necromancy had been possible, before the Ruining. No—not quite possible, because what the would-be necromancer had raised was only a mindless, shambling corpse. The dead wife he had wanted to raise remained beyond his grasp, her soul safe in the land of the dead. Or simply not existing anymore.

Juliet's voice broke into her thoughts. "What are you waiting for?"

"Hm?" said Runajo, looking up from the glowing letters.

"You were going to turn me in, weren't you, after we survived the library?" Juliet didn't sound angry, just curious. "We're alive. What are you waiting for?"

"They'll kill me too," said Runajo. "Or at any rate, punish me, and I won't be able to read the scrolls anymore. I need some good answers first, so I can convince them to keep exploring the library. So I can save the city."

"You don't ask for much, do you?" said Juliet.

"No," Runajo said, and nearly went back to her reading, but she couldn't quite look away from Juliet's face, expressionless except for the little wrinkle where her eyebrows had pulled together.

"You're surprisingly calm about being turned in," said Runajo.

"Don't you remember?" said Juliet. "I'm already dead. And I always knew my life would be poured out for others. I don't mind seeing Romeo again."

"Why do you think you'll see him?" Runajo demanded. "I thought outsiders couldn't walk the Paths of Light."

"They can't," said Juliet. "Neither can I. So we'll have a little time together, before we fade into nothing."

Runajo stared at her. "What?"

"Only those with true names can walk the Paths of Light," Juliet said patiently.

"And only the Catresou know how to bind names to people, I know, I have *heard* your superstitions before," Runajo said impatiently. "But you're . . ." She trailed off as realization hit her. "You're the Juliet."

"Yes," said the Juliet. "I have no other name."

The Paths of Light were folly and superstition, and Runajo did not believe in them at all. It still made her utterly furious to see this girl calmly explaining how her family had stripped her of *everything*, and not resenting them for it in the least.

"So you give up your life *and* your death for them?" she said. "I thought you believed in justice."

"I give them up so I may protect." Juliet's mouth twitched up. "I thought you believed in prices."

"I believe you're stupid," Runajo said, "if you can for one moment reverence something that treats you so unjustly."

Juliet snorted. "The Paths of Light are not a *person*. They did not decide to cast me out." Then she looked Runajo in the eyes. "Confess to me and tell no lies. If there were such beauty—you don't have to believe in it, but if there *were*—you'd not despise it, would you, though you could never touch it?"

"I could never accept," said Runajo, "that there was such injustice at the heart of the world."

"Yes, you do," said Juliet. "You still agree with your sages, don't you, that your soul goes out like a candle when you die? You love that beauty you glimpsed as a child, though you don't believe it will save you."

"That's different," said Runajo. "That was . . . that is just the way of things."

"It is the way of things that I cannot walk the Paths of Light," said Juliet, "and yet I count myself more blessed than you, because at least I know they exist."

I count myself blessed that my family never tried to destroy me, thought Runajo, but she didn't say anything. She could feel Juliet's belief, passionate and overflowing, and she couldn't entirely want that to go away. It seemed to be her only consolation, and soon she would be dead.

Soon she would be dead. The thought made her feel a little dizzy. She had thought that she was used to death, because of the long years she had spent watching her mother and father die. But because they had taken so long to die, they had been dead in her heart long before they closed their eyes. Now she tried to imagine Juliet gone, and her mind stuttered. If those eyes closed, that barely leashed energy stopped—

Juliet had seen justice. She had held infinity within her mind. And yet in a moment she could die and stop existing. It made Runajo want to scream against the order of the world, and she had thought herself resigned to it years ago.

I don't need to turn her in yet, she thought. *There's still the necromancer to catch, the scrolls to read. And when I do tell the Sisters about her, maybe they will want to keep her alive for a while, so she can help more of us get down to the Sunken Library.*

Maybe. If I can convince them.

She went back to her reading.

I have to convince them.

25

"PARIS TELLS ME YOU KNOW something of the Catresou arts," said Vai to Justiran.

After escaping the Catresou compound, they had gone back to Justiran's house. Even though it was the middle of the night, Justiran was still up, carefully mixing powders in a pair of little glass vials.

"Something like that," he said mildly.

"Good." Vai dumped the satchel they had filled with Lord Catresou's notes on the table. "Tell us what he's planning."

"It's likely to take more than a few minutes," said Justiran, raising his eyebrows.

"Well, we need a few minutes to plan our next move anyway," said Vai.

"Take the evidence to the City Guard?" said Romeo.

"Not yet," said Paris.

"If this is to protect your family," said Vai, "well, I do sympathize. But we have to stop them."

"No," said Paris. "It's to get the Master Necromancer. I really don't think he's Catresou. You said that the Night Game had been running almost since the Ruining, right?" He looked at Vai, who nodded. "We've had four Juliets since then. If the Catresou were behind it this whole time, they would have already carried out whatever plot they needed *this* Juliet for. And when I overheard Lord Catresou talking, he mentioned something about a 'Little Lady' they were using as leverage."

"The girl in the cage," said Vai.

"Probably," said Paris. "*And* they said they couldn't speak to the Master Necromancer just yet. That's not someone living in the Catresou compound, taking orders from Lord Catresou. If the City Guard raid the compound, they won't find him."

"Then we get in and unmask the Master Necromancer first," said Vai. "Sounds impossible. I like it. Except it is pretty impossible. You don't happen to remember anything else extremely useful that you've omitted to mention until now?"

"Er," said Paris.

"That was actually a joke," said Vai.

"I'm not good at jokes," said Paris. He'd remembered last

night, as he was trying to fall asleep, and he'd been trying to get up the courage to say it ever since. "I think my brother goes to the Night Game."

They both looked at him. Paris was horribly aware once more of his naked face; if he couldn't wear a mask, he wished he could get *used* to it.

"My oldest brother, Meros," Paris went on, and even after everything, it still felt like a betrayal to name him in front of outsiders. "I heard him talking about the Night Game. With my other brother."

That dinner after Tybalt's funeral, when Amando had complained about being old enough to "join in your Night Games." At the time, Paris had assumed they were talking about prostitutes. But now—

"Meros Mavarinn Catresou?" said Vai. "That's excellent. I know where he lives. I can rob him."

"How will that help?" asked Paris.

"They send out invitations," said Vai. "That's the story, anyway. The invitations name a meeting place—different for every guest—and when you go to the spot and present your invitation, you're blindfolded and taken to the Night Game." He shrugged. "So they say."

"Then we go in his place," said Romeo, starting to sound excited. "Find out what they're doing and stop them."

Vai looked at Paris. "Your brother—does he need to be saved from the Game?"

Paris had steeled himself for mockery, but Vai's quiet voice sent a wave of hot shame washing over him. He should be used to knowing these things about his family by now. He wasn't.

"I don't think Meros wants to be saved," he admitted.

"Do you mean that?" asked Vai. "Because I assure you: I plan to do as much damage to the Night Game as I possibly can, and if you don't ask me to spare your brother, I won't take any pains to keep him alive."

Paris flinched. "I don't want him *dead*," he said. "I thought you meant—I don't believe he'll listen to us."

Vai nodded thoughtfully. "I'll see what I can do."

"Why ask about him in particular?" asked Paris.

"Because there's nothing that will stop me from doing my best to destroy Lord Catresou," said Vai. "Your brother, I don't hate so personally." He wrinkled his nose thoughtfully; it was a curiously young expression on him. "So. The three of us, against the Night Game."

"You'll want to hear this first," said Justiran, looking up from the table. His voice was low and grim.

"What?" asked Paris. This was going to be bad, he could tell.

"I know what they were doing with the Juliet," said Justiran. "They wanted a key to the gates of death."

Paris waited for him to say more, but Justiran only looked around at them grimly, as if he'd already given them terrible news, when it was nothing they didn't already know.

"But they're already necromancers," said Romeo, evidently thinking the same thing as Paris.

Justiran shook his head. "This is worse. You've heard legends, haven't you, of heroes who walked into the land of the dead while still alive?"

"Yes," said Paris. "But that's . . ." And he meant to say *not possible,* but then he remembered how the land of the dead had appeared around them when Romeo tried to bond with Juliet.

"I believe it was actually possible once," said Justiran. "I used to study the Ancients. Their word magic gave them incredible power. Perhaps even the power to walk into the land of the dead. Most of that knowledge was lost when their empire fell, but the Catresou spells for creating a Juliet are a remnant of that art. These papers? They describe how to adjust the adjurations written on a Juliet's back so that she will also become a key to the gates of death. So that she can bodily walk into the land of the dead."

"But why would they need to?" asked Paris. He could feel a flare of hot, murderous rage from Romeo, but it was still important to think through the situation logically. "We already know how to walk the Paths of Light."

"You are forgetting that they're evil," said Vai. "I don't think the Paths of Light are their concern."

"And they *already* know how to bring back the dead," said Paris, glaring at him.

"That's a very good question," said Justiran. "Clearly, they want to accomplish something more drastic than necromancy."

"Could they be trying to end the Ruining?" Paris asked hopefully. That would at least be an honorable motive.

"There is nothing *honorable* about destroying your own daughter," said Romeo. His fury was fading from the bond, but there was still plenty of it left to color his voice.

"I didn't say it was right," said Paris.

"I can't tell what they intended," said Justiran. "But whatever they meant, I don't think that opening the gates of death would end the Ruining. The opposite, in fact." His fingers drummed against the table. "I've long believed that the Ruining started when the first true necromancer raised somebody from the dead; that such a fundamental violation of the world's order destroyed the balance of life and death. Maybe it was once safe for the Ancients to walk into the land of the dead—though who knows what precautions they might have taken—but now? I suspect that any such attempt could destroy the separation entirely. When they came back from their journey, there might be no difference at all left between the worlds of the living and the dead."

There was a long silence. Paris tried to comprehend what

Justiran had just said. He couldn't. He tried to disbelieve it, but he couldn't do that either.

There weren't words for this depth of treachery—against what it meant to be Catresou, against everyone in the city. Against Juliet.

She had accepted becoming the Juliet, though it meant she lost all chance at the Paths of Light. And her father had planned to use her devotion for *this*.

"Then Juliet's death saved us all," said Romeo quietly. "She would have liked that, at least."

Paris swallowed, wishing that he wasn't feeling Romeo's grief prickle at his own eyes and tighten his own throat.

"They're going to make another Juliet," he said.

"We'll stop them," said Romeo, quietly certain. "We won't let them hurt one more girl that way. I swear it." He paused. "I have an idea for that, actually. You two can be the guests, and bring me along as your sacrifice. That way I'll be in a position to help free the other sacrifices when we make our escape."

Paris had thought he was used to the horrifying idiocy that came out of Romeo's mouth, but apparently he was still able to be shocked.

"No," he said, "that is absolutely—"

Then he realized that Vai was looking at Romeo with a terrifying smile.

"I think I can work with that," said Vai.

Paris didn't have any other plan to suggest, but he didn't have to like it. After Vai had left, he said furiously, "I cannot believe you would propose such a plan."

Romeo only smiled. "You've been telling me and thinking at me since we met that I was an idiot," he said. "*I* can't believe this would surprise you."

Actually, he had a point. Using himself as bait for human sacrifice to get them into the Night Game was entirely typical of Romeo.

"I thought you'd stopped trying to get yourself killed," said Paris. He remembered how hollow-eyed Romeo had been at first—how every touch of his mind had *ached* with grief. He had changed so much over the last few days. Still sad, but also alive.

"I'm not trying to get myself killed," said Romeo. "I'm trying to avenge Juliet. And save people from these necromancers."

"If you meant that," said Paris, "you wouldn't have proposed such a foolish plan."

"It's a *good* plan," said Romeo. "Vai thinks so too, and he's taken over half the gangs in the Lower City, so he should know something about strategy."

"He's probably lying about that," said Paris bitterly.

"It's a good plan," Romeo repeated. "We ought to do it. And *I* ought to be the bait because—" He cut himself off, but they both heard the words that he thought: *Because I'm disposable.*

"You see?" said Paris. "*That* is why you are completely useless."

At that, Romeo turned and met his eyes. "I'm not being useless," he said. "And I'm not trying to die, either. I'm being realistic."

"No," said Paris, "you just think it would be poetic to die like Juliet. Without even a thought for the people you would leave behind."

"Because there's nobody!" Romeo shouted, flinging his hands up in the air and sending a wave of frustration through the bond. "Do I need to make it any clearer? Juliet is dead. Makari is dead. Runajo never needed me. Nobody will miss me when I die."

I would, thought Paris, and then slammed the wall between their minds.

But that just made it worse, because once he wasn't drowning in Romeo's frustration, he was able to imagine Romeo being dead. And it felt awful. Worse than when he'd thought he would lose his duel in front of Father and be sent to the City Guard.

Romeo was foolish and ridiculous and a Mahyanai. He had killed Tybalt and helped get the Juliet killed.

And somehow, without Paris noticing it, he had become a friend. The only friend that Paris had ever had.

Romeo didn't seem to have noticed anything; he went right on ranting. "Not to mention that I killed *your cousin* and will probably be executed as soon as the Guard catches me. Of course I'm disposable. But that's not even why I want to do this. It's for Juliet's sake. Not because I miss her. Because I want, just once, to do something that would make her proud."

He paused, and though Paris had blocked off his emotions, he could still see the raw vulnerability in Romeo's face.

"I'm not like you," Romeo said quietly. "I never cared about my clan. All my life, I never cared about anyone except Makari and Runajo. Then I met Juliet, and I cared about her more than anything. And she cared about *everyone,* all of the city, even though none of them cared the least bit about her." He paused. "I don't think she ever realized just how selfish I was. I'm not sure she could have loved me if she had. But that's why I have to do this. For Juliet, and for her city, and so I can be a little worthy of her before I die."

"Because it's correct," Paris said quietly.

"Yes," said Romeo.

"That is not dishonorable," said Paris. "That is . . . not unlike *zoura.*"

He remembered sitting with Juliet in the cool silence of the sepulcher. It seemed he could never resist caring about people who cared about *zoura*.

Maybe that wasn't entirely a bad thing.

26

FOR THE NEXT TWO DAYS, Runajo studied the laments with Vima and studied the scrolls with Juliet. It was curiously peaceful, except when she remembered the revenants beneath their feet and the necromancer somewhere within their walls.

She remembered often.

But Vima was one of the less insufferable people who had ever been put in charge of her. And Juliet was surprisingly . . . Runajo honestly didn't hate Juliet. It was rather strange.

On the third day, Sunjai was waiting outside her door when she got up.

"You're going to go see Inyaan," she said, and for once she wasn't smiling.

"Why?" asked Runajo.

"They won't let me see her because I am too attached and

might *disturb her meditations.*" Sunjai rolled her eyes as if it were a stupid joke, but her voice was quick and tense. "They will let you."

"But why should I go see her?" asked Runajo.

"I need to know how she's doing," said Sunjai. "You need me not to slander you to the Sisters." Then she paused, looking suddenly more unsure than Runajo had ever seen her. "Besides, we're comrades, aren't we?"

The fact that they had sat in a room weaving the city walls and hating each other meant precisely nothing, except that they were all very good at weaving, and they all hated each other. Runajo nearly said that. But she remembered Sunjai warning her about Miryo, and the matter-of-fact way she had said then, *We're comrades.*

If Sunjai had really meant that, she was a fool.

"We are nothing to each other," said Runajo—and why did Sunjai dimple at that? "But I will look in on her if you leave me alone afterward."

She thought about sneaking in during the middle of the night, but in the end it simply seemed easier to tell Vima—who still, bafflingly, liked her—that she wanted to see Inyaan, and Vima arranged for her to bring Inyaan's daily flask of bloodwine.

Despite the name, bloodwine was not made with blood, nor was it red—it was a clear liquid fermented from a cactus whose thorns were traditionally used in penance. Regular bloodwine was the favored drink of the Old Viyaran nobility, but in the Cloister, bloodwine was brewed with special herbs and drugs. It speeded healing and gave strength to withstand blood loss; it could also dull pain. It was used mostly by Sisters who were very old, or very new and still adapting to heavy penance.

Inyaan's daily portion was insultingly large. Somebody did not think her strong enough.

There were special rooms set aside for ascetic seclusion; their white walls were painted with twisted red patterns of thorns. Inyaan sat cross-legged on the floor, her back to the wall, her hands resting in her lap. Six slender white tubes grew out of the wall, and three bit into each of her arms. Where they plunged into the skin, they blushed dark red; farther away, they faded to white veined with pink, and then to pure white.

Her eyes were screwed shut. Silently, between deep breaths, she was mouthing words to herself.

Runajo remembered her own penance—the awful, unnatural horror of living stone jammed into her skin—and Sunjai's worry seemed a little less absurd.

But this was the Cloister. They were the Sisters of Thorn. Inyaan had known that when she came, and if she couldn't bear it, that was her own problem.

"I brought your bloodwine," said Runajo. "And Sunjai wants to know how your glorious seclusion is going. You'll surely be famous among the novices for this."

She wouldn't be so famous if the amount of bloodwine she needed got out. All the Sisters loved to boast of how much penance they could take without drinking it.

Inyaan opened her eyes and briefly glowered at her; then she looked at the floor.

"You're as friendly as ever," said Runajo. "I'll pour for you."

The little red cup sat next to Inyaan on the floor; Runajo poured the bloodwine and held it out to her.

No movement.

"Nothing will ever make me like you, so you don't need to try to impress me by looking strong."

Inyaan lifted her head. "You," she said venomously. "You're like my brother."

Like the Exalted, ruler of Viyara and descendant of the gods? Inyaan's insults needed work. Unless she meant that Runajo shirked all her duties.

"The point is, I'm not a cup holder," said Runajo. "Do you want it or not?"

Inyaan let out a heavy breath and looked away from her again.

"Enjoy your seclusion, then." She set down the cup and rose.

"Don't leave me," Inyaan whispered suddenly, desperately. "Please."

Runajo stared at her. "You don't even like me."

"But you'll stop me," said Inyaan. "Won't you? If I try to kill myself. Like the others." Her golden eyes were wide with fear. "Please stop me."

It felt like the floor flipping over to leave her hanging upside down. Runajo had never considered what the other novices might be thinking of the deaths. Inyaan had no idea the Sisters had been murdered, that there might be a necromancer at work. She only knew that two Sisters had killed themselves without warning, and the High Priestess did not want anyone asking questions.

What could she think, except that some strange power was forcing them?

"I know I'm a coward," Inyaan muttered at the floor. "But I don't want to die."

"Then you shouldn't have come to the Cloister," said Runajo. "Don't they tell you royal children what we do here?"

Inyaan started laughing. Choking, nearly soundless laughs that were almost sobs.

"We know," she gasped. "We *are*."

The pain in her voice was making Runajo's skin crawl. She didn't want to see this. She didn't want to *know* this. Inyaan wasn't supposed to be this gasping, helpless girl; she was haughty and composed and never afraid. She was too busy despising them all as beneath her, too . . . silent and refusing to meet their eyes.

For the second time in as many minutes, Runajo felt like the ground was sliding out from under her. What if she had always been wrong about Inyaan? What if her silences had been fear instead of disdain?

"We have the blood of the gods. We have to shed it *every* day." Inyaan's mouth twisted. "I couldn't bear it. I cried every time. So I ran away to the Cloister, where you only have to bleed when you're assigned." She took a shuddering breath that was almost a sob. "My brother . . . thought seclusion would be amusing. He's going to keep me here till I die."

"You think the Exalted arranged this for you?" said Runajo. She could imagine the Exalted was that cruel—she'd heard enough terrible stories about him—but she couldn't believe he would take that much trouble.

Inyaan's mouth twisted. "You really think the people outside don't control us?"

There were tears on her cheeks. Runajo knew that she was supposed to feel compassion, but all she felt was a sense of stomach-churning revulsion. She had thought, when she entered the Sisterhood, that at least she would escape people weeping over things.

"You aren't going to kill yourself," she said. "Atsaya was murdered. I saw the body. Tell anyone I told you and I'll slit your throat. Try to stop being a coward."

Her hand shook as she whirled and left.

She found Sunjai in the water gardens. They were vast: the lower half of the city spire was honeycombed with halls where lamps glowed ceaselessly with the same white-gold light as the sun. Beneath the lamps, corn and rice, tomatoes and carrots, peas and strawberries, bamboo and flax—and a hundred plants more—grew in giant glass vats of water. Beneath their roots swam shoals of fish, nibbling at algae, living and breeding and dying, food for the plants and food for the people.

It was an elegant arrangement, all things eating each other. Like Viyara in miniature.

Sunjai was kneeling, hands pressed against the glass walls of a vat, blood smeared between her fingers as she adjusted the magic governing the water. When she heard Runajo approach, she dropped her hands and stood.

"Well?" she asked grimly. "How is she?"

"Weeping," said Runajo. "Blaming her brother." The words jangled and scrambled out of her mouth. "I don't think you should go see her; you might stop adoring her, if you saw her act so pathetic. Though she does think she's been sent to seclusion to die, so maybe we can excuse her a little."

There was a sharp crack as Sunjai slapped her face.

"How could you," she said.

It wasn't as hard as she'd hit Runajo in their first week together. There was no reason for the cold feeling behind Runajo's ribs. It was not as if they had ever been friends.

"I went to see her," said Runajo. "I told you the truth about her. Was there something else you wanted?"

She knew that she shouldn't be saying these things, but she couldn't seem to stop herself. It felt like the only way to stop Inyaan's horrible weeping from crawling under her skin and infecting her.

"Did you expect me to care about her?" she asked.

"Yes," said Sunjai. "We are comrades. We weave together. It has always been the three of us—"

"You nearly broke my nose because I didn't worship her enough the first week," said Runajo.

"You were bullying her," said Sunjai.

Runajo remembered the fear in Inyaan's face—if it had always been there, if those lowered eyes and mumbled words had never been disdain—

If she had, all this time, been horribly cruel.

"And then you changed," said Sunjai. "When you started being kinder, I thought you changed. So I thought we could be friends."

Changed? Runajo had just decided it wasn't worth the trouble to say what she thought of them. How could Sunjai have been stupid enough to mistake that for friendship, and why was that thought like trying to swallow acid?

"Why do you care about her?" asked Runajo. "She's nothing."

"She is my friend," said Sunjai. "If you had a heart, you'd

understand." She shrugged. "But I suppose you don't. Good-bye."

And then she walked away, without looking back.

Her face was sticky with blood from the hand Sunjai had used to slap her.

"Why do you hate her?" asked Juliet that evening, when Runajo came into her room to read the scrolls.

"Who?" asked Runajo.

"I don't know her name," said Juliet. "But I caught a glimpse. A girl tied up and bled like an animal for slaughter."

"It is an *honor* and she should feel it." Runajo's voice was icy. "Besides, she's a murdering Sister of Thorn. Shouldn't you want her dead?"

Juliet was silent.

"Her name is Inyaan," said Runajo. "She's always hated me. Maybe. I've always hated her, definitely. She's in ascetic seclusion, and Sunjai is furious that I didn't weep for her. Don't feel that angry. You wouldn't have wept for her either."

"No," said Juliet. "But Romeo would have wept for her. He even wept for me."

"Romeo was a fool," said Runajo. "And it doesn't matter. I have no tears in me. I didn't weep for my own mother or father. You think I'd care about this girl enough to cry?"

"I think Romeo was better than any of us," said Juliet. "He would care about anyone. Mahyanai, Catresou, Old Viyaran, it didn't matter. He wept for me. He smiled for me. He thought I should have a name. You, who have always had one, cannot understand what that meant."

And she was right. Runajo couldn't understand it. But she could imagine a little of it, because she had spent years practically nameless in her own home, watching her mother and father cling to each other—watching her mother long for death—knowing that she was nothing more than an afterthought to either of them. A trinket, kept to prove that their love had been fruitful.

"If you have felt that way," said Juliet, "how can you despise her?"

"I still don't understand why you have suddenly decided that we don't all deserve death and suffering," said Runajo. "How recently did you tell me that we lived in a charnel house?"

Through the bond, she felt something like a flinch from Juliet. Then there was silence, and the sense of a wall between them.

After several moments, Juliet said quietly, "I do not—perhaps—wish to see you dead."

"That's boring and inconstant," said Runajo. "If we deserve death, then wish us dead. Don't indulge in half measures and wish us alive to keep on killing."

And then she did feel something from Juliet: pure, righteous fury.

"You don't understand," said Juliet. "You cannot possibly understand. All of us Catresou, we know from birth that the rest of you despise us. You prove it to us every day. You tolerate us—you have need of our blood—but you despise us. But Romeo did not. Romeo loved me, and he loved even what was Catresou in me, for all that he neither believed nor understood it, and I cannot—I loved that in him. I find I cannot dishonor it."

"Are you saying that you don't want me dead?"

There was a silence between them. And then, very softly, Juliet said, "Yes."

It felt like there was no air left in her lungs. The same revulsion she'd felt toward Inyaan was curdling in her stomach. But Runajo didn't look away from Juliet. She looked right into her eyes and said, slowly and deliberately, "I'm going to turn you over to be killed. Because *I* made a mistake and dragged you back from death. You know that, don't you?"

Juliet looked straight back at her, like a Sister of Thorn facing the final knife.

"Yes," she said.

And then Runajo had to look away. "I don't mourn," she said quietly. "I don't often feel pity. I don't see the point. Everyone dies anyway. People delude themselves that they'll live forever—they say they are mortal, but they still weep when they die, when they lose somebody close, and it makes no sense. They already knew. I've always known, so why can't they understand it?"

Without looking, she picked up another scroll. Her fingers tightened on the metal caps at either end.

"I know I should be kinder," she said. "We're all dead, all dying. The whole world is dying. What's the point?"

"What is not eternal is supposed to be nothing to me," said Juliet. "But I thought your people were supposed to find beauty in transience."

Runajo laughed softly. "You'll be very surprised to hear I am not a good Mahyanai."

If she were a good Mahyanai, she would not mind that the world was dying. She would find it sad, and she would contemplate its fleeting beauty, and she would prepare herself to face the end with calm stoicism.

But she was the worst of all Mahyanai. She wanted to live, and she wanted the world to live, and she was furious that the world was dying.

Death did not care. That was the first lesson everyone ever learned. Maybe not Romeo—he'd always lived a charmed life—but Runajo knew it. Juliet knew it. Everyone who cared to look over the walls of Viyara, across the water, knew it.

The world was dying, and death did not care who mourned.

All the world is dying, she thought, and the scroll was warm in her hands.

No: it was hot, almost too hot to touch. Runajo looked down, and saw that she was holding the corroded, damaged scroll. But now the glass tube glowed with a brilliant light, and the corroded metal caps hummed in her hands. As she watched, the glowing letters appeared in the air. They flickered and twisted—and they changed. The unreadable symbols that she had seen before rewrote themselves into perfectly comprehensible text.

If you can see this, then you have thought that the world is dying, and you have believed it. You have known it.

You live in the same cataclysm that we do.

I presume much, by writing this: That we will succeed. That there will be a world and generations after us. That someone in those future generations will sin as we did. (That last is not presumption; it is fact.)

My name is yn-Iacha Ra, servant to the Imperial Princess ketu-Indaratt Ai. I have seen the dead rise and walk. I have seen the white fog of death rise out of the earth, and I know that Death herself is angry at us.

Ketu-Indaratt Ai means to offer herself as a blood sacrifice when the moon is new. To flay the skin from her graceful feet and dance before the Mouth of Death. She will cripple herself to save this last remnant of our people, and yet we five of her handmaids fear it will not be adequate payment. So we have made our compact: to walk into the land of the dead first, and bargain with Death herself.

We have blasphemed by writing such sacred words upon

our skin as should open the gates of death. Four have gone, and nothing has changed.

I remain. Tonight I walk into death; this evening I write down a record, for any who come after us.

Our Emperor sought to live forever. Through unspeakable arts, he found the sacred word that means Life, and he wrote it on his body.

The world changed. The dead crawled forth. And we, who never sinned against Death, must pay the price.

Know this, O future generations: Death has a face. Death has a voice. Death will parley with those who unlock the gate, pass the reapers, and come to meet her.

Death will always win.

And yet we face her, one by one, and hope.

Then a new hand began writing:

I was once ketu-Indaratt Ai. I was once princess of an empire. Now I have lost my kingdom and renounced my name, for my father sinned, and everyone has paid, last of all my beloved handmaids.

I add my words to testify: Iacha succeeded. She bargained with Death and made an end to the ruination of our world. For my part, I have sworn to remain here forever, guarding the Mouth of Death. In friendly recompense, Death has given me Iacha's dead body back again. She lay still in my arms as I mourned her, and so I know the curse is ended.

Iacha believed that someday, our descendants might sin as we have sinned, and need the same recourse. Yet the last scribe who knew the sacred words is dead; that lore is lost. Therefore I have carved Iacha's breastbone into a key, and will preserve it for future generations. Perhaps this bone that walked into the kingdom of death and returned will be enough.

"It happened before," Runajo whispered.

Her whole body felt numb. This flicker behind her ribs, it wasn't joy—it was something even more elemental. Fire. Ice. Light. (Hope.)

She had heard the story of how Viyara was founded from the Sisters—how the last princess of the Ancients had gone to bargain with Death—and she had considered it a myth. In three thousand years, how much might be forgotten?

Now she knew. They had remembered the fall of the Ancients, but they had forgotten how it happened, that the world had been dying just as it was now. They had forgotten how the world had been saved.

By speaking with Death.

It didn't seem possible. Death was not a person, was not somebody with a face and a voice and the ability to strike bargains. Runajo had always believed that. And yet it didn't seem possible for the scroll to be a trick—who would write a lie that could only be read after a disaster that nobody had yet imagined?

Runajo had not come this far to ignore any chance at saving the world. If she had to question and then change everything she believed, she could bear it. She was brave enough.

The world can be saved, she thought, and didn't feel a thing except the terrible lightness in her chest.

"It happened before," she said, meeting Juliet's eyes. "Look. There's even a picture of the key they made after."

It shimmered in the air before her: a bone ring with six bone strips radiating out of it. Vima's heirloom. She could hardly believe it had been so close all along, but her heart was pounding with hope.

Runajo pushed the scroll at Juliet; the other girl's eyes flickered back and forth as she read it. "You think this is real?" she asked when she had finished.

"Maybe," said Runajo. "If it is, it changes everything. That key in the picture? It's Vima's pendant. It's right here in the Cloister. We have to tell her."

And then she went still, the hope turning to cold sickness. It was a risk for Runajo. For Juliet, it was a certainty.

Juliet was dead. Therefore she had to die. And Runajo was a necromancer, and therefore she probably had to die as well, but there was at least a little chance she might be spared. It was terrifying, but it was not the same.

We live as those already dead, said Juliet silently.

"How can you say that?" Runajo's didn't mean for her voice to be so soft and harsh, but she couldn't seem to help it. "How can you *say* that?"

Dead was dead was dead. She should be able to bear the thought. She shouldn't be afraid.

"I've been preparing to die for a lot longer than you," said Juliet.

Runajo clenched her teeth and admitted it: she was afraid for Juliet to die. Maybe even more than she feared her own death.

If she couldn't stop being afraid, she could at least stop being a coward.

She stood abruptly. "Enough," she said. "We're going."

Juliet stood in one fluid movement. She said, "You forgot to make it an order."

Runajo glared at her.

Juliet smiled back at her, strangely gentle. And then—even more strangely—she reached forward and smoothed down Runajo's hair.

Runajo allowed the touch. Allowed herself to look at the smile. Allowed herself to take a slow, steady breath.

Then she picked up the scroll and marched out of the room.

Thus with a Kiss

WHEN SHE HEARS THE KNOCK at her window, she realizes that she has been waiting for him.

In an instant she has bolted her door; in another, she has tied the mask back on her face. Then she draws her sword and opens the casement.

He is clinging to the balcony outside; he would surely have been caught and killed already, if not for the tree that grows so close to her window. There was a brief rainstorm after the revelry ended, and his hair clings to his pale forehead in damp, dark strands.

He is startled when she holds the sword to his neck, and she shivers as if she is startled too. When she looks at his dark eyes, nothing seems sure.

"You dance very well," she tells him. "But you are my enemy."

"Lady," he says, "I am only a poor pilgrim, like those who once walked to this city barefoot and bleeding from the ends of the earth to fulfill their vows."

She can't stop the smile from tugging at her mouth. "Your people have always despised the gods, and mine despised Viyara. That is a very poor argument for me to let you live."

"If you hate the pilgrims who vowed themselves to Viyara," he says earnestly, "then corrupt me from my purpose, and make me yours."

"You," she tells him, "are utterly a fool. You know who I am. Why did you come?"

"Because," he says, "I know who you are."

"Better than my father, who gave me this sword?"

"Yes," he says.

The truth is, she feels that she knows him too, and when she looks at him, she feels as if she has a true name.

"Tell me what you know of me," she says, "that my own father doesn't."

He grins, for all the world as if there were not a sword at his neck. "I know you will not instantly strike down an enemy at your window."

"You did not say, 'will not eventually,'" she says.

"That part," he admits, "I have yet to discover."

And what sort of traitor is she, that she nearly laughs with him so easily? But she pushes away the impulse.

"I cannot let you live," she tells him. "You have trespassed on our home."

"Is that your wish?" he asks. "To kill me?"

"Yes," she tells him. "I have no purpose but defending my family, and no dream but protecting my city."

The words slip out easily into the quiet night: the dream she has not yet dared tell to anyone in her family. That someday she might protect the whole city and life within it, not just the lives of her clan.

His eyes widen slightly: he understands what she has said, that there is a piece of her heart that is not entirely given over to her duty. But he doesn't doubt or mock her. He looks up at her, earnest and unafraid, and asks, "Am I not part of your city?"

"Yes," she whispers, and she lowers the sword.

In an instant, he has swung himself over the railing of the balcony, and they are standing together with no bars between them, only a breath of air.

"So you are now my pilgrim," she says. "Did you come with a petition?"

"Yes," he says. "Lady, may I see your face?"

"I am Catresou," she says. "I am the most sacred of all the Catresou, even more than my father."

"Yes," he says.

"Then why do you even dare to ask?"

"I am going to live and die for you," he tells her. "I would like to know your face."

"You will certainly *die,* at any rate."

"And for the past three hours I have lived, so my prophecy is true already."

She does laugh then; and with a twist of fear in her stomach, she realizes that she is going to say yes.

"You cannot tell anyone," she says.

"How could I dare to boast of it," he says, "when you have seen my face as well?"

She can feel her pulse in her fingertips as she lifts away the mask. And then they are face-to-face, and she is defenseless, and she should be ashamed that she has shown so much trust to an enemy.

But she is not ashamed. She is incredulous and afraid and delighted, and unashamed.

Slowly, he reaches forward. She does not draw back, and very gently, his fingertips touch her face. They slide along the line of her cheek and trace the curve of her ear. She thinks he is going to kiss her, but he only looks at her as if he can drink her up with his eyes. His fingertips brush against her neck and draw away. The breath stutters in her throat.

All her life, she has been reverenced and alone. Even when she takes off her mask—before Tybalt, before her father—she is still the sword of the Catresou.

Here and now, she is only a girl. Here and now, she is not alone.

She is the one who leans forward. She is the one who presses her lips to his.

The next instant, somebody inside the house knocks at her door. "Go," she whispers, and he vanishes into the night. She is alone, and her heart is beating very fast and her naked face is blushing, and she will never be the same again.

27

"WE'RE GOING STRAIGHT TO VIMA," said Runajo. "She has the key, and she'll listen for at least a little while before she orders us both killed."

They were walking down the halls of the Cloister together. Runajo's heart was beating very quickly. This was it. This was the moment when everything she'd done, everything she'd fought for—this was when it all became worth it.

If they could convince Vima to listen. If the scroll was telling the truth.

If.

They were almost to the door of Vima's quarters when they heard the scream.

It came from inside.

Runajo's hands slammed on the door, but it wouldn't respond. It was locked.

"Vima!" she shouted. Desperately, she wrenched at the spells, trying to release them. She hadn't thought that she cared about anyone, but now that she knew Vima was in danger, could *hear* her in pain, all she could feel was panic and *no, no, no.*

With shaking hands, she sliced her arm, smeared blood on the door, and tried again. Finally it gave way. Runajo flung herself inside—

She was too late.

Vima lay glassy-eyed and still on the floor. A reaper crouched over her body, using her blood to draw the same spiral pattern that Runajo had seen painted around Atsaya.

Juliet made a choked noise, and Runajo gasped for breath as well, because she could feel it too: the terrifyingly ponderous weight of a great magic, rolling toward them like an enormous and inevitable wheel.

The other Sisters had all been blood sacrifices.

Now the magic was complete.

The reaper hissed, and shivered, and then—it was as if it remembered that it was meant to destroy all human life. It sprang toward them, and Juliet launched herself at it with a yell.

No, Runajo thought numbly. *The reaper didn't remember. It was released.*

Reapers did not reason. They did not work necromancy and

they did not hesitate in killing anyone around them. If this one did . . . someone had commanded it.

Light and shadow swirled in the air over Vima's body.

Whatever she had been killed for, it was happening now.

Juliet and the reaper were still battling. Runajo knelt by Vima's body, wondering if smearing the lines of blood would stop whatever was happening.

Then she saw what had fallen on the ground by Vima's hand: the bone pendant that was the key to death. The chain was broken. Vima had torn it off her neck—why? What had she known?

Runajo half saw, half sensed Juliet ripping the reaper's head off. At the same moment, the air shivered around her. She looked up and saw the tangle of light and shadow go still. Then the light flared, so bright and sudden that it was like a punch to the face.

She thought she had fallen over, but she couldn't quite feel her body. The only clear sensation was the cold air in her throat as she panted for breath, driven by a panic that was half hers, half Juliet's. Because neither of them could move.

She couldn't see right. Everything was too light or else too dark for her to make out the details. This much she could see: a gap opened up in the air. A man stepped out. Her vision was too blurry to make out his face, but she could tell he had pale skin and dark hair.

He leaned over. He must be picking up the key. Runajo tried to reach for it, but she couldn't do more than flop her hand. He chuckled—a soft, dry sound—and her heart spasmed. She felt Juliet trying desperately to move. They were both helpless. They were going to die.

Then she heard his footsteps as he went to the door, stepped through, and walked away down the corridor.

A necromancer. In the Cloister.

Runajo tried to sit up. It felt like her body was loose and kept sliding out of place. Her thoughts kept sliding, too—where was Juliet? What had happened here?

A necromancer.

More than that. The unholy *rip* in the world. It felt like death. The necromancer had himself been dead, she was sure of it, and he had commanded the reaper to make the sacrifices that brought him back.

It is the presence of death in life that summons them, Vima had told her about reapers.

Was this what happened, if a soul somehow resisted the pull into the Mouth of Death? Then why didn't Juliet have the power to call forth reapers?

Runajo managed to sit up. Her head had started throbbing.

"What is this?" demanded the High Priestess from the doorway.

So here she was, back in the Hall of Judgment, facing a circle of priestesses.

Again? said Juliet. *You do not have the wisest habits.*

At least I haven't died yet, said Runajo.

They had told the truth. All the truth, because Runajo needed the Sisterhood to know exactly what they were supposed to do now, and Juliet would never lie.

So far, the priestesses had refused to believe that a ghost used Vima's blood to form himself a body and slip out of the temple. They admitted that Vima's pendant was ancient, but proclaimed no knowledge whatsoever of any key, and they swore that the scroll would not show them anything but blurred, corrupted text. That the fall of the Ancients had been a similar cataclysm they dismissed as Runajo's wild fantasy.

They did believe that there was a reaper, and that Juliet had once died and therefore must die again. They blamed her presence for its spawning, which Runajo had to admit was fairly logical.

"Mahyanai Runajo," the High Priestess said finally, "you have shown devotion to our city, but also extraordinary pride and blasphemy."

Don't tell me you ever expected anything different, Runajo thought, and heard the quick huff that was Juliet's replacement for a laugh.

"I am ready to pay for my sins," said Runajo out loud.

"Good," said the High Priestess. "You will sacrifice the Juliet, here and now, in recompense for the necromancy you both have perpetrated. In time and with sufficient penance, you may be counted one of us again, but I do not guarantee it."

Runajo heard the words with a sense of absolute calm. She had known this would happen. It was not a surprise.

Still she said, "Could she not be useful to us for a little while—"

"If you were not a child," said the High Priestess, her voice low and harsh with an anger that Runajo had never heard before, "you would know that there is no such thing as 'a little while' when it comes to cheating death. I myself have slit the throats of six necromancers, and all of them desired only *a little while* with their beloved dead. Count yourself lucky, *child,* that I believe you foolish and naive."

Runajo's heart was beating fast; her stomach and her fingertips were tingling. Her breath was also coming quickly, but that was something she could control, and did. Slowly she breathed in and out. Then she said, quite calmly, "So there are necromancers at large after all? Is lying the duty of every Sister, or just the High Priestess?"

"There are no necromancers at large because we kill them all," said the High Priestess. "And my duty includes preventing panic. What do you consider your duty, besides obeying your every whim?"

"Telling the truth," said Runajo. "So believe me when I say I am a Sister of Thorn, and I will obey."

She had known it would come to this. And it was right. Juliet's life could only throw the world more out of balance—and if Runajo was obedient, and lived, she might still be able to convince the Sisterhood of the truth.

Her mind was filled with the terrible absence of surprise from Juliet.

I also knew that it would come to this, said Juliet. *When he was a killer, and yet I took him to my bed, I knew that I would die for it.*

Oh, now you can bear to speak of love without blushing? asked Runajo.

I am almost dead, said Juliet, and there was a peculiar, heart-breaking triumph in her thoughts. *I have no more need of shame.*

Somebody had taken her hand. It was Miryo, and she wrapped Runajo's fingers around the hilt of a sacrificial dagger.

"You must do it now," said Miryo. Her voice was almost gentle.

We live as those already dead, thought Runajo. *There is no time to waste.*

She turned. She laid a hand on the side of Juliet's neck. Fitted her thumb to the side of her jaw. She could feel the swift heart-beat beneath the warm skin.

The knife was razor sharp. It would slide in very easily right below Juliet's ear, where the tip of Runajo's thumb rested now. There would be one quick, easy slice; after the first blood had sprayed across Runajo, Juliet would sink to the floor, where her heart would pump out the rest of her blood in less than a minute. Runajo could see it all in her head, and her stomach twisted as she realized that Juliet had probably seen it too.

I have watched the Great Offering every year, said Juliet. *I am not ignorant of how this works. You'll get a better angle standing behind me.*

You cannot be this calm about it, said Runajo.

Juliet's face was set like stone, but her silent voice trembled with laughter. *I promise you, I can. After all, I am going to find my husband, before he fades away entirely. You're the one who will still have problems to solve.*

She wasn't lying. She was perfectly happy to die, to leave Runajo alone and covered in her blood.

Runajo's body felt like it had turned to ice and stone, but her mind was whirling faster than it had ever gone before.

She had always known she could sacrifice anything. That was still true. But Runajo had excelled in the sacred mathematics. She knew how much blood was in Juliet's body; she knew the different ways of shedding it, and exactly how much power that would give the city. She could put a price on her life.

Inkaad. Cost and price. The Sisters said that was the heart of the world. That Juliet, in her essence, was no more than blood and breath and bone, and the power to be gained therefrom.

But Juliet had hungered after justice, something infinite and eternal, and that meant she had *thought* of it. To think of something was to hold it in your mind, and to hold something infinite, you must be in some way infinite yourself.

And that meant there was no appropriate price. To treat Juliet as something bought and sold and bargained for—

That was wrong. That was *obscene.*

She could not kill this girl who had infinity behind her eyes, and that meant she could not kill anyone, because the capacity to comprehend the infinite lay in all people.

And that meant Viyara and the Sisterhood were built on a lie.

Runajo had lived and been prepared to kill for a *lie*.

And she had only moments left to find a way to save Juliet.

She dropped her hand from Juliet's neck. She looked Miryo straight in the eyes and said, "Please. First, may I speak to my novice mistress?"

She could see the surprise in Miryo's face—she could *feel* the surprise from Juliet, but she ruthlessly thought of stone, because Juliet wouldn't understand this.

"I have done you wrong," Runajo went on, still looking at Miryo. "And before anything else, I want to beg your forgiveness."

"You don't want my forgiveness," said Miryo, once they were in a little side chamber together.

"No," said Runajo. "I want to point out that you're a fool if you let that girl die."

Miryo raised an eyebrow.

"Think," said Runajo. "That is the Catresou's Juliet, bound to serve their every command. Only now she is bound to me. What do you think that would do for our clan, if the Juliet were ours to command?"

And though Runajo had never found a single thing to admire

in Miryo, now she found this: the woman visibly choked back the insults she wanted to fling at her, and thought over what she had said.

"Do you really believe you can make her obey you?" she asked at last.

"Yes," said Runajo, desperately, recklessly. She knew how much she was offering. "She has to obey me. She has no other choice."

For several infinite moments, Miryo looked at her, obviously thinking through the situation. Runajo waited, remembering Inyaan's voice as she said, *You really think the people outside don't control us?*

Inyaan had better be right. (Sunjai would laugh if she knew Runajo was following Inyaan's lead.)

Then Miryo said, "If you have strength enough, there might be a solution."

Immediately, she gripped Runajo by the ear and dragged her back into the Hall of Judgment.

"I have spoken with her," she said in a clear, ringing voice. "And I do believe she has repented. I also believe that this punishment is too lenient and too wasteful. Let her and this undead Juliet both do penance for several days first, so that when she cuts her throat, it will not only be an act of justice, but a sacrifice that will strengthen the city."

"That will not suffice to make her one of us again," said the High Priestess.

Miryo snorted. "Nor should it. But neither should she be allowed to cut away her sin before she has been made to fully understand it."

Runajo could see the confused glances, the eyebrows raising or drawing together in surprise. But this one thing was in her favor: everybody knew how much she and Miryo hated each other. So nobody would suspect that they had conspired together.

"Very well," said the High Priestess, after a long silence. "But you will be given charge of her."

What are you doing? Juliet demanded as they were led from the hall.

Saving you, Runajo replied, not looking at her.

What are you hiding?

Nothing that will dishonor you, said Runajo. *Trust me.*

The next two days were difficult. Miryo kept her to a rigorous schedule of prayer and penance; even with the healer's ointment and the bloodwine, the cuts and holes in her arms never had the chance to fully heal. They barely took any blood, so she was in no danger of dying, but she was barely allowed any food, either.

She couldn't stop being afraid of the cords stabbing into her skin. She tried to be brave, but she couldn't.

And she could never relax, because Juliet was always there in her head, and had to be kept out.

Juliet was always there, and Juliet was always *furious,* because she could tell when Runajo drew the knife across her skin, and when the slender strands plunged into her arms, and when she had been on her knees, head up and back straight, for over an hour.

Runajo could tell that the other girl was undergoing some kind of penance herself, but she couldn't sense the details as well, or maybe Juliet was better at shielding them. She certainly didn't seem to think it was important how much damage was done to her own body.

Juliet was already dead, and Runajo probably shouldn't care about how much she got hurt on the way to her final death, but she did.

Besides, if the Sisters had been wrong about sacrifice and *inkaad,* then perhaps they were also wrong about Juliet needing to die.

Runajo hated that she had been wrong; she hated far more that she had assisted in the Sisters' ceremonies—even if she had never held the knife herself, she had willingly helped. She had woven the power they gained by blood into the walls surrounding Viyara. She had felt proud of herself for doing it.

And yet that power, however ill-gotten, kept the people of Viyara alive day after day.

Sometimes she thought of the key, and of the necromancer,

and she wanted to scream in helpless frustration. They'd had hope. They'd had a chance, and then he stole the key and now was going to do who-knew-what with it, and nobody would believe her.

That was another reason she had to survive and get out and keep Juliet alive: she had to track down the necromancer and the key, and Juliet was the only one who would help her.

If you told me what you were planning, said Juliet, breaking into her thoughts for the hundredth time, *then I could comfort you.*

I do not need comfort, said Runajo. That statement would probably be more convincing if she were not lying sprawled on her stomach, hardly able to bear the feeling of her clothes on her back, because this time Miryo had hooked her into the city by her spine. But then, Juliet couldn't see her.

And Juliet couldn't read her thoughts anymore, because she was being *very careful.*

It turned out that all she really needed to become good at shielding her mind was absolute desperation.

You're crying, Juliet pointed out, and Runajo squeezed her eyes shut against the betraying sting.

You shouldn't be able to know that, she said.

In fact, said Juliet, *it is much easier to hide specific thoughts than to conceal physical sensations. This bond was made for my Guardian, do you not remember? We were meant to fight the enemies of our clan together. We must be able to tell when the other is injured and how.*

Runajo breathed slowly and thought of stone. *You will just have to trust me for a little longer,* she said.

I do, said Juliet, and Runajo blamed it on her back when she started shaking with tiny, snuffling sobs.

Juliet would be so terribly angry at her, when she found out. But there was no other way to save her—not only from the Sisters, but from her stupid, stubborn loyalty to the family that had used and nearly destroyed her.

They had taken her name away from her; they had taken away her hope—false, but still *hers*—of eternal life. They had molded her into a weapon, made her proud to declare that she had no other purpose, and they had prepared to shackle her to a keeper so that even her thoughts were not her own. They had made her ashamed of loving, and they would have branded her a whore and an outcast if they found out she had loved anyway.

The slow burn of hatred was deeply comforting. It would serve them right when their Juliet belonged to the Mahyanai. It would serve them *right*.

And someday, Juliet would forgive her for it. Someday, Juliet would understand that family should not make you into a slave.

28

"I'M NOT SURE HOW YOU Catresou put up with wearing these masks all the time," said Vai as they walked down the darkened street together.

"You're complaining about the mask and not the dress?" asked Paris.

He hoped his voice sounded normal. They'd had to wait eight days for the next Night Game, and at the time, it had felt like forever. Now that they were on their way, it was all happening much too fast, and Paris was horribly afraid. If they failed, they would all be dead or worse.

Vai twirled, the skirt of his dress flaring out. "Not everyone is as obsessed with trousers as you lot."

It was certainly true that among many of the peoples that had ended up in Viyara, the men wore some sort of tunic or robe. But the dress Vai wore was a very definitely female piece of clothing by anyone's standards, and it was a little frightening how good he was at moving in it. Not to mention how feminine his slim neck and high cheekbones were capable of looking.

But if the Night Game realized that Paris was bringing the King of Cats to their party, things would get very unpleasant very quickly. Vai was the one who had come up with the idea, and who actually had to wear the disguise, so Paris couldn't very well object on the grounds that *he* was feeling a little uncomfortable.

"At least neither of you is blindfolded," said Romeo, who was gripping Paris's arm so that he didn't walk into walls.

"Blindfolds are much more comfortable than masks," said Vai.

Paris rubbed at the edge of his mask. Vai had gotten it for him; it was made of blue-painted leather, nice enough material and reasonably broken in, but subtly molded for someone else's face. He'd thought it would be a relief wearing a mask again, but now it just made him remember all the ways in which he wasn't a worthy Catresou anymore.

But there was no time for regrets; they were making their way to the Night Game. Vai had stolen the invitation from Meros's study, Paris had flushed all over with shame because there didn't seem to be *anyone* in his clan who cared about *zoura,* and now they were on their way to the meeting place.

It was a nook between two buildings, beside a little fountain that dripped water unenthusiastically from a lion's-head mouth. They only had to wait a few minutes before their escort appeared: three men in dark clothing, unmasked, their faces bland and unmemorable, drawing with them a small carriage with no windows.

"Invitation?" asked one of the men, and Vai handed over the piece of creamy paper.

The moment that the man spent examining the invitation seemed to go on forever. Paris wondered what would happen if the man realized it was stolen: would he attack them, or only turn them away?

Did he work willingly for the Night Game, or was he one of the living dead? What color would he bleed?

"Get in the carriage," said the man, handing back the invitation, and Paris felt dizzy with relief.

They climbed inside. Because there were no windows, they weren't blindfolded, but that still left them in utter darkness as they jostled through the streets.

Their destination turned out to be a house in one of the richer neighborhoods. It was made of pale stone, with the faces of all nine gods carved into its facade. A footman answered the door; when Vai presented the invitations, he drew the door wide to reveal a hallway with a red-and-gold floor, and three guards. Paris strongly suspected that there were also guards behind them, hidden in the shadows of the garden.

The footman led them past the guards and down a narrow, twisting stairway. It was impossible not to imagine that they were descending into the land of the dead.

Then they reached the bottom of the stairs, and it was—if not like the land of the dead—like another world.

The room was huge, and round, and hung with red-and-gold tapestries. To one side of the room, musicians played a slow, elegant dance; on the opposite side sat an iron cage full of men and women and children, all blindfolded. They also all seemed to have been drugged; none were trying to escape, and some had curled up to sleep, while others sat with heads lolling to one side.

In the center of the room danced a crowd of lavishly attired guests who all wore masks—huge, elaborate masks decorated with strings of beads and sheaves of feathers. That part, at least, should have felt familiar to Paris, but there was something slightly off about the way that the masks were shaped and decorated. He could tell that none of them had been made by a Catresou, and that made the whole scene feel even more like a nightmarish fever dream.

Right before them stood a man wearing a comparatively modest gold mask. He held out his hand and said, "Invitation?"

Paris handed over the paper.

"Sacrifice?" said the man.

Trying to keep his face calm, Paris shoved Romeo forward.

"And your wish?" asked the man.

They'd worked out a story ahead of time, but now Paris couldn't remember it, couldn't even open his mouth.

"My little sister," said Vai. "We want her back." And now he even sounded like a woman. He didn't try to change the pitch of his voice, but he spoke so sweetly and demurely that even the low notes sounded feminine.

"Perhaps you will be granted her." He bowed. "Welcome to the Night Game." He snapped his fingers, and another servant approached to lead Romeo away.

They're drugging the sacrifices, Paris said silently as he vanished around a corner. *Don't drink anything they give you.*

Well, Romeo said a few moments later, *they didn't manage to force it* all *down my throat.*

"Aren't you going to dance with me, darling?" asked Vai, batting his eyelashes.

"Right," said Paris, and took her—no, *his* hand. Vai was not a woman, and if he wanted to survive this evening without utterly embarrassing himself, he had to keep that in mind.

He had a really strong sensation that Romeo was silently laughing at him.

Paris had never been terribly good at dancing, but this was a simple one, which he could do even while worrying about the lurking necromancers. Vai, of course, glided through the steps with perfect grace.

"How do you know all this?" Paris demanded.

"My sister," Vai said cheerfully. "We had ambitions of rising in the world. So we taught each other to dance, and that meant learning both parts."

"And both wearing a dress?"

"You'd be surprised how often that kind of disguise comes in handy."

"It's . . . convincing," Paris admitted.

"To me it feels like I'm still dressed as a man, but that's because the hair's all wrong. Among my people, the women shave their heads."

"Who *are* your people?" asked Paris. Even in the Lower City, he'd never seen any women like that.

"I'm Ozani," Vai said, as easily and fluidly as he'd said all his lies.

"I've never heard of them," said Paris, though he supposed that wasn't surprising. He didn't know that much about the peoples who didn't belong to the three high houses.

"That's because I'm the very last." Vai singsonged the words as if he were teasing.

"Except for your sister," said Paris, dubiously.

"Except for my sister, who doesn't count because she is dead. And a woman. My mother and grandmother are still alive, but they can't carry on the family name. I can, so let me know if you have any pretty cousins you need to marry off. Ready to dance casually toward those doors in the back?"

"Right," said Paris.

They had to get some kind of useful information out of this evening before Romeo was slaughtered.

They also had to get the other sacrifices out, but Paris was starting to doubt if it would be possible. When they'd talked over their plans ahead of time, they'd hoped that creating a commotion would be enough, but Romeo had seen the listless, dead-eyed stare of the men and women in the cage. They probably weren't capable of running.

The steps of the dance spun them around again—and Paris felt like his heart jumped in his chest, because sitting with one lady on his lap while another kissed his forehead was Meros.

"What?" asked Vai.

"My brother," said Paris. "How can he be here? We stole his invitation!"

"Well, he is altogether handsome," said Vai after a moment. "From the nose down, anyway. Forget cousins, do you have any sisters?"

"He might recognize me, stop babbling, and realize this is a disaster," Paris whispered.

"Stop craning your neck to look at him, it makes you obvious," said Vai. "You're wearing a mask in a great crowd of masked people. We can get past him."

Paris didn't tell Vai that he and Meros were both Catresou, and used to recognizing people from only the nose down. He didn't have to tell him, because at that moment Meros looked right at them and stood, dumping the girl off his lap.

"You go," said Vai, pushing him toward the doors at the edge of the room. "I'll distract him."

Paris went, slipping through the crowd of people. Silently, he called out, *Romeo?*

Yes? Romeo said after a moment. He sounded . . . muffled.

Meros is here. We may need to run soon.

Run, Romeo slurred, and yes, he was definitely drugged. This was not going to end well.

The nearest doorway was hung with thick velvet curtains. Paris slipped through; suddenly the noise of music and chatter was muffled. He was in a narrow little hallway, dark and cool; there was light coming under the door near the end.

And then he heard Lord Catresou's voice. It was too muffled for him to make out the exact words, but he'd know those cadences anywhere.

Paris crept closer. And closer. Right up to the door, and then he could finally make out the words.

"—to see you again," said Lord Catresou. "I'm sure you've already heard about our difficulty?"

"Is that what you call your prize servant killing herself?" said someone else. It was another man; something about the tones of his voice seemed familiar, but Paris couldn't place it.

"I assure you," said Lord Catresou, "we will be able to make another much sooner—"

"We don't need her anymore," said the man. "I've found a new key."

An icy rush of dread spread up Paris's back. This must be the Master Necromancer. This was the man who had plotted with Lord Catresou to unlock the doors of death.

"And this one's just a bit of bone, not a girl," said the man. "It won't give us any trouble."

"I see," said Lord Catresou. "Do you want to use it tonight, as we planned?"

"I see no reason to wait. And you, do you have the Little Lady ready?"

"Of course," said Lord Catresou.

This was bad. This was worse than bad. They were going to destroy everything, *tonight*, and Paris wasn't sure how to even begin stopping them.

"Paris! It *is* you. You have gotten bold, haven't you?"

Hands grabbed Paris and spun him around, and then he was looking up into Meros's face.

"Quiet!" Paris whispered, trying to push him back down the passage.

"No, no," Meros went on, his voice loud and cheerful, "I'm not going to report you to Father. Not that he could do anything, now that you belong to Lord Catresou. I just want to congratulate you on finally becoming a man. That girl you had hanging off you is—"

The door behind them opened. Paris wrenched himself out of Meros's grip and bolted.

Unfortunately, that was right when two guards came into the hallway from the ballroom. They knew what to do with people fleeing the Night Game in a panic; they seized Paris by the arms and held him.

And then Lord Catresou emerged from the room where he had been talking. He took in the whole scene in a moment, and he let out a little breath of satisfaction.

"Finally," he said, and looked at Meros. "Did you catch him?"

Meros looked at Paris.

It was nothing that Paris would ever have expected: their eyes met, and for a moment he thought that maybe, *maybe* Meros was actually doubting himself.

For one moment, he looked like the brother that Paris remembered from when they were all very little, and nobody had told Meros that he was clever yet.

But then he smiled and said to Lord Catresou, "I believe I did. Though I'm still not sure what was the offense. Besides, of course, the obvious."

"Trespass," said Lord Catresou. "And disobedience. I'll believe you didn't help him if you leave now."

"Fair enough," said Meros, and turned away. "Sorry, little brother." He slapped Paris's shoulder as he stepped past him. "This is for the good of the family."

"He's betraying us," said Paris, but Meros only kept walking. "He is going to destroy us all!" Paris shouted after him.

Of course he didn't listen. Meros never listened; Paris had no idea why it hurt so much to see him walk away. It was no surprise and no change.

Then another pair of guards entered the hallway, dragging with them Vai, and Paris knew that they were truly doomed.

"I admit I'm impressed that you got this far," said Lord Catresou.

The guards had dragged Vai and Paris into a small room that looked like it might be the laboratory of a magi—or an alchemist. There were books and papers piled high on the desk, along with complicated bronze instruments that Paris didn't recognize. Vai and Paris were tied into chairs; Lord Catresou stood over them, looking down his nose.

Paris didn't say anything. He was trying to call silently to Romeo, but he got no response, only a vague sense of his presence somewhere nearby.

He was also trying not to vomit in terror. Because he and Vai were tied up with nobody to save them, and any moment Lord Catresou was going to get tired of glaring, and then they would die. They would die, and the whole world would die with them, and Paris couldn't stop remembering the old man turned into a revenant.

"I'm impressed that you're able to carry on a festival of this size without the whole city finding out," said Vai, who was either not afraid at all or hiding it really well. "Just how many of the City Guard have you paid off, or did you just skip straight to killing them and bringing them back as puppets? And are you the one managing the Night Game, or are you just the favored guests? We have such a lot of things to talk about!"

"Why do you want to open the gates of death?" Paris blurted.

Lord Catresou sighed. "It's amusing that you want to keep trying, but very soon it won't matter what you two know. This is the end. As you are a child of our house, perhaps I'll let you watch."

And then he turned and left them, which would be a marvelous opportunity to escape—except that they were tied up. In a locked room. With a guard outside.

"We're going to die," said Paris.

"Eventually," said Vai, "but not right now."

The joke wasn't funny when *eventually* meant *tomorrow morning*. Actually, the joke wasn't funny anyway.

"Did you not notice that we got captured?" Paris demanded.

"Don't worry," said Vai. "I have a plan."

"Does it start with not being tied into a chair?" asked Paris. "Because that's not very helpful."

"No." Vai tugged at the ropes without looking the least bit concerned. "It starts with admitting that we can't solve this problem."

"That's just giving up," said Paris, his heart sinking a little. Of course they were doomed, but it didn't feel right for Vai to admit it.

"Step two," said Vai, "is getting us a problem we *can* solve. Normally that might involve a lot of shouting or setting things on fire, but I'm betting that if nothing else, we're too useful as necromancy fodder to be left alone for long."

Paris wasn't sure there was any point to saying, *What do you mean, you are insane,* all over again.

Vai lifted his head. "Listen. Here comes our savior now."

The door opened, and Master Trelouno strode in.

It was bizarre. Paris knew that Master Trelouno was a necromancer who was probably about to kill him, but his first reaction was shame that he was slouching in his chair. Posture was the foundation of dueling. Master Trelouno had told him so.

"If you surrender now," said Vai, "I'll let you off easy. Otherwise, when we cross swords, you're getting thrashed."

Master Trelouno stopped, his mouth pressing into a thin line under his red mustache. He looked at Vai as if he were a bug, and he was considering whether to squash him or pull his wings off.

"You can't possibly want to do this," Paris said rapidly. "It's against *zoura*. It doesn't make sense."

Master Trelouno strode toward him, and Paris's voice speeded up as he said, "It's a betrayal of the Juliet. Of all our people. How can you—"

His hand slapped across Paris's face, hard, and for the next few moments Paris was blinking back tears, his nose stinging.

"Don't talk of what you can't understand, boy," said Master Trelouno.

"Can you understand a challenge to a duel?" asked Vai. "Because I am really starting to wonder."

Master Trelouno turned to him languidly. "I am here to bleed you dry."

"You are here to fear me and tremble in my presence," said Vai. "Unless you're prepared to fight me. Then I'll consider that you might be brave."

Master Trelouno's breath hissed out between his teeth.

"You can't—" Paris started.

"Be a good boy and shut up," said Vai. "I'm trying to provoke this man into killing me. Death in battle, it's the most honorable way to go, for my people."

"If you are not Catresou," said Master Trelouno, looming over him, "then you have no name. And if you have no name, then you can have no honor."

"And yet I'm Vai dalr-Ahodin, King of Cats and captain of the Rooks, who is renowned for keeping every one of his promises. There isn't a more honorable man in the Lower City, except for, oh, five or six men. But that's not important right now. My point is, what do your people remember you for? And are you brave enough to fight me or not?"

Master Trelouno's mouth curled in scorn. "You want to fight me? Very well."

He raised a hand and muttered under his breath. The ropes tying Vai to the chair loosened and then slid to the ground. Vai stood.

"This is insane," Paris whispered.

"This is a duel," Vai whispered back. "Pretend that I've already defeated the best of your clan in a fair fight. Oh, wait. I have."

"He's a necromancer!"

"That's not the same thing as a champion with a sword, and anyway, we had no chance of escaping when we were tied up. Now we just have a very, very small chance, right?"

Master Trelouno tossed a knife at him. "Think you can beat me with this, boy?"

Vai grinned and saluted. "I know I can."

29

"THAT WAS A TERRIBLE PLAN," said Paris.

Vai snorted. Paris could feel the puff of breath against his neck, because Vai had an arm thrown over his shoulders and was leaning rather heavily on him. Because Vai had gotten sliced in the side with a knife that Paris highly suspected was poisoned.

"It worked, didn't it?" he said.

It *had* worked. And really, it was Paris's fault that Vai was injured, because when Vai's sword was at Master Trelouno's throat, Paris had blurted, *Don't kill him.*

He wasn't even sure why he'd said it. Master Trelouno was a traitor, murderer, and necromancer. Paris had been sure that he no longer thought of him as a teacher. And yet he'd been afraid when he thought he would die.

Probably Master Trelouno would have pulled out the knife whatever happened, but if Paris hadn't distracted Vai, maybe he would have dodged. Now Vai was injured. He had still managed to knock out Master Trelouno, and Paris had gotten them out of the house, but they hadn't been able to save Romeo.

"Not your fault," Vai mumbled, and Paris tried to raise the walls around his mind before he remembered that this wasn't Romeo. Vai hadn't read his thoughts, he'd just guessed them.

"Romeo's still in there," Paris said bitterly. "As soon as Lord Catresou gets a look at his face—"

He hadn't been able to sense him at all, since they escaped the house. Would he even feel it, if Romeo died?

"Sorry," Vai muttered, and it just made everything worse because he did sound sorry, and he *had* gotten them out of that house against all odds. And as the only person not drugged out of his mind or seriously injured, it had really been Paris's decision not to go after Romeo.

It was the logical decision. Paris couldn't possibly have carried both Romeo and Vai out, even if Romeo hadn't been caged right in the middle of the ballroom. It made much more sense to get out and get help.

Paris had spent all his life afraid of failing, but none of that was remotely as horrible as the sick, endless waves of fear that were rolling over him now.

If Romeo died tonight, it would be all his fault.

If he and Vai didn't do something, everyone would die. Everyone.

When they finally reached Justiran's house, Vai was barely conscious. Paris was terrified that Justiran would be asleep and impossible to wake, but there was a light inside. He only had to pound on the door once before Justiran pulled it open.

"Help," was all Paris could manage to say.

Luckily, Justiran was more than equal to the occasion. He helped carry Vai inside and lay him on the table.

"I think it was poisoned," said Paris. "The knife." Vai had collapsed so fast, even though there hadn't been a lot of blood.

"It's going to be all right," said Justiran. "Get me that box on the third shelf." As Paris went to the shelf, he added, "I'm afraid I'll have to cut her dress open."

Paris was confused for a moment before he realized that Justiran had only met Vai once before, and obviously didn't recognize him through the disguise.

"It's all right," he said, picking up the box and turning around. "Actually—"

And then stopped. Because Justiran hadn't wasted any time; he had sliced Vai's bodice right down the front.

And it was suddenly very obvious that Vai had been so good at looking like a girl because Vai was, in fact, a girl.

After one moment of staring in surprise, Paris whirled away to look at the wall, his face burning. *I suppose that explains a few things,* he thought numbly.

"You can look now," said Justiran after a moment, sounding faintly amused. "I covered her up."

Awkwardly, Paris turned back around and saw that Justiran had draped a cloth over Vai's chest. He had cleaned up the slice on her side, but it was still oozing blood, and there was an odd, greenish sheen to the edges of the cut.

"It is poison," said Justiran, "but I can fix it. She'll be all right. Give me the box."

Paris handed it to him; Justiran flipped up the clasps and opened it to reveal . . . a pen and a bottle of ink.

"What?" said Paris.

"Regular medicine won't be enough," said Justiran. "Stand back. This is a little dangerous, and also perhaps defiling to a true Catresou."

Paris was no longer in any position to call himself a "true Catresou," but he still stepped back and made the sign against defilement. He didn't look away, though, as Justiran carefully, gently drew curving symbols all over Vai's stomach and side. There was something hypnotic in his slow, gentle movements; the air itself seemed to grow still, listening.

When he had finished, he laid down the pen. Gently, he touched two fingers to the center of Vai's stomach.

The ink sank into her skin and disappeared.

Vai drew a deep breath and coughed.

"Paris?" she said hazily, and that was when Paris whirled to face the wall again, because she was barely clothed, and now that she wasn't on the verge of dying, that was a lot more embarrassing. And improper. And kind of attractive, which he was really trying not to think about right now.

"How do you feel?" asked Justiran.

"Half naked," said Vai. "Otherwise all right, which is a surprise given that I just passed out from a knife wound."

"Poisoned knife wound," said Paris, not looking away from the wall.

"I will burn your house down and kill you if you tell anyone about me," Vai went on, "but otherwise, thank you."

"It's no trouble," said Justiran. "I think I have some spare clothes that you could borrow."

"Men's clothing," said Vai. "Not a dress. It's important."

"Of course," said Justiran, whom apparently nothing could ruffle, and he went upstairs.

"You could take off *your* shirt, and then we'll be even," said Vai.

Paris took a deep breath and didn't say anything.

"It's all right," said Vai. "Truly. I took a vow to be a man, so I'm not embarrassed."

"Were you ever embarrassed when you were a girl?" Paris demanded.

"Not often," Vai admitted.

"Why did you take a vow?" asked Paris. "Did you not like being a girl?"

"Oh, no," said Vai. "I would have made a very happy woman. But it was my duty to become a glorious man instead."

"Duty?"

Vai was silent for a few moments. Paris wished he could see her—his?—face, but he still didn't turn around.

"My father had twin children, a brother and a sister. The brother was too inquisitive. He followed rumors of the Night Game. He returned bleeding black, and before I killed him, he had slaughtered most of our family." Vai's voice was soft and low but didn't waver. "There had never been very many of my people, and then—then there was only me. And my mother, and grandmother, and women cannot lead a family. My people, we have a custom—if a family has no sons, the daughter can take a vow to be a man. So. Now I am all the daughters and also all the sons of my father's house."

"How does that help?" asked Paris.

"Simple," said Vai, sounding more cheerful. "I take a wife and give her permission to have a lover. As soon as I finish taking control of the Lower City, I'm going to have *many* sons, and my people will not be lost. I really was serious earlier. If you have a sister or cousin, let me know. I promise I will be an excellent husband."

"Catresou women aren't supposed to have lovers," said Paris, because that was the easiest part to respond to.

"What, not even in obedience to a husband's command?"

"There are limits to obedience," said Paris. "And I don't think any Catresou women would see you as a man."

He heard Vai get off the table and step closer. His back prickled.

"What about you, Catresou boy?"

Paris wished he could turn around and see the expression on Vai's face. He couldn't imagine putting on a dress and pretending to be a woman, much less believing that it truly made him one.

But he did understand about duty.

"I'll try," he said. "If you want me to. It's just—after I saw—" He stopped, his face burning again.

Vai laughed softly. And then said, just as softly, "You have to keep my secret. But I don't mind if you see me as a woman. I would have very much liked to be one."

Paris's throat tightened. He wanted to comfort Vai, but he knew how useless comfort was when family duty was involved.

Justiran returned with clothes a moment later. "Where's Romeo?" he asked, and Paris felt the dread roll back over him.

"Captured," said Vai. "We need to get him out. You can turn around, Paris—I have a shirt on. I'm going to call up my men."

Paris turned around, discovered he was still embarrassed, and looked at the floor. "It's worse than that," he said. "Before they caught me, I overheard them say the Master Necromancer found another key."

"Well," said Vai. "That's not good."

And Paris knew. He knew what they had to do, what he should have done long ago.

"We have to tell the City Guard," he said. "I mean, *I* have to, since they'll arrest you."

"They'll arrest you too, and ask your family to bribe them," said Vai. "There aren't a lot of honest guards about the Lower City."

"I have to try," said Paris. "Can you show me where the nearest garrison is? And then, well—"

"If you think I'm going to sit out this fight," said Vai, "you've greatly underestimated my manhood. And also my connections. I happen to know one guard who's honest *and* has a score to settle with the Night Game, and I'll be happy to introduce you."

"Won't *you* get arrested then?" asked Paris.

Vai grinned. "Oh, no. We have an arrangement."

"What sort of arrangement?" Paris asked cautiously.

"Mostly, we have other people we want to destroy first before we get to each other," said Vai. "But I'm pretty sure she'd be willing to help us out with this."

The guard was named Subcaptain Xu, and when Vai brought her into Justiran's house, Paris couldn't help flinching, because she was the guard who had questioned him and Romeo after they chased the revenant through the streets.

She raised an eyebrow. "Vai, why am I not surprised that he was involved with you?"

"He might not have been, when you met him," Vai said cheerfully.

"Why am I not surprised that he *ended up* involved with you?"

Though they'd managed to catch Xu at the end of a late-night watch, she didn't seem tired. Or frightened. Or surprised. Or anything except ready to start fighting necromancers.

"I can't vouch for all my guards yet," she said. "But I have a pretty good list of ones I can trust."

"You think some of them are working for the Night Game?" asked Paris.

"I think some of them have been killed and raised again," said Xu, looking grim.

"I did tell you about the blood test," said Vai.

"Yes, you did," said Xu. "But I can't have my men slicing their hands open every day any more than you can. I've lost good men because of that." She grimaced. "Well. We'll get them now."

"The only question is where," said Vai. "They know we got out. They must think it's possible that we'll tell somebody."

"Do you know where any of their previous meetings have been held?" asked Xu. "Maybe they would retreat to one of those locations."

And suddenly Paris knew. He knew where Lord Catresou was going to hold the ceremony, and even now, at the last desperate instant, he didn't want to tell. Because he knew what it would mean for his people, living and dead.

But he had made his choice when he agreed to ask Xu for help. There was no going back now.

"It's going to be in the sepulcher," he said.

"Why?" asked Xu.

"Because they're Catresou," said Paris. "A ceremony dealing with death? They wouldn't hold it any other place. It would be blasphemy."

"I'm not sure they still care about that," said Xu.

"They do," said Paris. "I'm Catresou. I know. That *always* matters to us. Juliet, when she was trying to bind Romeo as her Guardian—which was very blasphemous already, let me assure you—she did it in the sepulcher. Because it was a holy place. They are going to be there, I assure you."

"They'll have to do it at dawn," said Justiran. "You don't have much time to decide."

Xu looked at Vai. Vai looked at Paris.

"I'll risk it," said Vai.

"All right," said Xu, and turned to Justiran. "Are you sure it will be at dawn?"

"Nearly sure," said Justiran.

"Three hours," said Vai.

"It's enough," said Xu. "I'll call in all my favors."

"I'll call in all *my* favors," said Vai.

"Tell your favors to stay away from my favors," said Xu, "or there may be a few more arrests than you want from the evening."

"Don't worry," said Vai. "My people can handle themselves."

In the pale, predawn light, the white dome of the Catresou sepulcher looked almost blue. From the outside, there was nothing wrong: the garden around the sepulcher was pristine and empty. Guards stood at the door just like always.

Paris walked toward them without trying to hide.

At first he'd meant to wait, to go with Vai and Xu when their forces were assembled. But he couldn't stop thinking about what it would mean when outsiders breached the sepulcher. Would they be content with arresting Lord Catresou, or would they desecrate the graves as well?

How could he ever help them do it?

So he'd told Vai, "I have to go there first."

"That sounds like a stupid way to get killed," she had said. "Do you have a reason?"

"I have to see if I can stop them," he'd said. "Without outsiders."

"They are not going to listen."

"Maybe some of them will. They're my people. I have to try." Paris had drawn a ragged breath. "Are you going to stop me?"

Vai had smiled, her teeth bright. "From doing your duty to your people? No. Try not to get dead before the rest of us turn up."

He'd nearly said *thank you* before he realized how strange that would sound. But it was actually thanks to Vai that he was walking straight toward the door now. Because he'd decided she was right: when you had a problem you couldn't solve, you needed a new problem.

There was no way he could sneak into the sepulcher without the guards seeing. So he walked right up to them instead.

"I'm Paris Mavarinn Catresou," he said. "I need to talk to Lord Catresou."

They did not reply. Their faces were pale in the dim light, their masks stark, featureless white. Paris was suddenly struck by the horrible suspicion that perhaps they were the living dead.

One of them grabbed him by the arm and hauled him without a word into the sepulcher.

So his problem was no longer getting inside. It was being a prisoner about to face Lord Catresou and an unknown number of necromancers. As Paris was dragged down the stairs, he tried to remember the speech that he had worked out on the way there.

Paris?

He stumbled. It was Romeo. Awake. *Alive.*

It's all right, said Romeo. *The drugs wore off, and I managed to get the other prisoners out.*

Other? said Paris. *You mean* you *didn't get out?*

Well, said Romeo. *No.*

There was something strangely intense about his voice. He'd never spoken so clearly when they weren't in the same room.

What are you not telling me? Paris demanded. They were underground now, down in the sepulcher proper, walking through the lamplit passageways with their walls carved into elaborate filigree.

I'm probably about to die, said Romeo. *Lord Catresou has a knife and he's not happy. I wanted to tell you—*

Shut up, said Paris. *You're not allowed to die and you're not allowed to say anything. Where are you?*

Coffins, said Romeo, and an image of the room flickered into his mind. *But if—*

No, said Paris. He wrenched out of the guard's grip and bolted forward, deeper into the sepulcher. Romeo wasn't going to die. He had to get there in time.

He's starting the ceremony, said Romeo. *You have to stop it. Any way you can.*

Shut up, Paris said again, and flung himself around the final corner.

It was the largest room in all the sepulcher, the vault owned by Lord Catresou's close family. The white stone of the ceiling was carved into a frothy, whirling mass of decorations. At the center of the room, the stone froth dipped down, like soap bubbles dripping off a hand.

Around the edges of the room lay coffin after coffin, and among the coffins stood Lord Catresou's men, all masked. But at the center of the room stood no one, not Lord Catresou and not Romeo.

Nothing but a whirling globe of light and shadow, tall and wide as a man.

A whirling, *whispering* globe. As Paris stood staring in the doorway, he realized that he could hear the many-voiced song of death again.

And he knew what this was. It was a door into the land of the dead, one that Lord Catresou was opening right now.

Romeo was inside.

A hand landed on his shoulder. Paris lunged forward and flung himself inside.

There was darkness, and again that sense of cold, infinite emptiness stretching out around him. And there was light: swirling, interweaving streams of light in an ever-shifting lacelike pattern that unspooled itself from a single point: a little bone circle with six tines growing out of it. The bone circle hung in the air at the height of Paris's heart, and it slowly turned over and over, swirling the streams of light in a ceaseless rotation.

On the other side of the bone and the light stood Lord Catresou, a bloodied knife in his hand. Romeo was on his knees, hands tied; one of his sleeves was wet with blood, and Lord Catresou had grabbed him by the hair, while with the other hand he held a knife to his throat.

"Wait," Paris blurted.

"You," said Lord Catresou, his voice full of impatient loathing.

Romeo met Paris's eyes. Silently, he said, *You have to stop him. No matter what.*

"You can't—please, my lord, this is against the honor of our people." Paris's heart hammered against his ribs. It would take just one twist of Lord Catresou's wrist, and Romeo would be dead. "It's against *zoura*."

"This is *zoura*," said Lord Catresou: "to protect our people."

"But if you do this," said Paris, "if you open the gates of death, it might not fix the Ruining. It might end everything, right now. You could make the whole world into the land of the dead."

He knew it was probably pointless to argue, but every moment that he kept Lord Catresou talking, the man wasn't slitting Romeo's throat.

Lord Catresou laughed. "Haven't you noticed? This whole world *is* the land of the dead. Viyara is the last living remnant, and it is dying. There is no saving it. But if *we* are the ones to open the gates of death—we will live on, no matter who dies around us. We shall be the masters of Death. We and all our kin."

He's going to kill me no matter what, said Romeo. *I think it's part of the magic. You have to move now.*

Not yet, *I don't,* said Paris.

"We know how to follow the Paths of Light," he said out loud. "We don't need to fear death."

"Look around you," said Lord Catresou, his voice low with disdain. "Do you see any Paths of Light? They're a story for children. There is no escaping death, only mastering it."

The song of death whispered all around them.

The darkness was so vast. So empty. Paris tried not to wonder if Lord Catresou might be right.

"I will save our people," said Lord Catresou. "I will save us, if I must destroy the whole world to do it. And when the gates of death are unlocked, and I rule the dead, I can call back whomever I choose. Even Juliet."

Paris felt Romeo's flinch.

"She's gone," Paris said hollowly. "She's dead and she died without a name, all because of *you*. There's nothing to call back."

He had thought he was horrified before at her fate. But now, standing amid the infinite darkness—imagining Juliet here alone, her voice and thoughts and memories withering away—

"We have raised up outsiders who were ten years dead," said Lord Catresou. "There is something left of her to bring back."

"As a slave," Romeo rasped. "You would make her even more of a *slave*."

Paris got only a heartbeat's warning: he felt Romeo gathering his strength, and the next moment, Romeo threw himself back against Lord Catresou. He staggered, the knife wavering, and Paris lunged.

It was unthinkable for any son of the Catresou to bodily attack the leader of their clan. So Paris didn't think. He pounded his fist against Lord Catresou's face, once, twice, three times.

He was still. Paris was shaking.

Slowly, he turned to Romeo and started to untie him, his fingers clumsy. "Are you all right?" he asked.

Romeo was gasping for breath, almost sobbing; his mind was churning with grief for Juliet.

"We left her here," he said as Paris pulled the ropes away.

"No," Paris said dully, each word feeling like a blow to the stomach. "My family left her here. We did this."

If they had not made her the Juliet, she would have had a name when she died. She would not have been lost.

They both stood. The bone key still floated serenely in the air, turning over and over in a ceaseless dance with itself.

"We have to destroy it," said Paris.

"Wait," said Romeo. His eyes were wide; the light swirling off the key glittered in them. "We could also use it to walk *into* death, couldn't we?"

"She's not there anymore," said Paris. "It's been too long."

"Lord Catresou said—"

"He's a liar. A murderer. I don't believe him." Paris drew a shaky breath. "We can't bring her back. That would just make her a slave again. And you can't join her. She wouldn't want you to die, and—and—"

He'd lost everything else. He couldn't lose Romeo.

Romeo stared at him. Then he nodded, picked up the knife, and held it out to Paris.

"They're your family," he said. "You should get to set it right."

The knife was slippery in his grip. Paris thought his hands were sweating, and then he realized that the hilt was slick with blood. Romeo's blood.

His family had so much to answer for.

He slashed the knife at the key to death.

The blade caught against the bone. There was a stomach-churning moment where it felt like the knife and the key were still, and the whole universe was rotating itself around them.

With a tiny, dry crack that Paris felt through his whole body, the key snapped.

Light burned everything up.

Paris woke up with Vai poking one of her fighting sticks in his hair.

"Open your eyes," she said. "I know you're not *that* dead."

All the memories came back in a rush, and Paris bolted up. "Romeo—"

"Still unconscious," said Vai. "He's lost a lot of blood. I bandaged him up, but it doesn't look good."

They were still in the sepulcher. But this time, there was no swirling of light and shadow, no magic about to be unleashed.

Now there was a squad of the City Guard, and there were Catresou being cuffed, their masks stripped from them. Paris saw Lord Catresou standing in the corner—his face bruised, his nose bleeding—and he looked away with a shudder.

He turned back to Romeo. He was like Vai had said; unconscious, very pale. The blood had started to soak through the bandage on his arm.

"You're awake," said Xu, stepping toward him. Her uniform was still immaculate, for all that she'd just led guards into combat. "That's good."

"I have to go," said Paris, gripping Romeo's shoulders and starting to raise him. "I have to get him to—I have to get him home."

She'd helped them, and Vai seemed to trust her, but he didn't think it was a good idea to tell her about the strange magic that Justiran could work with ink.

Xu nodded. "That injury is no small matter," she said. "You need help?"

"I'll help," said Vai, sliding an arm under Romeo's shoulders.

Xu half smiled. "I'm sure I don't need to tell you to come back for questioning," she said to her. "But you." She looked at Paris. "I will need to hear your testimony against Lord Catresou."

Paris swallowed, not looking toward the prisoners. The whole city would know him for a traitor to his kin.

"I understand," he said.

"Don't worry," said Xu. "The worst is over now."

Paris nodded, thinking bitterly that she could say that only because she wasn't Catresou. He knew that he should feel relieved—all Viyara had nearly died—but all he felt was tired and sick at heart. He might have destroyed his clan. He was sure that they would never take him back.

After all that had happened, after all he'd learned, he wasn't sure if he *could* go back.

As he and Vai carried Romeo up the stairs, he wondered if it was really true that the threat was over. Because if the Master Necromancer had been at the sepulcher, he had been masked like the rest of the Catresou men, and not taking an active part in the ceremony. He hadn't stepped with Lord Catresou into the darkness as he opened up the door into death.

And there was the Little Lady—the strange, doll-like girl locked up in Lord Catresou's laboratory, neither dead nor alive. Had the Master Necromancer gone to find her? Who was she, and what was she to him?

Then—as they left the sepulcher—Paris glanced to the right and saw somebody slipping away between the buildings: a tall Mahyanai man in simple dark robes.

Paris nearly lost his grip on Romeo. Because he had never seen the man before, but he recognized that lean, angular face from Romeo's memories.

Mahyanai Makari.

"What?" asked Vai.

Makari was already gone, vanished into the half-light of the early dawn.

"Nothing," said Paris, his heart pounding. There was no time to go chasing after him. They had to get Romeo back to Justiran's house as quickly as possible.

But as they trudged back through the streets, it was all Paris could think about.

The Master Necromancer had brought back Makari.

He had brought him back as a slave, just like Tybalt. It was horrible, it was unthinkable, and Paris probably should have expected it.

How would he tell Romeo?

When they arrived, Justiran looked over Romeo carefully, painted three symbols on his forehead, then announced he would be fine once he woke up and put him to bed. As soon as Justiran came back downstairs again, Paris looked at him and said, "You know magic."

"Yes," said Justiran.

"What you did for Vai, and for Romeo . . . I've never heard of any art like that."

Justiran raised his eyebrows. "You learned that when we met. What are you asking now?"

"The people that the necromancers bring back," said Paris, "I know they always come back as slaves. Is there a way to free them?"

"Who is it?" asked Justiran.

"Romeo's tutor," said Paris. "The dead one. I saw him alive at the sepulcher, I'm sure of it. If he can't be saved—it will destroy Romeo."

This, Paris was very sure about. Romeo had only just barely pieced himself back together after losing Juliet. Paris had felt how important Makari was to him as well. If he found out that he was alive and yet worse than dead . . .

"I have to save him," said Paris.

"You can't," said Vai, her voice flat.

Justiran examined them both. "There may be a way," he said, and went out of the room. A moment later he was back, carrying a bone medallion on a chain. The medallion was intricately carved with a mess of swirling, twining lines that wove all around each other, and seemed almost on the verge of forming a picture. Paris found he was staring at it and had to force himself to look away.

He wondered if this bone would crumble as easily as the key had.

"I made this for somebody else," said Justiran, setting the

medallion on the table. "Only . . . well, I never had a chance to test it out. So I don't know for sure. But I think it might help your friend."

"What do we do with it?" asked Paris.

"Just touch it to his skin," said Justiran. "That should be enough. If it works."

"It won't," said Vai, and for once there was absolutely no laughter in her voice. "Those things they bring back are puppets. Not people anymore."

"I have to try," said Paris.

"No," said Vai. "You have to stay alive, and that means not doing anything stupid."

He wanted to say, *You don't understand.* But of course, Vai did understand. She had killed at least two people brought back by the necromancers—one of whom had been her brother—and both of them had returned as killers. She had every reason to believe it was impossible to save them.

But Romeo would never not believe that Makari could be saved. So Paris owed it to him to try.

"Promise me," said Vai, stepping closer, "that you won't do anything stupid."

"I promise," said Paris.

Trying to save somebody wasn't stupid. Especially when he had an actual plan.

"Good," said Vai. "I've got to get back to my men. But I will be seeing you again, and if I find out you broke your promise, I will make you regret it."

Then she left, and Paris was alone with Justiran. As Justiran started cleaning up the mess that they had made over the course of the night, Paris sighed and looked out the window.

Halfway down the street, Mahyanai Makari looked back.

30

IT WAS BARELY DAWN WHEN two Sisters came to Runajo's cell. They had dragged her out before she was half-finished waking; they already had Juliet with them, and they took the two of them down to one of the great halls where the Sisters often chanted prayers together. The entire Sisterhood had been gathered; at the front of the hall stood the High Priestess, her face grim.

"You know why you're here," said the High Priestess, when Runajo stood before her. Her voice was flat and emotionless.

Runajo's heart started pounding. "Yes," she said, except she didn't. Juliet had been kept just outside the room; that seemed to argue that she wouldn't be asked to kill her this instant. But she couldn't be sure.

The High Priestess looked at her for a moment, as if searching for something; then she let out a breath and said, "Strip her of the habit she has defiled."

She was being cast out. Runajo knew she was meant to feel ashamed, but all she felt was deep, utter relief. If they were casting her out, they weren't going to make her kill Juliet. Nobody but a Sister of Thorn was allowed to cut throats in sacrifice.

Sunjai came forward, along with another novice, and she met Runajo's eyes for a moment. Her face was set; Runajo couldn't tell if she was angry, or gloating, or sad.

She stared right back. It didn't matter what Sunjai thought. None of the Sisters mattered to her anymore. She was being cast out of the Sisterhood, which meant her plan must have succeeded.

Unless they just wanted to cast her out before killing her. She dared a glance at Miryo, but the novice mistress's face was unreadable.

When she was naked, the two novices shoved Runajo to her knees and held her in place.

"Mahyanai Runajo," said the High Priestess, "you have disgraced your name and defiled your sacred calling. You are no longer worthy of this Sisterhood, not even to die on our knives; therefore we cast you out, unmourned and unremembered, to live as you can with your shame."

The High Priestess stepped closer and looked down at her. "Have you anything to say?"

According to the ceremony, Runajo should now confess that

she had done wrong and kiss the High Priestess's feet. She would receive in return the promise that after ten years of public penance, she would be allowed to petition to die as a sacrifice, redeeming herself in the eyes of the gods.

"I am not ashamed," said Runajo. "I have no regrets."

A moment later, her head was ringing from the High Priestess's strike. Then the Sisters hauled her to her feet and turned her around to face the crowd.

She could feel everyone's eyes upon her. She was not ashamed, but her skin crawled.

"Go," said the High Priestess.

There was an empty path through the center of the crowd. As Runajo walked down it, she kept her chin up, her hands loose at her sides, her steps neither swift nor slow. She had done nothing wrong. She would not act as if she were ashamed.

But she was relieved when she got to the door, and there was waiting a Sister with a red tunic—hers, from before she had joined the Sisterhood. Someone in her family must have saved it.

They would all be laughing, because they had all predicted that her joining the Sisterhood would end in disaster.

I will avenge this, Juliet said silently, and Runajo was startled by the cold fury in her thoughts. *I will find a way.*

It's all right, said Runajo. *I knew what I was getting into.*

And there was Miryo. "Come with me," she said, and led them down the corridor.

You should have killed me when you had the chance, said Juliet. *Now I will be just as dead, and you have lost your place.*

I didn't want it anymore, said Runajo.

What of Viyara? asked Juliet. *Do you think you can save it when you're dead?*

Runajo felt a sudden stab of grief as she remembered Vima laughing at the idea of her of becoming a revenant.

I can't do anything more to save it from in here, she said. *The Sisters will never trust me again. And we're not going to die.*

As if in answer, Miryo said without looking back, "I hope you appreciate how lucky you are."

"I do," said Runajo.

"When your family came to negotiate, the High Priestess very nearly had you killed at once. You had better please them, because if they ever regret this bargain, they will know how to get back in favor with her."

What is going on? Juliet demanded.

Wait, said Runajo. *Trust me.*

And then they were in the visiting rooms, and there was Lord Ineo, the head of the Mahyanai clan and Romeo's father. He was a tall, handsome man, just starting to gray at his temples.

Runajo bowed deeply and said, "My lord."

"This is truly the girl?" he asked.

"Yes," said Runajo. "This is Juliet Catresou. She has been bound to me with her own people's magic and therefore must obey me." She looked over her shoulder at Juliet and said, "Bow to him."

Juliet bowed, perfect and polite, as she said silently, *You cannot do this.*

I must, said Runajo. *I am.*

She looked back at Lord Ineo and said, "She was also secretly married to your late son Romeo."

"Indeed," said Lord Ineo, and turned to Juliet. "We all mourn his loss."

Juliet's face remained impassive. *He's a liar,* she said silently. *He never cared if Romeo lived or died. You'd trust him?*

To love us like a father? said Runajo. *No. To protect us and the interests of the clan? Yes.*

"I want you to know," Runajo said out loud to Lord Ineo, "we fully appreciate what you have done for us, and we want to repay you."

"You will have the chance soon," Lord Ineo promised.

Runajo knew there was something serious and urgent afoot, because when Lord Ineo had brought them to his house, he didn't send her to the baths along with Juliet. He brought her into his study for a private conference.

But she really wasn't expecting what he said to her.

"Necromancers," she repeated. "Among the Catresou."

By now, she should be numb to the idea that nowhere was

safe. Hadn't she been learning it all her life? Hadn't she seen necromancy performed in the heart of the Cloister? Then why was this cold, sick fear winding through her body?

Really, she should have expected it. She had raised the dead and a ghost had raised himself from the dead, so why shouldn't the Catresou have a turn?

"Yes," said Lord Ineo. "Lord Catresou himself, and many of his high-ranking kin. The City Guard caught them in the act this morning at dawn, but we believe they have many more associates. They have yet to tell us anything of use. But I believe that if they could see that the Juliet was ours, they might be intimidated into talking. You know how superstitious they are about their darling slave."

"She can do more than intimidate them," said Runajo. "She can sense when somebody has killed. If you took her to see the rest of her clan—"

"We could root out everyone else who has killed to perform necromancy," said Lord Ineo. "Yes, that is excellent. Then you see why I must ask you to tell me exactly how far she is compelled to obey you."

Runajo paused. She didn't want to tell him this; she knew that Juliet would scream at her not to trust him, and whatever Juliet might think, Runajo did not actually have many illusions about Lord Ineo. After all, she had been right there to watch him neglect Romeo while he was growing up.

But it didn't matter now whom she did or didn't like. She had to keep Juliet alive; that was the task she had given herself, since nobody else was concerned with it. She would not go back on it. And that meant not only keeping Lord Ineo happy, but also making it very clear exactly how essential Runajo was to any plan that involved Juliet.

Besides, if the Catresou were engaging in necromancy, they absolutely had to be stopped, for the safety of the whole city. The key that the necromancer had stolen from Vima had to be found.

And that led her right back to the same conclusion: like it or not, she had to keep Lord Ineo happy, because he was the only one who might possibly give her the resources to stop the Catresou and search the city.

"She must obey any direct order that I give her," said Runajo. "She cannot even try to fight it. If she can find a loophole in the order, she can take advantage of it, and if she *cannot* do what she's ordered, she doesn't acquire the power."

"Interesting," said Lord Ineo.

"I think she knows in her heart that her family has wronged her," said Runajo, deciding that she could live with stretching the truth if it made Lord Ineo regard Juliet as more person than weapon, "but she doesn't want to admit it, because she is loyal. If she learns they are necromancers, though . . ." Runajo let the words trail off, partly to let Lord Ineo feel like it was his idea, and partly because she was suddenly struck by a wild hope. Juliet did not in any part of her heart believe herself wronged—for all she had questioned her family, she was proud to be the Juliet still—but if she could be brought to see the Catresou for what they really were . . .

"Listen," said Runajo, "we might as well be honest with each other. You want me to manage her for you, and I am happy to serve my clan. I *want* her to repudiate the Catresou. But there is one thing that I would like in return."

He raised an eyebrow. "Oh?"

"I know you have the ear of the Exalted." She knew, in fact, that he practically ruled the city, since the Exalted didn't want to take the trouble—but it would sound insolent to put it that way. "His sister is in the Cloister. He had her sent into ascetic seclusion there, and it is not . . . He did it only on a whim. I'd like you to persuade him to get her out of there."

"She's a friend of yours?" asked Lord Ineo.

"She's nothing to me," said Runajo. "But"—she remembered the awful, lurching moment when she realized that Inyaan had never been what she thought, and all the moments after as she learned just how awful heavy penance could be—"you could say that I owe her a debt."

Lord Ineo looked at her thoughtfully. Then he said, "I'll be direct with you as well. I mean you and your friend no harm, but our clan must always come first. You have trained as a Sister; you know how fragile our city is. The Exalted does not care to rule, while the Catresou plot our downfall. I will use you and the Juliet however I must to protect us."

A little of the tension in her stomach uncoiled. It was a ruthless speech, but it was exactly the sort of thing that Runajo might have said, if she ruled the clan. She knew how to deal with that way of thinking.

"But what you're asking is a small enough favor," said Lord Ineo, "and fair besides. I can do it."

"Thank you," said Runajo, feeling a little dizzy. She had bargained with Juliet's obedience as her price. There was no going back from this path. "Shall I fetch Juliet?"

"Yes, but you can take the time to bathe first," said Lord Ineo. "And one more thing before you go. The Juliet is bound to avenge the blood of the Catresou family, isn't she?"

31

RUNAJO HAD NEVER THOUGHT SHE missed her home. But as she walked into one of Lord Ineo's guest rooms, having washed in a properly scented bath and wearing a silky blue robe of exactly the kind she had grown up wearing, she felt strangely comforted, as if something hanging out of place for years had shifted back. There was a traditional calligraphy scroll hanging on the wall; the bedroll was the right size and shape. There was a slightly different smell to the air, and Runajo couldn't say what it was, but it felt *right*.

Juliet, on the other hand, clearly didn't feel that things were all right, and Runajo didn't need the bond to know it. The other girl paced back and forth in the little room, her hands restless.

"Well?" said Juliet, spinning to face her. "What did he say?"

The servants had dressed her in Mahyanai robes as well, dark crimson embroidered with gold, and coiled her dark hair up on her head with sticks. The outfit sat flawlessly on her, and yet Runajo could tell she was uncomfortable with it from the way she moved.

And now she had to decide which bad news to break first.

"He will protect us," said Runajo.

"And the price?" Juliet asked flatly.

"You need to become the Juliet," Runajo said bluntly, all in a rush. "Our Juliet. You told me the seals aren't yet complete, right? There's still a final ceremony before you are bound to avenge your clan?"

Juliet went still, and Runajo could feel her horror through the bond.

"You can't," she said. "There are no magi."

"Do you need them to draw the seals?"

"It would be a blasphemy," Juliet said slowly and deliberately, "to finish it without them. Do not ask it of me."

The problem was that Runajo didn't have a choice. The Mahyanai were the only ones with the power and the will to protect Juliet from both the Sisterhood and the Catresou, and they weren't willing to do it unless they got a Juliet of their own in return.

Not to mention that if the Catresou necromancers weren't stopped, the whole city could be revenants in a week.

"I don't care if they kill me," said Juliet. "I am willing to die. I would rather die."

"You are trying to preserve the sacred rites of the people who made you a slave," Runajo snapped. "And who are confirmed necromancers. Did you ever suspect that, when you served them? Your father and several of his closest friends have been arrested for necromancy."

She felt Juliet's sudden, stabbing sense of betrayal, and she knew that *she* was the one who Juliet felt had betrayed her.

"That's a lie," Juliet whispered.

"They were caught in the act this morning," said Runajo. "Lord Ineo himself told me."

Trust me, she wanted to say, but she couldn't, not even through the bond. Not when Juliet was looking at her like this, her face hard-edged and bitter.

"Lord Ineo said so." Juliet's voice dripped with scorn. "And of course he bears my people no prejudice."

"Of course he hates them and wants to believe the worst of them," said Runajo. "But he is not going to stake our clan's reputation on arresting somebody without cause. Your people betrayed you. They would have betrayed you if they only made you the Juliet and did not turn to necromancy. Why do you cling to them?"

"They are *my people,*" said Juliet. "Tell me the truth, would you do differently?"

"Yes," said Runajo. "I did differently when I stepped over my own mother's body so I could join the Sisterhood. And when I left the Sisterhood so I could save *you*. I will always do what is right, and not what my family tells me." She took a breath, trying to get control over her temper. "And I will not let you stay a slave to your family. Tell me how to complete the seals."

Without another word, Juliet undid her sash and turned, pulling down her robe to expose her back.

Halfway between her shoulders and hips, right over her spine, was a symbol painted in swirling calligraphy. It was about as big as Runajo's palm. Over and around it was outlined a shape like a crescent moon with the horns turned downward. Inside the crescent was a series of little symbols so densely intertwined it was hard to tell where one ended and another began.

"The downmost stroke of the symbol," said Juliet, her voice emotionless. "Add a teardrop hanging from the tip, and the word for justice will be complete. Put the family seal underneath, with lines connecting it to the crescent. That is all."

"Do we need a special kind of ink?" asked Runajo, kneeling to look more closely.

"Not at this point," said Juliet. "The seals have their own power by now. But please. Do not do this."

The *please* hurt more than the raw misery Runajo could feel through the bond. Juliet had never begged for anything before, and Runajo felt sick, but there was really no other way.

"Among your people, the wife joins the husband's family, doesn't she?" she said. "You're already one of us."

"Then Romeo should be the one to write the signs on me," said Juliet. "Send me to the grave so he can do it with his own hand."

Runajo hesitated, then laid a hand against Juliet's shoulder. Felt her flinch, but refused to let go.

"You think you're just a weapon," she said. "You think that we will treat you as just a weapon. Neither of those things is true. And someday, you will thank me for this."

Juliet's emotions had gone away, hidden from the bond. "Just get on with it," she said wearily.

"Lie down on your stomach," said Runajo, and fetched a brush and some ink. Slowly, carefully, she painted the Mahyanai crest at the base of Juliet's spine. She drew lines from the left and right of the crescent to connect it.

And then she laid her brush to the word for justice and drew the final teardrop.

For a moment nothing happened. Then Runajo felt something like what she had felt standing over Vima's body: the slow, terrible weight of an enormous magic that was about to begin.

I can bear it, she thought, and then everything went dark.

It turned out she couldn't bear it. Fire seared through her mind. Her body. There wasn't a difference. It felt like all the world had turned to fire: fire and light and *meaning*, too terrible and intense for her to comprehend. She would have screamed, but she didn't seem to have a voice left. She didn't have any breath left, either. She was smothering and she was burning and she forgot everything except the pain.

Slowly she came back to herself. She was lying on the floor with Juliet—fully clothed again—sitting over her, face expressionless. The sunlight coming in the window hadn't changed; she hadn't been unconscious for long.

At first all Runajo could do was breathe. Breathe, and feel desperate, helpless relief that her body was whole and not in pain.

Juliet said nothing. She didn't move. Runajo couldn't feel her through the bond, either, and after several moments Runajo's mind started working enough that she realized it might be a bad sign.

She managed to sit up. "Are you all right?" she asked.

"We nearly died," said Juliet, her voice strangely calm. "The ceremony is not supposed to be like that."

"We've nearly died before." Runajo rubbed at her forehead; it still ached.

"I wish we had," said Juliet, still calm, and then Runajo was *burning*, just like before, only this was worse because then she had been too dazed to fully feel it, and now she could.

"Stop," Runajo managed to choke out, and abruptly the fire

was gone; she was doubled over, gasping for breath, with tears in her eyes.

Memories. Juliet was using her memories against her. She knew she should have expected this, but it still felt like betrayal.

Until you, too, would rather be dead, said Juliet, with precisely the same viciousness with which she'd told Runajo that she lived in a charnel house.

She wondered how long Juliet had been saving up *drive her to suicide* as a loophole in the order *don't kill me.* Probably she should admire her determination, and sometime soon she would, but right now—right now she *hurt.* The fire hadn't just been physical, and the whole inside of her mind felt like it had been scraped raw and bleeding.

"Stay out of my head," said Runajo.

She gulped a breath. She was shaking. With exhaustion, and remembered pain, but mostly with fear. And grief. Because she had thrown away everything for one girl, and now that girl would never stop trying to kill her.

"Don't play with my memories." Her voice was rough in her throat. "Don't share your feelings. Don't talk to me, and if you can figure out a way to give me dreams, don't do that either. Stay out of my head as completely as you can until I give you specific and unambiguous permission."

"As my master commands," said Juliet, her voice dull and emotionless.

They were truly back to the beginning. Runajo would understand this and not blame her for it soon, but right now—right now she wasn't able to face it.

"Get up," she said. "Lord Ineo wants to see us."

Lord Ineo was waiting for them in his study. So were several members of the City Guard, including a subcaptain—a tall, Old Viyaran woman, with her white hair braided in a crown around her head—and two middle-aged men, dressed in fine clothes that were rather rumpled and dirty. They both looked Catresou, but they had lost their masks. One of them had a bruised face, while the other had a drooping red mustache and a goatee.

Runajo didn't recognize them.

But Juliet stopped in the doorway and said hollowly, "Father."

The taller prisoner, the one who was bruised, looked at her. What little color he had drained from his face.

"Juliet," said Lord Catresou.

"My lord Father." Her voice sounded distant and dreamy. "I am sorry."

Then she crossed the room in two strides, kicked his legs out from under him, and when he fell to his knees, she snapped his neck.

It happened so quickly that nobody could react. As his body toppled to the floor, she turned and reached for the other prisoner. But the guards were lunging for her now, as Runajo shouted, *"Stop!"*

Juliet stopped. She might have been a statue for all she moved, for all the notice she took of the guards holding her arms. Her eyes were wide, staring at nothing.

"What is this?" the subcaptain demanded.

"A regrettable accident," said Lord Ineo.

Runajo felt numb. Nothing seemed real: not the sprawled body, not the panicked gasps of the surviving prisoner, not Juliet's terrible stillness.

Lord Catresou was dead. Juliet's father. She had killed her own *father*.

"I am the Juliet. I belong to the Mahyanai. That man shed Mahyanai blood." There was no expression to Juliet's voice whatsoever. "He had to die. So must this one."

"Don't touch the other one," Runajo said. "Don't. Don't."

"I once thought an order from my Guardian might stop me from obeying the adjurations," said Juliet. "I was wrong."

All of a sudden she dropped, like a puppet with its strings cut, her arms twisting out of the grip of the guards. They scrambled to catch her, but it was too late: she had already caught the man with the red mustache and snapped his neck.

Then she went still again.

"Ineo," said the subcaptain, her voice dangerously low with fury, "what have you done?"

"It's my fault," said Runajo. She felt like she was hearing the words from far away. "I saved her when her people betrayed her, and I bonded her to us. You see what happened."

"It is the right of the Juliet to mete out justice," said Lord Ineo.

"Your people were granted no Juliet in the Accords," said the subcaptain.

"The Catresou were granted no necromancers, and yet they have them," said Lord Ineo. "We can settle questions of the law later. Right now, the question is: are we going to rule the city tomorrow, or will the necromancers? Because I believe this girl can help us."

They argued a little longer, but Runajo hardly listened. She knew what was coming, and she was trying to think of a way out, because no matter how much the Catresou might deserve this, Juliet did *not*.

Lord Ineo turned to her. "Runajo," he said, "I don't want to risk you in the fighting. Order the Juliet to obey me as she does you, and I promise I will bring her back to you safely."

It was impossible. She couldn't do it. She'd thrown everything away to save Juliet; she couldn't hand her over to this awful fate.

Juliet didn't look at her, but waited silently. As if she knew what Runajo was going to do.

And there was only one thing that she *could* do.

Blood for blood. Price for price. Runajo needed somebody to shelter Juliet from the Sisters of Thorn. She still needed to save Viyara, and that meant freedom and resources to find the necromancer and the key to Death.

Lord Ineo was the only one who could give her any of that. And there was only one currency he would accept.

She remembered speaking to Vima: *I never go back on my plans.*

"Juliet," she said, calmly and clearly, "until tomorrow, obey Lord Ineo as you would me."

32

JULIET CAME BACK TO HER that evening.

Juliet came back to her after an endless, horrible afternoon full of blood-curdling rumors. The Catresou were all dead. The Catresou were slaughtering the entire city. People were fighting each other in the streets.

Runajo listened to every rumor, no matter how sick she was with dread. She had sent Juliet to this fate. She had known how many terrible things might happen, and accepted them all as the price of Juliet's life. She had no right to shield herself from any part of it.

When the sunlight slanted low and golden across the roofs, Juliet came back with Lord Ineo. They were both cheered in the courtyard, because they had helped save the city. The Catresou were pacified, the necromancers wiped out. All was well.

She was spattered in blood, but it didn't seem to be hers. She moved calmly, each step graceful as she followed behind Lord Ineo.

He bowed to Runajo when he approached her—deep enough to show true gratitude, not just politeness—and Runajo bowed to him in return.

"My lord," she said. Juliet wasn't meeting her eyes, but that was hardly surprising. Runajo could feel nothing through the bond from her, but she'd commanded that.

"You have done us a great service," said Lord Ineo.

Runajo bowed again, very deeply, and said, "I am honored to serve my clan."

Her voice didn't tremble. Her hands didn't shake. She was the only person left who could possibly protect Juliet, and that meant she had to be perfect.

"She's a little tired now," said Lord Ineo, in a bid for mastery of understatements. "Take her back to her chambers and have her cleaned up."

"Of course," said Runajo, and looked at Juliet. "Follow me."

Juliet followed her silently. But as soon as they were alone inside the hallway, she said quietly, "This is your fault."

Runajo choked on tears or a scream, she wasn't sure; then she grabbed Juliet's wrist and dragged her back to the room.

"Tell me what happened," she said. "How many of them were guilty?"

I'm sorry, she wanted to say. But Juliet wouldn't accept it. Not when Juliet had been forced to know how well her kinsmen deserved their death.

Something tilted the edges of Juliet's mouth. It wasn't exactly a smile. "Not nearly enough."

"What?" said Runajo, confused. Why would Juliet want *more* of her kin to be guilty of murder?

"Did you command me only to kill the guilty?" asked Juliet, her voice soft and patient.

"No," said Runajo. It felt like the world was turning end over end. Nothing made sense. "Why? How many did you kill?"

"As many as your Lord Ineo told me to. What did you think he would do with me? What do you think he ever wanted, besides the destruction of the Catresou?"

Runajo flinched, but she made herself meet Juliet's eyes and say, "I know you think that now. But without your father—"

Juliet laughed, a harsh, bitter sound. "You think I only killed my father today?"

"No," said Runajo, sick with guilt, "but the necromancers—"

"I destroyed the Catresou," said Juliet. "Lord Ineo got the Exalted to give him an order of death for the whole clan. He gave everyone in the compound a choice: renounce their names and submit to his rule, or die as Catresou. And I killed them. Nearly half would not renounce, and I slaughtered them with my own hands."

It took Runajo a moment even to understand the words.

She had dreaded so much death and destruction. But not this. Nothing like this.

"That's not possible," she said. "Why would he do that?"

Viyara was at peace. Viyara would always be at peace. A hundred years ago, when they drew up the Accords, the three high houses had sworn that there would never be war between them, because they were all that was left of the world. Runajo didn't entirely trust Lord Ineo, and there were many things she didn't like about her clan, but they weren't bloodthirsty monsters. They weren't insane.

They were supposed to be *better* than the Catresou.

"Command me to show you my memories as proof," said Juliet, "and I will."

Runajo swallowed convulsively. "No," she said.

She could never let Juliet in her mind again. She didn't dare.

She didn't deserve to have Juliet in her mind, ever again.

"Most of my cousins." Juliet drew out each word, leaning forward toward Runajo, clearly relishing each flinch. "All the lords of the Catresou. Most of their advisors. Many of their wives. Anyone who got in my way or who would not submit, I killed them. And it is all your fault."

"I didn't know," Runajo whispered. "I'm sorry."

Juliet looked her in the eyes. "I will never forgive you," she said, her voice calm and absolutely certain. "I will never forgive you. I swear by my soul that no Juliet will *ever* forgive you."

33

PARIS TURNED AWAY FROM THE window. His heart was thudding; his hands were numb and stiff. But he didn't hesitate. As soon as Justiran went into the other room, he picked up the medallion and bolted out the front door.

He had promised Vai he wouldn't do anything stupid, and he wasn't. It was entirely logical to go after Makari right now, because if he didn't, there was no telling if they would ever find him again. Besides, he needed to try this before Romeo woke up. Because once he woke, there would be no hiding the secret from him, and he would demand to be included in whatever attempt they made to free Makari. And if Makari couldn't be freed . . .

Paris remembered the *crack* as Vai snapped Tybalt's neck. How easily she had done it.

Romeo wasn't Vai, and he probably couldn't survive losing

Makari a second time. Paris hadn't been able to do a thing to help Juliet, but he could do this much for Romeo.

Makari didn't run from him. He walked away with long, leisurely strides. Paris caught up with him quickly and then stopped, two paces away, his heart hammering.

For a few moments they stood looking at each other in silence. Makari was meeting his eyes, but there was absolutely no expression in his face.

"Are you . . . are you free now?" asked Paris. Had disrupting the ceremony somehow shattered the power that the necromancer held over him? That didn't make much sense, but if Makari was still enslaved, he surely would have tried to kill or capture Paris by now.

"I'm going to help you," said Paris. Slowly, his hands only shaking a little, he stepped forward and pressed the medallion into his chest.

Makari took a deep breath. Paris looked up, desperately hopeful—

And Makari smiled.

"Did you think I was a slave?" he asked.

"You were dead," said Paris. He couldn't seem to think past that. Makari had been dead, and he could only be alive if he'd been raised by the necromancer, and that had to make him a slave—

"Dead and returned," said Makari, and Paris must have

absorbed more of Romeo's memories than he had thought, because he could tell that there was something slightly yet stomach-churningly wrong about Makari's voice, his smile.

Perhaps he had gone mad. Being dragged back by the necromancer's power and then set free by his death must be terrible enough to shatter a mind.

"Listen," Paris said. "We can help you. Romeo's here. Do you remember him?"

"Of course I do." Makari drew his sword. "That's why you're going to die."

Paris tried to run, but Makari was too quick for him. In a moment he was backed against the wall with the sword point against his throat.

Makari clucked his tongue. "You don't get to coward out of this. Draw your sword and fight, little boy."

He should have waited for Romeo. He should have listened to Vai. He should have gotten used to danger by now, but Paris's hands were still shaking as he drew his sword.

"We haven't hurt Romeo," he said, in case Makari was confused about that. "He wants to see you again—"

Makari snarled and lunged. He was taller and heavier than Paris, and faster even than Romeo. Every time he lunged, he cut another shallow slice into Paris's skin: arm, leg, cheek, the other arm. Paris staggered, gasping in pain. His heart was thundering in his ears, but his body seemed to be moving slower and slower.

"I really can't believe you were even *second* in line to protect the Juliet," said Makari. "Did you know she's alive again?"

For a moment, the words didn't make sense. It wasn't possible. Juliet couldn't be a necromancer's slave—not the girl who had been so fierce and righteous in her grief, who had loved *zoura,* who had said she could bear anything if she could protect her people first.

She had never been allowed to protect them.

Paris shook his head. "No," he said desperately.

"I thought I wouldn't need her," said Makari. "Dead keys are so much easier to use than living ones. But now that you broke the other one, I'll hunt her down and drag her out by the hair."

There was a dull thump against his ribs. Paris looked down and saw Makari's sword embedded in his chest.

It didn't hurt a bit. He thought, very calmly, *I've been stabbed in the heart.*

"I am the Master Necromancer," said Makari. "I helped begin the Ruining. I have died fifteen times since then, drenched the world in blood so that I could walk back from death of my own accord. And you thought you could *save* me."

He pulled the sword out. There was one moment of pure agony, and then all Paris could feel was wet wet red. He realized that his knees had given out, and he had fallen to the ground.

Makari knelt beside him. He gripped Paris's chin and turned it so they were looking eye to eye.

"Romeo was obedient," said Makari. "He was mine. He was not going to give me any trouble. And then you got hold of him."

Romeo was always defiant and always belonged to Juliet and always, always would give everyone trouble. But Paris couldn't say that, because he couldn't breathe. His heart couldn't beat anymore, and he couldn't breathe.

He was very cold.

"You're dying," said Makari. "I'm going to sit here and watch the light go out of your eyes. And then I'm going to raise you back to life. You'll be perfectly obedient."

Paris thought, *Then why don't you kill Romeo?* But Makari couldn't hear him. Nobody could hear him now, not even Romeo. He was going to die alone.

He'd always been alone.

"I'll go back to Romeo," said Makari. "I'll tell him that you worked for the necromancers all along. I'll tell him that you betrayed him, and did your best to enslave me. And you'll provide whatever proof I need."

Romeo won't believe it, Paris thought. *Vai will certainly kill me. If Juliet is even half alive, she will find a way to stop you.*

But maybe Juliet was too deeply enslaved. Maybe Vai wouldn't kill him fast enough. Maybe Romeo would doubt him long enough, trust Makari for long enough—he had loved Makari, Paris had felt it, this was going to kill him, and Paris tried, desperately, to move. To stop this from happening. But his whole body was numb now, and he could hear the song of death.

Water, singing with many voices.

He'd heard it twice before. But this time there was nobody for him to save, and nobody to save him.

Makari's hand ruffled his hair, as if he were already an obedient pet, and it was wrong wrong wrong, but he couldn't speak, couldn't move.

This time, the song of death wasn't terrible. He felt like he was going home, and he would have sobbed if he'd been able, because he knew he wouldn't get to stay.

He thought of Romeo and he thought, *I'm sorry.*

And then the world went away.

In Lovers Meeting

MASKS GLITTER IN THE LAMPLIGHT. The scent of smoke and jasmine floats on the air.

They are the least of the three high houses. But on the Night of Ghosts, the Catresou rule the city. The Old Viyarans hold their bloody penance services so that the dead will stay dead. The Mahyanai burn candles in memory of the dead, who they believe exist no more.

But the Catresou—whom everyone else calls dour, mysterious, and death-loving—on this night, they dance for the dead. They throw open their gates, offer sweetmeats and wine to all passers-by, and dress themselves in the gaudiest costumes and masks that they can find.

And anyone who wears a mask may dance with them.

The boy's mask is simple: leather, embossed and dyed to look like leaves. There is no reason for it to catch her eye as she enters the courtyard of her father's house. And yet she looks twice at him: a slender boy, probably no older than herself and certainly no taller, standing a little apart from the rest of the crowd, not laughing or drinking or flirting. Watching.

His masked face turns toward her and stops. He is watching *her.*

He is curious to see her, of course. All know of her, but since her training is not yet complete, very few have met her. And all can recognize her now: by the white dress she wears, and the white filigree mask, and the short sword she carries in her hand.

This is her duty and her right: to perform the sword dance on the Night of Ghosts, because alone out of all the daughters of the Catresou, she is permitted to bear sharpened steel. This is the first year she has been old enough to do it.

She takes her place. The music starts. And then there is nothing but her and the dance and the naked blade. Sometimes she whips it around as if striking invisible foes, sometimes she tosses it in the air and catches it, sometimes she whirls her body around it as if it is the axis of the world.

The sword has always been her heart and her life.

And then she realizes that he is walking toward her.

He moves in slow, careful strides, keeping time to the music. She watches him. She does not slow in her dancing. She sees him count her steps, track the way she moves. He has the eyes of a duelist.

When she next throws the sword up into the air, he spins into the sphere of her movement and catches it, then whirls away.

The next few minutes are the strangest dance the Night of Ghosts has ever seen. She does not miss a beat as she spins after him, leans into him, reaching for the sword. He catches her wrist and spins her out again. Her finger crooks around his. She will not be let go, and she draws him in again, catches the sword from his fingers—

He lets her take it, and takes her waist instead, lifting her up and spinning her around.

When her toes touch the ground again, at last their eyes meet.

She has seen the way he grips the sword, and knows that he is Mahyanai. She should be angry that one of their enemies has dared to break in upon her dance, but finds that she cannot. Not when the music is thrumming and laughing, and he is smiling that terribly bright, innocent smile.

And they play. As simply and easily as children, they play, catching and capturing the sword back and forth between them as they keep time to the music. They whirl, and his back presses against hers; they duck, and her fingers wrap around his wrist for one brief moment before she snatches the sword away.

The dance lasts but a minute, or perhaps ten thousand years. When the music stops, they are a pace apart, both their hands wrapped around the hilt of the sword.

Then he lets go. Still he does not speak.

"You dance as if you knew the sword," she says. "But how many have you fought, and how many killed?"

"None," he says, still breathless and still smiling. "And you?"

"None *yet*," she says, and cannot help returning his smile.

He grows solemn then. "I will not lie to you," he says quietly. "I am Mahyanai Romeo."

As the music starts again, she says, "I am the Juliet. I am the sword of the Catresou."

And in another time, another place—soon and very near—she will be his enemy and perhaps compelled to kill him. But this is a night for ghosts, and revelry, and impossible things.

She holds out the sword hilt first, a clear invitation. "If you think that you are strong enough to dance with me a second time—let us begin."

Acknowledgments

First of all, I have to thank Sasha Decker, Tia Corrales, and Megan Lorance, for being the kindest and most supportive friends that any writer could hope to have.

Hannah Bowman continues to be a fantastic agent who believes in my stories even when I don't, while Kristin Daly Rens still amazes me with how hard she works to make my novels the best they can be. I'd also really like to thank Jenna Stempel and Colin Anderson for the gorgeous cover, as well as the entire Balzer + Bray team.

Bethany Powell, Natalie Parker, Brendan Hodge, and R. J. Anderson all read various drafts of *Bright Smoke, Cold Fire* and gave not only excellent feedback but also some desperately needed encouragement. Also, while E. K. Johnston didn't read the manuscript, she still gave some world-class encouragement.

Finally, I have to thank Sergei Prokofiev and Jean-Christophe Maillot, whose ballet *Roméo et Juliette* convinced me that I loved this story—and William Shakespeare, who wrote the play to begin with.